MAY AND TED

J. D. Robertson

ISBN-Digital: 978-1-7782160-1-5
ISBN-Print: 978-1-7782160-0-8

Edited by: Margaret Morris
Cover design by: Shaun Stevens

To Kevin and Richard, wherever you may be.

1973

May

It's the first day of school. I'm in second grade, and I don't really like it. But there's this boy I can't stop looking at. Teddy. He has white curly hair, and his eyebrows are always scrunched together like he's thinking hard. He sits at the front of the classroom and always puts his hand up when the teacher asks a question. His hands are clean.

I didn't go to this school last year. I sit at the back and try not to get asked questions because I'm not ready to know anything yet.

Whenever he raises his hand, his curls bob backwards because he's looking up at the teacher. She always smiles at him. I think he's a good person to know because the teacher likes him.

When school is over, I start walking home, and I see him walking too. He's in front of me. I decide to follow him and be a spy. Mom says I shouldn't spy all the time; it isn't polite. But Mom is stupid. I stick close to the bushes and walk a little slow so I don't catch up to him. He stops and looks at everything. He picks up a garbage can lid and a stick, and then he's sword fighting trees, using the garbage can lid as a shield. I want to play with him pretty bad. But I wait.

When he gets to his house, he disappears into the backyard. I'm not allowed in the front door at my house either. Mom says the front door is for company.

The house is pretty nice. It's got lots of flowers under the front window. I think they're roses. And the outside is all sparkly bits of glass and rocks. There's a really big Christmas kind of tree in the front yard. I stand behind it a bit and wait to see if he comes out to play.

I'm going to be brave and go knock on his door. But just as I step from behind the tree, there he is, and he's carrying a pole. It's got a painting thing on the end of it.

I duck back behind the tree and spy on him from a peeky hole through the branches. He starts walking down the street, and I sneak out to follow him. But then he stops again. I almost yell at him because he's being hard to spy on. He takes the painting thing, I think it's called a rolly, and rolls it on the grass. When he lifts it up, it's covered in dog shit. I can smell it, even! I have to bite my cheeks so I don't laugh.

He keeps walking down the street with the rolly thing pointed straight ahead like he's a knight and that's his spear. He's almost running. I pretend I'm on a horse, hunting him. I hold onto my reins and trot slowly. Then he stops, and I pull up on my reins and stop too. This time, I don't even hide. He must know I'm playing too.

He's looking at something beside the sidewalk. Maybe it's a foxhole, and he's waiting to stab the fox with his spear. He takes the rolly thing and starts painting whatever it is with dog shit. I giggle. Finally, he looks at me. I smile at him like he's a big piece of birthday cake, but then I feel stupid because he's got a very angry look on his face. Maybe I should have pretended a bit longer. I think I was playing a different game than him. His stare makes my face feel hot.

He throws the rolly pole out into the street. Not like it was a spear at all. I think he doesn't know how to throw. And then he walks away. It feels like I got punched in the stomach. I watch him go, then I walk over to the place where he was painting.

It's a white cat. It's dead, and one of its eyes is gone. I wonder if he took it.

It smells like dog shit and something else, and it makes me want to barf. I pinch my nose with my fingers and get down on my knees. Flies are landing on the poo lumps that the boy painted on its fur. The cat's tummy is caved in, but if I stare really hard, it looks like it's still breathing.

I touch the place where the eye is missing. It's cold, and the hair feels pokey on my finger. Then I push my finger into the hole. The inside is dry, like a scab. I look around the ground to see if I can find the eye so I can put it back in the cat's head, but I don't even know what an eye looks like when it isn't in a head. I curl my finger a little so it hooks onto the bone around the eye and I can lift the cat's head like Dad lifts a fish by the gills. I look underneath the cat. No eye. I let go, and the head falls back down. It doesn't make any noise when it lands.

Ted

There's a blue flower growing out of a crack in the sidewalk. I bend down to look at it. The petals get huge and surround my face. I'm wrapped in purplish walls that are thin enough to let in the light. I laugh so hard I can't catch my breath. And then I really can't catch my breath because a giant petal blocks my nose and mouth. I try to lift my hands up to pull it off my face, but my hands won't move.

"Time to get up, buddy." It's my mom's voice. The petals turn into my blue sheet with the planets on it. She isn't in my room. She always calls me from the bottom of the stairs on her way to work. She says she can't look at me to say goodbye in the morning. Her heart will break, and she'll want to skip work to be with me.

"Don't forget your backpack. I love you."

"I love you too!" I yell it loud so she can hear me.

This is how we do things, me and my mom. She has to go to work early, and we can't afford a sitter, so I get up and get ready all by myself. She likes me to sleep in so I can stay up later with her at nighttime. I've been doing it since first grade. Nobody knows, except Mrs. Benhowser. She's my mom's friend from down the street. She's old. She says I can always call her if I need help. I never call her.

I get up and look out the window to watch Mom leave. She looks up from the driveway and blows me a kiss. I pretend the kiss knocks me over, and I fall backwards onto the floor. Then she drives off.

I get dressed in my blue overalls and my striped blue T-shirt. Blue is my favourite colour because the sky is blue, even at night. Kind of.

When I go downstairs, there's a bowl and spoon and a little plastic jug with milk in it. We tried using the full carton, but I spilled it all over. Then, when I was older, we tried again. I was strong enough to pour from it, but I always forgot to put it in the fridge before I went to school. Milk is really gross when it's sour. I always have Alpha-Bits because they help me practice my letters. I never finish all my cereal. Today I leave C, A and T floating in what's left of my milk and take it out to the deck for Ghost.

The first time Ghost came for breakfast, I had never seen him before. It was just starting to be dark in the mornings, so Mom had left the kitchen light on. I started eating my cereal, and there he was, sitting on the back deck outside the kitchen, watching me. It was funny because his eyes went from my bowl to my mouth, my bowl to my mouth, my bowl to my mouth—as if they were attached to my spoon. I held my spoon in the air, and he looked up. I moved my spoon in a circle, and his head moved in a circle.

That first day, I left him the letters R and P, because I didn't really think about it. And a little bit of milk. I opened the back door, and he ran off. I thought maybe I'd scared him away, but then I saw the tips of his ears peeking over the edge of the deck. So I put my bowl down and went back inside to watch him from the window. As soon as I closed the door, he ran up to the bowl and started drinking up the milk. He was so big and white. His fur was shiny and smooth like he was milk too. And his tail twitched like an angry snake behind him.

A few days later, Ghost started walking to school with me. Well, not really to school, only as far as Mrs. Benhowser's. And not really walking with me—he would sneak out from under bushes and cars and run past me and disappear, then he'd show up again a little further along the way. Sometimes, he would jump out and attack my leg with a swat of his paws and then take off. That was funny. I think I could hear him laughing too.

But this morning, Ghost isn't on the deck waiting for his milk. I step inside and watch through the window, and he still isn't there. I wait a long time. And my stomach feels empty, even though I just ate breakfast.

I walk to school really slow, waiting for him to jump out at me. But he doesn't. I'm almost at Mrs. Benhowser's, and I think maybe I'll walk home again because I feel pretty lonely. Then I see something white in the ditch. I think it's snow at first, which is stupid because it isn't even winter yet.

When I get closer, I see one of his legs is sticking up straight in the air. It makes my stomach jumpy. He's so bright and white and clean. He looks like some kind of stuffed toy. He doesn't move, even when I start to walk away. Stupid cat. Why is he doing that?

I have a lump in my throat I'm so mad.

The bell rings, which means school is finally over. I like school, but today I don't like anything. The teacher even said my attitude was bad when she asked me to answer some stupid question about the story she read us. I don't tell her about the lump in my throat. It doesn't go away when I swallow.

I walk home really slow. I wish I knew a different way. I stop a lot along the way, trying to decide how to walk past Ghost without seeing him. Or maybe I do want to see him. Or maybe I want him to be gone when I get to where he was. I'm pretty sure he's dead. If he's gone, then maybe he isn't dead. But when I get to Mrs. Benhowser's house, I can see the white of his fur sticking out above the sidewalk, so I decide I'll just go and visit Mrs. Benhowser. She always has cookies. Maybe I'll even tell her about Ghost.

But when I knock on her back door, she doesn't answer. Her car isn't even in the driveway.

I sit on her back step for a bit with my head on my hands and my elbows on my knees. Thinking. She has a really good backyard for thinking. There's two crabapple trees and lots of roses. The grass is full of yellowish lumps where the crabapples have fallen out of the trees. They smell like warm applesauce. And there's lots of buzzing from wasps.

She still hasn't put away the giant paint roller from when Mom and I helped her paint the ceiling in her kitchen because her roof leaked. Mom said if we didn't wash it properly, the fuzzy part would go hard. Mrs. Benhowser said she was going to throw it away. She said the next time the roof leaked, she'd be in an old folks' home. I wondered what an old folks' home was.

It's leaning against the house near her back door. There's spiderwebs and leaves on the fuzzy roller part. It's long because we put the regular roller on a broomstick. Then I get an idea.

I take the roller and bang the fuzzy part on the sidewalk to shake off any spiders. I try to carry it in one hand so I can get down the narrow path beside her house, but I end up using two hands and walking sideways.

Then I start looking for some mud. There's no mud because it hasn't been very rainy lately. But I find a really big pile of dog poo. It's super gross, but that's exactly what I need. I smush the roller into the poo and roll it back and forth. It's really stinky; it must be just pooed today. When the roller is covered in poo, I hold it carefully in the air, walking over to

7

where Ghost is in the ditch.

He's still really white, but now one of his eyes is gone, and there's a kind of hole there with some pink on the fur from blood. His leg isn't all up in the air now. I lower the roller down near his neck and then paint the poo down his body, right to the end of his tail. I roll it back and forth, back and forth, until the cat on the ground isn't Ghost anymore. It's just some dirty old dead cat lying in the ditch. The lump in my throat gets really big.

I hear someone laughing. There's a girl watching me. I remember her from school, she's the new kid. She's smiling really big at me. I hate her. She shouldn't be watching me. I throw the roller into the street and walk away. Now I'm crying, big gulpy crying like when my dad didn't ever come home again. I want to run, but I don't want her to think I'm running away from her. I'm not afraid of girls.

When I tell Mom about Ghost, I cry. She holds me on her lap so I can snuggle up, and she kisses the top of my head. Then she rests her chin on my head; her breath tickles my hair. I know she's crying too because her breathing is shaky. It's the same as when she told me Dad wasn't coming home. But not really.

May

The boy is in class, but I don't see him after school when I walk home. I think he doesn't like me.

I walk past where the dead cat was, still kind of looking for the eyeball. The cat is gone now, like it was never even there. I get down on my knees at the edge of the sidewalk to have a better look. I'm thinking maybe I dreamed the whole thing—maybe there never was a shit cat.

"Pretty gross, huh?"

His voice makes me jump out of my skin!

I look up at him and think I should pretend I don't know what he's talking about. But then I remember yesterday, how mad he was.

"Why'd you do that?"

"Do what?"

I think, *Now who's pretending?* "The shit," I answer.

He smiles a tiny smile that's like when a bird flits by. And then it's gone.

"I wanted him to be dirtier. He was too clean."

He's weird. Maybe I don't like him. Then a tear dribbles down his cheek. He isn't really crying. It's just one tear.

"Too clean to be dead." There's that fast smile again.

"Oh," I say. Then I get up and start walking down the street for home. He's weird. Maybe I feel sorry for him, but I don't know how to be when kids cry. That's for grown-ups to take care of.

It's hot. The sun is baking all the dead leaves that have fallen off the trees. When I crunch them with my feet, they smell like dirt and Grandma's kitchen. When the boy catches up to me, I can smell him too. He smells like new sneakers and sweaty hair. He's walking beside me, and I smile inside because what he did to the cat was cool, and maybe he's only a little weird.

"Was it your cat?" I ask.

"Nope."

I get to the corner of Elm and First Street and step off the sidewalk to cross the road, but he doesn't. I guess his house is the other way. I start to cross the road anyway. Am I supposed to say goodbye?

"But I knew him," he says from behind me.

I stop in the middle of the crosswalk and turn back to him. "I live down there," I tell him, pointing down First Street with my head. My thumbs are tucked in my backpack straps so he can't see my hands shake. I'm pretty excited that he's talking to me.

"Oh." He shrugs. He walks away from me down Elm.

I have so many questions: Why's your smile so fast? Why're you going that way? But I don't ask him anything. I walk across the street and keep walking.

Then he's beside me again. "Wanna go climb a tree?"

I grin at him.

Ted

The girl is at the ditch where Ghost died. She's got her knees bent so her bum is almost on the ground and her hands are on her kneecaps. She's looking down into the ditch like if she stared hard enough, she would see Ghost anyway. But Ghost is gone, so I don't know why she's doing that.

I want her to know I'm not afraid of her, so I say, "Pretty gross, huh?" I think I surprised her because she loses her balance, and when she looks at me, she has red blotches on her cheeks. Her hair is flat and straight and brown. And her eyes are black and really big.

She asks me why I painted Ghost with poo, and I tell her he was too clean. As soon as I say that, I get a tear in my eye, like when you hurt yourself and you cry before you know it hurts.

Then she starts walking away, but I catch up with her. She asks me if Ghost was my cat, and I tell her no. Then she starts to cross the road, which isn't the way to my house. I wish she was still walking with me. Mom says sometimes I'm too shy and people think I don't like them because I answer their questions with little words. I call out, "But I knew him!"

She stops and tells me she lives that way and points down First Street. I say, "Oh." I start to walk home. There I go again with small words! I turn around and run to catch up with her. "Do you want to go climb a tree?"

She does.

"Your name is Teddy, right?" she asks.

I try to tell her my name is Ted, because it's more grown-up, but it comes out "Ted—dy," because nobody calls me Ted. Not even me.

"I'm May," she says. "But you can call me Cleopatra if you want because that's my favourite name."

But I don't want to call her that because that isn't her name.

We go to the woods near my house, between the Watson's and Mr. Chee's store, where he sells licorice cigars. My climbing tree is where I go after school and watch for my mom to get home from work.

I have to give May a boost because she doesn't know how to swing up to the first branch like I do. She climbs fast. I don't think she knows trees too good because she climbs all the way to the top where it starts to wobble, and some of the branches are too bendy to hold you. She keeps kicking stuff into my hair. I've only ever climbed trees with my cousin Geoffrey, but he never kicks stuff at me. I wonder if she's being mean.

I sit on my favourite branch and, after a bit, she climbs back down and sits on the branch on the other side of the tree trunk. "Look! We can see the school."

We sit and watch. We see teachers going to their cars and kids still going home from school. We even see Mrs. Benhowser carrying the poopy paint roller to her garbage. I feel bad that I wrecked it, and my heart sinks a little.

May starts giggling. "What if she didn't know there was shit on it and she started painting something?"

I think that would be awful. "Ew! Then her house would be stinky all the time!" I can't help laughing a little. Mrs. Benhowser would wonder why her house was so stinky, but maybe everyone would be too polite to tell her.

"What if everyone painted their house with poo?" May says.

I think that would be even more horrible. "No. Just in their bathrooms. Then no one would have to hide their stinky farts!"

May giggles so hard she can hardly catch her breath— just like me when I laugh too hard. I like making her laugh.

"Then you could paint the kitchen with icing!"

Her eyes get big. "Or peanut butter." She rubs her tummy.

"And jam!" I say.

She spits out another burst of giggles.

We sit up in the tree, talking about more crazy things. I see my mom's car coming down Elm Street. "I have to go. My mom's home."

May's happy melts off her face. "No, you don't."

But I do because Mom worries when she comes home and I'm not there. It's part of our deal so we don't need babysitters.

"I'm hungry," I say, and I start climbing down.

She follows me. I think May is mad because she kicks more bark on my head when we climb down. She even steps on my hand—two times.

Most days, Mom is tired when she gets home. Sometimes, she even cries. I give her lots of hugs and try to help her out. But sometimes she just tells me to go play in my room. Like tonight.

I like my room. I have a ton of Lego from when Mrs. Benhowser cleaned out her basement and found her son's toys. And I have the *Encyclopedia for Children*, which is a bunch of books that tell you everything. I can read them because they have lots of pictures. I have lots of paper too, because Mom brings it home from the office when people make mistakes so I can use the empty side. I also have eight crayons, three pens (one doesn't work very good though), two pencils, and a sharpener. I like to write stories with pictures.

I draw a picture of me and May in the tree. I put big scratches of brown crayon on my head to show where the bark is. Then I scribble it out because it just looks like a silly hat.

While I eat my spaghetti with ketchup, because I don't like sauce, I tell Mom about May.

"Sounds like you made a new friend," Mom says. She's smiling her sparkly smile.

I shrug and bite my lip. I don't have any friends except Geoffrey, and he's my cousin. I don't know how a friend feels like.

"Have you ever heard of someone called Cleopatra?" I ask Mom.

She tells me Cleopatra was a famous Egyptian queen from a long, long time ago. After supper, she helps me find Cleopatra in my encyclopedia. She painted black all around her eyes. All the Egyptians did. It was fashionable, Mom says.

"Fool! Don't you see now that I could have poisoned you a hundred times had I been able to live without you?" That's what Cleopatra said. Maybe in a movie, I think.

May

It's the first time he's ever come to my house.

My mom is real nice to him because she always wants me to have friends, but Ted doesn't even talk to her.

"You can call me Max," my mom tells him. He smiles that funny little smile that disappears as fast as it comes.

"Some people think Max is a boy's name," Mom tells him, "but it's short for Maxine, and that's a girl's name."

"Like you could call me Cleo if I was Cleopatra," I say.

He looks at the picture of geese we have on the wall beside the kitchen table.

"Do you like geese?" Mom asks him.

He shrugs. I take his hand, and we go to my room to play.

My Barbies are all over the floor. Some of them don't even have clothes on. I think that makes Ted's ears turn red. He's cute when his ears turn red.

One of my Barbies has black hair, and I drew black eyeliner on her eyes once when I was pretending she was Cleopatra. I didn't do a very good job because I couldn't get the eyes even. Now I use her as the evil Barbie.

Ted picks her up. "Cleopatra?" he asks.

"No," I say. I take her away from him and throw her in the closet. I grab Growler, my stuffed black bear and give Ted the white dog that's called Scottie.

"We must kill all the Barbies before they take over the world!" I growl in my best bear voice. I make Growler stomp along the bedroom floor, kicking Barbies everywhere.

Ted is down on his hands and knees too. "We must destroy them!" he says in an English accent that makes me giggle. He makes Scottie stomp so hard on the Barbie Jeep that the windshield breaks off, and I laugh so hard that I have to run to the bathroom.

When I get back, we conquer Barbieland and have a tea party over the dead Barbies, with the Barbie queen all tied up in a sock.

Ted

I play at May's house after school. Her mom is very beautiful but kind of scary because she's tall and has a very loud voice. But she gave us cookies. Her name is Max. Like a man.

We went to May's room because her mom kept asking me questions, and I was being shy.

Her bedroom floor is covered in toys. I feel embarrassed because I don't have that many toys because me and Mom don't have that much money. I hope May doesn't find out.

I see a doll that has black hair and black around her eyes like an Egyptian. It looks like May drew the black herself. I wonder if she got in trouble for it. To make her feel better, I pick it up and ask if it's Cleopatra. She yanks the doll out of my hand and says no.

I think she's mad at me, but then she gives me a really cute Highland terrier dog to play with. She tells me his name is Scottie. I think that's a good name for a Highland terrier because Mom and I read about them in a library book once, and they're from Scotland. Which is a country where they speak funny. Mom can speak like them. When she does, I laugh.

On my way home, I put my hand in my jacket pocket, and there's something round and hairy inside. It doesn't wiggle, so I'm not scared. It's Cleopatra's head. I didn't steal it, I swear. I will put it in her backpack tomorrow when she isn't looking.

(1974)

May

I like making Ted nervous. I like when he doesn't know if he should smile or be serious. And I like watching him hold back his tears. He's so in love with me, I can make him do anything.

Ted is the teacher's favourite. He does all the right things: he's nice to other kids; he does his homework; he's quiet, and he always knows the answer when a teacher asks a question.

I tease him about Miss Webber because she always gives him special things to do, like deliver stuff to the office or hand out spelling worksheets. Even the principal, Mr. Reid, always stops by Ted's desk when he visits our classroom. Mr. Reid is like a grandpa—he always wears a sweater that's the same colour as mustard and a bow tie, and he always squats down to talk to us kids. His voice is low and growly, and he smells like the pipe he keeps in his sweater pocket.

Today, Mr. Reid leans with his bum against Miss Webber's desk, his arms are crossed, and he's watching us as if we're some kind of show. Second grade is almost over, and it's summer outside. All I want to do is go out and play with Ted.

Miss Webber is talking about transportation. Everything is about cars and trucks and trains and buses this year. If five children get on the bus at one stop and three children get on the bus at the next stop, how many children are on the bus? We've coloured pictures of fire engines and even trucks that have cars on them. Miss Webber reads us stories about canoe trips and balloon rides. I think I'd like to go on a balloon ride with Ted. But now I'm bored of talking about transportation. I want to ride my bike or play in the park.

Miss Webber has a bunch of things on the table at the front of the classroom. There's a couple of wheels; I think one is from a bicycle and one is from a wagon; there's a plastic horse, which I wouldn't mind having because it fits Barbies; there's some matchbox cars, and even a boat in a dish of water.

She points to the table and asks the class, "What do all these things have in common?"

Ted's hand pops up like it does whenever she asks a question, while the rest of the class answers her like one robot voice, "Transportation."

She sees Ted has his hand up, "Ted?"

"Transportation," he says, his cheeks pinking up like they always do. "They're all things that move."

"And why is that important?" she asks him.

"Because it helps us get places faster—it's like making the world smaller."

Miss Webber keeps talking, but I'm not listening anymore. The air is hard to breathe: it's thick with the pukey smell of library books and the tang of sweaty kids, even though the windows are open. I watch Ted. He's listening. He always listens.

Mr. Reid walks around the classroom like he always does, his hands are behind his back like Miss Webber makes us do when we go to assemblies. It stops us from poking at each other, she says. He stops at Ted's desk. Ted sits behind Mary Riley, in alphabetical order. I wish my last name was Riley. Or Russell. That's Ted's last name.

When Mr. Reid bends down to talk to Ted, Ted gets up and follows him out of the classroom.

I'm pretty sure Ted isn't in trouble, but he's gone a long time, and I start to worry when the day looks almost over. Miss Webber is even a little worried. She keeps checking her watch and then the looking at the door or Ted's empty desk.

Ted comes back just when we're getting ready for the

17

day to be over. Everyone's cleared their desks. Sam Walters is closing the windows. Audrey gets to erase the blackboards today. Ted's cheeks are bright red. I think I see a smile hiding behind his face.

The bell rings, and I run to him. "What happened? Did you get in trouble? Do you have detention?"

He smiles at me. "Nothing. We just went to the library and looked at some books. I told him about Saturn."

"Really?"

"Yup."

"Why is your face all red?"

"Because he raced me back to the classroom!"

I put my hands on my hips and glare at him like my mom does when she knows I'm fibbing. "Bullshit."

His little grin pops up again. "We raced in the hallway! And I even beat him!"

"You're a suck," I tell him. And I walk home without waiting for him.

Ted

Mr. Reid has his hand on my shoulder when we walk down the hall. I don't say a thing because I know I'm in trouble. But I don't know why.

But instead of going to his office, we go to the library. Now I know why I'm in trouble. I took a book and forgot to sign it out. And I didn't bring it back yet. I meant to, but it's me and Mom's favourite book now. It's about birds and the songs they make. We have fun when we read it because we try to do the birds' songs ourselves, and sometimes Mom laughs so hard, she cries.

Mr. Reid points to a table in the corner near the

encyclopedias and dictionaries. The books in that corner are big and heavy, lined up in alphabetical blocks of blue or red. Important books like that are always blue or red, and they always have gold letters on the outside. Nobody goes in this part of the library unless they're a big kid and they have to find out stuff for a project. Nobody but me, that is. But Miss Webber usually tells me I should look at books you can take out of the library. Like the bird book. I look at the blue-and-black block of *Encyclopedia Britannica* and remember another book I took by accident this year. There's a gap between Q–R and U–V. I remember I almost dropped it when I hid it in my backpack. So many things start with *S*. Satellite. Sea. Sentinel. Sea turtle. I start to shake. I'm in so much trouble.

Mr. Reid talks to Mrs. Hill, who takes care of the library. She smiles and nods. Reaching under the counter, she pulls out a bunch of books and hands them to him. He brings them over to our table and sits down beside me. The top book is *Physics of the Planets*. I've taken it out of the library six times. He opens it up and flips through the pages. "I've heard this is one of your favourite books," he says. He gets to where there's a huge picture of Saturn, so big it doesn't even fit on the page. "Can you tell me about Saturn's rings?"

I look at him to see if he's laughing at me. "Because you don't know about them?"

He nods.

So I explain to him how the rings are like moons, only they exploded a long time ago, and there used to be three moons or maybe more.

"Anything else?" he asks.

I feel silly. I know he's asking me because he thinks I only look at the pictures. I tell him how scientists calculated the distance of the rings from each other and from the planet, and how dense they are because of the gases in them. I think I'm babbling. I can't quite remember the formula for the density calculation.

". . . and the gases on Saturn are mostly hydrogen and helium. They couldn't stay on Saturn if it wasn't for grav—"

Mr. Reid interrupts me. "What do your parents do for work, Ted?"

I tell him my mom works at the doctor's office.

"Is your mom a doctor?"

I giggle. My mom hates doctors. "No! She doesn't even like blood!"

"Does she know how smart you are?"

I roll my eyes. "She calls me her 'boy genius.'"

Mr. Reid smiles.

We look at a few more books. He asks me questions, and sometimes we just talk about the books. Mr. Reid knows more about machines than about planets. When we look at the book about tanks and guns, he tells me he fought in World War II.

"Wow," I touch him because he's still alive and because he must have been scared. He's also way older than I thought. "Are you okay?" I ask.

He chuckles in his growly voice. "I think so," he says.

Mr. Reid checks his watch. "I guess I'd better get you back to Miss Webber."

I shrug. But I don't want to go back to the classroom.

May

Mr. Reid took Ted away from the classroom again this morning. Ted is gone until lunch. I don't even ask him about it this time. I don't want to talk to him anymore. There are only eight days of second grade left.

Ted

"There are only eight days of school left!" is written on the board. Every day, someone gets to change the number. Today, Michael Peters got to change it. But it's still Monday. I always feel lonelier on Mondays because my mom won't be home after school. It's better now that May is my friend though. I turn to smile at her. I know she'll be looking. She always looks at me.

There's a knock on the door, and then Mr. Reid walks in. He always does that, knocks and just walks in anyway. May says I should do that when I visit her, but I don't like walking into someone's house unless they answer the door. May's mom still frightens me.

Mr. Reid talks to Miss Webber really quiet. Miss Webber nods. "Teddy?" She makes her finger waggle at me. I get out of my desk and walk to the front of the classroom.

She looks down at me. Miss Webber is very tall. I don't know why she has to wear high heels. "Mr. Reid has some special work for you," she says. She smiles super nice, like she always does when she talks to me. I smile up at her so she thinks I'm okay with going. I'm not though. May said I was a suck when I went with Mr. Reid last time. And she didn't even walk home with me that day. I can feel her eyes staring at me as Mr. Reid puts his hand on my shoulder and steers me out of the classroom.

"Don't worry. It won't be hard work," he says when we get into the hallway. He squeezes my shoulder and then lets go. "I think you may even like it."

"Okay," I tell him. I hope May doesn't get too mad. I take a big breath. I really like Mr. Reid. His footsteps echo because he wears hard-soled shoes. We aren't allowed to wear shoes like that, only sneakers. I don't even have shoes like that. My footsteps sound like whispers next to his.

We go to the library again. There is a teacher there who looks like a mom, my mom, not May's mom. She is wearing a big white shirt that looks like a man's shirt and a red tie like Mr. Reid's, only skinnier. She has corduroy pants on, beige, the same colour as mine. Hers still have the fuzzy lines on the knees though. Mine don't.

"Hi, Ted, I'm Sally," she says. She puts her hand out to me. Am I supposed to shake it or kiss it? I put my hand in hers and pump it up and down, and she smiles.

She asks me questions about how I like school, and what are my favourite things and who my friends are. She's really nice.

"How would you like to try some of these worksheets for me?" she asks. She gives me three worksheets with lots of questions on them. "I'll be back in a bit."

I usually like worksheets unless they're boring. "Okay," I say. I'm a little angry that she's leaving me alone.

But the worksheets are fun. They have good questions with numbers and history and science. There's even some grammar stuff that I don't mind.

Underline the wrong word in this sentence.

Circle the largest: molecule, atom, proton.

What continent is Egypt on?

Find the next number: 1, 2, 3, 5, 8, __ (That one was fun.)

I finish as fast as I can even though there is no one to be faster than; it's just me. Then I wait. And wait. I'm getting hungry because I missed recess. I know because I heard everyone else in the hall. I rip off the top corner of a worksheet and chew it until it's soft enough to swallow. I rip off another corner and chew. If I was lost in the wild with nothing to eat but paper, this is what I'd have to do. I am a survivor. I eat seven corners before Sally comes back with Mr. Reid.

Sally takes a package of Oreos out of her purse. "You must be getting hungry. You missed recess."

I nod, swallowing the eighth corner. I tear into the package of Oreos and take a bite out of one before remembering to split it open. I look to see if they notice, but Sally is just looking at my worksheets, nodding her head, and Mr. Reid is watching her with his eyebrows raised. He's nodding too. I split the cookie in half and peel the icing off with my bottom teeth.

Finally, Sally looks up at me. Her eyes are all twinkly, and she has a big smile. "You're a bright little boy, aren't you, Teddy?"

Mr. Reid slaps his hands down on the table, which makes me jump. "I told you!"

I wipe the crumbs off my face with the back of my hand. Then I look down at the table because it's weird that they're both smiling at me. Uh oh. There are crumbs on the table too. I put my hands over them and carefully slide them over the edge.

"Can I go outside for recess now?"

Mr. Reid laughs. "Recess? It's almost lunchtime!" He stands up. "Come on. I'll take you back to class."

I slip another Oreo into my hand before I get up, thinking I can give it to May. Sally pats my arm. "We'll talk soon, Teddy, okay?"

"Okay." I walk away quickly in case she tries to shake my hand where the Oreo is hiding.

I wish Mr. Reid never took me back to class. I walk to my desk, and May starts whispering to Josie, who sits in front of her, staring at me the whole time. They both giggle. She doesn't talk to me at lunch, and after school she leaves without me.

At home, the house feels very empty. I stand in the kitchen and try to remember what I used to do before May was my friend. And I remember Ghost. That makes the lump in my throat turn into tears in my eyes. But then I see there's something yellow bouncing around the railing on the deck. I wipe my eyes to see better: I think it's a bird from my book. There's actually a bunch of them all over the mountain ash tree. I try to count them, but they keep moving. I sneak away to get my bird book, the one from the library, and come back, sitting very slowly on the kitchen floor in front of the sliding glass doors that open onto the deck. It's a cedar waxwing.

The book says the waxwing is a fruit-eating bird. Its song sounds like "bzee!" and then a long sigh. Their song slips through the window, and I practice it very quietly. They must be coming here for summertime. Suddenly, a car door slams, and they all flit away. Mom's home.

"Hi, Mom!" I run to her and give her a super big hug before she even puts her bag down or takes her coat off.

"Oh!" She stumbles a bit because I hug her so hard. "You're home early! Everything okay?"

I almost get the lump back in my throat, but I force myself to remember the birds instead of May. "I saw cedar waxwings. You scared them away. They make a song like 'bzee ahhh.'"

Mom laughs and gives me a good squeezy hug. That makes everything good.

"Okay, buddy, let me get my shoes off."

We're eating noodles for supper, my favourite. Mom mixes hers up with hamburger and peas, but I don't like it that way, so she puts my hamburger bits on one side of my plate and my noodles on the other. She puts the peas in a cup so they don't get ketchup on them. I eat my peas with a spoon because it's easier. And I eat them first to get it over with.

Mom puts down her fork. She's watching me, so I suck up an entire noodle into my mouth to make her laugh.

"I had a phone call today. You'll never guess who it was."

I can't guess because I'm chewing all that noodle, and it's gross to talk with your mouth full.

Mom smiles. "Mr. Reid!"

I chew fast and swallow.

She reaches across the table and squeezes my hand. "Why didn't you tell me about the tests?"

"Tests?"

She smiles like she does when I tell her something new that I learned. "With a lady named Sally Corbert?"

"Those were tests?" I didn't know they were tests. I should have studied, I think. I shrug. That was maybe two days ago? May hasn't talked to me since then, that's all I know. Which reminds me of the cold feeling I had inside my tummy all week.

"Honey? Don't worry. The tests were to see how smart you are. And"—she taps on the table with her finger—"you"— tap—"are"—tap—"very"—tap—"smart!"

"Mr. Reid wants to put you in a special program for third grade. What do you think about that?"

"I don't know." I think May will never be my friend again. I wish I didn't do so good on the tests. "Why is it special?"

"You'll get school work that makes you think a bit more, and the teacher will give you special projects to work on so you aren't bored."

"Will the kids laugh at me?"

"Of course not."

After dinner, we watch the science show with Julius Sumner Miller.

May

When school got out, me and Mom and Dad went to the beach and stayed in a cottage and rode horses and went on boat rides and did lots of swimming. Dad even let me bury him in the sand except for his face. It took almost all day. Mom fed him beer through a straw so he wouldn't get thirsty.

We were gone so long Uncle Jake moved into our house, and when we came back, he didn't leave. He sleeps in the bedroom downstairs.

Sometimes, Uncle Jake takes me in his room, and we play tickling. He lies on top of me and tickles me all over, even between my legs! It feels very funny when he does that. He says he likes to watch my face when he's tickling me. Most of the time, he wets his pants, and then we have to stop. He's says I can't tell Mom about the tickling because he doesn't want her to know he still wets his pants. His room is stinky.

But this morning, it's boring. Mom and Dad went to work, and Uncle Jake is still asleep. I'm not allowed to wake him up because Mom says he works at night.

I have my Barbies out on the coffee table. We're watching *As the World Turns*. Lisa is so beautiful. Everybody wants to marry her, but she doesn't have to marry anyone. Stupid Grant had his chance with her. She should kill him.

I wonder about Ted. He probably misses me. I haven't played with him since he went with Mr. Reid that second time. But I bet he's sorry now. He shouldn't spend so much time with teachers like that. It's weird.

I'm going to go find him.

Ted

I'm up in the tree, high enough to see the school. It's the highest I ever go. It isn't as high as May likes to climb. But I'm Ted, not May. There's nothing to see at the school because it's summer holidays. Mrs. Benhowser takes care of me in the summer. I go to her house in the morning for breakfast, and she sends me out to play when her "soaps" come on because I'm not very quiet. Soaps are the TV shows she watches that make her cry. She drinks tea and knits while she watches them. I don't know how she can knit when she's crying and watching TV.

I used to climb the tree by myself all the time before May was my friend. I can watch the world from here.

Looking down my street, I see May, and my heart gets nervous. She hasn't talked to me since I did those tests. She has new friends, and they always laugh at me. Today she's alone.

She disappears when she walks into the woods towards the tree, but then I can see her again when she's underneath me. I try to stay very still. I'm kind of scared. She hasn't been very nice to me.

"I know you're up there, Teddy!"

I almost don't answer her, but then I do. "Hi."

"Watcha doin'?" she asks. She starts climbing up to me. She got taller, so now she can get up without me helping her.

"Nothin'," I say.

"Well, let's do something," she says. Like nothing ever happened.

May is talking to me again! But I don't know if she's going to be mean or nice. My heart is all jumpy. She stops climbing halfway up to me.

"Wanna come jump on my trampoline?" she asks.

"Okay," I say.

We walk to her house and go to her backyard. I didn't know she had a trampoline. It's orange and blue, and it creaks when we jump.

At lunchtime, we go inside. May says we can have peanut butter and icing sugar sandwiches because her mom isn't home.

May gives me a spoonful of icing sugar. "Eat it," she says.

I put it in my mouth and try to swallow it, but I cough instead. All the icing sugar blows out of my mouth, and it lands on May's face. It makes her eyebrows turn white, and the powder sticks all over her hair. I laugh. "You look like an old lady!"

May's face stops smiling. She puts her whole hand in the peanut butter jar and takes a handful of peanut butter out. I am still laughing because who does that? She takes the handful of peanut butter, and shoves into my mouth and slides her palm up against my nose so peanut butter goes up inside. I can't even breathe.

When she takes her hand away, I have tears in my eyes. She laughs. "You look like you ate shit!"

She takes my hand, and we go find her dog Rex and let him lick our faces clean.

May

I'm on my way to meet Ted. I have a package of cherry Jell-O to share. I picked cherry because it will make my lips look red, like I'm wearing lipstick.

Usually, Ted waits for me in the tree, but today I'm meeting him at the playground at school. That way, we can sit in the concrete play tunnel nice and close, and he can lick the Jell-O powder off my hand like he's my puppy.

Ted's on his hands and knees outside the tunnel. He looks like he's afraid to go inside. Maybe he's pretending it's a cave full of monsters. I call to him. "Teddy!"

I think he hears me because he stands up and brushes his hands off on his pants.

A girl comes out of the tunnel who I don't even know. She's one of the big kids, I think. From fifth or sixth grade even. She has scratches on her knees, and her red hair is real messy. She looks at Ted, and he says something to her, his hand reaches out to touch her arm, but she just nods her head and starts to walk away.

I run across the field to get to him and make sure she goes away.

Then my Uncle Jake comes out of the tunnel! What was he doing in there? And why were him and Ted playing with that girl?

"Wait!" Jake calls to the girl.

She stops and turns around.

"You're okay, right?" He gives her his special smile that he only gives to me.

She looks at Ted, then Jake. Her eyes are twinkly, and her lips are pulling into a grin, "I'm—" Then she sees me, and her stupid grin goes away. She nods her head just one time.

"What are you—?" His words stop like he forgot what he was going to say. "Oh, hey, sweetheart!" He looks from me to Ted. "You didn't hurt her, did you, Teddy?" He points his chin toward the girl.

I can't even speak I'm so angry.

Ted's ears are red, but his face is so white his freckles look like dirt. He shakes his head, no, and stares at the ground.

I finally find enough words to spit out, "Who. Are. You?" The girl turns and runs.

Uncle Jake watches her go and shrugs. He bends down to kiss me on the forehead. "You're just in time! I was going to go get some ice cream." He takes my hand and then reaches for Ted's. "Care to join me?"

Ted looks like he doesn't even know where he is. He just stares at us. I glare back at him and pull at my uncle's arm. Uncle Jake shrugs again, and we head for the road. His hand feels all sweaty, and he's breathing funny like when we have tickle fights.

When we're about halfway across the field, I look back. Ted's kneeling down, looking in the tunnel. I holler, "Ted!" He jumps up and runs to catch up with us.

Ted is too shy to talk to Uncle Jake, and Uncle Jake doesn't even try to talk to Ted. He probably invited Ted just to be polite. I have to do all the talking, which is just fine because otherwise Uncle Jake will talk about cars or football, and that's too boring. I talk about different flavours of ice cream we could invent, like Alpha-Getti ice cream. Nobody laughs.

We finish the ice cream, and Uncle Jake goes home. Me and Ted go to the climbing tree.

Ted climbs higher than he ever does, to where the tree gets skinny. I follow him, but then the tree starts to bend, and I go back down a bit. "What are you doing? You should come down here."

He doesn't even answer me. Probably because he's too scared up there. I went up that high when I first climbed up here and I remember it made my heart go fluttery.

I wait, looking up at his bum and skinny white legs. He looks stupid. His arms are wrapped around the trunk like he's a koala bear. I think he's going to break the tree. I wish it would get windy, then he'd fall off and he'd never go that high again.

"Do you want some Jell-O? It's cherry." I wasn't really hungry because of the ice cream, but I know Jell-O is his very favourite thing. It's like when I try to get a squirrel to take a peanut from my hand. I feel the tree shake; he's climbing down.

He sits across the trunk from me, and I pour some Jell-O powder onto my hand and take a test lick. I lick my lips so they are red. Then I reach around the back of the trunk and poke him with my thumb. "Here," I say. I have to hold on to the trunk with my other hand, so I'm all twisted. Ted has to twist too, but then he just pops his leg over the branch so it's like he's riding a pony. I copy him. He takes a lick from my hand, and it tickles. Now our knees are touching, and if the tree trunk wasn't in the way, we could kiss.

When he looks up, I make sure my lips are pushed out like they do in magazines. I think it's the first time he's looked at me today. He smiles and puckers his lips like he's a fish.

He's making fun of me. I turn my hand upside down and wipe the Jell-O off on the tree trunk. "What did you do to that girl?"

He doesn't even ask what girl; he just looks down. But his ears are red, so I know he did something. I've spent too much time looking at the top of his head today. "Did you hurt her?" I hope he did. But he doesn't answer me, he just keeps staring at the ground.

"Do you like her?" This time, he shakes his head, *No.*

Do you want more Jell-O?" He looks up at me and nods. His lips are red. At first, I think it's from the Jell-O, then I see a tiny cut on his lip and it's bleeding. "You're bleeding," I tell him.

He wipes his lip with the back of his hand, looks at the blood smear and then wipes it off on his jeans. Then he puts the same hand out, palm up, and says, "Jell-O?"

I pour the Jell-O powder onto my hand and hold it up to his mouth to lick.

Ted

I'm going to the playground at the school to meet May. She said yesterday that she took a box of Jell-O from their kitchen. It's so good. Last time we had orange Jell-O. It tasted so sugary my tongue went numb before we finished the box. Our lips and our faces turned orange too. When mom asked why my lips were orange and I told her, she laughed and made me take a bath and brush my teeth! She said I shouldn't eat so much sugar.

I told May I would wait in the tunnel for her. We like to pretend we're dogs and it's our house. It's not very big for a house. But it's big enough that the sixth graders sometimes hide in there to smoke cigarettes or kiss. One day, I saw smoke coming out of both ends of the tunnel, and then Mr. Reid went stomping up to it, and five kids crawled out! He made them go to the office.

Someone's in the tunnel now. I can hear them making weird squeaking noises. I think it's May. She's probably being a puppy. I get down on my hands and knees so I can crawl in —it's not May! It's mostly Uncle Jake. And a girl. I think he's tickling her. She's on his lap and giggling and wiggling. She keeps saying, "No, no, no!" but she keeps giggling. Her dress is all twisted, and I can see her bare bum.

Jake's long hair is hiding their faces like a curtain. He tucks it behind his ear and then he sees me. His eyes look like May's before she does something mean. I stand up. There's a noise in my head like the ocean inside a seashell.

Uncle Jake whispers, "Hey!" just as the girl's head pops out from the tunnel, and she grabs my leg, then my pants and my arms, climbing up me like I'm a tree until she's standing in front of me. She looks straight at me as if she's surprised I'm there. My skin is crawling from where she touched me, and I want to move away because my head is roaring even louder, and she smells like sweat and metal.

She has red hair and freckles everywhere, there's patches of sand stuck on her skin from where she was sitting. Her lips look white and wet. Her face is wet and muddy.

She keeps staring at me. I think her eyes are stuck open, because they're so wide I can even see white all around the blue and she doesn't blink. She has crusties on her lashes like she just woke up and didn't wash her face yet.

She makes a kind of squeak in her throat. It sounds like she might cry and I know what that feels like, so I think I will try to give her a comforting pat, but she jumps like I poked her with a stick. She starts to walk away.

"Wait!" Jake's voice echoes out of the tunnel, then his head sticks out. He has to crawl because he's too big to be inside there. "You're okay, right?" He takes a deep breath.

I look at the girl. She's stopped, and she is nodding and doing her best not to cry, but her body is shaking like she's already crying inside. There's some blood on her thigh.

But then Jake says, "Hey, sweetheart!"

And then May is beside us, she's breathing hard, just like Jake. I think maybe she was playing with them. She looks mad.

"You didn't hurt her, did you, Teddy?" Jake says.

"Who?" I say. But I didn't hurt anyone. Except May is mad, so I'm pretty sure I hurt her. I'm afraid of what Jake will do to me. Did that girl hurt May too? I look at May's legs for blood. I shake my head. I didn't hurt anyone.

"Who. Are. You?" May growls.

I hear the girl run away and Jake laughs. When I look up, May is walking away with Uncle Jake. She's holding his hand. I guess we aren't going to have Jell-O, but I think I will sit in the tunnel for a bit anyway. I feel my legs melt from under me. There's something inside the tunnel. I think it's a sock.

"Ted!" For a second, it seems like May's voice is coming from the tunnel but it's just her echo. It's too big to be a sock. It's pink. I jump up and run to catch up with her. Maybe she isn't mad.

May

Ted has a snake. He named it Charmer. You would think it was the only thing in the world. He even put it in his pocket so he could bring it up the tree with him. Now he has it out, and he's kissing the top of its head.

I hate snakes. They're stupid. And crawly, like spiders. They can bite you, and you can die. That's what Mom says.

Ted

Every day almost, May meets me at the tree, and we walk to the store or the playground, or we just go to her house to hang out. Her mom is at work almost always, but her uncle lives at their house too, so she isn't really alone. He sleeps most of the time. He has a bedroom in their basement. Whenever he wakes up, May tells me to go home. I can't go home unless my mom is back from work, so I usually go back to Mrs. Benhowser's.

This morning, Mrs. Benhowser gave me pancakes for breakfast. Now it's time for her soaps. I'm going to the tree to meet May, and then I see a stick move. Of course, it isn't a stick! It's a garter snake! I bend down and pinch it gently between my finger and thumb and I hold it close to my chest. Snakes like warm because they are cold blooded. Its skin feels like my mom's leather jacket she got from the thrift store, smooth and cold. I'm going to call him Charmer. Snake charmers are from India.

He wiggles a little bit, but then he stops because of how cozy warm I am.

Snakes are so cool. They're just like a spine that moves by itself. And they have secret legs that are too small to even show on the outside of them. I learned that in my reptile book.

I stay still, and he wraps his long self around my wrist. It feels like we're holding hands. Rubbing my face on his skin, I can smell his snakiness.

I can't really tell if he's a boy because I don't think you can tell too easy with snakes, but I think he's probably a boy because of how nice he is to me.

"Hi?" May is suddenly beside me, and I didn't even notice her.

"Hi!" I say. I am so happy to see her because I have a snake. I hold up my hand, all wrapped up in snake to show her. "This is Charmer!"

May pulls away from Charmer like he smells bad. "Eww!"

"I found him just down there," I say and point down the pathway.

"Why are you playing with a snake? That's gross." She makes an ugly face and sticks her tongue out at him when he uses his to sniff at her.

"Touch him. He feels really neat."

She pokes him hard with her finger, which makes Charmer unwrap and wiggle. I bring my hand back to my chest so he can feel safe again. He coils up and settles down.

"He likes me because I'm warm," I explain to her.

"At least somebody likes you," she says.

I feel a little squeeze in my stomach, that wasn't a very nice thing to say. I'm not sure if she is being mean or funny, so I don't say anything back.

May swings up on the bottom branch of the tree and starts climbing really fast. I drop Charmer into my shirt pocket and follow her. She keeps climbing really high, but I stop at one of the good sitting branches and take Charmer out of my pocket. I'm worried that I shouldn't have brought him up here because I might drop him, but he wraps around my wrist again, and I watch him sniff with his tongue.

When May comes back down, she sits on the other side of the tree trunk. She reaches out her hand with a finger pointed out, and I reach my snake hand out to her. She touches Charmer, really lightly this time, and my heart feels warm. Her fingernails are all painted with felt pens from yesterday, and so are mine.

"Wow," she whispers. "Can I hold him?"

I unravel Charmer from my hand, holding him gently behind his invisible ears. "You just hold him like this, not too tight though," I tell her. "Then he'll wrap around you."

She takes him carefully like I showed her, but instead of letting him wrap, she holds him in her fist and takes his tail with her other hand, pulling him like a rope.

"No!" I shout at her, trying to reach across to swat her hand. "He doesn't like that!" Charmer is twisting, trying to get free.

May looks at me like she does when she's going to stop talking to me, but then she kind of smiles and squeaks. And drops Charmer.

I watch him fall, bouncing off branches. I can't even breathe.

In the blur from the tears in my eyes, I can see May wipe her hands on her jeans. "Sorry," she says. "I just didn't like how he wiggled."

I start climbing down the tree to see if I can find Charmer. If he is even still alive.

"Where are you going?" May calls down to me. I don't answer her. From the bark and twigs falling on my head, I know she is following me.

I find Charmer on the ground right beside the tree trunk. He's on his back, with his white belly showing all the ridges that help him move. But he isn't moving. I dig a little hole for a grave. I even say a quiet prayer even though I don't know if God is real. I know Mrs. Benhowser would have said a prayer, so I thought it was a nice thing to do.

May sits on the ground against the tree, tossing pine cones. Sometimes they hit my back, and she giggles. "Oops!" she says.

May

It's the first day of third grade. The bell rings, and we pile around the playground where Mr. Reid and two lady teachers stand with clipboards in their hands. I didn't know Mr. Reid taught third grade. I hold on to Ted's hand. I don't want to let him go. I got to be with him almost every day this summer. The smell of his skin and his voice and his laugh stay in my head all the time like a good dream.

Mr. Reid blows a whistle, and we all shut up.

"Welcome back! And to those of you who are new, welcome to Whitman Elementary. This is Miss Thompson," he says, pointing to the tall skinny teacher with a big nose and a flowery dress. "And this is Miss Frey." He points to the other teacher, who looks kind of like him, without the beard. She wears her glasses like a necklace, and she keeps picking stuff off her mustard-coloured sweater. I don't like her. She's ugly. I bet she even smells bad.

Miss Thompson calls names first. I am May Carlisle. She calls my name after Corey Anderson and Sandy Barber.

I squeeze Ted's hand and whisper in his ear, "I'll wait for you." I let my lips touch his skin when I whisper, and I know it tickles him because he scrunches his shoulders. He loves me so much.

"May Carlisle?" Miss Thompson calls my name again. Wow, she's stupid. "I'm coming!" I shout at her. I stomp up to stand with Corey and Sandy.

She calls about a hundred other kids' names. I stare at Ted, and every time he looks at me, I move my lips to say his name, "Ted Russell." Like the teacher is going to call him next. He almost always smiles, but he hardly ever looks at my eyes.

Mr. Reid starts calling names. I look back at Miss Thompson to see if he interrupted her, but she's bent down talking to a kid in our group.

Every time Mr. Reid calls a kid, they go up to him, and he shakes their hand.

"Ted Russell?" he calls out. I watch Ted strut up to Mr. Reid like he's going to get some kind of award. Mr. Reid reaches his hand out to Ted, and they shake. Ted's face lights up with one of those twinkly smiles of his. He doesn't look at me at all. Mr. Reid's kids surround him; there's only seven of them. He says something, and they all laugh. Then they walk together through the office doors. Ted has his hands folded behind his back, and his head is turned to listen to Mr. Reid as they talk. His ears are red. He never even looks back at me.

"May?" It's Miss Thompson. "Time to go, honey." I look up, and the rest of my class is already lined up at the side door. I didn't even notice they were gone. I'm shaking, and I can't catch my breath. Miss Thompson puts her hand on my shoulder and says, "Come on, honey."

I shake her off and start toward the door where the rest of her class is. As she walks by me to lead us in, I mutter, "I'm *not* your honey."

Inside the classroom, there is a name card on every desk. I find mine in the very middle of the room. Kids are talking and laughing, but it sounds like I'm listening to them from inside a closet. I sit down and stare at the top of my desk.

"Okay, people!" Miss Thompson calls out. "Let's settle down!" Everyone shuts up. She has a really big smile with giant front teeth.

Madison Cooper pokes me in the back. "Wow, that's a nasty set of fangs!" she whispers.

I giggle even though I'm still mad.

When Miss Thompson raises her eyebrows at me, I fold my hands on my desk and give her my best smile. She nods and smiles back with her goofy teeth. She says thank you to me with her lips but not her voice. Maybe she's nice.

"Let's put these desks in a friendlier way, shall we?" She lets us pick one friend we want to sit with and then gets us to put our desks in groups of four. It gets really noisy. When we're done, I'm sitting with Madison Cooper, Shelly Weise and Tara Leeds. We play together at recess, and by lunchtime, we're best friends.

After school, we all leave together. Madison and Tara can walk my way home, but Shelly's mom always picks her up. Ted is standing at the door with a stupid smile on his face. I walk right past him with my new friends.

We're talking about what we're going to bring for social studies tomorrow. Miss Thompson wants us to bring something from a foreign land. Shelly is telling me about something called a kimono.

Ted comes up beside me. "Mr. Reid got us a tiny classroom with a couch, and we get to go to the library whenever we want!" he says.

I stop and stare at him. "Who are you?" I ask. Shelly and Madison giggle.

You'd think I'd just slapped him across the face the way Ted looks back at me, all pink skinned and hurt. He starts to say something, but I cut him off. "Get the fuck away from us!" I walk away with giant steps so the girls have to run to catch up with me.

Miss Thompson is probably my favorite teacher ever. And I am her favourite student; I know because she always smiles at me. She always picks me to be her office messenger and to hand out worksheets. Her teeth hardly even bother me anymore. She doesn't even get mad when I talk too much.

Ted

Today is the first day of school, and I'm pretty excited. May meets me at the end of my street, and we walk together to the schoolyard. She's pretty grumpy. My mom says maybe she isn't a morning person. I try to stay quiet, but I can't help myself.

"I wonder if the twins will be in our class?" No answer. "What teacher do you want?" Nothing.

I don't tell her what Mom said about Mr. Reid wanting to give me "special opportunities."

When we get to the schoolyard, May takes my hand. I feel odd because no one else is holding hands, but I think she is nervous, so I squeeze her hand to make her feel better. Together we walk to the doors near the principal's office. That's where the third graders are supposed to wait. I know because my mom told me. There's a lot of kids waiting around and there's Mr. Reid and two teachers I don't even know.

Mr. Reid blows a whistle to get everyone's attention. He tells us the two new teachers are Miss Thompson and Miss Frey. Miss Thompson has a flowery dress and a nice smile. I hope she's my teacher. But then I look at Miss Frey, and I see she is nervous and shy like me. She doesn't look at us students very much; she is mostly worried about her sweater being old, I think, because she picks at it a lot. She might be a nice teacher too.

May tightens her grip on me when the teachers start calling out names. Miss Thompson goes first and she calls out three names, and then she calls, "May Carlisle?" I feel a little panicky because May will be away from me, and she's been with me almost all summer. I'm worried we won't be in the same class. And also, that we will be in the same class. Which would mean May would see Mr. Reid treating me special. And that would make her mad.

May puts her face really close to my ear and whispers, "See you soon." I scrunch my shoulders and pull away because it almost feels like she is kissing me in front of everybody. I let go of her hand, but she stays close until Miss Thompson calls her name again.

"May?"

"I'm coming!" May shouts too loud, and she stomps up to stand with the other kids in Miss Thompson's group.

I wait and listen for my name. It's very noisy and hard to hear. I look at May and she's moving her mouth like she's saying my name. That makes me laugh so I look away because I don't want to miss my name. When I look at her again, she is still staring and saying my name.

Miss Thompson calls Shelly Weise. She skipped my name, I'm pretty sure, because Shelly always comes after me in the alphabet. I look away from May and don't look back. Then Mr. Reid calls Jonathon Kendall. Everyone stops talking.

Jonathon is really quiet and shy. I feel bad for him getting in trouble from the principal on the very first day of school. He walks up to Mr. Reid, and Mr. Reid smiles and shakes

Jonathon's hand. Then Jonathon stands beside him, looking at his toes.

Two more kids get called up. They shake hands with the principal and stay up there with him.

"Ted Russell?"

My heart thumps right into my throat. I look up at Mr. Reid, and he nods his head once at me. I walk up to him. His hand is already out for shaking and he is smiling his big crinkly smile. I think May's eyes are trying to burn a hole in the back of my head.

"Hey, buddy!" Mr. Reid says. "Welcome to the enhanced learning class!"

A whole class? Not just me and Mr. Reid? "Thank you," I say. Out of the corner of my eye, I see May's class start to move toward the door. Except May. She's standing by herself, still staring at me. I move over to stand with the other kids and look at my feet, just like them. Maybe everyone is being stared at.

"Okay, my friends, let's go find our classroom!" Mr. Reid starts walking away, and we walk with him. Not even in a line, just like a group of friends. As soon as we get in the school, we look at each other and smile. It's like Mr. Reid just saved us from the bullies. For the entire school year.

He takes us to a little room beside his office. It's like a classroom only smaller, and there's mobiles of planets hanging from the ceiling, and real pieces of engines on one of the shelves and guitars and bongo drums on another. There's an old red couch in the corner with a bunch of cushions. The couch looks like the one in my grandma's basement.

Mr. Reid says, "Pick a seat, folks."

I think someone just piled the desks into the room this morning because they're all over the place—some in the middle, one against a wall facing out, and one against a wall facing the wall. There's more desks than there are students. Nobody takes the one facing the wall. I take one that's near the couch.

Mr. Reid sits on the corner of the teacher's desk, just like he did in Miss Webber's class. He folds his arms in front of him. "Wow, you guys are pretty quiet."

We let out a nervous giggle, then it's quiet again. Smart kids are usually quiet.

"So you may have heard me mention that this is the enhanced learning class." He looks us over. Some of us, like me, nod. "That means I'm going to push you a little harder this year. We're going to really explore your potential." He looks up at the ceiling and shakes his head. "Sorry, does anyone know what *potential* means?"

Before I even get a chance to answer, one of the fourth grade kids shoots up her hand and blurts out, "How good we can get!"

Mr. Reid smiles. "That's basically it. The idea with this class is for you to keep trying. If you're doing a worksheet or a project and you find it's too easy, take on the next level."

Mr. Reid talks a little bit longer; then he gets us to write out five questions. They can be about anything we wonder: math, science, history, or anything. He says not to ask questions about school because we can do that anytime. We get to use our pencil crayons and can even draw pictures.

I really like third grade. I can't wait to tell May how neat my class is. I wait by our corner after school because my class has different recess and lunchtimes than hers. She finally comes out, and she's smiling. She's in a good mood! I run up to her, but she is talking to someone else. I don't think she sees me because she keeps walking. I follow her and just start talking because it's me and she says we're best friends. We're going to play together this afternoon.

I call after her to get her attention. "Guess what?" I puff out when I catch up. The girls she's with look back at me, but May doesn't. "Mr. Reid got us a special tiny classroom with a couch and sciencey stuff, and we get to go to the library whenever we want!" I'm talking super fast, but that's because the other girls are there, and that makes me nervous.

May stops and turns to look back at me. She squishes her eyebrows together. "Who are you?" she says.

I think she's being funny at first, so I smile a little and say, "Ted," and keep walking with them.

But she turns and shouts, "Get the fuck away from us!"

I stop, and she stomps away with the other girls, who are giggling. I get my throat lump and take deep breaths to make it go away. Mom told me that can help a lot.

Inside the house at home, I stop breathing so deep, and my lump isn't there anymore. I have lots of stuff I want to do for school tomorrow. Mr. Reid says we don't have to call it homework; we can call it preparation. He says that's what he calls it when he gets stuff done at home for the next day.

I like May a lot. But I think school's easier.

May

Madison, Tara, and Shelly are a lot like Ted. They want to do anything I want to do. Only they aren't dorky-brained.

Before school started this morning, I dared Tara to take Michael Stevens's chocolate chip cookies out of his lunch bag. He always gets two cookies for his lunch.

We have quiet reading just before recess. I get my library book about dogs out of my desk. Shelly and Madison do the same, but Tara heads for the back of the classroom where we keep our coats and backpacks. Everybody is chattering.

"Okay, everyone, settle down," Miss Thompson says, standing at her desk. She's looking at the class over her glasses, which are halfway down her nose. I think she likes quiet reading time. "Tara? Back to your desk, please!"

"I forgot my book in my backpack."

Mrs. Thompson puts her hands on her hips and shakes her head. "Okay, hurry up."

I look back and see Tara has Michael's backpack open, her head buried inside. Doesn't Mrs. Thompson even know Tara's backpack is pink, not green? I turn back and open my book, staring really hard at the pages so I don't laugh. Tara comes back to her desk with a book about beetles. I think that's Michael's book, because her library book is about dogs, just like mine. Tara is terrified of bugs.

I look over at Michael. His glasses are sitting on the corner of his desk. Miss Thompson says some people only need glasses to see far away. She needs glasses to see close, so she keeps hers on a necklace around her neck. Michael's got a book open on his desk with his finger pressed onto a page.

It finally snowed! I walk to school with Tara and Madison. Shelly always gets a ride to school, so we just meet her in the playground. At the playground, I pick up a handful of snow. It's icy wet and melts into dribbles between my fingers. While Tara is walking in front of me, I push my handful of snow down inside her collar. She squeals and runs away. Then I feel a thunk on my back. Madison just threw a chunk of wet snow at me, but she doesn't throw very good, so I hardly feel it. I grab more snow, shaping it round in my bare hands. Then there's a smack of sharp ice on my face and my eye. It's so cold it burns. I turn to see Shelly with a big smile on her face that disappears fast.

She catches her breath. "Oh! Oops! Sorry." She runs to me, reaching out to brush the snow off my face.

I take the snow in my hand and grind it into her nose and face. "Facewash!" I scream right into her ear. Then Madison and Tara are on top of us, throwing snow and wrestling and laughing so much I forget I was going to kill Shelly. The bell rings, and we go inside. Shelly has a bit of blood on her lip, but she wipes it off with her pink mitten.

When it snows, everyone has to take their boots off at the door and put them in the boot racks. Then we walk in our socks to get to our classrooms where our inside shoes are. It's pretty stupid because everyone gets wet socks and then we have to be in wet socks all day. Wet socks stink.

I take off my boots and see Ted near the other side of the hall taking off his. His are big green ones with fluffy stuff around the tops and laces. They come up to almost his knees. He doesn't notice me because he's facing the other way.

At recess, we are playing in the snow at the edge of the schoolyard, and some dog has left a shit near the big tree. The snow around it is yellow.

"That's so gross," says Madison. "What if we stepped in it?"

"Eww!" Shelly doesn't even want to look at it.

Looking at the poo reminds me of Ted and his stupid dead cat. And that reminds me of his boots. And that gives me an idea. "Wouldn't it be so gross if someone stepped in it and then walked into the school?"

My friends all respond with another, "Eww!"

Then I grin my best twinkly grin and look first at Madison and then at Shelly. "Wouldn't it be even grosser if they had poo inside their boots?"

Madison giggles. "May! You wouldn't!"

"Nope, I would never do that," I say, shaking my head, still smiling. "But I bet Shelly would."

Madison and Tara crack up. "Shelly would never ever!"

I look over at Shelly. She looks worried. She's chewing her lip and not really looking at me. She knows I'm mad at her for the snowball this morning. I rub my face where it hit me. "I don't know," I say, "I think Shelly is pretty crazy. Right, Shelly?"

Shelly looks down at the lumps of brown fudge in the snow. She breathes in deep with her mouth and blows out hard. She looks up at me and Madison and Tara, taking the baggie from her recess snack out of her pocket, and nods her head. "Yup, I'm really crazy." Her hands are shaky when she picks up the poo though, so I know she isn't all that crazy.

The bell goes, and we run for the doors. Shelly keeps her hand careful in her pocket to hold the poo. There's kids all over taking off their boots in the hall. It smells like fresh air and stinky feet. Shelly has her boots off and is holding them in her hand, looking at me. I lean into her and say, "Those big green ones at the end."

She walks over and bends down like she's going to put her boots away and drops the turds into one of Ted's boots. She drops the baggie in the other boot.

Madison snorts out a giggle. I grab her by the arm and drag her to our classroom. I'm holding back my giggles too. When we sit down at our desks, all four of us burst out laughing.

Miss Thompson smiles at us. "Did you have fun in the snow, ladies?"

Ted

The boot room stinks of dog poo. I hurry to get my boots on to get away from the smell and because school is over. But as soon as I put my boot on, I feel something squishy inside, and the poo smell puffs up into my nose. There's poo inside my boot! I struggle to take my foot out when I hear May call out, "Who has poo on their boots?"

The kid next to me is staring at me. He's littler than me; I think he's in first grade. He picks up his boots and steps back, pointing at me. He doesn't laugh. He just points and stares. Everyone else laughs. Especially May.

I shove my foot back in my boot. "No! It is not me!" I lift one leg at a time to show everyone the bottoms of my boots. My ears burn. The laughing stops. May is standing across from me, her arms folded and her eyes spark like they do when she's done something that no one else thinks is funny. She's laughing inside herself.

I walk home, mashing the poop between my toes every time I take a step. May and her friends follow me.

In the kitchen, I squirt the soap for dishes inside them. I'm crying because winter only just started and these are my only boots. Mom was very worried looking when I wanted them so bad at the store. She even put things back from the shopping cart until there was just my boots and a big box of those weird napkins she always buys but doesn't even use.

The house stinks of dog shit. Which reminds me of when Ghost died. That makes me cry even more. I hate that I cry. I hate May. I hate that she makes me cry.

The front door opens, and Mom calls out, "I'm home!" and then, "Oh God, what on earth?"

I'm standing on a chair at the kitchen sink, soap suds all over me and my boots. My face is wet from sweat and crying and bubbles.

"Teddy! What have you done?" She tiptoes into the kitchen, scowling, but when she sees me, she smiles.

I look across the kitchen floor and see trails of poopy

sock prints. "Sorry, Mom." Then I get back to scrubbing. "Someone put poo inside my new boots."

Mom looks angry again, but she doesn't say anything. She just gets a mop.

May

Summer is here, third grade is over and we're moving to England to live with my Granny. We're flying there tonight. I am so mad. Mom says I'll love London. "You'll make new friends," she keeps saying.

I don't want new friends!

This morning, Mom is at work for her last day, and Dad is packing boxes, putting them in the garage. Mom made me pack up my toys last night. She says we have to put everything away so other people can live in our house while we're gone. I don't want anyone to play with my toys, so I put extra tape on the boxes.

I think I might run away. I take my backpack and put socks in it and my toothbrush. I go to the kitchen to get some snacks to keep me going until I find somewhere to stay. But all the cupboards are empty. There's only milk in the fridge. This is so stupid! I don't even have any money because I had to buy a Troll doll.

I put my shoes on and sneak out the back door so Dad doesn't see me. I realize I'm heading for Ted's house. He has to go to a babysitter when there's no school, so even when I knock on the door, I know he won't be home. His babysitter is creepy and old. I'm not going there. Maybe he's at the tree.

When I get to the path, I look around the street to see if he's anywhere before I go into the woods. I haven't been here for so long I forgot how many ferns and trees there are. And how quiet it is. At the bottom of the tree, I look up so far my backpack almost makes me fall over. I don't see anything that looks like a bum or a boy on any of the branches. I call up, "Is that you?" really loud. But no one answers.

I wait for a bit and then holler again. Nothing. Maybe Ted doesn't climb trees anymore either. I decide to go to the playground at the school and swing for a bit.

Nobody is at the playground. Why is everyone so boring anyway? Tara and Madison are both away, and Shelly doesn't even live close enough to play. I sit on the swing forever, but nobody shows up. I guess I'll go home. At least I can watch TV if Dad didn't pack it already. I'll look at the tree one last time though. I should say goodbye to Ted in case I don't run away.

"Is that you?" I can see his bum about halfway up the tree. He doesn't answer. I start climbing. I hate climbing this stupid tree, especially when he isn't behind me to catch me. He's at his usual spot. I sit on the other side of the trunk from him. He looks at me but doesn't say anything. He's playing with one of those blocks that you turn and twist to make the colours the same on every side.

"Anyway. I just came to say goodbye," I say. He still doesn't say anything. I hate it when Ted acts stupid. "I'm moving today."

He finally looks around the tree trunk at me. "So?" he says.

Why is he being stupid? No wonder I don't play with him anymore. "I'm going to miss you," I tell him.

"Huh," he says.

He starts twisting the block. Most of the colours are in place, but they start going everywhere as he works. He is doing it backwards. His fingers are dirty around the knuckles, like

50

the white squares on the block. His fingernails are full of dirt underneath. So are mine, but I have pink nail polish on them.

"I'm sorry I didn't play with you at school," I say. I pick at the pink on my nails. This is boring. I wish he would just give me a Ted smile and we could go play. "I didn't want you to think I was stupid. None of my friends would have been nice to you anyway. Madison and Tara are mean to everyone. So is Shelly."

"I know," he says, still not looking.

I reach out and try to smack that dumb cube thing out of his hand, but my arms are too short. Instead, my hand just taps his thigh. "C'mon," I say. "Let's go do something."

"Like what?" he says.

My heart jumps. Finally, he stopped being stupid! "Let's go to the playground," I say, already climbing down from the stupid tree.

1982

May

We finally moved back to our old house. It's really odd to be here. Mom is going back to work today, and Dad starts teaching at the university tomorrow. And I have to start school. Puh.

I've changed ninety-two times since I got up this morning. In London, I just wore a uniform. I didn't need to decide anything but how to do my hair. I'm finally on my way out the door in one of Dad's white dress shirts, my black leggings, and Doc Martens. Freshman year, here I come. I wonder if Ted's still here. I almost went to his house yesterday after I got my stuff unpacked, but Mom wanted to go shopping.

It's so hot already my pits are wet. I think I might turn around and get changed again. But I'm desperate for a fag, and Mom and Dad still don't let me smoke at home. I pull out my pack of Camels and light one up.

There are a few kids on the street heading the same way as me. No one I recognize though. That's okay. From what I remember, there was nobody worth knowing on this street. Nobody worth knowing anywhere around here really. Except Ted.

When I get to his street, I slow down. The street is empty, but it looks brighter than I remember. Then I realize there's houses where the climbing tree used to be. Wow. I guess I have been away a long time.

I walk past the elementary school, and it's different too. It's beige now. It used to be blue. It looks weird with no kids in the yard, but they're already inside because the little kids start earlier than us. Two more blocks, and I'm at Timberland High. It's fucking huge. Everyone is standing in little groups, laughing and talking. I look at my watch and see I'm early—like, by ten minutes. I keep walking past the school and light up another fag. I walk around the block along the fence that surrounds the football field, listening for the bell. My heart is whackadoo. Fuck school. Why the fuck should I go?

There's an opening in the fence, and I walk through to take a seat on the bleachers. I can see the school across the field and I can hear the voices of the kids. The bleacher seat is damp from morning dew, which sucks because now my ass is wet. I flick my cigarette butt onto the grass and lean back.

"Got a smoke for me?"

I jump out of my fucking skin. There's a guy under the bleachers—his head popped out between the benches above me. His face is pink with zits, and he has long black whiskers randomly sprouting around his chin and lips.

"Jesus! You scared the fuck out of me."

He grins and wedges his head back under the seats, appearing seconds later in front of me. "Hi, I'm Mike," he says. He looks at me expectantly.

"May," I give him. He's hard to look at, not just because he's got zits but because the sun is blasting right behind his head. So I look at my boots.

"You startin' here this year?" he asks, taking a seat beside me. I get a whiff of Aqua Velva and Old Spice mixed with BO. Why do so many guys not know about showering?

He pushes a greasy lock back over his head. "So how about that smoke?"

I look him up and down. He could clean up nice. "How 'bout a quarter?"

"Seriously?" He shakes his head and has to stand back up to dig into his jeans pocket, and I'm guessing, to adjust his boner.

He comes up with two dimes and three pennies. "I owe you two cents."

I take the cash, dig out my Camels, and tap out two

sticks. He has a lighter ready and gallantly lights mine first, cupping the flame and leaning in close. He inhales deep, and I wait for him to cough it out. He doesn't disappoint.

"You're new," he says.

"Kinda."

"I never seen you before."

"I was away for a few years." I let my London accent pour through as I speak. I started talking like a cockney when we were over there so the kids wouldn't make fun of me. At first, people, especially grown-ups, would ask me where I was from, even though I was copying their accent, because apparently you can tell what part of England a person is from by the way they speak. But I got better at it, I think, because people stopped asking.

"Let me guess. Freshman?" He's cool enough not to mention the accent.

"Sophomore," I lie.

"Nice. An older woman," he says.

We sit for a bit, our legs stretched out, elbows resting on the bench behind, watching the sun pour morning over the school as the noise of kids gets louder. The bell rings. My heart chokes my breath.

"You goin' in?" Mike asks. He hasn't moved.

I don't answer. The schoolyard empties. My heart settles. I reach and press my hand over his crotch. Of course, it's hard.

"Let's go take a shower," I say, squeezing at the sausage pushing against his fly.

"Okay," he squeaks.

He stands up quick enough I think he's going to pass out. His skin is pale and sweaty, making his zits glow like puss-capped volcanoes along his neck and chin. That BO has won out over the Aqua Velva, and the smell is enough to make my stomach turn. He reaches a hand down to help me up, but I ignore it.

"On second thought, I think I'll head in," I say. I start walking across the field toward the empty schoolyard.

"Me too," Mike says, scrambling to catch up.

Ted

I won't actually skip any more grades, but I'll probably graduate next year. The class I'm in is called accelerated learning. They've given us the curriculum for all the sophomore courses, and we just have to meet the requirements at our own pace. Easy enough. All I want is to get to university where I can do some real learning.

Miss Bluth is only twenty-three. She is working on her PhD in education, and teaching us is not only her job but part of her research. Her glasses are nearly as big as her face, and her bangs are clipped back with bobby pins that don't seem to be working.

"So you guys are my lab rats. That's okay, right?" We already knew this because our parents had to sign a release to let her study us. "I promise I won't manipulate you. As a matter of fact, my research is based on not manipulating you, although I can't say there won't be the odd pizza party."

There's a guy sitting across from me. He's gorgeous. He must be from another school. He's got grey eyes, the colour of blindness, that seem so contrary to his Mediterranean features. His arms are tanned almost black. I watch the muscles in his forearms flex as he lets his pen slide between his thumb and index finger, letting it drop to the desk and then pinching the bottom to let it slip through again. The name on his notebook is David.

"Things you need to do to stay in this program." Miss Bluth writes a number one on the chalkboard, punctuating it with a sharp tap that shatters the tip of her chalk. "Oh, shit. I mean, shoot!"

The class roars in laughter, but when she turns to us, her cheeks are bright red and there are speckles of chalk on her face. We stop as suddenly as we started. She looks like a little girl getting bullied, and we all know how that feels.

"I guess I need to learn to write on a chalkboard, huh?" She grins at us as she wipes her dusty hands on her skirt. I watch David smile at her, and I wonder what he's thinking.

Things we need to do to stay in the program:

1. Score 90% or higher on everything. Rewrites are allowed on assignments but not on tests.
2. Take part in at least one extra-curricular activity. Check. I am in band.
3. Complete eight sophomore-level courses. Once that's done, we can start on senior-level ones.

"We have the science lab on Tuesday and Thursday afternoons. You're welcome to stay as late as you need." She pauses and then adds, "Unless I have a date."

Everyone laughs. David rolls his eyes. Then he looks at me, eyebrows raised. What does that mean? My face burns, and I regret my new haircut because I know my ears are flamboyant red.

This is going to be an amazing year. Or a horrible one.

May

It's Ted! He's beautiful. He's walking in front of me, down the hall. I'm sure it's him. His hair: still the same blond curls but now the curls are just on the top, shaved on the sides. His ears, probably his worst feature, still stick out like a bat's.

I remember when I learned that bats see with their ears, I started calling him Batman. He thought it was cool until I told him why. And his stride: a little wide, as though he has a huge cock to contend with between his legs.

"Ted!" I shout down the hall. He's disappearing into the mess of kids changing classes. I push my way through like a running back pulling yards. But I lose sight of him amongst chests and arms and legs. Fuck being short. I stop shoving and stand in the hall. Kids bump past me and give me nasty looks. I glare back at them, willing someone to say something. My temper is hot. I'd love to fuck someone over. But no one rises to the challenge. The hall empties with me still in the middle of it. Where did he go?

I kick a locker with the full force of my Doc Martens. The sound echoes in the hall. I'm about to kick another one, but a teacher has appeared from one of the classrooms, so instead I walk in the opposite direction, toward an exit sign. Fuck school.

Ted

Being part of the accelerated learning class is like wearing a sign that says Kick Me on your back. We are the brunt of the entire school's entertainment. Walking down the hall? You can be guaranteed there will be a leg stuck out for you to trip over. Standing in a crowd? Oh dear, I accidentally knocked your binder to the floor. Eating lunch? I believe that sandwich belongs to me.

The only good thing is, we get to commiserate with each other. It's like returning from battle every time we come into the classroom.

◆ ◆ ◆

It's Tuesday, and I have my cello with me. The hard case bumps against my leg because I'm trying not to touch anyone else with it as I go down the hall. I've done that before and ended up with a black eye.

Speaking of black eyes, I see the bulk of Zack Bilton coming toward me, and my heart starts to fumble. He's got a couple of his friends with him; one looks like a skinny rat; the other is twice as wide as Zack with pig eyes and no neck. They split up, so one stooge is on either side of me, and there's Zack's big zitty face almost close enough to kiss.

"Hey, turd." He tilts his head. "You forgot to say hi to me." His breath smells like mouldy cheese.

I roll my eyes and try to step around them. I feel a tug on my cello case. Fuck. Here we go.

"What's in the case?" he asks, poking it with his foot. The rat pulls the neck of the case up and is opening a clasp. I keep a grip on the handle and pull the case close with my spare hand. Which makes my backpack slip off my shoulder and swing precariously close to Zack's nuts.

He grabs my collar, of course, and shoves me towards a locker. The rest of the kids in the hall are taking a wide path around us. My head clanging against the metal is like a starting bell, and everyone seems to move a little faster as our scrimmage moves to one side of the hall. That, or I'm fighting consciousness. Then Zack staggers sideways, and David is there, all fists and kicks and grunts. My cello case gets heavy again as the stooge beside me lets go.

A voice hollers, "Gentlemen!"

David drops all aggression, and Zack and company walk off as if they were just part of the hallway traffic. Miss Bluth comes scurrying down the hall with as much authority as she can muster.

"You guys okay?"

David hasn't even broken a sweat. He looks at me with that incredible grin, eyebrows lifted, pale eyes on me. On me.

"We're good," I hear myself say, eyes locked on David's. A smile is tugging at my lips. Of course, my ears are flaming. I scratch the back of my neck to break the intensity of our eye contact.

"Do I need to get the principal involved?" Spoken like a true victim, Miss Bluth knows exactly what the risks are when shitheads like Zack get in trouble for bullying. They attack outside the school.

"No," I say, still looking anywhere but at David. "It was nothing."

"Okay. Let's get to class, guys." She leaves us, her bulging briefcase making her bend sideways as she walks.

David puts his hand on my shoulder. "C'mon, kid."

I finally risk looking at him. Those eyes. I can't speak, because I can't breathe, but I think I nod.

I think we both know we have to touch. That afternoon, we're eating lunch together in the classroom.

"Where did you learn to fight?" I ask him.

He shrugs and finishes chewing the bite of peanut butter sandwich in his mouth. I watch his Adam's apple bob as he swallows. "My dad got me in kung fu as soon as they figured out I was going to be smart." He starts to take another bite, but stops, and says, "Want to learn some moves?"

We're in his basement. He's teaching me some moves to protect myself. Blue vinyl mats line the floor, like at school when we do wrestling. We're in bare feet and no shirts, just our jeans. No one's home.

"Try to kick me."

I giggle. *Fuck. Get yourself together, Ted. At least have some decorum of cool.*

David shakes his head, a smile tugging at the corners of his mouth.

"It helps. Really. Once you know a few moves, you won't be so easy to intimidate."

I take a deep breath and exhale, trying to control the feelings racing through me. Where do I kick? His chest? Like that would be possible. His shin? I go for it, taking two steps in and aiming as strong a kick as I can muster right at . . . Oh fuck.

He blocks my leg and grabs my foot before I connect with his crotch. I fall to the mat. He's laughing and standing over me. His torso a dark muscular *V* rising from his jeans. "Okay. So we need to teach you how to kick too."

But he's getting down on his knees, straddling me. I don't move. His hands hold my wrists. I don't move. He's lowering his head. I realize I'm holding my breath, and I don't want to blow it out in his face, so I slowly exhale through my nose. The sound is ridiculously loud.

David smiles.

We kiss. It's like taking my first breath. Lips touching dryly, parting to touch warm, wet tongues. That tickly feeling I get in my cock rushes in like a powerful ache that only wants more. My hands lose themselves in his taut form. I want. So bad I want. The scent of skin and breath mingles. Urgent joy.

We're going to sign up for the cross-country team. We've been running together for the past couple of weeks, and we set a pretty good pace. I ran almost every day this summer, and David, well he can do anything.

This morning, Coach Milton got on the PA and announced there's going to be a cross-country team. "We've been invited to the city's cross-country meet in October, and I think we can make a show of it," he growled over the scratchy speakers. "I need at least ten of you to get us in the game. Meet me at the track after class today if you think you've got a three-mile run in you."

The only thing is, it won't just be David and me. There are a bunch of kids out there already. My breath starts to catch. Funny how my tiny world that revolves around David makes me forget all the other assholes we go to school with.

Our trysts are rare. But it's enough to know David wants me as much as I want him. When we stand near each other, there's an actual current I'm surprised no one can see. Actually, I'm glad no one can see. We get enough abuse.

I give him a light bump, walking close enough that I brush against him, as if by accident. It's our way of holding hands.

"Is this a good idea?" I ask as we get closer to the group of kids, mostly in gym shorts, mostly of the jock variety. Some of them are stretching, pulling a foot up behind them, or especially the girls, bending down over straight legs to touch their toes, their butts on full display. I'm scanning the group, looking for anyone who gets a particular pleasure from torturing me. I don't recognize anyone. I take a steadying breath.

David bumps me back. "Of course, this is a good idea."

The coach, whistle bouncing off his jiggling chest, is strutting across the field. It's now or never.

David slaps my shoulder. "You get to show all these suckers what a good runner they made of you!"

Then a girl is between us. I fight the urge to run. Girls can be the nastiest. She's beaming up at me instead of David, which is weird, because girls don't look at me.

My head roars in panic. She's saying something and putting her hand on my face. I step away and glare down at her, remembering what David keeps saying about not being a victim. I reach deep for a masculine growl, "No!" But I don't think anything comes out. Behind her, David's body tenses into a fighting stance.

"Oh my God, Ted!" she says, closing the space I made and putting her hand back on me. "It's me, May!"

May? Oh! A little rush of weakness goes down my legs, and some kind of squawky giggle comes out of my throat. I'm so cool.

"May? You're back?"

"Miss me?" She's wrapping her arms around me. I remember laughing so hard, deep in our imaginary world, the warm feeling I got when she was being nice. As if I was the only person in the world. I remember dog shit in my boots. My snake falling. Her tears and my freedom when she finally moved away. I take her hands by the wrist and get out of the hug, moving closer to David. My ears are burning, my heart is pounding. I think I'm going to throw up.

David's looking at me like a lover being introduced to a wife. I want to stroke his hair. *No, babe. She's a nightmare. She's nothing.*

"David"—my lover, my everything—"this is May. We went to the same school when we were kids."

He looks down at May and gives her a nod and half a grin.

May turns her cleavage his way as she slips her arm

around my waist. "We were best friends until I had to move," she chirps.

What the fuck is she doing? I scowl over her head to David.

"Where'd you move?" He asks her. But he's looking at me, and I realize he's doing his best not to laugh.

"I was in London with my folks." That explains the stupid accent.

"And you two didn't keep in touch?" he asks, still fighting a smile.

I'm biting the inside of my lower lip, holding off my own laugh. I love him so much.

The coach's whistle breaks the awkward air, and I take a big stride out of May's grasp, joining David's side. I put my hand on his shoulder and lean in to mutter in his ear, "Help."

He snorts, and we're both doing our best not to burst. "Deep breaths," David mutters as we take our place in front of the coach.

May shoves between us and stands in front of me. She gives me a flirty glance over her shoulder and crosses her arms.

It's too much. I'm gone. And there is nothing worse than laughing when the coach is talking. I back away and head for the school. David's right there beside me.

"Okay," he says, once we're out of hearing distance. "So, I guess cross-country is out."

I'm going to laugh all night. Wow.

Now that I've seen her, I can't unsee her. Not just the stuff I remember, but it seems the school just got smaller. No matter what time of day I'm in the hall, May's there too. Most of the time, she's wrapped around that Steve guy. He's a severe jock. But he's never given me any trouble. I always make sure I smile and wave if she sees me. And she always sees me. Probably because she feels my eyes watching her every move. That's what you do when you're walking past a snake. You make sure it doesn't attack.

"Hi, Teddy!" She's peeping around Steve's bicep, a massive hunk of flesh that can't be ignored. She's got her hands up around Steve's neck, and he's got his on her ass. "How's it going?"

I shrug and pull my lips into a smile, baring my teeth. "I'm good," I call back, bobbing my head in agreement with myself. "How about you?" I keep walking. It'll be over soon.

"We should hang out someday!" she calls out. Then she squeals. I assume Steve's hand has slipped.

"Sure thing!" I call back over my shoulder. And it's over.

May

I like to run. I actually joined the track team in London so I could skip class. We were always heading to other schools for track meets—and they always happened during the day. Turns out I was pretty much the best that school had ever seen. So that's why I'm showing up for track instead of going home after school today.

Ted's here. Oh my God. He's on the track team? Poor boy doesn't stand a chance when he sees me in these shorts. He's talking to a guy who's hot in his own right. As I walk up to them, my heart's all excited, and so's all that between my legs.

I step between them. "Remember me?" I say, beaming up at Ted.

He doesn't smile. He just says, "No."

I realize they're both staring right down on my tits, and

my tits are definitely something to stare at. I reach up to Ted's face, but he pulls away. That pisses me off.

"Oh my God, Ted! It's me, May!"

His face goes from "Who the fuck are you?" to "Wow! It's you!" instantly. There's that grin.

"May? You're back?"

"Miss me?" I ask, and I wrap my arms around him. His waist, that is. He's so tall, my head is against his chest. I can hear his heart and it's beating hard. He takes my wrists and unwraps my arms, stepping out of our hug, but he can't seem to let me go. His hands are still gripping me. I know it's hard for boys. He probably doesn't want to pop a woody in his gym shorts.

"David, this is May," he says, finally letting go of my wrists. "We went to the same school when we were kids." Ted's voice is shaky, and his ears are pink.

David gives me a nod. "Hi." He's the same height as Ted but dark all over. His heavy-lidded eyes look down at me like he could take me right there.

"We were best friends until I had to move," I explain to David. "But I'm back!" I slip my arm around Ted's waist to let David know not to bother trying to pick me up.

"Where did you move to?" he asks me, but he's looking at Ted.

"I was in London with my folks. My dad was working there."

David tilts his head. "You two didn't keep in touch?" he asks, still looking at Ted.

The coach's whistle blows, and he has his arm up in the air. "Okay, folks, let's gather 'round!"

I look up at Ted and slide my hand down to his ass. "Shall we?"

David walks on ahead of us, and Ted picks up his pace, so he slips out of my grip. He catches up to David, and they lean their heads together. Ted talks into David's ear and squeezes his arm. David nods and smiles at him. It all looks a little gay. Poor Ted. No wonder he gets bullied. I catch up and cram myself between them, standing in front of Ted so I can see what's going on.

"First off, thanks to all of you new people for coming out. This is going to give us some fighting power in the city meets. We'll do a warm-up and then divide you up into groups. I want juniors over here"—he points to his left—"and seniors, yes that's you, Mr. Williams"—everyone laughs—"over here."

I lean back to rest against Ted, but no one is there, and I stagger. I look around and see Ted and David are halfway across the field, headed to the school, walking so close together they bump.

"Hey there, you okay?" It's the notorious Mr. Williams. He's lean and black and putting a gentle hand on my shoulder. The sun makes a halo out of his afro.

"Yeah, I just tripped a little."

He keeps his hand on my shoulder. "C'mon. Seniors are over here." He puts a hand on his chest. "I should know."

I take another glance back at Ted and David as I walk toward the senior track team.

"Do I call you mister? Or do you have a first name?"

The coach starts hollering. "Juniors! Jumping jacks! Seniors! Give me a lap!"

We start jogging together. So, I'm a senior. Who knew?

"You can call me Steve. Or God, if you prefer."

"I don't believe in God."

"Okay. Do you believe in Steve?"

He's funny. I like that. I laugh.

"I might. Does he like sinners?"

"Steve loves sinners!"

Ted and David have disappeared into the school. I'll deal with that later. For now, there's Steve.

Ted

Supper is done, and we're watching the news. David sits on the loveseat with his legs up, and I sit cross-legged on the floor, leaning against the loveseat. Mr. LeClair is in his big green leather recliner, and David's mom clatters dishes in the kitchen. I offered to help her, but she just laughed and sent me out to the living room "with the men."

Bob Gentry has been elected to Laguna Beach city council in California. He's the first openly gay government official elected in the US. The newscast is weighing in with judges, CIA agents, and other city councillors at Laguna.

I don't look at David, but I see his toes wiggling out of the corner of my eye. I think of walking along a sandy beach, hand in hand, openly in love.

Mr. LeClair slams the recliner footrest down and stands up. I nearly wet myself. He shuts the television off. "An abomination in the eyes of God," he says, and he walks away, muttering, "Fucking faggots."

I crane my neck to smile at my sweetheart. He's staring straight ahead. His eyelashes are wet. I reach up to touch him, and he swipes my hand away.

Mom knows. I think she does. She's never asked, and I've never said anything. But I don't feel like I'm hiding it from her. Or maybe I am? I've never talked about what it's like to kiss David, or how much I love him. But I do talk about him all the time. And she never questions when he comes over and we lock ourselves in my bedroom for hours.

May

Steve and I are actually dating. Turns out he is the school's super jock. All we do is fuck and run and get high. It didn't take too long for him to figure out I was only a sophomore, but by then he was smitten. He's all about attending classes and stuff though, because he wants a scholarship. Whatever. I still consider afternoon classes optional. And mornings sometimes too.

Today is one of those mornings. We had a late night. Steve came in through my window at about midnight, and we were at it until he looked at the window and saw the sky was turning grey. "Holy shit! My folks are going to be up soon!" And he was out of me and my room in seconds flat. I guess I fell asleep because now it's ten o'clock, and I'm still lying here.

I put on my pink cowl-neck sweater, black leggings, and my pink high-tops. I get Mom's amethyst earrings out of her jewellery box and fifty bucks out of Dad's wad in his sock drawer. I'll take Steve somewhere nice for lunch. Just before I leave, I grab a benny out of the medicine cabinet. I love the energy they give me.

I always look down Elm Street when I pass. Today's no different. Winter has knocked all the leaves off the trees, and I can see the red door of Ted's house. I stop and blow a smoke ring. It circles the door. How is that not a sign?

I take a few steps down Elm and blow another ring. This one circles his bedroom window. What else can I do?

And now I'm in his backyard. The leaves from the big maple are raked into a giant, inviting pile. I flop down into them; they crunch as I land. I love the smell of dried leaves. The back deck looks freshly stained. It's dark brown and smooth. Almost like a chocolate bar. I want to lick it. I guess I'm getting a little high. I laugh. Perhaps I'll go inside . . .

I check, and the key is still hidden under the stone turtle that sits on the deck beside the sliding glass doors. I always thought it was stupid to lock glass doors. Anyone wants in, they can just smash the glass, right?

But I don't want to smash today. I look at my reflection in the window as I slide the key in and turn the lock. I look like a magazine model posing for fall fashions, fetchingly peeking around the doorframe, the maple behind dripping gold and yellow leaves. I give my reflection a lick. The glass is cold and smooth.

I step into the kitchen, and I'm surrounded by Ted. There's a box of Froot Loops on the table and an empty bowl and spoon in the sink. I take the box and wander through the house, nibbling on sugar-coated pastel loops and touching everything.

Upstairs in the bathroom, Ted's shaving stuff is tucked in a corner by the sink, muted by his mom's cacophony of cosmetics and hair doodads. I put on some of her mauve lipstick and kiss the toilet seat.

I saved the best for last. I'm in Ted's room. There are bits of science stuff everywhere. A collection of crystals on his desk, one of them is the same colour as the earrings I'm wearing. How did he know? I slip it into my pocket. On the shelves, there are books about physics and ancient Greeks and chemistry. He's got a bunch of bugs pinned to a block of Styrofoam and a jar filled with what looks like snakeskin. He's still a dork.

The bed has the same quilt it's always had, some old thing made by his grandmother, I think. It's made from every scrap of fabric you can imagine, even corduroy. I think he told me it was all his mom's old clothes. As I stare at it, the rectangle shapes start to ripple. I bellyflop into the waves and inhale his pillow. It smells like cookies and shampoo. I shove it between my legs and milk it against my clit until the tickly ache inside me bursts into a full-body tingle.

The bean is in full power now. Too bad, because I would love to take a little nap on Teddy's bed. Another time, I guess. I sit up, cross-legged on the pillow, and take in all that's around me, turning my head from side to side, up and down, enjoying the blur that happens with quick movement like a movie on fast-forward. Blur . . . books! Blur . . . rocks! Blur . . . jar of weird stuff! Blur . . . fish tank! Fish tank? But there's no water in it. I get up and walk towards it. It's a little high up for me to see inside, but I see a branch and some sand and . . . Oh shit! It's a snake. It's a fucking snake. Its scaly skin is pressed up against the glass like a two-toned green blob. I'm fucking gone.

Sliding the deck door closed, I realize I left the key up on Ted's desk. And the Froot Loops. Fucking snake. I'm not going back in.

I head to the school. Might as well find Steve.

Steve and I are coming in from lunch. He has to go to English, or he isn't allowed on the football team or something stupid. We had cheeseburgers and oral sex for lunch. I'm breathing onions and cum. He's draped over me like a piece of meat, and I'm all tucked in under his arm. Ted and David are coming towards us. I lick my lips. "Hey there, Teddy!"

Ted beams at me. "Hi, May!" There's that blush again. So cute.

I feel Steve's body tighten up. "Fuckin' faggots."

I pull out from under his possessive arm, checking behind me to see if Ted's doing something stupid, but he's not.

He's maybe walking a little faster.

I step in front of Steve. "Who's a faggot?"

"Your buddy there," he says, nodding in Ted's direction.

I grin, reaching my hands up to his shoulders.

He bends down, "Baby, I gotta go—"

He stops talking as my thigh connects with his gonads. It should have been my knee. I hate being short.

"What the fuck?" He's got tears in his eyes.

I walk away. I've got nothing more to say to him.

I guess Ted's the one. Always. As far back as I can think, Ted's been mine. Forget that he's a dork and his ears turn red every time he looks at me. He's mine. After that morning in his bed, I can't get him out of my mind. And he's no faggot. He wants me bad. I need to take care of that.

Ted

It's been raining for two days straight. All the golds and yellows of the leaves have been washed out, and all that's left are shit-brown mush piles in gutters and corners where they'd been brushed by the wind. Inside, Timberland smells like dampness and wet sneakers. The halls are empty, and I'm heading to the boys' room, thinking about the snow that's supposed to come this weekend. And David. And David in the snow . . .

"I'm sick of this shit."

I might have actually screamed. But probably not, because no one came out of a classroom to see what the fuss was about.

May. Walking beside me. Head tilted up to look at me. "The fucking rain. Every day."

And, in the same breath, "We have to get together!" She

squeezes my arm.

"Sure, yeah." I focus on walking. *Let go of me, May, God, please just let go of me.* I hardly remember her, but what I do remember isn't that great, and how I feel when I see her is worse.

She stops, and her grip on my arm makes me stop too.

"No, I mean it." She's got that anger in her eyes that my body remembers enough to feel nauseous.

I swallow. She watches my Adam's apple. "Why?" I ask.

"Oh, babe! We have so much to talk about!" Now she's all bright and bubbly twinkly again. Phew. Maybe.

I start to walk again. I really need to pee. "I gotta, um . . ." I point to the washroom.

She giggles, and she walks alongside me.

"Okay, see ya," I say, giving her a little wave as I push through the door, but she walks right in behind me.

"Ummm . . . you can't be in here."

She puts her finger to her lips, shushing me. I escape into the stall.

"Why don't you use the urinal?" she calls out.

I don't answer. I undo my fly and let loose. I'm surprised I can even pee with her in here. I'm also surprised she isn't looking over the stall.

"Okay, I'll wait outside."

I check my watch. Another twenty minutes until class gets out. I can't stay in here the whole time, especially since she doesn't seem to have any qualms about coming in.

I hear the door squeak open, and someone walks up to the urinal. I listen. They pee. And they leave. They don't wash their hands. Gross.

I flush. At the sink, I scrub my hands like a surgeon, killing time. She can't still be out there. She must have a class to get to.

She's there though. Of course. She walks beside me as I head back to class.

"Hey, Ted?"

"Yeah?"

"I'm sorry if I come on too strong sometimes," she says. She sounds like the little girl I remember. "I don't know too many people here. And you were always so kind to me."

She's stopped walking. Picking up my pace, I pretend not to notice.

"Steve and I broke up." Her voice is almost satanic as she chokes back a sob. Not her intention, I'm sure.

God, I'm an ass. What is my problem? Why am I so afraid of her? And mean? She probably just needs a friend. I can be nice, right?

"Okay," I say. My problem is, I'm gay. I could never tell her that. She couldn't handle it. She would destroy me. And David.

"Your mom, is she good?" May asks.

I start to answer, but she's still talking.

"Did you see the tree? The entire forest is—of course you did!" She giggles. "It's on your street."

"Yeah, that happened in fifth grade," I say. We spent hours in that tree. "I came home one day, and it was gone." I remember wishing I'd climbed it one more time, but by then, I'd stopped climbing trees.

"Can we go for coffee after school?" she asks. "I've got a Cleopatra story I want you to hear."

That makes me smile. "Fact or fiction?"

"Both?" I can't tell if she's being coy or she doesn't know

what the word *fiction* means.

We're stopped just outside my classroom. My hand is on the door handle.

"Meet me at Tardy's at four-ish?" she asks.

I say, "Sure," even before I'm sure.

She smiles like she won a prize, her bright pink lipstick emphasizing the yellow of her teeth. "See ya!" she says, and she skips down the hall as I escape into the classroom.

My stomach is fluttering away. I'm not sure if I'm excited or terrified. I almost feel like I need to go to the washroom again.

As I walk to my desk, David makes eye contact with me, his eyebrows raised to ask, "Are you okay?" I give him a nod and take my seat across from him. Of course, my ears are red. Of course, he noticed. I sink my focus into the notes on my desk. I feel like I've cheated on him.

Tardy's is like a 50s-themed diner, except it isn't a theme. Tardy's has been around since the 50s and they haven't changed a thing, not even the waitresses. On every table, there's a history lesson on Timberland High School carved into the yellow Formica: R. B. plus S. L.; I love Johnny; Fuck; Grad 1974. The table I sit at has "State Chumps" scratched into it. It looks like the *u* was an *a* at one time.

It's crowded and damp. Fortunately, the smell of coffee and cheeseburgers wins out over the ripe smell of wet teenagers. I fidget with the menu, then the salt shaker. I hope she won't come.

I didn't tell David. Not sure why. I think it's because of how he reacted that day on the field. Or how May acted that day on the field. I know I'm gay; David knows I'm gay, so why am I so hush-hush?

"Coffee, Teddy?" Glennis, the waitress that came with the place, is smiling down at me, coffee pot at the ready, lipstick on her teeth. She knows my mom.

I cover the coffee mug on the table with my hand to stop her from pouring. "Can I get a hot chocolate instead please, Glennis?"

"Of course, dear!" She grabs the mug off the table, knocking into May as she turns.

May scowls at her and takes a seat. Glennis doesn't flinch. "And what can I get you, young lady?"

May rolls her eyes. "Well, old girl, I think I'll have a Coke and some fries with gravy."

Glennis laughs. "Alrighty, sweetheart," she shoots back.

She's out of earshot when May snarls, "I'm not your sweetheart, you old bat."

I shake my head, feeling the familiar rush of nerves I always felt when May was being bad and she was on my side. Now I know why I'm here. I wanted to taste that feeling again.

"You can't rile her, you know," I tell May. "She's suffered through every teenage asshole that ever went to Timberland."

"You're calling me an asshole?"

Fuck. "No!"

But she's smiling, so we're still good.

"So do you still climb trees and play with snakes?"

"And do you still put makeup on your Barbies?"

She grins. "We still have the trampoline. It isn't set up though, or I'd make you come jump with me."

"That would be horrifying! Don't you think I'm a little tall for a trampoline?"

She giggles like I'm the funniest guy in the world. "I missed you so much when I left. I thought my heart had broken."

"We were only eight."

Her lids lower. She's going to turn angry again. Glennis arrives with my hot chocolate and May's coke and fries. May glares at her.

"I missed you, too," I blurt out, deflecting her wrath. "Tell me about England."

Between fries, May talks about the school she went to, how they wore uniforms but made up for it with wild fashion. "Like my purple hair," she says, twirling a strand around her middle finger. "They even put safety pins through their cheeks and lips."

"Eww. Why?" I find myself searching for pinholes on her face. Through the dense layer of makeup, I can see the outline of a couple of zits, but no holes.

"Right here." She puts a finger on her lower lip.

I squint, but see nothing, and nod as if I did. "Wow. Did it hurt?"

"It bled like fuck! The girl who did it for me passed out!"

My brain screams bullshit, but I just laugh.

"And everyone fights. My boyfriend would go out on a Friday night just looking for someone to beat up," she says. She's twirling the purple strand faster now, like she's excited. Apparently, that's how a girl flirts.

"You ever get into a fight?" she asks.

"You're kidding, right?" I shake my head. "I've been on the receiving end of a fight, if that counts."

She reaches across the table to touch my hand. I fight to not pull away. "You should try it," she says, biting her lip. "It makes you feel like you own the world."

"David is teaching me some kung fu," I hear myself say. Stupid. I didn't want to bring David into this conversation.

"Who's David?" May asks.

Huh. Who's David? He's my world. "He's just a friend."

"We should, right?" She's leaning towards me. Her boobs are squishing up against the table and almost popping out of the top of her T-shirt. "Find a fight?"

"No! Why would we do that?"

She flops back in the seat, looking away from me. "Because it's something to do."

"Or"—I'm thinking fast here—"we could go to a movie?"

And there she is, all sparkly smiles again. "Yes!"

Fuck, fuck, fuck. Did I just ask her out on a date? No. It isn't a date if I bring David, right? Well, it is, but it's me and David's date. Oh God, why did I do this? How did she suck me in?

"What's playing?" she asks. "I wonder if there's a newspaper around here?" She cranes her neck, stretching out of the booth.

"There's one over there," I say, getting out of the booth. "Just a sec."

I'm headed to the front of the restaurant. I know they stash any newspapers left behind on a rack at the front door. I take a quick look behind me. May is hidden back in the booth, waiting for me. It wouldn't be hard to leave.

I pause at the door, picking a paper from the rack, check behind me again, and then open the door to the street.

The rain is coming down in steady grey sheets. A car splashes by as I step out. I forgot my jacket. Fuck. Do I go back in? I'll get soaked. The rest of the world is smart enough to stay out of the rain, except me and that lump of passion under the eaves of the old Wells Fargo building across the street. It's hard not to notice bare flesh in the rain. She's up against the wall, and he's got his hand under her skirt, her naked leg wrapped around his thigh to accommodate him. Him.

It's David. I stand very still, trying to take my next breath. Trying to scream. Trying not to scream. He's supposed to be at kung fu. Rain drips off my hair and runs down my cheeks.

I go back inside Tardy's.

We go to *Rambo: First Blood*. Not my pick. I vaguely notice May's hand on my thigh, and the tickle of her breath on my neck, the weight of her sitting too close to me.

She watches Sly save the world while I replay David's infidelity over and over in my mind.

She whispers, "Rambo turns me on."

I nod.

When it's over, I pay a taxi to take her home, ducking from her final attempt to kiss me as I press more than enough money into the driver's hand. It's stopped raining, and the world smells like garbage.

I go home and wait for David to call. I pick up the receiver and dial most of his number before I stop myself. What would I say? I was out with a girl, and I see you were too? But I didn't do anything.

At school the next day, he's sweet enough, but then he takes off at lunch, and in the hall, I see him draped over Macey Phillips. She's definitely the bare leg from the night before. She's almost as tall as him, and she's wearing a little kilt-style skirt that barely covers her butt. Our eyes meet as he's bending down to do something with his mouth to her ear. He must see I'm blinking back tears. He shrugs and buries his face in Macey's slippery straight hair.

I get it. I get why David is with a girl. If his folks ever found out he was gay, he'd be off to military school or worse.

I go to the office and ask to use the phone to call Mom.

"I'm sick," I tell her. There is no noise in the background. She must have taken the call in her boss's office.

"Oh, baby! I'll be right there!"

"No, it's okay. I can walk home."

"Are you sure?"

"Yeah. Can you tell the secretary?"

Mom taps on the door. "Hey, muffin-man." Her pet names seem to become more absurd when she's worried about me. "That snake of yours was hollering at me last night. I think he needs a walk or something." She talks through the door.

I lift my head off the pillow. "I've got a lot of homework to do."

"Maybe we could clean his cage?"

"I cleaned it last week."

"There's that Jack Cousteau show on tonight."

I roll my eyes. She pronounces it "Jack" instead of "Jacques." Normally, I find it funny.

"I'm busy." I've been lying in bed since I got home from school this afternoon. I didn't go down for dinner. This is her second attempt at coaxing me out.

"And *I'm* lonely," she says.

I know. But that's not new. She's been lonely for a while.

Ever since I started seeing David, she's hinted that she misses my company. I never had a social life before. It was always just the two of us. Oh, well. That's over. You get your little boy back now, Mom. Tears are spilling out of my stupid face again.

"Ted. Come on. Open the door." She's trying the handle.

I hear the faint jingle of the phone ringing downstairs. And in the silence that follows, my heart starts to beat again. Then a second ring. I'm already blasting through the door. It's him. He's calling. I forgive him.

I hear Mom mutter, "Jesus!" as I head down the stairs, swinging on the handrails to take five steps at a time. I think I might have hit her with the door.

I slide down the hall in my sock feet, and halfway through the fourth ring, I catch the receiver off the phone. "Hi!" I say, so sure it's him.

She gives off a sultry giggle. "Well, hi!"

"Oh." Nothing else comes out except my disappointment.

"So? What are we doing tonight?"

At school, May is beside me. She's always beside me. Laughing and chattering, arm hooked through my elbow. She thinks we're going out, even though I never touch her. But I haven't pushed her away either. The past few days, I've just been numb. It could have been George Michael beside me and my heart would hardly beat.

I have no desire to do anything with May. I think even if I weren't gay, I wouldn't be attracted to her.

I see David fitting into groups of kids I hardly know. He's like a photograph that's going out of focus.

◆ ◆ ◆

It's the end of the day. When I get out of class, May is standing at my locker. I want to go home. I want to be alone.

It's been one week and one day since I touched David. I load a weekend's worth of homework into my backpack and slam the lock into place, giving the combination a spin.

"Oh God, there's Steve," she says, pushing me around a corner.

"Who's Steve?" I ask, stumbling a little as she guides me.

"Wow, you're an idiot," she says.

"Oh. Steve. I thought you guys broke up?"

"Yeah." She pushes through the doors into the teacher's parking lot. "Kinda?"

I'm pretty much running. "Are you kidding me?" I look over my shoulder.

She grabs my hand and sets a wicked pace. Across the teacher's parking lot and down an alley. My backpack is bumping against my back with a rhythm all its own.

She stops at the elementary school playground, where we spent hours playing. May style. We're catching our breath. She leads me under the firepole platform. I have to crouch; she has clearance. She turns and wraps her hands around my neck, and on her tiptoes, she's kissing me. Sticking her tongue in my mouth. She stinks of makeup and hairspray. Her mouth tastes like lipstick and stale cigarettes. I gag and push her away.

And she's going to kill me. Oh well, it's her or Steve. Or my broken heart. I slide down against one of the supporting posts and sit in the dirt.

She wipes her smeared lipstick with the back of her hand. Her face is red.

"What's your fucking problem?" She's standing over me, her eyes taking on that darkness that usually frightens me and her upper lip quivering into a snarl. "Are you fucking queer or what?"

I take a deep breath. "Yeah, I am." The words deflate me. It doesn't feel like enough. All this time, never saying it out loud. Even with David, we didn't discuss what we did. We didn't put a label on it. "Queer. I'm gay," I clarify for her, for me.

And her snarl turns into a smirk. "No, you're not!"

She starts to straddle me. I stand up real quick, bashing my stupid head on the platform overtop of us. Wincing, I duck and back out of the shelter. I head across the playground to First Street, taking big angry strides. Angry at myself for telling her. Angry at David for hurting me. Angry at myself for not even being able to kiss a girl.

May

I hate him. He doesn't understand what we have. Fuck, he's stupid. Gay. Right. And I'm Cleopatra. I'm so mad I'm actually crying.

What does that even mean, to say he's gay? Does he actually have sex with other guys? I'm picturing him with a cock in his mouth, and my stomach turns. He must be lying.

I slam through the back door into the kitchen. There's a wave of steam and cigarette smoke, and a scratchy Rolling Stones album is playing in the background. Mom is cooking supper, a cigarette in one hand and a soup ladle in the other. I must have startled her because the ladle is in the air, and she has what looks like pea soup on her cheek.

"Well, hello to you too! What's happening?" Mom thinks she's cool. She isn't.

She sees I'm crying and puts the ladle down. "Now

what?" she asks.

Bitch. I never cry. I wipe my eyes with the back of my hand. "Nothing."

"Bullshit," she says. She leans back on the kitchen counter with her cigarette, taking a nice long drag. Sometimes, I think she does that just to tease me. Because we pretend I don't smoke. I take a chance and reach for her pack on the counter, pulling my own lighter out of my jeans pocket.

"Well?"

"Just boy problems."

"Figured as much. Fuck 'em." Then she laughs. "Actually, don't. Or use a condom or something." She takes another drag and blows a smoke ring. "You'll be over him in a week."

I blow my own smoke ring and three more. "Nope. Not this one."

She raises her eyebrows.

"Have you ever had a guy tell you he's gay? To break up with you?" I ask.

"Oh, honey!" She laughs. "What did you do to the poor boy to make him say that?"

I look at the ceiling and shake my head. "Nothing."

"Well, he's an idiot for saying that, isn't he? Just the other night, they busted up one of those queer bars. And the cops don't mess around with that kind of shit. It's all billy clubs and beatings." She turns to the cupboard behind her—which only hangs from one hinge—and takes a glass down, then pours from the bottle on the counter. Scotch.

"I just don't get it. I'm sure he's lying," I say. I can't even imagine him touching anyone but me. I'm running my fingers through my hair as we talk, splitting up the hair-sprayed clumps.

Mom plops some ice cubes into her drink and takes a good sip and then notices what I'm doing. "Oh, honey, don't do that!" she says, reaching out to stop my hand. "You'll break your hair."

I slap her hand away. She grabs my hand, hard, crunching the fingers. I duck my head in anticipation of a follow-up blow, but we both realize she still has the drink in her other hand.

She smiles instead and hands me the glass. "I'll get another one."

I take a sip. The heat of the alcohol seeps over me. I take a bigger sip, wondering whether we're going to have a good talk or a bad one.

She pours her drink and wanders into the living room and over to the couch, patting the space beside her. "Come. Sit. We haven't chatted in a while."

I take a seat in the overstuffed chair across from her. The coffee table between us adds a safe distance.

"Are you liking school?"

"It's okay, I—"

"What about that Steve guy? He's not the one who dumped you, is he?"

"No, it was—"

"I remember a guy, just before I met your father. He was so hot." She nods and lifts her brow. "We had a thing going for a while, but . . ." She sits back and swirls her drink.

I do the same. I've never had scotch in a glass before. Usually just straight out of the bottle.

Mom smiles. She likes it when I copy her.

"He probably turned gay after I was done with him," she continues. "I saw him a few times after, but never with a girl."

She's quiet for a bit. I watch her feet. She still has her work clothes on. Her red toenails are muted under taupe stockings.

There's nothing left of my drink except the ice cubes. I suck on them.

"Do you think that's how it happens? They just turn gay?" I ask.

She's lighting another cigarette and takes a thoughtful puff. My own smokes are stuffed down the front of my pants. I'd take them out, but she would recognize the brand and probably think I stole them from her. Which I did.

She blows out a solid sexy stream of smoke and squints through the cloud as she answers. No wonder I like smoking. She makes it look so good.

"They're sick, honey. It's something wrong with their head." She leans forward. She's got her professor cap on, or should I say Dad's professor cap. "From what I understand, they need to undergo treatment in a hospital. Sometimes for up to five years. Even ten.

"But I hear the Catholics have their own way of taking care of it." She sits back again, looking enlightened. "It's like an exorcism." She points to her temple with the hand holding the cigarette, tapping with her ring finger. I wonder if her hairspray will catch fire. "Demons in their head," she says.

She holds up her empty glass. "Can you get me another drink, love?"

I get up and take our glasses into the kitchen.

"When you think about it, it's all the same, right? Sickness and demons." She's talking louder so I can hear her. "I always thought that about your uncle." She chuckles. "Not that he was gay, no chance of that."

My uncle. He was a favourite topic. I want to watch her

face. I pour two drinks, add ice, and hurry back into the living room.

Mom takes the glass from my hand and a shadow of anger crosses her face when she notices I have one too.

"You go easy on that. It's your dad's good stuff. Costs a bundle."

But you drink it like soda, I don't say out loud. I take up my spot in the chair and ask, "Uncle Jake?"

She's sloshing the booze around in her mouth, as if she just remembered how quality it is. Swallowing, she closes her eyes in ecstasy and then pops them open again, like an idea. "Yes! Jake. He was in trouble since day one. Always taking things, breaking stuff, lying. Mom and Dad—Grandma and Grandpa—used to have to beat the crap out of him daily." She laughs. "I guess it was a blessing, kept their attention away from me, especially when we were teenagers."

She's getting out another cigarette and this time offers me one. Her nails are red and perfect. Or not. I notice a little burn mark on the index fingernail when she flicks the lighter for me.

I curl back into my chair.

"But after he got out of jail the first time, I don't know. He was—well, I guess we both were—grown-up. He was living with us, you remember? Grandma and Grandpa wouldn't take him. Their own son." She shakes her head. "Mind you, your dad wasn't too keen on him either."

I sit very still, wondering if she'll mention how Jake played with me.

"His temper was—violent. Do you remember? The slightest thing would set him off. I remember he plugged the kettle in while the dryer was on one day. Blew a fuse. All the lights went out and everything, he came out here and he threw the kettle across the room."

She gets up on her knees to inspect the windowsill behind her. "There," she says, running her finger over a large painted-over dent on the window frame. "That's where it hit. And I was sitting right here in this same spot. Fucking crazy." She laughs again and sits back down, knees tucked under her, linen skirt stretched tight. "But I always knew how to calm him down. Her hand slides across her thighs. Your dad wanted him out. But I know how to calm him down too!" She winks at me.

I hate it when she gets all sexy like that. Not that my mom isn't always sexy, but it just feels awkward. I take my chances and try to get her back on topic. "You said you thought something was wrong?"

She frowns. She doesn't know what I'm talking about. Her drink is finished already.

To remind her, I say, "With Uncle Jake?"

She smiles, her eyes brighten. "Oh, right. I often wonder if he should have been put in an institution."

"Because jail isn't an institution, right, Mom?" I don't say out loud.

"This time, anyway. It's like the homosexuals. He can't control himself. I mean that girl. You probably don't remember any of this. Of course, she was young, but every day she walked past this house. And Jake, he watched her. But there's only so much a man can take, you know."

I think she might be getting teary eyed. Then she frowns. "Stop sucking on those. You look like a retard."

I spit out my ice cube. She holds out her glass, and I get up to fill it.

"No more for you," she mutters.

I walk into the kitchen, and she calls after me, "You can have some of that lemon gin, in the green bottle, corner cupboard."

I know where the lemon gin is. I take a swig of the good stuff right from the bottle and then pour each drink. This is going to be the last round; she's going to turn soon. I can feel it. But it's almost six. Dad will be home soon, and that will be my escape. I check to make sure my shoes and purse are by the back door. I can run faster scared than she can drunk.

One more time, I take a safe seat across from her. But this time, she won't have it.

"Sit with me." She pats the couch to encourage me, as if I'm some kind of lap dog.

I giggle. "Actually, I'm kinda stinky. I didn't get a shower after gym today."

She wrinkles her nose. "I thought I smelled something." She motions with her head. "Go clean up then."

I stand to go, and there: she's turned. This time for sure there are tears. She blinks to make sure they spill out of her eyes.

"No. Stay." She sniffles. "Sometimes, I need to talk." She wipes her eyes with the back of her hand. "You know? That was hard with Jake. People called him a predator. Can you imagine? My little brother?"

She pats the couch again, and I take a seat at the far end.

"He told them he couldn't help himself. We hired a good lawyer. Found pictures of that chick in cheerleading outfits and doing cartwheels. You don't do the splits like that and expect to not attract attention."

She sniffles again and then sobs. "I miss him so much." *No kidding. You've been drinking since he went to jail.* Her hand reaches for mine. "If that cunt's little brother had kept his mouth shut, none of this would have happened. Why would they let a kid on the stand like that?"

The kid on the stand. I've heard the story a thousand

times. From her and Jake. Jake always says he's gonna kill the little bastard if he ever finds him.

Mom visits Uncle Jake in jail all the time. I go when I can. He teases me and says he'll marry me when he gets out. He touches my face and rubs his thumb on my lips. "We're going to have so much fun," he says. But he looks so old now.

I sit with her gripping onto my hand, wondering what any of this has to do with being gay. Or crazy. Except her.

Ted

She acts like nothing happened. Today she's hanging on my arm, even though my arm is trying its best to be unwelcoming.

It's scary, because I expected her to be mad, and she isn't. Which isn't always a good thing with May. It only means she's decided on a different tactic to get back at you.

"How you feeling today, sweetie?" She rests her head on my arm. The other arm is shouldered with my backpack. Maybe I should start hooking both arms through. The perfect defence.

"I'm fine," I answer, as cold as possible.

We get to my classroom, and she lifts herself onto her tiptoes, puts her hands on either side of my face, and kisses me on the lips. It feels like there's a spotlight on us.

She whispers into my neck, "We're gonna fix you up, babe. Don't worry, 'kay?" She takes a step back. "See you after school." Then she turns and wiggles away. It looks as if she forgot to get off her tiptoes.

I stare after her. I want to kick her.

"Come on, lover boy. Time to take a seat." It's Miss Bluth, standing in the doorway, waiting to close the door.

I walk in and take a seat. Everyone is watching me.

Except David.

May

I know what to do now. I can help him. He just needs to find out how good I feel. Inside.

There he is. He's walking ahead of me up First Street. I run to catch up, slipping my hand through his arm.

"Hi! You going my way?"

"Hi," he answers. I can feel the tension letting go in his arm as I hold him. He was worried about us. Poor sweetie.

"I missed you. Did you guys go away this weekend?"

"Yeah."

"Your grandma's?"

"Yeah." He's walking fast, and I almost have to run to keep up with him. Sometimes, his strong-silent-type act is a pain. I have to do all the talking.

"And how you feeling today, sweetie?"

He says he's fine. Of course, he is. People like him probably don't even know they're sick.

At the school, he opens the door for me.

"Steve," he says, shaking his arm so that I have to grip onto him.

I giggle. "Don't worry about him. He's seeing Tanya now. I saw them together on Saturday."

The hall is crowded with kids and noise about everyone's weekend. We head to his locker, and I let go of him so he can do the combination. I think he's the only kid in school who doesn't know how to pop the lock. I slam the door with my fist. It swings open.

He shrugs and takes off his jacket.

"Did you know my Uncle Jake is in prison? Remember him?"

The bell rings, and everyone starts moving, including Ted. I get up close to him so my boob is rubbing against his arm.

"He should be out in a couple of years. Mom says it wasn't his fault."

"Really," Ted says. He sounds sarcastic.

"I'm pretty sure he did it on purpose though. I remember our tickle fights. He likes that kind of thing."

Ted shakes his head. He's such a forgiving guy. Not even letting me insult my own uncle.

We get to the door of Miss Bluth's room, and Ted stops, taking my hand. People are filing in, and I see David coming down the hall toward us. Time to mark my territory.

I get onto my tippy toes, cup his cheeks in my hands, and he bends down to meet my lips. I push my tongue against his lips, but he holds them tight. He's so innocent.

I whisper, "We're gonna fix you up, babe. Don't worry, 'kay?" As I step away, I can see the confusion in his eyes.

"I'll see you after school, baby." I walk away, knowing he's watching my ass.

I hear Miss Bluth say, "C'mon, lover boy."

How can he even think he's gay?

I'm waiting for him at his classroom. He's one of the first ones out, and he stops still when he sees me. I know I have this big stupid grin on my face. I can't help it. We have such a connection. One of the kids bumps him back into reality, and he steps closer to me.

I give him a hug. "What's the plan?"

He's staring down the hall. "Nothing," he says.

He's got his red ears going. Is he pissed at that guy who bumped him? Isn't that David? I wonder if he wants to smack him around a bit, because I'm up for that.

We walk down to his locker, and he gives the door a slam like an old pro. Yeah, he's pissed. Kinda sexy.

He gets his stuff and then tries to close the locker the same way, which you can't do, so it hits him in the face. Or maybe he's just punching it? I hate that he's such a dork. Maybe a smack in the head would do him good. I lift the handle and close it for him.

Not even a thank you. He's watching David down the hall. I take his arm, feeling his pulse under my fingers. His Adam's apple slides in his neck as he swallows. It looks like he's going to cry. Oh, my god.

He's hot for David.

"Stop it!" I yank him out of his trance.

"What?" He's fucking oblivious.

We start heading to the doors.

Okay, I have to keep it together. That's his gayness kicking in. He can't help himself.

"It's okay, hon. I understand. I think the important thing is that we stick together." I slide my hand into his back pocket. "The more me you get, the better you're gonna feel. I know, David's gorgeous. He's even kind of feminine. Put a set of tits on him, and he would be almost as hot as me."

I'm babbling. Therapy is not my forte. It's almost like he's pretending he's sick. I'm losing patience.

He turns around, nearly snapping my wrist in his pocket, so I have to pull it free. He's walking away from me. "I can fix you, Ted. Let me help you." He keeps walking. I raise my voice, "It's illegal, you know!" I get everyone's attention but his.

So I scream. "I'll report you!"

That seems to work. He slows down. Mr. Watson, my social studies teacher, is walking towards Ted. Oops. I catch up to my love and slip my hand through his arm.

Watson's got a thing for me. I can see the rage in his eyes as he looks up at Ted.

"Report you for what, Mr. Russell?"

I hesitate for just a beat. Should I play the maiden in distress? Better not. I give a little sigh to get Watson's attention. "Oh, sorry. Just a lover's spat, Mr. Watson." I wink at him.

We walk home. Ted doesn't say a word. Neither do I. I think I overdid it.

At Elm Street, I ask him to come to my place. He backs away from me like I'm a rabid dog.

"I'm sorry. I just want to help," I say.

He turns away from me and heads down the street. He's so sensitive sometimes. It isn't cute at all. What the fuck do I see in him?

I light a cigarette and watch him walk away. He walks with that little bounce, just like when he was a kid. It's like his body wants him to run, but his brain won't let him. It makes me smile to watch him. I guess I like the chase.

Ted

At the end of the day, she's outside the classroom. Binder hugged to her chest, leaning against the wall. How do I end this? David bumps me as he passes. I tingle, watching him walk away. Then May is in my face.

"What's the plan?"

"Nothing," I say, heading to my locker. She scampers beside me. I see David walking alone, up ahead of me. Did he and Macey split up? I give the door to my locker a hard smack with the back of my fist, and it pops open. There's a trick to it. If you do it right, you don't need to take the lock off. I get it about half the time.

I grab my jacket, load up my backpack, and slam the metal door closed, depending on the same trickiness. The door bounces back into my face. Like I said, about half the time.

"Let me get that for you," May says. There's a bit of bite in her voice, like she's getting mad. Finally.

The door slams with a metal clang as I stare down the hall after David's ghost.

"Stop it!" May snarls, hooking her arm in mine.

"What?"

I head to the door, away from David. I don't want him to see me with May. I remember how he saved me from Zack Bilton. Would he save me from May if I asked?

I stop and turn back to follow him, dragging May like a piece of toilet paper stuck on my shoe.

She lets go.

"It's illegal, you know!" she shouts after me. The few people still around look—at her, at me. I keep walking.

"I'll report you!"

I slow my pace.

There's a teacher walking up to me. I don't know him. He's carrying a car bag that spills over with papers, grey-tonsure comb-over, jingling keys in his hand. He smiles. "Report you for what, Mr. Russell?"

Teachers always know who I am. I shrug. He smiles up at

me, then down at May, who is hooked onto my arm again.

"Oh, sorry! Just a lover's spat, Mr. Watson." She twinkles at him.

We walk home in silence. I stop at Elm Street and unhook her from my arm.

"Come to my place?" she asks, reaching for my hand.

I say nothing and back away.

"I'm sorry," she says. "I just— I just want to help." She almost looks remorseful.

Really? I shake my head and turn to walk down my street. She doesn't follow me. I feel a lightness come over me, like I'm walking out of a bog onto solid ground.

May

I write him a note: "Ted, I know I can be too much. I'm sorry. Please know I care about you and that's why I said those things. I hate the thought of you getting into trouble. I will always remember the fun we had together, and you will always be in my heart. Love, May."

Since then, I've left him alone. I'm a little pissed that he hasn't tried to contact me, but I need to play this better. I know that. It wouldn't be the first time we've taken a break from each other.

I wave at him in the halls and say hi every time I see him. But I keep my distance otherwise.

Ted

She's stopped bugging me. I see her in the halls, and she just waves, like nothing ever happened.

It's the last day before Christmas break. Miss Bluth

has us doing presentations on the science and history behind Christmas. Not very Christian. It's awesome. David is presenting on the Star of Bethlehem.

He draws as he speaks: first the stable with Mary and Joseph, then Earth as a big circle that the stable sits on, then the Sun on one side of Earth and Jupiter on the other side with an arrow coming out of the top to indicate its heliacal rising. He draws the manger again, with Jupiter hovering above, apparently paused over the manger as Earth laps the larger planet and then the Moon, landing overtop of it, in front of everything, creating the classic Star of Bethlehem. Finally, he draws a stick Baby Jesus inside the manger, in stick Mary's arms.

"Any questions?" He looks straight at me. For the first time in weeks. Which means I don't have any questions. I can't speak with my heart in my throat.

At dismissal, he's beside me.

"Not bad for an atheist, right?" He bumps against me like the old days.

"Who, you or Jesus?" Am I cool or what?

He laughs. "I don't think I'll ever outdo Jesus."

"I beg to differ."

"Really?"

I smile and nod. We're at my locker. He hits it open for me.

"I'm sorry," he says. I have my head in my locker, loading my backpack. I pull out my jacket and put it on.

"It was my dad." We head to his locker, as though we never took a break, as though Macey didn't happen.

"I think he started to suspect something, and then he introduced me to her. She's one of his friends' daughters."

He opens his locker and pulls his coat out, wrapping a scarf around his neck.

"I thought that might be the case."

"He kept ranting about fags, how they should all be put away. Fix 'em or kill 'em, he kept saying. I thought I could try . . ."

I touch his arm. "I understand." I don't want to, but I understand.

We walk in silence back to my house.

At home, in the hallway, he takes my hand in both of his, bringing it to his mouth. He inhales deeply then kisses the top of my fist, stepping closer, so our hands are the only things separating our lips.

He looks into my eyes, lifting his brow, questioning.

"And risk certain death?" I quip. I'm not nervous. My ears aren't burning. I'm angry. And I'm brave. But I'm not nervous.

He nods, once. I move our hands from between us and kiss him like it's the first time.

All joking aside, we have to be more discreet. San Francisco may be ready for fags, but the rest of the country isn't. We decide to meet downtown on Saturday. I need to do some Christmas shopping.

The chaos of downtown is safe. We let our conversation drown in the crowds and traffic. We talk about running away together and finding a place where it's okay to be in love.

"Europe is good. There have always been fags in Europe. Amsterdam . . ."

We get our picture taken with Santa, telling Santa's helpers we're brothers and want to give it to our parents as a gift. And we'll need two, because they're divorced. The elf ladies almost come to tears, hearing the story we weave.

We're waiting for the bus. David has the photo out. We are on either side of Santa, each resting a hand on Santa's shoulder. It's a great photo.

"We don't look like brothers." He tucks the photo into the micky pocket of his jacket.

May

It's Christmas Day. I want to celebrate with him. I want to share Christmas morning with him, in our pyjamas, sipping rum and eggnog. We'd exchange gifts and then make love over and over again.

But instead, I'm sitting on the floor. There's wrapping paper everywhere. The end table beside my mom has a selection of bottles: perfume, lotions, and a bottle of wine. There's a pair of red lace panties draped over the rum bottle, a Christmas present for her from Dad. Dad has his legs on the couch with his feet on Mom's lap. The matching bra is wrapped around his knees, one kneecap in each cup. They've been drinking since last night. I found them on the couch this morning when I woke up. Snoring.

I brought them coffee.

She got me a rabbit-fur bomber jacket. It's the real deal. And leg warmers. Dad got me a carton of smokes.

A few drinks later, they pass out again.

I open a bottle of Coke, chug some down, and top it off with some rum from the open bottle left on the kitchen table. I don my new jacket and leg warmers and head out.

Ted's always been good about shovelling the walk and the driveway. He's always trying to be the man for his mom. The house looks warm and welcoming. There's a plywood

Santa on the lawn all decked out in peeling red paint and black boots. Christmas lights hang off the gutters, red-blue-green-yellow, red-blue-green-yellow. The back deck is shovelled too, right up to the turtle where the key is hidden. I knock, then unlock the door. Ted and his mom always go to his grandmother's on Christmas Day after they've opened their presents.

The tree lights are still on. They're old-school, screw-in bulbs, the same colours as outside. They've cleaned up the wrapping paper, and all their presents are carefully arranged under the tree. His mom got a set of silver wine goblets, earrings, and chocolates. Ted's pile is huge: jeans, T-shirts, chocolates and a tin of nuts, a calculator, *Raiders of the Lost Ark* and *Caddyshack* videos, a popcorn popper.

I take a mandarin orange from the fruit bowl on the table and sit back in the overstuffed chair, watching the lights flash on and off, on and off. The decorations on the tree are old and fragile looking. Glass ornaments with painted scenes of poinsettias or churches, bits of silver tinsel garland draped over branches, paper snowflakes, and school projects. There's a popsicle stick reindeer. I remember we made that in second grade. The year we met. I never thought to put mine on our tree at home.

It always feels so quiet and safe in this house. I sip my rum and coke, wishing this was my home. Sometimes, when I came over, we'd play checkers on the rug in front of the fireplace. You would think a guy that smart could win at checkers, but I always won, and he'd be super sweet about it. Then one day, he wins, three times in a row. I decided we would play tea party instead and made him eat a red checker. He broke it into pieces first. I wasn't hungry.

There are pictures of Ted with Santa along the mantel of the fireplace. Little Teddy with his blond curls, the guy I fell in love with, beaming on Santa's knee. Older Teddy, from the years I was away.

I start to drift off, slipping into a dream where I'm walking in the snow. Ted is on top of a hill in front of me. I step towards him and slip. I try again and slip, and the snow turns to mud. I keep trying. Ted has his hand out, kind of reaching for me, but not really. It's more like a handshake he's going for. Someone is standing behind him. Someone tall. Then I'm back in the living room, and the someone is standing behind me.

I jolt awake and spring to my feet. No one is there. My bottle is still in my hand, and coke splashes on my fingers. I laugh and chug the rest down. And I see another Santa picture on the kitchen counter. At first, I think it's Ted with his mom. But she's not tall at all. It's David. He's got his hand on Santa's shoulder. They both do, but Ted's looking at David like there's no one else in the world. I toss the photo in the cold fireplace. And head out.

Ted

It's Christmas Eve. David is here, and we're playing Parcheesi, Mom's traditional Christmas Eve game.

His family doesn't do much on Christmas Eve, so he stays late. At the back door, we sneak a kiss goodbye. He reaches into his pocket and hands me a box wrapped in blue foil. "Don't open this until tomorrow morning." He gives me another peck on the cheek. "Promise?"

Christmas Day is always delicious. Me and Mom wake up early. She's just as excited as me, maybe more so. We stay in our PJs and have hot chocolate and a mandarin orange, and then we take the plate of cookies Santa never eats over to the living room, sit down next to the tree, and open presents.

"You used to tell me ours was one of the last houses on Santa's route," I say, setting the cookies on the floor beside me. "And he was too full from everyone else's cookies to eat ours."

"That started because I forgot to make it look like he'd been here one year—I think you were about three or four. And you were devastated that he hadn't touched your cookies. I had to think quick!"

Mom starts handing me my gifts. "I hope you like it," and "This is from Aunt Betty," and "I hope this fits."

I pass her a box wrapped in red paper and trimmed with white and black to look like a Santa suit. "This is for you, Mom." I lean across and give her a kiss. "Merry Christmas."

I'm aching to open David's gift. I see it out of the corner of my eye as I watch Mom unwrap her silver wine goblets.

"Oh! Teddy! They're beautiful!" She leans across and wraps her arms around me. I've also given her a card, handmade, as always. This year is a sketch of a doe and a fawn with white sparkles glued on for snow. Inside, I've written: "Mom, I know I've always been a little different, and I know that's made it a little harder to be my mom. But you've always been my champion, my safe place, my home, and I want you to know how grateful I am. Love, Teddy."

"I kinda went all Hallmark on you," I say, watching her read the inscription. Her eyes well up—mission accomplished.

I glance at the blue box under the tree and then begin unwrapping one of the gifts Mom has placed in front of me.

Mom puts a hand over mine and nods towards the blue gift. "C'mon. I'm dying to see what it is."

I take it and begin to tear at the paper, revealing a gold cardboard jewellery box. As I begin to open it, it occurs to me that this might not be a gift I want my mom to see. But when I look up and see the excitement in her eyes, I know it doesn't matter.

Inside, lying on a white cotton bed, is a red coral corno pendant on a gold chain. Handwritten on the inside of the box top is: "The Italian corno (not porno) is an amulet worn to protect from the evil eye. Wink. Merry Christmas, David."

May

I'm in the visitor room with Jake. His hands are on the table because they have to be.

"So, they bought you a hooker jacket?" He says it loudly enough that people look my way.

I blush. Jake can be a bit of an asshole.

One guy keeps looking at me after the others have returned to their conversations.

I make eye contact with him. Jake notices and isn't impressed, but he's pretty weird that way. He puts his hand on my cheek and turns my face in his direction. "You don't want to look at anyone here, sweetheart. They're all bad people."

"Including you?" I give him a sassy grin and lean across the table, lifting my chin so he can get a good look at my cleavage.

He stares and nods. "My girl."

I'm waiting at the bus stop outside the prison. It's blinding bright and warm enough that the snow is melting and there are puddles everywhere. So different from inside that hole of a building. A car pulls up in front of me, super slow so he doesn't splash me. It's the guy who was watching me. He leans across and rolls down his window, letting a cloud of smoke out. I recognize the smell. "You heading into town?"

"Yeah," I say, opening the door.

He's sweeping crap off the passenger seat as I climb in. I don't think he expected me to. He hands me what's left of the roach on a clip that's a bluebird's beak. The paper is sticky with resin, and there's a little bit of lip skin on the end. I suck in without touching it to my lips. There's a hula girl glued to the dashboard; she has a broken arm.

"Sorry, it's left over from a couple of days back." He laughs. "I forgot it was even here."

As I hand it back to him, he reaches out a hand to shake mine. "I'm Ron, by the way."

"Joanne." I give him the tips of my fingers to squeeze. His hands are callused and meaty. He has oddly perfect teeth, except one is missing on the bottom left. It's off to the side though, so you can hardly tell unless he smiles.

"Visiting your old man?"

I snort, how deliciously vague. "Sure. I'll go with that. You?"

"My brother."

We chit-chat all the way into town.

"So do I drop you at a bus stop? Where do you live?"

"Where do *you* live?" I tease.

"Oh. Okay." He puts his signal light on. "We can do that."

He lives in a three-storey walk-up, on the ground floor. We go in through the patio doors. There's a guy and a girl on the couch, watching TV. The girl is wrapped in a blanket, curled up against the guy, one bare leg stretched across the couch. Her hair is perfect except for a matted wad sticking out the back. Her eyes are black with old mascara. He has the remote in one hand and a cigarette in the other. His arms are skinny, and one has a homemade tattoo, but I can't figure out what it is.

"Hey." Ron tilts his head at me. "This is Joanne."

They grunt. Ron takes a couple of beer out of the fridge

and grabs my hand, leading me down the hall. As he opens the door to his room, he says, "You're sixteen, right?"

I laugh and push past him.

Suddenly, I'm face down on the bed, and his weight is on me. He has a handful of hair and he's licking the back of my neck. I giggle and try to roll over, but he has me pinned. I buck and kick, struggling to get up. He whispers, "It's okay. You know it's okay." And I do. He tries to slide a hand down the back of my jeans, but they're too tight. And then his weight is off me. I roll over. He's standing with his legs wide, undoing his jeans. I smile, pop the button at my waist, and slowly lower the fly.

Ted

It seems like May actually figured it out. She's stopped hounding me. She doesn't even look at me when she walks by. Her shadow of crazy still haunts me—I'll see her and panic rises inside me, but then she just ignores me, and I realize I'm safe.

David is my life.

We spend our days together in school, and we manage a few nights together too. Mom loves having him over. Sometimes, I think she knows, but then she'll say something about us chasing girls or mention someone's daughter and say, "You should really meet her."

David's parents are another story. They can't know. David's dad wants him to go into the military—do his time for his country, just like every man in the LeClair family. Mr. LeClair did two tours in Vietnam. "We had to set them gooks straight. They're primitive, you know. Can't think for themselves. It's America's duty to protect them from Communism." David says his father nearly came to tears when Nixon pulled us out.

He talks about sending David to military school. Sometimes, it's a threat, and sometimes, he's just saying how great it would be to have the opportunity. He's even suggested, more than once, that we both go. "It would toughen you up," he says. "And you're both so smart, you'd be officers before you know it."

So we do things to make Mr. LeClair proud. Practice kung fu. Go to church. Play pool. David has a poster of Farrah Fawcett over his bed and steals his dad's *Playboys*. And when we get harassed by other kids, we fight back hard. Physically. Okay, mostly David fights, but I don't run away. That's pretty ballsy for me.

The plan is to graduate and get somewhere safe where we can be together.

It's Friday night, and we're walking home from *Return of the Jedi*. Winter has made a final attack: heavy wet snow sits in clumps on top of heather bushes blushing purple with new bloom. The sky is dust and orange. We schlump through the slush, splattering wetness, keeping to back alleys where we can brush up against each other and where our whispered conversation is safe.

"New York," I say. "Their gay community is actually a gay community. They've got a decent university . . ."

"Too close. I want to get the fuck out of here. At least California, maybe Amsterdam."

"Amsterdam? Really?"

"Why not? Imagine the ancient University of Amsterdam? Rotting our brains in the halls of such greats as —"

"How do you even get into a place like that? Don't you need to speak, what is it? Danish?"

"Spraken de Dane?" David responds in a distorted accent of German and Swedish.

I laugh. "We'd better start applying. A lot of these places won't take me because I'm too young."

"Au contraire—they'd be all over a boy genius like you."

"What about Canada? The West Coast? I have an aunt out there, in Vancouver." My mom's little sister was one of the flower children who migrated to the West Coast in the late 60s, then slipped up over the border with a bunch of friends.

"She's the hippy?"

My face is in the slush. I hear a *whump* as I try to close my mouth against the gritty sludge. Someone is kneeling on my back. David is grunting beside me. I struggle to lift my head, fighting the hand that pushes me down. I see David's face just as a boot connects with the back of his head, propelling his forehead against mine. There are three, maybe four of them. Legs, hands, heavy breathing, giggles.

I smell alcohol on the breath that whispers, "Fucking faggots," into my ear.

Then hands grip my head, grinding my face into David's. I stare into his eyes until the salty slush stings them closed. Teeth cut into lips and turn slippery with spit and blood.

"Does that turn you on, faggot?"

Then the hand is off my head and on the waistband of my jeans. Oh God no. Oh God no. I feel my wallet slide from the back pocket. The weight is gone. I start to push myself up, to grope for David. Something light falls on my head.

"Good thing you have cash."

Pain sears up through my groin. I'm not sure if I scream. I'm not sure if I black out.

Then all I hear is breathing. David's. Mine. A hand touches my face. I flinch. "It's me," David says. "You're okay. We're okay."

We struggle to our feet, and the light from the street

touches his face, and he smiles, blood smeared across his mouth and teeth pink with blood. "You look rough," he says.

I laugh and reach up to stroke his dripping hair. "Your head?"

He rolls his head in a semicircle and takes my hand away, giving it a squeeze. "I'm fine. Strong neck, remember? I practice self-defence!"

"Jesus."

We start limping toward the street, brushing ourselves off.

"So tell me about Vancouver," David says, shoving his hands deep into his pockets as we turn onto the sidewalk.

May

I haven't talked to him in weeks. It's the hardest thing I've ever done. I do my best not to follow him or watch him. And when I can't help myself, then I don't let him see me. I watch his locker or his classroom door from the end of the hall and walk in a different direction when he appears. I tell myself I'm just checking to make sure he's okay. It's like trying to quit smoking. I remind myself that this will be worth it.

He and David are never apart. They walk too close together. They act like there's no one else in the world. But there is. I'm here. Always.

I take out my frustrations on Ron. Our sex is wild and rough. I scratch and bite. He leaves bruises where his fingers dig into my flesh. I hurt him, he hurts me, until we cum, ripping at each other to reach a violent euphoria.

Ted

Should I believe her? David does, and he would think me a true asshole if do anything but support a childhood friend. She isn't even trying to touch me. She looks like she's been crying all night. I don't remember much about her dad. But I don't remember much about my dad either, just shadows like old movies: him lifting me up at the zoo, him at the bottom of the slide promising he'll catch me, and him sharing a Twinkie under a blanket fort in the living room.

She seems blinded from her tears. I have to guide her out of the school. When she tucks her hand around my arm, I try not to cringe.

We walk to her place, and she catches me up. I've read about cancer and watched *Love Story* of course. But I've never known anyone who has it or died from it. It's hard to believe someone can cough blood and not go to the doctor about it. Maybe he knew. I have questions, like "Are the tumours on the outside of his lungs or the inside?" "Can you hear them when he breathes?" "Does he feel them?" "Does it hurt?"

But I don't ask. He could die any day. I brace myself for the nightmare of her loss. Maybe the mourning process will soften her.

At the door, she fumbles with her keys. Her hands are actually shaking, so I take over and unlock the deadbolt. A wall of heat hits us when the door opens. May kicks off her shoes and mutters, "It smells like cancer in here." Then she disappears. It sounds like she's opening a window.

I wait in the kitchen, which seems beaten since I last saw it. There are chips of paint off the cupboard doors, one of which hangs at an angle, missing a hinge. Crusted plates sit in random stacks on the counter, and pans crowd the stove. One looks like there's still something stewing inside; bubbles form on the surface of its dark contents, despite the fact the stove is off. A bottle of Canadian Club is by the sink, three fingers left. The lid is gone. I don't think what I'm smelling is cancer, but

J. D. ROBERTSON

something has definitely died in here.

She comes through the kitchen like an attack. Wrapping her arms around my waist, her face buries into my chest. I'm not sure if she's laughing or crying. I pat her back. I can do this. She just needs someone to hold her. She reaches for my shoulders, and we stumble backwards into the counter. I steady her with my hands on her waist. Then her face is in mine, and I flinch, turning my head.

"No!" It comes out of me the same way we tell David's dog Marco not to jump up on us. I even lift my knee against her. I try to soften it. "Please, no." But it's too late.

She starts screaming at me. She wants me to fuck her. She's climbing up on me, trying to lick me. Her bloodshot eyes are wide, her pupils pinpoints of rage. I shove her away and head for the door.

As I reach down to get my shoes, something hard hits my head and clatters to the floor. She threw a fucking frying pan at me? I reach up to touch my head as the floor flies towards me.

May

I'm crying, face in my hands, my forehead pressed against his locker. Full sobs. I can feel kids watching me as they pass, some slowing down. A couple of people have come to me, put a hand on my shoulder, asked if I'm okay. I shrug them off and growl, "Go away," and they leave quickly. Most kids are afraid of me.

Out of the corner of my eye, I see him and David round the corner and come to a full stop when they see me. I drag my fingers across my eyes, actually touching my eyeballs, and the burn starts immediately. Real tears. Hairspray coated fingertips. They start to walk away, but I run to them and grab Ted's arm. He freezes.

"It's my dad," I gasp, looking up at him through burning

eyes. "Please." He looks down at me, and I see his face visibly change from hatred and anger to pity. Oh, Ted. You are so kind.

He looks at David, who nods, his arms folded. And then Ted touches me. My arm tingles at his caress. "He has cancer."

"Oh God," Ted says, still looking at David.

"Hey, I'm so sorry," David says softly. He touches me too, an awkward pat on my back. His hand feels like ice.

It takes everything I have not to glare at him. Instead, I drop my head and let another shudder of despair take my body, grinding my fists into my eyes. Fuck, it burns.

David knows he isn't welcome and is smart enough to get away. "Ted, why don't I catch up with you tonight, and we can go over that chemistry?"

Perfect. I keep my head down and grab fistfuls of my hair, trying to wipe the hairspray off my fingers.

"Yeah," Ted responds, "come by after dinner?"

I watch David's feet step away.

"Take care, May," he calls softly as he walks away.

Ted takes my arm and guides me back to his locker. "Let me just get my stuff," he says. As we head out of the school, he asks, "Do you want to go for coffee?"

"Can we just go to my place? I like to keep near the phone in case the hospital calls."

"Oh, May. Yeah. Sure."

We walk to my place. I hold onto his arm, and he lets me, and I deliver my story. I tell him about how Dad started coughing blood, and Mom finally talked him into going to the doctor. But by then, it was too late. The ambulance took him away this morning after a night of hacking and puking. My mom followed them in the car. She wouldn't let me come. Oh, and he only has a month to live.

Okay, it's actually Ron's story, from when he was a kid. But it's working. Ted hangs on my every word. And when I look up at him, I see his guilt. And his desire.

"Thank you for listening," I say as I struggle to put the key into the back door. My hands are shaking, which is a nice effect. Ted thinks I'm a basket case. "I didn't want to come back here alone."

"Here," he says. He takes the keys out of my hand. "Let me."

Inside is hot. I open windows, muttering, "It smells like cancer in here."

When I walk back in the kitchen, Ted is standing there, awkwardly waiting for me to tell him what to do. I'm a show, don't tell kind of girl, so I wrap myself around him, burying my head into his shoulder, and start sobbing.

He pats my back. His breathing is shaky, and his breath is hot on my hair. I wait for a kiss on the top of my head. Nothing. I lift my head and place my hands on his shoulders, pushing us backwards into the counter.

"Hey!" Ted tries to laugh.

I lift myself onto my toes to kiss his lips.

He turns his head. "No!" He tries to step sideways, but my hands are holding the counter tight on either side of him. "May, please don't."

My eyes fill with tears. Real ones this time. Raging, angry tears. "Why not, Ted? Why can't you just give me one pity fuck? Is that too much to ask?"

I'm shouting right into his face, and his eyes squint from the volume of my words. He turns white. "But your dad . . ."

"Whatever." I grab his face and wrap a leg around his, grinding against him, my lips parted, tongue searching. He shoves me off him with the full force of his weight. I almost fall, but the stove saves me. Ted starts to move to the door. But now a frying pan is in my hand, greasy with cold fat from last night's pork chops. I watch as my arm swings it in some sort of discus throwing arc, and then it slips from my grip. It should have hit him in the back, but he bent down to get his shoes. It thunks into his head, then clatters loudly to the floor. Ted hesitates, puts his hand to his head, and then he clatters to the floor too.

"Ted! Oh God, Ted! Are you okay?" I roll him onto his back, straddling him, touching his face, kissing him. Kissing him. Kissing him. He doesn't turn his head away. I'm so turned on I ache. I start to undo his zipper but stop when I realize he could end this just by waking up. I give him another quick peck. "Wait there," I whisper and run to Mom and Dad's bedroom.

Dad has six neckties. He wears them at funerals and weddings and for the big company Christmas do. I take two. One I use to tie his wrists together behind his back. The other, his ankles. He wakes up just as I prop him up against the couch.

Ted

Edges of light slipping through blackness. Pulsing into sharp, deliberate stabs of pain. I feel something lumpy against my neck. My cock is wake-up hard. I feel a tug at my fly. My arms won't move. I pull words out of my darkness. "What are you doing?"

My eyes pop open as cool fingers wrap tightly around my erection. Jesus, it's May. "No!" Stop. Oh my God, stop touching me! I'm propped up against the couch on the floor in her living room. My hands are tied behind my back. My legs are pinned under her. I pull away, kicking with my legs and trying to roll over, but she digs her nails into my balls. My cock wilts.

"What the fuck are you doing?" I shout. I'm sweating.

Shaking. She takes me in her mouth, and the hardness returns. I look away. David. I'm so sorry. She's moaning and grunting, and then I'm inside her. It's silky and hot and wet, and she's licking my ear and—fuck! I cum. Just like that. She's going crazy on top of me. I am nothing.

Then she's done. Her cheek presses against mine. She's whispering something. My detachment burns into rage.

Her hand goes over my mouth. "See?" she says. "You aren't gay at all."

I open my mouth to bite her, but her hand is gone. She's untying my hands.

May

He's sitting on the floor against the couch, legs straight out in front of him. It doesn't matter if he comes to now. I tug his fly down and feel his body tense.

He whispers, "What are you doing?"

Show. Don't tell. I slip my hand inside his pants and find what I'm looking for. It's warm and fleshy and stiffening as I pull at it, working it out over the elastic of his underwear. Wow, I'm not disappointed. He's circumcised. The head pushes up, dark and proud. My hand barely fits around it. I slide the skin up and rub my thumb over the wet drop forming on the tip.

"No." He's talking to his dick, I'm sure.

I grin, "So much for being gay, right?"

He starts to wriggle his hips. He's getting into it. Then he bucks and tries to turn sideways. I tighten my grip and cup his tight little balls in my hand, letting the fingernails brush against the skin. He gasps. The bucking stops. His dick loses a bit of its turgor. I can fix that.

"Just enjoy, baby." I kiss his cock lightly, letting my tongue tease around the head and then lick the length of it, smearing the spit with my hand as it pumps.

Everything becomes energy. I'm touching myself, pulling my panties aside under my skirt, grinding my wet cunt against him.

"Please, no," he whimpers. His entire body is shaking.

I slide him inside me, place my hands on his chest, and dig my nails in, pumping and grinding with my hips.

"Oh, Ted, my beautiful man. I wanted you so bad!"

He won't look at me, won't let me kiss his lips. I lick at his ear, feeling the hard curves under my tongue. It takes seconds. His shaking turns into shuddering quakes, and then a low moan comes from his throat. I feel his cock unload inside me, and I scream, pushing down on him, biting his neck, feeling my own orgasm spark through my body.

We're both crying. I rub my cheek against his, sharing our tears.

"It's everything, right?" I whisper. "Just like I told you." I reach between my legs, exploring the wetness of our passion. I suck one finger clean and then press my hand to his lips, smiling softly. "See? You aren't gay at all, my love."

I untie his hands.

He growls and lunges at me, pushing me to the floor, fingers gouging into my arms. His face is red, his eyes squinting. He wants more! Look out, girl, you have unleashed an animal! He presses a hand against my chest to hold me down while he unties his feet. I run my tongue around my lips. Then both hands are on my shoulders. As a smile breaks over my face, he pushes hard against me. And stands up.

I reach a hand up to him. "Bedroom?"

But he's gone.

I catch him at the back door. As he opens it, cool air tickles my skin. "Ted, wait!" I'm still breathing hard from my orgasm, but there's something else—an ache, like I'm watching my soul walk away from me. "Don't go. Please. I love you."

He turns back, his eyes still wet, his eyebrows raised. "You raped me."

I smile like a Cheshire cat. "Did I?" I slam my forehead against the doorframe with everything I have. The pain is bright and sudden, glittering deliciously across my temple, erasing my post-fuck euphoria. I feel the cold trickle of blood down my cheek. "That's not how I see it, Ted. That's not how anyone is going to see it."

Ted

People are playing ball somewhere. I hear the crack of a bat. A cheer follows. My head bent down, I watch as my runners take steps forward on the gum-spattered sidewalk, like I'm watching a movie.

I'm not a rapist. I didn't do it. I swear nothing happened. I'm walking home from her place. Shivering. My dick tingles, and my balls are aching. I feel so ashamed. Am I just a pervert? How did that happen? I hate her. She disgusts me. But my fucking dick is like an alien.

I bite down on my tongue. Trying to hurt. Trying to stop thinking about what I did. Or what I did with David. Don't think about him. You were just experimenting. So was he. That wasn't real. I'm straight. There's no such thing as gay.

Mom's home. The car is in the driveway, and the sun glows yellow in the hallway through the tinted windows of our entryway. I step inside, and the warmth of home envelops me.

She calls from the kitchen, "Hi, honey!"

I want to run to her. I want to be six again, when I didn't care about boys or girls. We could eat spaghetti and sit on the couch and practice bird calls.

"I made spaghetti!" she calls, as though she read my mind, or maybe my nose influenced my thoughts. "How was your day?" she says, popping her head into the hallway. "Honey?"

"Yeah," I say. "I'm just going to have a quick shower. Then I'll be right down. Okay?"

She's standing with her hands wringing a tea towel, trying to decide whether I'm okay or not.

"Wait for me?" I reach out without touching her, oddly like a pat on her shoulder but not. Not while I stink of May.

My shower is hot, and I scrub my genitals with a brush. I can't look at myself. The soap turns pink. I slam my head hard against the tile wall. Just once. It hurts more than I meant it to.

Mom's at the bathroom door instantly. "You okay in there?"

"Just banged my elbow! Out in a sec!"

I rinse and towel off quickly, before the steam melts away from the mirror.

Mom puts my plate down as I step into the kitchen. She's been listening. I know she put the spaghetti on my plate as soon as she heard the bathroom door open. And the sauce on top as I stomped down the stairs. The green and red parmesan shaker sits in the middle of the table with the salt and pepper. Spaghetti night.

I have a forkful of pasta in my mouth before she asks, "What's going on?"

I glare at her, shake my head, and continue chewing.

She breaks eye contact first and spins her fork in her noodles. We eat in silence, our forks scraping against plates like nails on a blackboard. We never eat in silence. I can feel her watching me. I eat fast so she doesn't see my hands shake.

"Girl problems?"

I look to the ceiling and exhale big. Girl problems? Boy problems? Fuck if I know. "Mom, just leave it."

We finish eating without another word. Images of David and May flip through my brain in a nasty slide show.

She lets out a sigh and gets up to clear the plates. "Want to go to Grandma's with me this weekend?"

"Yes." I don't even hesitate. Out of town is the best place to be.

"Girl problems then." She concludes.

I get up to help her with the dishes.

"How's David doing?" she asks, handing me a tea towel.

She just can't leave it. Normally, I'd stomp off to my room. But I need to be with her right now.

I swallow. "Good," I say, shrugging my shoulders. Does she know? Is she trying to guess? I brush it off with, "I think he's good."

I wipe a plate, flip it over, and wipe the other side.

"Did you two have a falling out?"

I don't answer.

She pulls the plug from the sink, wrings the dishcloth, and goes to wipe the table.

"I saw May's mom the other day. I didn't know they were back."

"Yeah. She's at the school."

She puts her hand on a hip. "Well, that would have been some news worth sharing."

I shrug again and fold the dish towel carefully; I hope

she doesn't see my hands shake. I should probably just leave. There's nothing I can tell her. By the way, I'm gay? By the way, I'm a pervert? Oh, and a rapist—that too.

She watches me with that ache in her eyes, the one she gets when I'm hurt. Like she's hurting for me.

"Can we just watch a movie or something?" I ask. "I can make some popcorn."

She hangs the dishcloth over the tap at the sink. "Sure. I'll go put on my PJs."

May

I did it. I finally had my Teddy. My cunt aches with the sweetness of it all. I can't stop touching myself.

Ted

We're on the couch watching *Grease*, a bowl of popcorn between us. I'm melting a piece of popcorn in my mouth. I can't taste the butter or the salt. It feels like Styrofoam. *Grease* is a favourite for Mom and me; we watch it like comfort food. Usually, we bop and sing to the tunes, but not tonight—at least not me—Mom still hums and taps her feet.

Sandy's singing Danny's praises to her girlfriends while Danny grunts smut about Sandy to his boys. I love John Travolta. He has a look of David about him. And Olivia Newton-John is perfect as the good girl turned bad. At one point, I thought I had a crush on her, but I realized it was just solid admiration. Mom adores her.

"Did you know her grandfather won a Nobel prize for physics?" Mom quips. She loves it when she can deliver me anything remotely to do with science.

"Huh." I shovel some popcorn in my mouth to end the

conversation.

"He was Jewish. Isn't David Jewish?"

"No," I mutter, not taking my eyes from the screen.

"He escaped the Holocaust, you know." She reaches into the bowl, pinching a couple of kernels in her fingers. They almost make it to her mouth, but another thought hits her. "What a thing, huh? The Holocaust?"

I nod again and point at the screen, reminding her to shut up because I'm watching a movie.

Danny shows up at the end-of-year carnival all dorked up in a letter sweater when there's a knock at the door. My heart stops. Did May actually call the police? Jesus.

Mom starts to get up, brushing the popcorn off her lap. "Well, I wonder who that is?"

I put my hand up to stop her. "I got it." Best to face the devil myself. Maybe I can talk my way out of it.

I've never known the hall to the front door to be so long.

Our front door opens into a hallway that leads to the kitchen, and halfway down to the right is the door to the living room. The summer sunset beams down the hall from the back windows. Off the kitchen, to the left, are the stairs that take you up to the bedrooms. The hallway is crowded with coat hooks and a telephone table—our black phone sitting atop the five-inch-thick phone directory. The handle has an extra-long cord, tangled and twisted around the legs of the table. I feel a sudden urge to untangle it when the knocking starts up again. "Shave-and-a-haircut!" I am at the door in two strides and knock back. "Two cents!"

It's David. Here to work on chemistry like we planned a million years ago this afternoon. I open the door, and every muscle in my body becomes water.

He catches as me as I fall.

"Whoa, buddy!" he says. "Are you okay?" David is in heterosexual mode. He tries to prop me against the wall, pushing away from me. But I won't let go. He whispers, "Where's your mom?"

I kiss his neck, inhaling his salty summer skin. He giggles. "What are you doing?"

My hands take his face, and I pull him in for a kiss— pushing my tongue against his lips, like a baby needing to suckle. I feel his shaky exhale, and his tongue reaches out to mine. Our mouths close onto each other. It feels right. Soft. Safe.

"Honey?" It's Mom. David tries to pull away, but my hands are wrapped around his head. Her voice is closer. "Everything okay? Oh." Then I hear her footsteps back away. "Oh." She says it again as though it will help her make sense of what she saw.

David breaks away, pushing my shoulders against the wall, looking at me like I just confessed to murder. Not rape. "What the fuck, Ted?"

I take his hand and lead him down the hall, toward the living room. The credits are rolling on the TV. The entire population of Rydell High is singing the song "You're the One That I Want." And Mom is sitting at the edge of the couch, examining her fingers, like options, spread palms up in her lap.

Before I can say anything, she says softly, "It's okay. I knew." She takes a quick breath. "I think I knew."

David tries to release his hand from my grip, but I squeeze, and he stops. He's looking at the floor, waiting for a verdict. His body vibrates.

"And?" I demand, suddenly needing to know. I need to know I'm gay. And I need to hear it from her.

She looks up; her eyes are wet. "Oh, honey." She leans forward, reaching out to us. "Look at the two of you! How could

I be anything but happy for you?"

"Because it's illegal? Because it's okay to beat us up? Because David's dad will—God knows what he will do!"

David mutters, "Dad can't know—he just can't."

Mom stands up and comes to us, touching his arm, touching mine. "Of course not," she says. Then practical Mom appears. "Let's sit down and talk about this." She heads towards the kitchen.

David repeats himself as we follow her. "Dad can't know." His hand is damp.

We aren't talking. David and I watch as Mom makes us lemonade—Russell-style: two spoonfuls of lemon juice, a spoonful of sugar, and a tiny pinch of salt, stirred into a mug of tap water and ice. The sliding glass door is open. A robin begs plaintively for sex as the day disappears. We sit next to the only other window in the kitchen. The tiny Arborite table is like a gameboard between us.

Images of May's attack flash back into my brain. "Can't we just move somewhere safe?"

David is in the odd seat, next to me. Mom puts the mugs on the table and takes her chair across from me.

They begin bantering suggestions.

"What about San Francisco?" David quips, with a lisp and a flip of his wrist.

Mom's more serious. "Grandma has room for you," she says, looking first at me, then David. "Both of you."

"We could go to a college transfer program," David pitches back, restarting our old conversation.

"Your Aunt Betty lives in Canada."

"Amsterdam," David states, as though he's decided.

Mom laughs. "And how would that work?"

I take a deep breath. "Can we just go? Tonight?"

They both look at me as though I am the child in the room interrupting an adult conversation.

David snorts. "No?" It's a question. Directed at me. His eyes asking: What the fuck is wrong with you? Haven't you made enough trouble?

"I have to work, honey," Mom says softly, shaking her head. "You only have another year to go, if that—"

I shake my head, my lips pressed tight against the words I want to say. The words I don't know how to say.

David reaches across and strokes my hair, glancing quickly at Mom when he remembers our taboo. But she just nods. He continues.

The banging on the glass explodes the moment. David's hand drops to his lap. My heart stops.

Mr. LeClair's voice shouts, "David!" as he steps through the open door, and David jumps to attention.

I can tell by the look on Mr. LeClair's face. He saw us. He saw David stroking my hair.

"Hey, Dad," David's voice rattles. His lips seem to be turning blue.

"John!" Mom is up too. "How are you?"

Mr. LeClair stands, hands on his hips, legs wide like he's about to give a command. He stares at David. Then his tight mouth pulls into a sneer as he turns his glare at me. He shakes his head.

Mom clears her throat. "Can I get you some lemonade?" She wipes her hands on her shirt and then looks down, seeming to realize she's in her pyjamas—short shorts and Dad's green faded army T-shirt—and turns away, busying herself at the counter.

Mr. LeClair turns his gaze back to his son. "No. Thanks. This asshole was supposed to mow the lawn tonight. Seems he forgot—"

David's stance mirrors his dad's, his cheeks turning red, his tone belligerent. "I had chemistry homework!"

"I had chemistry homework!" Mr. LeClair whines. "You always have homework." Then he points his head to the door. "C'mon. Let's go."

David holds his ground for just a beat. Then his dad takes a step towards him. And the stance melts. His hands go up, palms out. "No! Dad! I'm coming."

He steps around his father toward the door, hands still up. Mr. LeClair reaches for David's arm and shoves him. "Git!" he barks.

"Hey!" Mom has turned from the counter. She's holding a teaspoon in her fist, hip height, as though it's a weapon. Mr. LeClair looks at the spoon and then at Mom's face. He snorts and shakes his head. Then he's gone.

Mom leans back on the counter, still holding the spoon.

"He won't hurt David," she says, staring at the door. Then she turns to me. "Will he?"

I bite my lip.

It must be three in the morning. I'd been staring at the ceiling forever, playing hide and go seek with my thoughts: May, David, Mom, Mr. LeClair, May again. But I guess I fell asleep because I'm awake now. And someone is in my room. I lie perfectly still. Our breathing roars in the darkness. Then there's a sob.

"David?" I'm out of bed, wrapping myself around the cold body huddled in the corner.

"We have to go," he says.

I stroke his hair, feeling a swollen and sticky bump under my fingers. He smells of metal and fear.

May

Mom's in the kitchen. I have my binder snugged to my chest, ready to head out the door. I usually stay in bed until she leaves. But today, I figure I can wait at the end of Elm Street for Ted, and we can stroll the rest of the way together. If we make it to school, that is. This heat could drive a girl and her boy to the lake for the afternoon.

"Oh my God, honey! What happened?"

I have a lovely bruise blooming around the gash on my forehead. I laugh it off. "You know me! I walked into a doorframe at school—turned too soon."

Mom chuckles, shaking her head. "You're such a klutz."

Actually, I'm not. Usually, if I walk into a wall, it's because she pushed me. But it's been a while.

"You're leaving early?" she asks. Mom has a smoke baking between her fingers, and I eye it, then the pack on the table. I have my own, but it's always nice to smoke someone else's. She watches my gaze. "Really?" Then she comes to me with her hands up, and I flinch, but she just brushes the hair from my forehead, inspecting the bruise. She reaches over to the pack and pulls a smoke out. "Okay, you can have one, but you're not going out like that. I have some makeup tricks just for situations like this."

The white embroidered cloth that protects the wood of her antique vanity table is smeared with ashes and rainbows of eyeshadow. The ashtray spills over, adding black smears to the colourful mess. There's a golden-edged burn hole on one side. She turns the chair so I'm facing her and gets onto her knees to work on my face. Her breath is sour, and clouds of smoke billow between us as she works. We keep making eye contact, and it's awkward because my throat tightens up and my eyes water. She wipes the tears with her thumb, once and then a second time. But the third time, she snarls, "For heaven's sake! Just close them and stop snivelling."

When she's finished, the bruise is gone. The cut is gone. She's done some sexy smoky shit to my eyelids too. "These things tend to spread. Might as well get that covered up before your eye turns black."

She gets some hairspray, and telling me to close my eyes again, she spritzes my face, then fixes my bangs over the worst of the bump.

She leaves the room without ceremony, muttering, "You're going to be late for school."

I look in the mirror and see shadows of my mother's face in mine. The sun hits something sparkly and spreads dots of rainbows over my face. It's her emerald earrings, dangling from the earring stand. I put them on and fix my hair so most of the bangs spike up and just a few strands cover the bump.

I'm not early anymore. I run up the street, but no one is in sight. School started ten minutes ago.

I walk through the school doors into empty halls and head for Ted's homeroom. I just need to see him. I just need to feel that spark. And I'm not going to wait.

Of course, the classroom door is closed. I give it a quick tap, pulling some sheets of paper from my binder. Miss Bluth opens the door a crack, like she's alone in her apartment. Too bad there isn't a chain on the door, sweetie.

"Hi!" I say, stepping forward, forcing her to take a step back. "Ted left this at my place last night." I beam, scanning the room for my man. "I think it's due . . ." My beam fades as I take in Ted's empty desk.

"Ted isn't in today." Miss Bluth reaches for the papers, but I let go of them, and they flutter to the ground. She scrambles to the floor to pick them up as I turn to leave. I hear her call, "Thank you."

I'm running. Ted's house. My lungs burn for air as I make the corner and charge down Elm. I should have reported him.

Ted

I wake up just before Mr. LeClair starts beating on the front door. His shouts cut across the morning breeze simpering through my bedroom window. "If you don't send that little shit out here right now, I'm calling the police!"

We're lying on our backs in my bed, the sheets scrunched in a pile between us. I turn my head to look at David, fully dressed beside me. His eye is swollen shut, and I wonder if he's still asleep. I reach for his hand and give it a squeeze. He squeezes back, shaking his head the tiniest bit.

I hear Mom open the door. "John?"

Mr. LeClair continues his rant in a demanding whisper. "I want that little prick out here, now!"

I imagine she has her ratty pink housecoat wrapped tightly around her waist and her hair in a sleep-knotted ponytail. My alarm clock says it's only six. She doesn't get up until seven. She has no idea David is in my room. "He's not here, John. I'm sorry," she tells him. It's a good thing she doesn't know. Mom's a lousy liar.

Mr. LeClair doesn't believe her anyway. His feet scrunch down the driveway, and he yells, "I know he's in there!" Just before he slams his car door and skids out of the driveway.

"I can't just walk away from everything, sweetheart."

Mom is perched on the couch, in a Bermuda-flowered dress and white heels, ready for work. Three mugs of coffee lay out a triangle on the coffee table. The blinds and windows are closed despite the heat. David and I are shirtless. We sit on the floor cross-legged, talking in loud whispers.

"You have to go to school. I have to pay the bills. David has to . . ." She looks at David. His right eye is red and swollen; the cheek and temple are turning purple-green. She shakes her head and takes a deep breath. "I'll speak with your father—"

"No!" he growls. "I'm not going back." The swelling of his eye gives him a weird permanent wink, like he's just kidding.

"Mom, you can't just—"

Knuckles banging on glass break our whispers. We freeze.

May

That little fuck. His mom's car is in the driveway. Something is definitely up. Maybe he's sick.

I'm banging on the glass patio door. "Ted!" I try not to scream. "Hey, babe, open up!" I stop and listen for sounds inside the house, but my breath is coming hard, and my pulse is slamming in my brain. I bang the glass again. "Are you okay?" Silence.

I try the door, but it's locked. I go to the stone turtle for the key, but it isn't there. This is bullshit. I pick up the turtle. It's heavy enough. I lift it over my head and get ready to heave it through the window, watching my reflection rage back at me, long and lean. And gone. The window slides open, and Ted's mom, Carol, is standing in the doorway.

"May?" She steps onto the deck as I lower the rock. "Honey? What are you doing?"

Ted's voice comes out of the darkness. "Leave her alone, May!"

Then he steps onto the deck. He's so beautiful. And all shy, pulling on a T-shirt to cover himself up. David is behind him. I drop the rock and push past Carol.

"There you are!" I say, reaching for him. "God, I was so worried!"

But he pushes me away. "You should leave."

I stare at him, smelling his musk over the cool morning air. "What's going on, babe?"

Then I look over at David standing there topless, hands on his hips, as if he's in charge. But his face is bruised up. I look back at Ted, searching his face, his arms for the same. "Are you hurt? Did someone hurt you?" I reach for him again, but he steps back.

"May, you need to leave." He catches his breath. He doesn't want David to know about us. Poor sweetie. "Now," he squawks.

David and Carol both look at Ted like he's an idiot. David is the one who steps up.

"How's your dad doing?" he asks. His hand touches my arm.

"My dad?" What the fuck does my dad have to do with this?

"There's nothing wrong with her dad," Ted sneers. Why is he acting like this?

Sweet Carol scolds her son, "Now, honey, stop this!" Then she is up beside me too. She and David, each touching me. They understand. They know Ted and I have to be together. It chokes me up a little, and I nod and give them a tiny, brave smile.

Ted takes another step back, and it's hard to hear what he says next, but it makes Carol and David look up. David has a smirk on his face.

Ted nods, and then he shakes his head, looking only at David. He speaks louder this time. "She raped me."

Rage boils up inside me. "Really? Really, Ted?" I wipe at the makeup covering my bruised face. I point at the bruise on my forehead. "That's not how I remember it."

Ted shakes his head, speechless as usual. He turns and walks back into the house. I go to follow him, but David grabs my arm. He's not smiling anymore. "You should go." His fingers dig into my flesh, and I kick at his nuts, but suddenly I'm turned around, facing the yard, my arm twisted behind me. He pushes me toward the lawn. I stumble. I look back, and they are both retreating into the house.

"I'm calling the police!" I shout. I grab the turtle rock and heave it toward the window, but it clatters on the deck. I hear the neighbour's window slide open.

"Everything okay, Carol?"

David stands in the window, watching me. He has a baseball bat in his hand.

I'll kill him. I'll kill them both.

"Carol?" the neighbour calls again. I leave the yard, anger tickling through my body like fear.

Carol's voice calls from somewhere inside the house, "We're fine, thanks, Marsha!"

Ted

She's here. I should have told them. Mom goes to answer the door, and I'm right behind her. But I'm suddenly aware of my nakedness and grab a T-shirt as I pass the laundry room. I feel David behind me as I step out onto the deck.

"Oh God. Her Dad," he says, feeling my sense of urgency.

"Something must have happened."

I shout, "Leave her alone, May!" as I step onto the deck.

She lunges at me, feigning concern. I push her away, surprising myself with a kung fu block. Where the fuck was that last night?

"You need to leave." My voice is soft and squeaky, like I'm trying to shout in a dream. I clear my throat. "Now!"

But David steps up to her, scowling back at me, as if I'm pure evil. He touches her arm. "How's your dad doing?"

She looks up at David, and I can tell she doesn't know what to say. She can't even remember her own fucking lie.

"There's nothing wrong with her dad," I sneer.

Mom goes to May, reaching out for her. Jesus. They have no clue. I step back. I want to run. "She raped me," I whisper.

David hears me. A smile tugs at the corners of his mouth, eyebrows raised. But when our eyes connect, I say it again, louder this time. "She raped me."

Mom backs away from May, folding her arms in front of her. "Perhaps you should leave, May," she says.

"Really, Ted?" May growls. She is rubbing at her face, wiping gobs of makeup off her forehead, uncovering the bruise she gave herself yesterday. "That's not how I see it!"

I turn and walk into the house. My ears are burning; my eyes are full of tears—I won't let her see me like this. When I look back, Mom is following me, and David has May in a half nelson, guiding her off the deck. Then Mom's arms are wrapped around me, and she's stroking my hair. David steps into the house and slides the glass door closed. He takes the baseball bat from the broom closet and stands at the doorway.

A rock bounces onto the wooden deck. David flinches, but he doesn't move.

May screams, "I'm calling the police!" her voice fading as she storms off.

David turns to me. "Raped you? Really?"

Mom is holding onto my arm. She leads me to a chair. I tell them the story. How May tricked me into coming to her house. There's a lump on the back of my skull the size of a chestnut and I touch it as I remember the moment the frying pan hit me. Mom strokes her hand over the bump and then busies herself getting a bag of ice.

"You need to go to the hospital, sweetheart," her hands are shaking as she puts ice into a plastic bread bag.

I can't look at David. I feel his eyes on me. His hand is on the table, not quite touching mine. I don't know how to tell the next part. I'm terrified he won't be able to forgive me.

"When I came to, I was on the floor in the living room. She'd tied me up, and she was unzipping my fly." I swallow. I can't—I won't share the rest.

Mom and David don't say a word. My palms sweat on the table. Mom gently touches my head, finding the contusion. She places the bag against it. When I reach up and take over, her hand drops.

"She smashed her head against the doorframe when I was leaving," I breathe. "And said I was the one who raped her."

There's silence. Then Mom says, "Okay," and she walks away.

David places his hand over mine.

I hear the clicking sound of the phone being dialed from the hall. Holding my breath, I count how many numbers she dials. Seven. Eight. Long distance. Exhaling, I look up and meet David's eyes. We exchange tiny, brave, minute nods. He squeezes my hand.

Mom's voice seems to echo down the hall. "Hello, Betty?"

1988

May

Jake leans across the seat and pulls my head towards his. His tongue pushes against my lips, and I open my mouth to let him in. I give it a gentle suck and then pull away carefully. His hand grips my hair, and I giggle. "I'm going to be late!"

The grip turns into a soft stroke, and then his hand is on the steering wheel. "Okay, baby girl. I'll pick you up at two?"

The door of the old Chrysler clunks as I force it open. Blue clouds from the exhaust push their way into the vehicle. "Yup! Love you!"

"Be a good girl, and get me lots of tips!" he says as I struggle to close the door behind me.

Crossing the street, I look at the overcast shield of grey clouds and then at my watch. It's quarter to five. I have fifteen minutes before my shift starts. When I get to the door, I look back at Jake. The neon glare of the Central Saloon sign reflects on the car window so I can't see his face, but I know he is mouthing, "I love you." I mouth it back.

I walk through the noisy bar, straight past the kitchen. Kisha picks up right behind me, empty drink tray in her hand, and we head out into the alley.

The steel door slams behind us, sealing the noise inside. She takes a joint from her apron and holds it up. "Tip, from table four," she says, nursing it to life with quick puffs over the flame of her blue Bic. Her fingers are long and skinny just like the rest of her. They're adorned with silver rings: a skull, a life cross, and a Pac-Man. Her nails have the chipped remains of black nail polish. She's twenty-one going on twelve—sexy and stupid all in one package.

She hands me the burning reefer. I take a long deep toke, holding the smoke down against the choking rebuttal of my lungs.

I pass the joint back to Kisha, watching as she takes her turn before I slowly exhale. Despite my best efforts, I cough. "Nice," I say, nodding my head.

And, as though on cue, Kisha coughs her fucking head off. I shake my head. Her eyes are streaming, washing thick black eyeliner onto her cheeks. She giggles her dorky snort giggle.

"They gave me the windows," she says, pulling up the waist of her black T-shirt to dab at her eyes. Her pierced belly button is decorated with a fairy stud that dances over the black Celtic tattoo wrapping her waist.

I can't help myself. I put my hands on her hips and bend down to lick a circle around the fairy. Kisha has her hands on my shoulders, giggling some more. I take the fairy in my teeth and give it a tug, feeling the quiver of her tummy stop, along with her laughter. "Oh," she says, and then, "Ow," as I tug a little harder. I twist my head a little and then let go.

When I stand up, she's still wiping her eyes. Then she lets her T-shirt drop, looking like a stretched-out hanky over her waist. "Why don't we trade? You can have the windows?" She passes the roach back to me.

I take another toke and then reach my hands around her neck to pull her towards me. Her lips open, and I blow the smoke into her mouth.

Jake doesn't know I do this. Play with Kisha. I think it's part of the attraction. I mean, I've been with Jake since he got out—and that was, fuck, four years ago? So that's a long time with just one guy. Jake's real possessive, though. I don't know who he'd kill first if he caught me with another guy. But with Kisha, it's not really sex, because she doesn't have a dick. If anything, he'd want to watch.

I take both her hands in mine and give them a squeeze.

We go back to the Happy Hour crazy inside.

Ted

Six years, and my stomach still flips when he smiles at me. The three-day conference on wastewater toxicity is an annual thing, and this is my first time presenting. David has come to cheer me on. Our hands are deep in our pockets to control any wayward contact. We are strolling along the waterfront in Seattle, meeting some friends for drinks at Central Saloon. The September sun is still bright, keeping a firm grip on the last days of summer.

We're talking about the work we've seen presented the past couple of days. "Do you ever regret not going into research?"

He answers without hesitation, "Nope. Not in the least."

David graduated as a pharmacist last year. He's working at a local pharmacy. Nothing glamorous or big money, but it takes the edge off. Since then, we've been able to move into a bigger apartment and—well, the pressure's off.

"What am I doing while you go to the lab at two a.m. to check on an experiment?" he says, poking me with his elbow.

"Sleeping."

"*Quod erat demonstrandum.*"

Central Saloon is part of the tradition for this conference. Our research group works with a team from Norway and another team from Atlanta, and this is one of the few times we can all be together in the same space and let our hair down, so to speak.

There are a bunch of people leaving as we go in. They hold the door for us, and we walk into the beer-scented room, scanning the crowd for Tippy and Stephen. Tippy is a seven-foot-tall Brazilian. He's hard to miss. He got into Georgia State on a basketball scholarship only to discover, and embrace, his inner dork and quit basketball to become a scientist. Stephen is the complete opposite of Tippy: Norwegian, wide and white, without an athletic bone in his body. They both study at University of British Columbia. We share a lab.

Stephen spots us first. "Yo, comrades!" he hollers across the room in his Scandinavian accent. There's a notable pause in the raucous conversation as the Americans absorb his odd accent shouting communist lingo. I shake my head—Stephen will do anything for attention.

We tuck ourselves into the cozy corner booth they've commandeered. There are two draft jugs on the table—one is empty—and about a dozen glasses.

Tippy pours for us while Stephen flags down the waitress for another jug. "You have to catch up!" Tippy shouts as he plops our drinks in front of us.

I oblige, knocking back the half-pint glass, but David just takes a sip. I scowl at him. He shrugs. He's too cautious sometimes, and I know he would never want to be out of control in a strange place.

"Aww, come on, David!" Stephen groans. "You can do better than that!"

He responds with his usual confidence, "Someone has to get you fools home at the end of the night."

"Taxi!" Stephen shouts, just as the waitress arrives with two more jugs.

"You need a taxi?" she asks.

"No, ma'am," Stephen says, suddenly focused on his beer glass and the table. Apparently, he hasn't had quite enough liquid courage to talk to the opposite sex yet.

She pulls out a notepad and a pen. "You guys want any food? It's wing night. Twenty-five cents apiece."

Tippy takes over, flirting with her. "Is that Pac-Man?"

She smiles and holds up her hand to look at the yellow enamel ring on her finger as if she just noticed it was there. "Yup." She bites her bottom lip.

"Classic, man," Tippy says slowly. He reaches for her hand, and she lets him take it.

David and I look at each other and shake our heads. Tippy is an artist. I'm just glad he's not gay—I wouldn't want to have that kind of flirt around David all the time.

We order fifty wings, to start. The rest of the team eventually arrives, including my advisor, Dr. Don Knudsen. I was in my third year of my undergrad when he invited me to join his lab to do my master's. He actually wanted me right away, but administratively I had to complete the course requirements for my bachelor's degree first. I challenged my final electives—Philosophy 420 and History 310—took some spring and summer courses, including a thesis program, and was ready for grad studies by September '86.

Don is gay too. Like us, he hasn't officially come out, but he lives with his partner, Patrick, in a one-bedroom apartment just across from campus.

I'm into my third beer, and I feel a little more than tipsy. Yeah, I'm a lightweight. David has slipped a glass of water in front of me, and I take a big drink. The conversation has ping-ponged from "What was he thinking?!" to sequencing the human genome, to "Why don't we all move to Seattle?" I need to pee. This is no easy task when you are in the corner part of a corner booth. I consider crawling under the table, but there are way too many feet.

I nudge David and announce, "Sorry, folks, nature calls." Everyone shuffles out until it gets to me. I stand up and feel my legs want to bend but grab the edge of the table before I visibly stumble. Everyone piles back into the booth as I focus on walking straight, racing my bladder to the men's room.

May

Fuck, it's stupid in here tonight. I swear I'm going to puke on the next plate of chicken bones. Wing night sucks. It's all cheap-ass college students in here. They get stupid drunk and gropey, and then, when they finally leave, they don't even think of leaving a tip. I've got only one table of executive types, a.k.a. good tippers. They're getting all my charm.

Sweet little Kisha is working her ass off too. She's got a couple of big tables, both full of university nerds from what I can see. She seems to be enjoying herself though. Good on her. I bet half the people at those tables didn't even order. God, she's naive.

I finally catch up with her in the galley. She's picking some meat off a chicken bone. Her fingers and lips are glossy with grease.

"Eww, that's disgusting!" I swipe at her wrist, careful not to touch the grease, and the chicken bone slips out of her hand, dropping to the floor.

"Someone saved it for me!" she whines, bending down to rescue the wing. "It's not like I'm picking off plates."

"Don't eat that," I say, shaking my head.

She rolls her eyes. "Duh!" she says and tosses the wing into the bus tray.

"Are you on break?" I ask her.

She gets up and starts arranging glasses on a tray. "Nope."

"Sure, she is." It's Greg, the manager. He's leaning on the corner by the kitchen doorway. I wonder how long he's been standing there? He looks at me. "Cover her tables? You can take

139

yours when she's done."

Kisha grabs an empty tray and heads back to the dining room, calling, "Back in a minute!" over her shoulder.

Greg lifts his hands in the air in exasperation. I follow her out and watch as she makes her way to the back table in the corner. She bends at the waist, ass out, and starts clearing glasses. Someone hands her a piece of paper and a pen. She puts her tray down and writes something on the paper. Then she walks away, coming back toward the kitchen, leaving her tray at the table.

A tall guy from the table picks it up and starts after her. He calls something, and she turns back. They share a laugh, and he touches her waist before she heads towards me and he fucks off back to his table.

What a little slut.

"I'm on my break now," she says as she walks past me into the galley.

I'm right behind her. "What the fuck was that?"

But Greg is still in the galley, and he's handing her a plateful of chicken wings and a napkin as she takes a seat at the little table. He looks up at me, eyebrows raised. "Can you let Gail know she's after you? So"—he checks his watch—"you go at eight thirty, and she can go about nine?"

"Did you just give out your phone number, Kisha?"

"Huh?" She's about to take a bite of a wing. "Oh, that. He was just asking where they should go for breakfast. They're at some kind of conference." She giggles and waves the wing, adding, "They're all scientists!"

She has no idea how much she hurts me sometimes.

Greg reaches across and pats her hand. "Well done, Kisha. It's great to see you girls go that extra mile."

She looks up at me and smiles, tilting her head in an I-told-you-so kind of way. I hold her eyes with mine and swallow my rage, nodding. "I'll let Gail know."

I get the bartender to pour me a jug of draft and make a beeline for the table of scientists. As I slosh it down on their table, they all chime in, "Nope," "Whoa," "We didn't order that."

The guy who got Kisha bending over is about a foot taller than the rest of them. He puts a hand up in a stop gesture along with a couple of others at the table.

I give them a puzzled look. "Oh? Huh. I could've sworn she said you guys," I say, scanning the group. They're mostly my age, mostly guys, and three girls. There's one older guy. Maybe he's someone's dad? Only one of the girls and the older guy make eye contact.

The older guy speaks up. "I wouldn't want to rob someone of their beer."

One of the boys in the corner draws my attention. He's looking behind me across the restaurant and nudging the girl next to him—the girl who's brave enough to look at me. He's saying something but not to me, and I can't hear him anyway. She calls, "David has to pee, folks. Let's slide!"

David? How fucking pretentious. Why not Dave?

He realizes I'm watching him and stops moving, muttering, "Never mind." His head is bent down, examining the wet rings of beer in front of him.

Old guy says, "I bet that beer belongs to that table over there. They look kind of wistful."

I smile, picking up the jug, keeping my eye on the David guy. "Alrighty, I'll give them a try. You folks need anything else?" I ask as I turn to go.

David looks up. "Actually, yeah. Do you have any pie? Or maybe Jell-O?" He says Jell-O extra loud. He's trying to look at me, but his eyes keep looking past me. He's shaking his head, no, as he speaks.

As I say, "Jell-O? No," I turn to see what he's looking at.

A guy is just stepping up behind me. "Sorry, folks, I'm back!"

I know him. Oh my God. I know him! Tears sting in my eyes. I whisper, "Ted."

He stumbles back a step and smiles. A bunch of people are spilling out of the booth, surrounding him. He's still smiling, looking at me.

I put the jug down and reach for him, grasping his hands in mine. "It's been so long. Look at you!"

He's still smiling.

"You two know each other?" I hear someone ask. "Duh," someone else responds. "Ted, you sitting or what?"

Then his hand is pulling away and that David guy is tugging at my Ted. "We were just heading out," he says, throwing a handful of crumpled bills on the table.

"No!" I say, "I'm on my break in a bit here. Stay, and we can catch up?"

But Ted is turning away. David—I remember him now— has hold of his arm and is steering him towards the door.

Ted

The toilet is miles away. I always feel so naked when I'm walking through a crowd like this. It's why I'm never this inebriated. What a fun word! *Inebriated.*

I know no one is watching me, but I know if I let loose one little stumble, all eyes will be on me. I focus on walking normally. Deep breaths. I'm not that drunk. The room isn't spinning. I probably just need to pee really bad.

So many chicken wings. I can't help but see tables as I go by. Piles of wing skeletons and crumpled red napkins surrounded by greasy faces and hands. Every chicken's nightmare. I stifle a giggle with a smile. Some girl sees me and smiles back. I quickly look away and refocus on my mission.

The men's room is surprisingly empty but completely disgusting. Cigarette butts in the urinals, the floor is covered in splatters of god-knows-what and crumpled balls of paper towels surround the empty trash can. It stinks of vomit and pee. I hear someone retching from a stall. Lovely.

Why do they put mirrors in front of urinals? The last thing I want to look at is my face while I pee. I've got that blotchy red thing going on on my neck. It shows up whenever I have a few drinks.

I wash my hands and splash some water on my face and then discover there are no paper towels left. I use my sleeve to dry my face and wipe my hands on the back of my jeans. One last look in the mirror to convince myself I'm sober.

Two guys come in, lighting a joint as soon as they walk through the door. One of them looks at my reflection in the mirror and nods toward the cigarette, offering me a toke. I hesitate for a second, then shake my head. I've only smoked pot once and only because I was really drunk, and I puked my guts out.

I feel fresher now. I walk back into the smoky bar and my legs feel solid. I almost feel like I could eat another wing or two.

A waitress is at the table. As I approach, I hear Gail hollering, "David has to pee, folks!" My God, she's loud. I'm still chuckling when I get to the table. The waitress has a full jug of beer in her hand, and she looks like she's taking it away. Have we been cut off? David is saying, "Jell-O" really loud. He's looking at me and shaking his head. Wow, what happened while I was gone? I hesitate, trying to read whatever he's trying to tell me. Whatever. "Sorry, folks, I'm back!" I say, loud enough to get the table's attention.

Then the waitress turns her head, looking straight at me.

My skin sparks in fear. She's reaching for my hands. Smiling. Talking. I'm instantly sober. Or am I completely stoned? The group from the table is piling around me, and it doesn't make sense.

Tippy asks, "Do you two know each other?"

Stephen responds with, "Duh."

She's saying, "It's been so long." She's crying, holding my hands. She hasn't changed. Her eyes are black with liner. Her hair is bleached white. Tiny. Maybe a little rounder than I remember. Her hands are cold.

My brain wants to say something—something to kick her down before she gets up. My teeth are bared in anger. I pull my hands away.

Don says softly, "Are you okay?"

Then David has his hand on my arm. "We're heading out," he says, turning me and guiding me to the door.

"No!" She shouts after us, demanding me, as always. She says something else, but I can't hear her.

Fuck you, May.

"We shouldn't go to the hotel yet." David's steady voice cuts clear into the dusk as the door closes us onto the street. He lets go of my arm.

I look over my shoulder as we head down the street. The door to Central Saloon opens again, and a bunch of people exit. I don't see May. We walk purposely, without saying another word, crossing the road and turning down the first street toward the waterfront.

I take a deep breath and exhale slowly. "Wow."

"I'm sorry. I tried to warn you," he says, "but—"

"I—I'm a grown man. She can't hurt me!" I stop walking. "This is ridiculous. We should go back."

"I didn't press charges, you know." She's caught up with us.

I turn to confront her.

I swallow. "For what?"

She has that pleading look on her face, eyes wide open, lips pressed between her teeth. Her apron is twisted and bunched to one side from running. Her tiny skirt is hitched up, showing the banded tops of her fishnet stockings.

She wipes sweat from her upper lip with a finger. Looking me up and down, she shakes her head. "You're beautiful, aren't you?" She takes a step closer. "How've you been? Why are you in Seattle? Do you live here now?"

The memory is like ice cracking through my soul. I feel her body on mine, the wetness of her tongue, the cigarette stink of her breath, her sweaty slippery body. But my hands are bound. Fucking bound together!

My lips pull into a sneer. I want to scream and slap her filthy smile. But my body starts to shake, and my chest tightens. "Go," is all that comes out. It sounds like a cough. Then, as though it's an afterthought, I muster another word, "Away." Then I remember to breathe. I inhale deep and slow and exhale through pursed lips. Yoga class.

"C'mon, Ted. Let's go." David's voice grounds me, as always.

May looks at him and delivers a flat, "Fuck off." She turns back to me, tilts her head, and smiles. "Do you want to—I don't know, get a coffee? Catch up a bit?" She has her hands at her sides, fingers twitching.

"No, May, I don't," I say.

She stares at me, her eyes darken, lids lowering. I draw in another lungful of air and blow out slowly. She grips onto her hips and straightens her spine. A smile peels across her face then disappears as she bites her lower lip.

I feel David's tension beside me, feel him shifting his weight. She turns her attention to him, sinking into her hip. "I had him first, you know. He could barely wait to be inside me."

"That's not true," I hear myself say. But I don't need to say that to him, do I?

His face is blank. He blinks slowly and takes a step toward her.

"He loved my hot wet cunt," she taunts. "Look at him now. He can hardly breathe he needs me so—"

"Shut up," he says in a soft growl, reaching for her.

May screams.

"Everything okay here?" A man with a duffle bag and a crewcut is instantly between May and David, his hand on David's wrist. His neck is thicker than a lamppost.

David drops his hands. "Yeah," he says, exhaling his rage, "we were just fooling around."

The guy looks at me and then at May. She's desperately trying not to laugh.

I feel a nervous giggle gurgle up inside me, and then I'm grinning. My brain is so stupid. I bite my cheek to make the smile disappear. I bite so hard it bleeds.

Then May has tears in her eyes, and she's nodding to the guy. "Yeah, we're okay." She looks back at her feet.

The tears seem to make the guy's muscles swell. "I think you boys had better leave."

Good idea, I want to say, but "Yes, sir," comes out.

May looks up just as we turn, a tear rolling down her

cheek.

May

I follow him.

I never stopped looking. Not after our lovemaking. I can still feel his cock inside me. Whenever Jake and I fuck, I close my eyes and think about Teddy and the ache in his eyes that day. His desire. He wanted me just as bad as I wanted him. And then he disappeared.

Rape. We'd both called it *rape.* I thought about reporting him, just so the police could help me find him, but I know leaving me wasn't his choice. I know my Ted wanted to stay. But his mom and David got all fucked up and possessive and took him away from me.

So I've waited. Watching for him. It's been five years, and now he's back. He couldn't stop smiling when he saw me.

I push through the crowd, and I'm almost at the door when Gail jumps in front of me. "Any clue when I get my break?" she asks.

I shake my head, pushing her aside. When I look again, they're gone, and the door is closing.

There's a massive traffic jam at the door. A bunch of big guys coming in, and a bunch of big guys going out. I hate being short. I grope my way through arms and torsos, Old Spice emanating from crotches. There's an "accidental" hand on my boob, and I bite the wrist it belongs to. The guy yelps, and the group opens up. Someone holds the door open to let me out.

They're crossing the road. Shoulder to shoulder, heads down.

I run to catch up with them. I know he's scared that I pressed charges. I know David is leading him away from me. I know we just need to touch. I can have him back.

He stops walking as I catch up to him, it's like he can feel me. "I didn't press charges," I say, catching my breath.

Then he's looking at me, and I melt. I'm breathing hard, and sweat beads on my face. I probably look like I just had an orgasm. And I could, looking at him again. I can't help but say, "You're beautiful, aren't you?" His blond curls are wild and tight, growing down past his ears, and he's got some downy whiskers happening around his lips. His eyes are steady and blue under thick eyebrows. No wonder David doesn't want to share him.

He's smiling and grunting something. He can't even talk he wants me so bad. He's breathing as hard as I am. Our eyes are locked. Oh, babe.

I'm reaching for him when David interrupts us, "Come on, Ted. Let's go."

I know I'm speaking for both of us when I tell David, "Fuck off."

God, David is a selfish prick. I realize I have to get this passion of ours away from that fuck wad. "Do you want to—I don't know, get a coffee?" I ask my sweetie. "Catch up a bit?"

"No, May, I don't."

It doesn't make sense. I smile. He's kidding, right? But he doesn't smile back. My pulse throbs in my head, just over my eyes. It's like black ink. Fuckin' David.

"I had him first, you know," I say, my eyes burning into him. "He could barely wait to be inside me. He loved my hot wet cunt. Look at him now. He can hardly breathe he needs me so—"

David whispers something and takes a step toward me. I see a super buff guy walking past us, and I scream.

Buff Guy is with me in a second. "Everything okay here?" he grunts.

David shrivels back into a little fag. "Yeah," he says, "we were just fooling around."

I stifle a laugh, deciding whether to let this guy loose on David, but then I look at Teddy, and he's choking on a giggle too! A big ole goofy grin is all over his sweet face. Aww, baby. I love you. I look at my feet, holding back the laughter until tears come to my eyes. I don't want this beast hitting my Ted by mistake.

I lift my head and show Buff Guy my tears. "Yeah," I tell him, "we're okay." I look back down at my feet again.

Buff Guy sends Ted and David on their way. That's okay. I can wait now. Until I get Ted alone.

Ted

We weave our way toward Hotel Theodore, crossing roads, wandering down alleys. David's adrenaline is still in fight mode.

"God that woman's crazy," he mutters.

I nod. "I thought you were going to attack her." I remember wishing he would attack her, way back in high school.

He laughs. "So did I! It's probably a good thing she screamed." He shakes his head. "Did you see the way she just turned the tears on? Like she flipped a switch?"

"I know. She scares the shit out of me," I agree. I don't tell him she was actually laughing. The feeling of her is slowly slipping off me. I glance over my shoulder. "She isn't following us."

"She won't," David says. He turns and takes a few steps backwards, searching the road behind us, then turns forwards again. He shrugs. "I think getting aggressive with her was the right thing to do. Or"—he puts a hand on my shoulder

—"maybe she's just not that into you anymore."

I snort a laugh, and he manages to hold a mischievous smile for another second before he's laughing too. "C'mon," he says, steering me into a corner store. "I need a chocolate bar."

In our hotel room, I close the curtains and put the chain on the door before I undress. Locking the bathroom door, I take a long hot shower without turning on the fan. Steam builds thickly in the tiny space, so when I step out and dry off, the mirror reflects nothing but light.

David lies on the bed, flipping through channels with the remote. I tuck in beside him, my head on his chest, eyes closed, listening to the sound bites between flips: canned laugher, an excited sports reporter, the rewarding ding of *Wheel of Fortune* letters. He stops at *NYPD Blue*, and Jimmy Smits's voice, along with David's heartbeat, sets the background music for the movie of May that plays like shock waves in my mind.

I try to keep her out of my head, but sometimes it takes an effort. She's like a ghost in the back of my thoughts whenever something makes me feel nervous, like presenting a seminar, or a stranger looking at me. And then she pops up when I'm having crazy fun too, sharing hysterical child giggles as though she won't let me have fun without her. Like the water "fight" David and I had last week in the apartment, where I made the mistake of attacking him with a squirt from the plant sprayer and he returned fire with the kitchen sink hose. We spent the rest of the day planning sneak attacks on each other until I upped the ante with a can of whipped cream and we ended up in the shower. I swear the whipped cream was her idea.

May

I run back to Central, dodging drunks across the length of the bar, making my way back to the galley. Kisha and Greg are just getting up from the table. Greg's holding her plate full of wing bones. "Just think about it, 'kay?" he says, disappearing into the kitchen.

"Okay." She turns her back to me and bends down, ass sticking out, to primp her hair in the little mirror we have stuck on the wall. What a fucking slut.

"I need your keys," I say, taking off my stupid apron.

She straightens and turns, reaching into her pocket as she shrugs. "Okay," she says as she hands them to me. "Where you heading?"

I leave without answering, heading towards the back door. She doesn't deserve an answer, and she doesn't deserve to know about Ted. He's mine.

Her car is in the parking lot across the alley. It's a 1964 Galaxie, with rusted-out fenders, a cardboard-covered window on the back-passenger side, and seats worn through to the springs. I think she paid twenty dollars for it.

I get in and fight the seat, trying to slide it forwards so I can reach the gas pedal, but that's not happening, so I end up sitting on the very edge, poking the gas pedal with my toes and peering between the steering wheel and the dashboard to see.

I go back to South Washington Street where I found Ted and drive slowly, looking down every crossroad. The car's rotting muffler has everyone turning their heads, and the stink of exhaust mixed with the sick sweet smell of Slurpee and the skunk of weed is enough to make me gag. I crank down the window and inhale some fresh air, then light a cigarette from the package on the passenger seat.

The streets are pretty empty in this stretch, and I turn left on Sixth, but then I'm stuck at Yesler. I go north, still looking, but Yesler's too busy. I think about going to the University. Kisha said they were scientists. Of course, Ted's a scientist. But there's no fucking way I'll find them there. Not without some help. I head back to Central. Might as well finish my shift. I'm pretty sure Kisha is hooking up with that guy from the dork table.

Gail glares at me when I walk back into the bar from the back, tying my apron. At the window section, I see Kisha delivering wings and a jug of beer to one of my tables. Gail stomps past me without a word, and Kisha saunters up with a big grin. "*This* is for you!" she says, pushing a ten-dollar bill into my pocket. "From that table of suits."

"Where'd the dorks go?" I say, looking over at their table, now filled with a bunch of bleached-blond coeds. Do they all use the same fucking hair dye?

"Oh, they left," she says. "Decent tip though."

Someone from my section is calling and waiving an empty jug in the air. Kisha starts to go to him, but I grab her arm and pull her towards the break galley. "Did you get a phone number? That guy was pretty hot for you." She turns away from me and shakes her head, whispering something. "I can't hear you! What's with you and that guy?"

She looks up at me, all round eyed like she's going to cry. I realize my fingers are digging into her arm. She thinks I'm mad at her for flirting. I tighten my grip. "You stupid slut. I want to see those guys. How do I find them?"

She grins brightly. "Oh, that's easy. Come for breakfast with us tomorrow morning!"

I let go of her arm. "Cool. Where are we going?"

"The Sherwood, around ten."

My brain goes clear as the tension melts away. There. I've got him now. I walk over to waving-jug table and give them my sassiest smile.

He isn't here. I scan the table. There are about fifteen of them, and not one of them is Ted. What the fuck? Kisha is snuggled up beside Tippy, the giant stud from last night. He's got his arm draped around her. I am guessing she slept with him last night. She waves at me, and people across the table from them move their chairs to make room for me. I'm stuffed between the old guy who was at the Central and some other dude who looks like a squirrel with zits.

"We didn't get formally introduced," says Old Guy as he reaches over to shake my hand. I give him my fingertips. "Don Knudsen."

I'm thinking about telling him my name when Squirrel sticks out his hand, long skinny fingers poking in my direction. "Martin Winkle," he says. His index finger has a dirty fabric bandage on it with a blob of black-red staining over the padding part. I'm not shaking that. I fold my hands on my lap and give him a nod.

"So you know our Ted, do you?" Don Knudsen asks.

"Yeah, where is he?" I try to sound casual.

"I think they got an early start," he says, pouring tea from a metal pot. The tea runs down the outside of the spout and lands in a puddle beside his cup and saucer. "Would you look at that. You'd think by now—" he grabs his napkin and blots at the spill.

"An early start on what?"

"The trip home," Squirrel chirps. "I think he wanted to get back to the lab. He's all excited about something."

This is good. I can see Ted working alone in a lab. "Where's the lab?"

Squirrel quips, "UBC," with an emphasis on the *B*, at the same time Don says, "How long have you known each other?"

I turn to Squirrel and say, "UBC?"

"University of British Columbia."

Oh. "That's in Canada, right?" I ask.

Squirrel nods, twitching his nose. "Vancouver. Our Vancouver, not yours."

Fuck. Canada. I picture a map in my brain, trying to remember where Vancouver is. I think it's close.

"You do know where Vancouver is, right?" Squirrel asks, cocking his head and raising his eyebrows. Before I can answer, he's rolling his eyes and shaking his head. "You fuckin' Americans." He actually turns away from me.

Knudsen laughs. "Martin! Settle down!"

I want to stab them both with my fork. "Fuck you," I say, standing up. The conversation around the table stops. I look over at Kisha, who is squinting up at me, her head almost resting on Tippy's shoulder. "We're going."

He whispers something to her, and she stands up. "Tippy's gonna give me a ride," she says, tossing the keys across the table. I watch them land on the floor beside me. I lift my gaze to glare back at her, but she's already running towards me. "Oops! Sorry!" She bends down and picks up the keys. "Here you go," she says, handing me the keys. I'm staring at her, hands on my hips. "Oh. You want me to come with?" I don't blink.

"Hey, Tippy? I gotta go, 'kay?" Tippy is standing. She blows him a kiss. He pouts and gives her a tiny wave.

As we walk away, I slip my arm around her waist and let my hand slip down to her ass. I know Tippy is watching. It'll either drive him crazy or it'll drive her crazy. Who cares?

Ted

We live in a decent-sized three-storey walk-up that looks down on the beast of a blackberry thicket separating us from the next tier of buildings down the hill. We're on the third floor. The apartment is old, but it gets lots of sunshine, and it's not too far from the university, without the high rent.

It's two bedrooms. Mom lived here with us until I turned nineteen, and then she moved in with Joe, "the boyfriend," as we call him, even though they've been together five years.

Joe glommed onto Mom the second he saw her, which was the day we came to this building to fill out a rental application. He owns the building and a bunch of others in the area. He calls the rentals his hobby. He's an electrician by trade and started investing in apartment buildings in his twenties. He still lives like a pauper even though he doesn't need to.

He and Mom live on the top floor of his building in North Van, albeit the penthouse with a fantastic view of Vancouver harbour, he could just as easily afford a place in the British Properties or right on English Bay. She still works her job at the seniors' home down the road. She loves it, doing crafts and visiting with grandparenty-type people all day. We still have family dinners on Sundays. We are a family.

I'm excited to get to work this morning. You might not know it though. David tackles the dwindling morning rush hour, and I'm silent and thoughtful beside him in the passenger seat. Inside my head is busy as it always is after a conference—revisiting new ideas and planning experiments that might just get me the results I need. We only have one car between us, so David usually drives me to the university in the morning and picks me up at the end of his day or when I'm done—whichever comes last.

As we wind our way through campus, he looks over at me. "I'm guessing you're going to be late tonight?"

I shrug. "I'll call you? It's just planning stuff right now." I reach over and touch his hand as he pulls up to the Life Sciences Centre. "Maybe we can squeeze in a run tonight."

"I'd like that," he says.

I get out, turning to look at him through the window as I close the door.

Campus is awake with students heading to early morning classes. Morning has broken with long cold shadows across pathways so people and leaves seem to skitter in and out of darkness. The effect sends a shiver down my spine, reminding me of May in Seattle. I look over my shoulder as though she might appear again. I pick up my pace, reminding myself she's in a different country and doesn't know where I am or how to find me.

My research stinks, literally. I'm looking at microbial methylation of mercury in sewage water. Once mercury gets a methyl stuck on it, it's deadly to us because it can get into our systems. And we all know mercury sucks. And when it's methylmercury, it sucks even more because it basically makes your body think it's allergic to your nerves—making antibodies against the myelin sheath, the stuff that wraps around every nerve. Needless to say, I use a fume hood and gloves and a mask and everything on experiment days. And I get my hair tested for mercury every month.

The conference got me all pumped again because someone was talking about the pH of environment affecting favourability toward methylmercury (nasty) or dimethylmercury (super nasty). The lower the pH, it seemed, the higher the tendency toward demethylation. So today, I'm figuring out how to lower the pH around my little bugs (bacteria) without killing them, so I can see if that's how they react to a basic environment. This means I'm tucked in our little office, doing chemistry equations and math.

I share this space with Tippy and Stephen. They come galloping in at ten—they're late-night boys.

"Ted!" Stephen barks. "You missed an amazing breakfast on Friday! Your girl showed up!"

I freeze. "I don't have a girl."

"Of course not, you fool, you're gay." Stephen looks to the ceiling and shakes his head. "The waitress."

"Tippy's waitress?" I ask, looking at Tippy as he drops his backpack on the floor and slumps into his desk chair.

"Nope, the other one." Stephen hangs his backpack on the hook near his desk and unzips it as if he just told me it's raining outside. "And she has quite the temper!"

Oh God. What did she do? I grip my pencil, waiting for the rest of the story.

He takes a stack of papers from his backpack and an apple and places them neatly on his desk. "Yeah, so Martin got all uppity about Americans being, you know, stupid about the rest of the world. No offense, Ted." He sits in his chair and takes a bite of his apple.

I look down at my desk. I don't remember May being patriotic, but Martin can be irritating. And May is easily irritated.

"She told him to fuck off," he says, still chewing. "And then stormed out, with—" He points his apple at Tippy, who seems to be dozing off, arms folded across his chest, legs stretched out across the office.

"Kisha." Tippy completes his sentence.

"Yeah. You seeing her again?" Stephen asks.

"I don't know." Tippy yawns and stretches. "Bit of a hassle to get to her, right?"

Stephen shrugs. "Get her to come up here."

"Nope. She's cute enough, but"—he points to his temples —"didn't see much happening upstairs."

"And your point?"

Tippy shakes his head. "Just not worth it."

I realize I've been holding my breath. I exhale slowly.

Stephen laughs. "So what about this chick, Ted? She sure looked excited to see you."

I sink lower in my chair. What do I say? She's my stalker? "Just someone I knew from when I lived back east."

"She knows you're gay, right?"

"Sorta," I say, then nod my head. "Yeah, I'm pretty sure she does."

May

"See you at work?" Kisha says as she pulls up to my apartment block. The building used to be pretty posh, but now the shiny Art Deco aluminum panels are faded, and the paint is peeling off the railings. There's a fancy entryway, with a sheltered walkway and a circular drive, both of which have dandelions and crabgrass spilling out from their cracks as though the earth is leaking. In the flowerbeds, daisies and rhododendrons fight with invading blackberry bushes.

I haven't said a word the entire trip back from breakfast. I reach over and put my hand on her thigh as she puts the car in Park. "Are you going to see him again?"

Kisha sputters, "No? No, I don't think so." She looks at me, trying to figure out the right answer. "They're all kinda weird, right?"

"I dunno. I thought that Tippy guy was kinda cute." I give her leg a squeeze. "Maybe we should pop up to Canada and give him a visit."

Her eyes get big. "Canada? Is that where he's from?"

Fuck. She slept with him, and she didn't even know what country he's from? "Seriously? I thought you fucked the guy?"

She giggles. "We didn't do much talking."

I want to slap her, but I have incredible control. As I slide my hand up her thigh, she looks down, willing me to go further. She might like boys, but she likes me better.

"Give him a call. I'm sure the three of us could have a blast."

She looks up at me, and I wink. I know it's her fantasy to have me with her when she's having sex with a guy. I make her feel safe.

"We could go up on Sunday." I lean in and give her a kiss on her neck, just below her ear. She shivers. My hand slides to warmer places.

"I can't," she says.

I look outside, glancing through the front, side, and back windows. "Nah, we're good," I say. My fingers tickle at her crotch. But she's gripping the steering wheel, and her body is shaking. God, she cums quick sometimes.

"I didn't get his phone number," she says.

"What?" I pull my hand away from her crotch and take her by the chin, turning her to face me. The smell of her wafts between us. I'm shaking too. Her eyes flit in every direction to avoid my gaze, like a dog that shit on the carpet. I relax my grip, remembering she asked Tippy to call her. "Don't worry. He'll call."

She gives a little nod. I get out of the car, close the door, and lean in through the open window. "Call me if you hear from him?"

She nods again, as she shifts the car into Drive. But her eyes are wet with tears when she turns to me. "He doesn't have my phone number. I'm so sorry."

I slam the roof of her car with my fist as she drives away.

I haven't slept in three days. I just have to get to Ted. I have to get us back together. I just have to get to fuckin'

Canada.

I quit Central on Saturday. Told them I have to move back home to take care of my dying mother. Greg was very sympathetic. Kisha cried. My final paycheque will be ready today. Jake doesn't know I quit. He dropped me off at Central last night; I blew him a kiss, and he drove off as I pushed through the main door. I went to the movie theatre instead. Watched *A Nightmare on Elm Street* and *Pumpkinhead*, then hung out at a coffee shop until just before two a.m. I was waiting at the front doors of Central Saloon when Jake pulled up.

I've been packing since Friday, slowly formulating a plan in my head. Stuffing things into my backpack. Forgetting stuff in the car—my boots, my sneakers, a jacket, a hoodie. Jake doesn't notice shit like that.

He's snoring on the mattress on the floor. I've never thought about leaving him because I never thought I'd find Ted. It's always been good. Not great, not always safe, but good enough. He has a bit of a temper, but so do I. I let him win. If I don't, he gets a little rough.

I don't know how he's going to react to my leaving, but I'm not going to find out. I do know he'll be pissed when he finds out I took the car, even though it's in my name. And the money in his sock drawer. But that's my money. My tip money. He always takes it when he picks me up, then gives me a couple of bucks back for "spending money." Of course, I only ever give him half of what I take in. I stash the rest at work. So I have some money, but he won't when I leave. He hasn't worked much since we got here. He'll get a job at a shipyard or at the docks, but he usually only lasts a few weeks. Someone will piss him off, or the work is too shitty. I get that. Most of the coin he brings in is from B and Es and selling a little weed or a little coke. He has a tendency to smoke the profits though. Or snort them. Can't say I haven't helped him.

I only need my birth certificate to get into Canada. I found that in a box my mom gave me when Jake and I moved cross-country. She'd cried and said, "You two take care of each other, okay?" She had no clue what was going on, or if she did, she didn't care.

I'll tell the guys at the border that I'm going to visit friends at UBC. No one's going to question a sweet little coed, right?

It's seven a.m. Central opens at eleven thirty. The clock on the wall ticks loud and rhythmically against Jake's uneven snores. The missing beats are driving me insane. I have to go now. I pick up my backpack and walk softly towards him. His jeans are lying in a crumpled ball beside the mattress. Bending down, I dig through their pockets, pulling out the car keys in my fist so they don't jingle.

My throat tightens as I stand up. I want to bend down and kiss him goodbye, but I'm not stupid. I tiptoe across the room, slip on my little black boots, and with my eyes on Jake, open the door slowly, and back out of our life together. Once I'm in the hall, I take big strides towards the stairs, then run down them two at a time. My heart's beating fast; my skin is tingling. I feel alive.

The sun is lightening the clouds as it rises. Rush hour rumbles in the streets. The starter doesn't grab the first turn. Fuck. Did I flood it? I take a breath and try to remember how Jake taught me to start it. I turn the key, listen to the carburetor gasp, then push the gas pedal to the floor. It catches. I exhale and smile. I got this. I back out of the parking spot and ease my way into traffic.

Ted

"Got everything?" I ask David as I climb into the car.

"Yes," he says. He reaches into the back seat and drops

my T-shirt and running shorts on my lap. I wait until we get into Stanley Park before I wiggle out of my jeans and change. He's already dressed for the run. "Did you eat something?"

"Yeah, an apple, just before I left."

He looks over at me, eyebrows raised. We both know I can be a bitch if I'm hungry after I run.

"I promise!" I laugh. We pull into the parking lot near the seawall. The after-work crowd is beginning to die down; so is the sun. It will be dark when we finish, but the trail is well lit.

"What are we running for tonight?" David asks.

"Roast beef sandwiches and potato soup at O'Malley's," I suggest. O'Malley's is a favourite little hole in the wall, and it's local, so we can walk home after a beer or two.

"Right."

We run a full ten kilometres—our usual distance—five out and back and then walk a bit to cool down. We're deep in conversation the whole time. David has only been working as a full pharmacist since graduating in May, so he has all kinds of learning experiences to share. Plus, there's always some interesting customer to tell me about.

"I bet you're dying to know how Mrs. Simpson made out this weekend?" he asks.

"Of course."

"Her granddaughter's wedding ceremony went off without a hitch. You should have seen her eyes light up." David does his impression of eighty-seven-year-old Mrs. Simpson's crinkly falsetto. "'Karen was such a lovely bride, and that young man she's marrying? A perfect gentleman!'" He clasps his hands together and tilts his head sweetly as he speaks.

"Ah, sweet Mrs. Simpson." I laugh.

He continues sweetly, "'But then that cunt of a motherfucker showed up at the reception!'"

I can't help but gasp. "Hah! No! She did not say that!"

"Yes, she did. She truly did," David assures me, nodding his head.

"Okay, so who is the"—I can't say the C-word —"motherfucker?"

"Why, Mr. Simpson, of course. Her ex-husband. 'With a dirty little tramp on his arm, younger than his own granddaughter.'"

"That dog!"

After a quick stretch, we stroll back to the car. A woman is walking towards us from the shadows. She's short but kinda bulky. Not May. Why would it be May? The woman walks between cars to avoid us. Women do that in parking lots, avoid strange men. David squeezes my shoulder as we part to get in our respective sides of the car.

He starts the engine, but before he puts it in Reverse, he looks over at me. "She's not here, Ted," he says. "She doesn't know how to find you." He starts to back out of the stall.

"Actually, she might," I say.

He slams on the brakes and shifts back into Park. "What?"

"She went to the wind-up breakfast on Friday," I say. "I think Martin told her where we're from."

"Fuck," is all he says, and he backs out of the parking spot. We drive home in silence and eat peanut butter sandwiches and chips for supper. We're on the couch, watching *MASH* reruns when he finally says, "Now what?"

May

I can't find him. This place is the size of a small city. I had no idea a university was so big. I've been all over the place looking for him—three days of my life wasted. Hanging out in lounges and coffee shops. Wandering through hallways and looking in every door. Sleeping in my car. This is fucking impossible.

Four o'clock on Wednesday, and the exodus begins. Kids start filing out of buildings. I sit at a bench near a fountain as a swarm of dorks sweeps over me. I try to watch everyone, looking for Ted or David. Or even one of the guys from breakfast last Friday. Everyone walks with their head down, talking or just walking alone. Way too much thinking going on here.

An hour goes by. It's getting dark, and I'm bored as fuck. The crowd thins out and seems to age as I sit here. Older professors and people in business suits. I get up and head back to my car, which is parked off campus about a mile away. I refuse to line up for an hour to spend ten bucks for parking. As I'm waiting to cross the road and leave campus, a little turquoise car turns left in front of me, one of those Hondas everyone's driving. It's David. I turn and chase the car, but it's going too fast. I head back to campus, feeling a little brighter.

Ted

It's David's birthday today, and—added bonus—it's Saturday. What a perfect combination. Except the rain kind of sucks. It hasn't stopped us from doing the birthday hike, something we've done since we got to Vancouver in 1983. Rain never stops the birthday hike, and more often than not, it's raining on December 16.

David picked Shannon Falls, and we hit the trail early so we would be back in time for supper at Mom's. The trail is muddy and slippery in some parts, maple leaves turning to gold and yellow mush under our feet. I have water dripping from my nose by the time we reach the base of the falls. My rain gear is doing its best, but I'm beginning to feel like a clam within it. There's a gigantic cedar about thirty feet up the falls. Its roots sprawl out across the rocks like an invasion, and its branches reach down in inviting j's, reminding me of the tree I used to climb when I was a kid. I point to it and shout over the roar of the rain and rushing water, "Lunch?"

David nods. We pick our way into the forest instead of climbing the falls to get to the tree. It's a little treacherous. The forest has grown over boulders that tumble from the falls. Spaces between the rocks are hidden by the detritus that lines the forest floor. My boot gets jammed between two rocks, and I tumble sideways, squealing like a little girl. David, ahead of me, turns and sees me lying on one elbow, on my side, legs crossed, looking like a scrawny version of the Burt Reynolds centrefold.

He shouts, "Are you okay?" as he scrambles down to help me.

I end up taking my foot out of my boot so I can twist the boot free. Nothing is broken, other than my pride, and I lace my boot back up. We continue our climb upward.

The tree is six feet in diameter, at least, with a pillow of dry moss at its base, perfect for sitting. Which we do. With our backs resting against the trunk. I pull slightly flattened ham sandwiches from my backpack and pour hot chocolate into the cup of the Thermos. We eat, watching the forest and the rain. Any other sound is silenced by the rampage of the falls.

David checks his watch and gives me a nudge. Time to go before the sun goes down and before we're late for supper. We pack up and head back down the falls, me in the lead. As usual —and we should know this—going down is way harder than going up. I'm completely focused on the strategy of getting down without breaking my ankle. The rain has stopped, but the moss on the forest floor is like a sponge, and the cedar spines lay out a slick surface over its bright-green carpet.

It isn't until I get to the bottom of the falls that I turn around and see David, lying face down about halfway down the hill. "David!" I scramble back up to him.

He's laughing, trying to cover tears of pain.

"Oh my God, babe!" I say as I reach him, forgetting to shout over the falls. But I'm right beside him, holding his shoulders and trying to support him. "What can I do? Are you stuck?"

He winces, using his full upper-body strength to pull himself upright, gasps in pain, and drops back down. "I don't think I'm stuck," he says, almost whispering, "but I think something's broken."

I climb down into the crevice where his leg is jammed between two rocks. There's a bend between his knee and his ankle that makes my stomach heave. I push at one of the boulders with everything I have, but it's a boulder, part of the earth. It isn't going to move.

May

I have this sense of calm now I've found him. Like my shadow is reattached. But at the same time, I'm feeling all shy—I'm not ready to go to him. Not yet. I'm just going to watch him for now. Today, I'm sitting against a horse chestnut tree just outside the Life Sciences Centre, sketching. I have a Mariners cap on and Jake's bulky old lumber jacket that I found in the trunk. Jackie Kennedy sunglasses. I don't look like me. I draw stick figures with boobs and cocks. Sometimes, I draw a tree.

He walks by me at 11:56. He's on his way for lunch with that guy Tippy and some other guy. He shoves his hands deep in the pockets of his Dockers, lifting his face to the sun. I watch him until he becomes part of the crowd. He'll come back at 1:04. Laughing and energized.

I was worried this morning. I didn't see him get dropped off. I actually had to walk down the hall and past his lab.

Fortunately, I heard his voice, so I didn't have to look inside and risk him seeing me.

I don't always wait for him at lunch, but I do on Mondays. I ache to see him after the weekend. And weekends are busy for me. At least this weekend was. Friday was dead, but I had three dates on Saturday and two on Sunday. The worst part is hanging out beside my phone waiting for a call. Or maybe it's those sick fucks that just call to jerk off at the sound of my voice. It's like they're stealing from me; they get off, and I get nothing. I thought the answering machine would help, but for some that's just a gift—they don't have to talk to me, and they can still get off. I guess I need a pager.

I know where Ted lives. I followed the Honda home on the first week. Some nights, I just park on the street and watch his apartment. I see his shadow moving from room to room. Sometimes, he steps out onto the balcony, and I get to see him, a glass of wine or a beer in his hand. I think he knows I'm watching because sometimes he has his shirt off or his bathrobe on. Sometimes, David comes out and joins him and just ruins it. I wait until the lights go out, knowing he's safe in bed, before I drive away.

Maybe tonight, I'll spend the evening with him. Follow him home. Maybe I'll skip work and spend the whole week with him. I want to know his life. We're getting close again.

It's 1:04, and there he is, surrounded by a bigger group of nerds. Doctor Don and the Squirrel are with them. I sink behind my sketchbook, peering between my shades and the brim of my cap. The Doctor seems distracted. He's walking outside the group, looking around. Ted's carrying a paper bag and a coffee, his afternoon snack. He talks to one of the guys, shaking his head, shrugging his shoulders. He looks worried. I hope he's okay. I grip my sketchbook, fighting the need to go and touch my boy, to stop whatever is bothering him. Doctor Don looks straight at me. Fuck him. I lift my head and stare back at him, anonymous behind the huge lenses of my glasses.

The little Honda didn't show up. It's six o'clock, and I'm parked in the loading zone at the doors of the Life Sciences building. Where the fuck is he? I was waiting in the parking lot, watching across the road for David to pick him up at their usual spot. This beast of a car is pretty noticeable, so I don't want to be right in their face, but when the clock clicked past five forty-five, I drove over to the building. If David doesn't pick him up, maybe I will. But this is ridiculous. I could be making money instead of waiting the fuck around for that selfish little prick.

I get out of the car and slam the door, leaving it running, the lights on. Inside the building, the hall is empty. I can hear the sound of some prof droning on from a lecture theatre. I follow the sound and step into the huge room, there's about fifteen students along the front row staring at a screen lit by an overhead projector. No Ted.

The lights are out in his lab. I wander the halls, trying doors, listening. I even go to the second floor. Check the washrooms. Nothing. He left without me.

I walk back to the car. There's a lump in my throat, and my eyes sting with tears. Sometimes, I think he just doesn't understand. He has to put some effort into this too. Men can be so cold.

I'll drive out to his place and see what's going on. But this is his last chance. I can't handle this kind of hurt.

Ted

I'm late, not that anyone cares. I had to park at the other end of campus today, and even then, it cost me five bucks. I'll have to figure out a better way to do this. David won't be driving for at least six weeks. Which means it's my turn to play chauffeur. I dropped him off at the pharmacy where he works, and then it was kind of easy to go against traffic through downtown until I got to the university.

Poor guy, what a birthday gift—a broken fibula and a trip down a mountain in a stretcher. He had to wait in the rain for me to run and get help. The doctor says it's a clean break though, and he should be running again by springtime, but no skiing this year.

It's a little lonely driving myself from his work to mine. I feel like I'm in the wrong seat. Which is odd, because I love it when I get to work before anyone else and I'm alone in the lab. That is definitely not happening today.

I leave the lab a little early, out the back doors, and hike across campus. I don't want David stuck waiting around. He is more than a little cranky about being immobile. I find him waiting at the side of the road in front of the pharmacy, his plaster cast neatly hidden under some very old-school wide-legged pants Joe lent him. He looks miserable, but he's hiding it with a strained smile. I pull up and get out to help him, but by the time I get to the sidewalk, he's already in the passenger seat and closing the door.

I get back in and give his hand a quick squeeze. "How're you doing?"

David glances at me and then faces the windshield and swallows. "Fuck!"

How do I respond to that? I pull out into traffic, feeling like I should try starting the conversation again. "Should we pick up something for supper? Or do you just want KD?" My voice is high with nerves. I don't like dealing with angry people, even if it's just David.

"No, I don't want KD," he mimics me in a squeaky fag voice. Then he sighs. "Let's just go home and watch some TV, 'kay?"

It feels a little like a punch in the stomach, but I remind myself he's not feeling well. He doesn't need to be an asshole though. The next few weeks are going to suck. We're almost home before he apologizes. "I'm sorry. You shouldn't have to put up with this pityfest." He touches my hand. "Why don't you go out somewhere tonight? Give yourself a break from me?"

I laugh with relief. "It's only been two days! You're allowed to feel sorry for yourself. You'll get used to it. We'll get used to it." I look over at him as I pull up across from the apartment building and put the car in Park. This side of the street has no sidewalk and drops down into a thicket of thorny blackberry bushes. "Do you want some help getting out? Or do you insist on falling into the blackberry bushes?"

He laughs and shakes his head. "I insist on you parking on the other side of the street. But first, let's go pick up some burgers."

I nod, pulling out onto the street again.

"I'm sorry, babe," David says.

May

I park my car at my favourite viewpoint and look up at Ted's apartment. The lights are out. Maybe he went for a run. He doesn't usually run on Mondays though. I roll my window down to stick my head out and look for the Honda, but a car is coming. I quickly wind up the window and sink back into my seat, waiting for it to pass.

It's them. Ted's driving. He parks in the space in front of me. My heart is racing. I stay perfectly still, even though every fibre of my being wants to go out and touch him. So close to me. Baby, I can feel you.

And then they're driving away. What the fuck? Did he see me? Why is Ted driving? Why the fuck is he making this so hard?

I follow them to the drive-thru at McDonald's and then back to their apartment block. I take a spot two cars behind them and open my car door. It's time to talk. I'm done trying to make this work. I was hoping to get him alone one night but — Oh, shit! Crutches? David's on crutches? I stifle a giggle and softly pull my car door closed. Ted walks slowly beside David, and they disappear into the building. I close my eyes and feel my shoulders drop with relief. Okay. This works. This works really well.

The suite is perfect for me. It's the basement of a house: a bedroom, a kitchen, and a bathroom all wrapped around the laundry room, the hot water tank, and the furnace. They say they've had no rats for two years now. Rent is only three hundred a month. That I can do. And it's furnished. I can't wait to sleep in a real bed instead of my car. That doesn't mean I'm giving up on Ted. It means I'm ready for when he comes to me.

It's nice to start building a life here. I don't hang out at the university all day anymore. Today, I went for a run along the Westminster Quay and actually went back to my own place for a shower. I've bought some clothes for work and found a hairdresser who might be trustworthy. I might even look for a real job. Ted's not going to want me whoring when he moves in. That would break his heart.

Ted

I sit on the seawall beside him, tying my runners. He's bundled up in a Cowichan sweater and has his crutches propped beside him and his cast leg stretched out. Girls walking by check him out.

"You're going to trip somebody," I say.

He lifts his hands and shrugs. "What can I do?"

I stand and reach my arms into the air, leaning to the right and then to the left, then bend down to touch my toes, giving my hamstrings a stretch. Standing straight again, I bend my leg behind me, lifting my right foot to my butt, and reach back to hold it with my hand for a quad stretch, do the other leg, and then I'm ready to go. "Want me to grab you a hot chocolate before I go?"

David is staring out to the water, mesmerized and content. He smiles and shakes his head. "I'll go get one in a bit. You go, young master. Run like the wind," he says, trying to sound like a movie quote.

I take off at a slow, warm-up pace.

We're at week three with the cast, and this is my second run on the seawall without him. The weather is holding off, and even though it's the first week of November, we haven't seen much rain. Today is unusually bright and crisp. There's still some frost on the path in the shady spots, but it's past noon, and the sun has warmed most of the pavement.

As I round the bend, I pick up my pace and feel my muscles fight the run as the blood rushes to soothe them. By the time I get under the bridge, my body isn't cold anymore, and my breath is an even rhythm in time with the sound of my runners on the pavement. The inlet opens up to Georgia

Strait here. The ocean's flat horizon is marred with freighters, waiting to come into port. Beyond them, the Gulf Islands wear tiny caps of snow at their high points, like kippahs—winter beginning its slow descent to sea level.

As I enter "the zone"—that meditative, endorphin-infused runner's high—I lose track of the scenery and become one with my breathing and the beat of my pace.

Thirty minutes later, I'm on my return, almost at the bend where the mermaid welcomes ships into Vancouver Harbour. Another runner is behind me, talking. The noise breaks into my headspace.

The voice speaks again. "You keep a good pace!" and my stomach turns in recognition. I swallow the bile in my throat as I lose my rhythm and run faster.

She's beside me, her breathing steady and even. "Ted, we need to talk."

"No," I squawk, increasing my stride to a sprint.

May

A Sunday morning run. What a lovely idea. At least that's where I think we're going as I follow the little turquoise Honda down West Georgia toward Stanley Park. They did this last Sunday too. I've been exploring the forest trails around there ever since.

They've parked and are at the seawall. David is sitting next to his crutches while Ted puts on his running shoes. I reach into the back and grab mine. I'm already wearing track pants and a T-shirt, perfect for today's weather. Even so, I'm actually dithering with excitement by the time I get out of the car, eyes on my Teddy as he does his stretches. It's going to be just him and me today. Finally.

He takes off at a slow pace; apparently, he trains like

an old man, and I run across the parking lot into the woods that back along the seawall. It's thick rainforest, just like the stuff around Seattle, a web of trails lined with bits of trash —McDonald's wrappers, empty mickey bottles, and the odd condom. I run parallel to the seawall. It's cold in here with the trees blocking the sun, and quiet; my steps thump on the red earth like it's hollow.

I get to the path well ahead of him, breathing hard and freezing as I wait in the shadows. Finally, he putts by. I give him a little space before I follow. He's going at a reasonable pace, but it's still hard to stay behind him. For one thing, I run way faster than him. For another thing, I'm so excited and happy, I want nothing more than to run beside him, talking and laughing.

I decide to play. Taking a deep breath, I slow to a walk, watching as he moves farther and farther from me. Then, when I can't stand it anymore, I sprint up to him: chasing him and catching him again and again. Each time I get close, I want to wrap my arms around him and inhale his skin. He's oblivious though. I won't let myself get close enough for him to notice.

I'm in sprint mode when he makes his U-turn and I blast past him. I keep running for a bit and then turn around to catch up with him.

Now. It's finally time to talk to my sweet boy. I watch him from behind for a bit—my eyes actually sting with tears— before I say, "You keep a good pace!" Wow. Is that what I wanted to say?

He stumbles a little. When I get beside him, I can see the grin light up his face and his Adam's apple bob in excitement. His skin is pink under morning whiskers.

"Ted, we need to talk," I say. It comes out all breathy and soft, sexy as hell.

It's too much for him, and he fights it. He squeaks, "No!"

and speeds up, running away from his desire for me. Unless—I sprint to catch up—he's playing my game! He knew I was with him the entire time. Sprint, slow down, sprint. Oh, babe, you know me so well.

I'm giggling when I get beside him again. But we can't play right now. Time is tight. I should have got to him earlier. We're getting closer to David, and he could ruin everything. I grab his arm, pinching the flesh above his elbow, but he's sweaty and slips out of my fingers. "Stop, Teddy. Please?" He keeps running. I keep up to him. He's pissing me off now. "C'mon, I'm not playing anymore."

His ears are deep red. "No," he puffs again. I know it's hard for him to run this fast.

I can't fuck around anymore. I hook my arm into his and stick my foot between his legs. As we tangle, he falls into me, and we hit the pavement together. People are coming to our rescue as he struggles to get up. I wrap my arms around him and start laughing and kissing him. The heroes back away awkwardly.

"Let go of me!" he growls, grabbing my wrists and pressing them to the ground like he's going to kiss me. I let my mouth open softly to welcome him.

He presses his knee into my thigh as he gets up, pinching the flesh against the ground. "Ow! Fucking ow!" I scratch at his thigh as I scramble to my feet. He's started running. The cedar and leaves that stuck to him are falling off like a winter storm. "Okay, wait!" I call after him "Ted, I promise this is important!"

He slows down and looks back at me. God, he's gullible. I fight the smile that's dancing on my lips and catch up to him.

Ted

Why am I stopping? What could she possibly have to say that's important to me? But I'm almost back to David, and I don't need him to be part of this. I feel my fists tightening as she gets closer. She found me. I kind of knew it would happen after Seattle. I actually want to feel the impact of my knuckles on her face. My face burns with rage and the heat from my run, but the ocean breeze is cooling my skin quickly, like a shiver.

She walks up to me with light in her eyes and her whole face fighting a smile. She looks like she's going to sneeze. "So, what's up baby?"

I stare at her, willing myself not to blink.

"I'm so glad I found you. Aww, look at your sweet ears!" She reaches for my ears with both hands, as though she's pulling me down for a kiss. I step back, and her hands drop.

"What do you want, May?"

"You," she says. "Just you."

I turn and start walking away.

She shouts, "This is what you need to know, Ted!"

My shoulders drop. I stop walking. My head is down, and I rake my fingers through my hair as she continues talking in a low mutter.

"We're good together, baby. You might think there's something between you and David, but that's because you don't know any better, but I do. And I'm not going to let you go this time. We will find a way to make this—you and me— happen."

I start walking away as she continues her babble beside me. "Our love is—it's everything. I know, because I can't stop thinking about you. I need you. We'll have an amazing life together, I promise."

I walk faster, rolling my eyes to the sky. She stops walking. "End it with David, Ted," she says in a calm steady voice. "Or I will."

The chill on my skin drops into my belly.

May

He waits for me. His fingers running through his curls. And those ears. Red as roses. They're like a mood ring. Why the fuck do I love those ears? At least they don't stick out like they used to. I want to touch them so bad, but he pushes my hands away.

And then I spill my guts to him, confessing my love, watching as he takes it in. He's such a hard thinker. That furrow in his brow, so cute when he was a kid, is getting stronger and deeper. "We'll find a way to make this—you and me—happen," I tell him.

He looks up at me, and I see the pain in his eyes. It's been so hard for him, this charade with David. He needs me to take the lead. I can see it now. But he walks away. Jesus fucking Christ. I catch up and stay beside him, waiting for his hand to take mine. For some acknowledgement. But nothing.

Grow just one fucking testicle, would you? Why do I have to do everything in this fucking relationship? Sometimes I wonder if it's just a complete fucking waste of time. I inhale deeply and blow out a slow sigh. It's not his fault. How can he know how great it's going to be? If that's what he needs, I'm here for him. I stop walking, and he slows down. Amazingly, I speak without screaming—God I'm a fucking saint—so only he can hear me. "I love you." He doesn't turn. "End it with David, Ted. Or I will."

Nothing. Not even a glance over his shoulder. Up ahead, I can see David hobbling out to the centre of the path. Ted starts running. I can't bear to watch. I step into the forest and make my way back to the parking lot. By the time I get there, the little Honda has left. That's probably a good thing, because right now, I'm not sure who I want to kill, David or Ted.

Ted

He was starting to worry. Standing in the middle of the path, waiting for me. So sweet. And when I get to him, he knows he had good reason. For one thing, I'm covered in leaves and twigs. There's a scratch down my arm from May grabbing me.

"You okay?" he asks me, reaching out to touch the scratch.

I look into his eyes and shake my head minutely, no. "Let's go," I say, turning toward the parking lot.

He's so patient. We're out of the park and stopped at the lights going onto Georgia. I still can't speak.

I examine the rear-view mirror and then reach back for my UBC sweatshirt, taking time to look out the back window. I pull the sweatshirt over my head before the light turns green and take the turn with the shirt around my neck. When the road is straight, David takes the steering wheel so I can slip my arms through the sleeves.

Her shadow is stuck on me. I find my eyes locked on the rear-view, searching for her. What kind of car does she drive? Did we beat her out of the parking—

"Whoa! Car!" David shouts.

I slam on the brakes before I even return my focus to the road. We stop within inches of the guy turning left in front of us. He gives us the finger through a rolled-down window as he makes his turns. "Sorry!" I call out, but our windows are closed, and he doesn't look like the type who would care if I was sorry.

"It was her," I finally spit out, gripping the steering wheel, staring straight ahead.

"Her?" It takes a beat for him to register and then, "Are you serious? Where? Did she talk to you?"

"I'm calling the police," I say, as I realize that's what I'm going to do.

"Why?"

I look over at him, not hiding the irritation in my voice. "You do remember, right?"

He nods. "Of course I remember."

"It's worse. She's been stalking me. She knew I was going to run by myself." I take a breath. "She told me to break up with you." I return my eyes to the road.

"Really?"

"Her exact words were, 'End it with David, or I will.'"

"Crazy bitch."

Traffic is heavy going onto Granville Street Bridge, and we stop talking as I negotiate through.

I'm in the centre lane and almost up to speed. David asks, "Do you think she knows where we live?"

I almost stop the car right there. Instead, I shoulder check, signal, and wedge my way back into the right-hand lane, turning onto West Second. Of course, she does. "Fuck," I acknowledge, checking my mirrors again to see if anyone is following us.

David adjusts his bad leg with his hands. I see him out of the corner of my eye, head cocked, looking at me with his eyebrows raised. "Where're we going?"

"Not home," I growl. "Maybe Granville Island? Lunch?" We hadn't been to Granville Island at all this year. It's a great place to have some lunch and get lost in the crowd.

May

Part of me feels a little guilty. I shouldn't have blown up at him like that. But the rest of me feels like it's about time I let him know what he has to do. Because he doesn't seem to know himself. And then I remember, that's part of what I love about him. How sweet and naive he is. My desire to keep care of him is—well, it's everything.

I want him so bad I'm actually touching myself as I get in the car. Thank God my pager is buzzing. It's Owen. He's getting to be a regular date. He lives out of town and works in the city, so he has a condo here. He called the first Sunday I put my ad in the paper and has called every Sunday since. Apparently, his wife has "let herself go," and he can't stop thinking about me.

I'll go straight to his place and take a shower. He can watch me. He'll like that. Then I'll pretend he's Ted and fuck his brains out. He'll like that too.

The condition I'm in, I'd better work all night.

Ted

Despite a lovely lunch at Granville Market, May keeps tripping through my head. I look over my shoulder as I park the car, checking the mirrors. David gets out before I do, lifting himself up with his arms and reaching into the back seat to get his crutches.

"Hey," he says. "Are you coming?" He's bent down, head tucked in the car, leaning on the crutches. I realize I still have both hands on the steering wheel.

"Yeah," I say as I come back to reality. "I'm sorry. I just can't get her out of my head."

"Do you want to go for a walk?" I ask him when I join him

on the sidewalk.

David looks at his foot, his crutches, and then at me, with a big grin on his face. "I think I've had enough, thanks."

"Oh my God, I'm an asshole!" I take his arm and start walking with him towards the building doors. But I can't stop looking for her. What kind of car would she drive? Is she watching us right now?

When we get to the door, David says, "Go. I'll wait right here. Check the rest of the block. I want to know as bad as you do."

I walk to the end of the block, systematically looking into each car I pass, feeling the reassurance of David behind me. I cross the street and head back to our building, realizing how deep a back seat can be, how easy it would be to hide in a car. But every car is empty. I cross the street back to David and shake my head, no. She isn't here.

"What are we going to do?" David calls from the couch as I put on the kettle for some tea. The stairs up to the apartment are still a challenge on the crutches. "Are you going to make that call?"

I walk to the balcony and step out. I don't recognize any new cars on the street since I did my inspection minutes ago. I go and sit beside him. "Should I?"

David shrugs. "Yes? She wasn't messing around today." He touches a scratch on my knee from when she tackled me.

It's nine o'clock, and there's a buzz on the intercom. Six hours. Apparently, stalker calls aren't a priority.

"Hello?" I answer. I always feel awkward talking on the intercom. Why says hello when you know they're just coming up anyway? But now there's May.

"Police," a voice growls through the static.

He doesn't sound very friendly. I press the buzzer to let him up.

I open the door to an older guy in wrinkly Vancouver Police black, silver badge at his hip, top coil notebook already in hand. He's thick around the shoulders and thick around the waist, his white hair buzzed close at the neck and temples. He looks at me and smiles, eyebrows raised. He looks like he's about to laugh.

I open the door wide enough to let him through. David says hi from the couch, his foot elevated on the coffee table. The officer follows me into the room, and I sit beside David, gesturing towards the easy chair for him to sit. He doesn't.

"Okay, so tell me what happened," he says, looking from me to David and then back.

And I do, from the rape, to the encounter in Seattle, to today's attack. He writes nothing down. His hands fold behind his back as he listens, mirth in his eyes.

"So you say she attacked you?"

"Yes, officer, she's attacked me twice, and I believe she'll do it again."

"Right," he says, finally flipping open his notebook. He looks around the apartment, probably calculating the homosexuality in the room. "Can you describe this lady?"

I nod. "She's short, about five foot nothing. Blond hair, dark—almost black—eyes."

Again, he looks at me and then at David and back to me. "You know, sometimes, when we're young, we can make the wrong decisions," he says in a fatherly tone, putting his notebook and pen back into his breast pocket. "Sometimes, we need to reconsider our choices. Before it's too late. Maybe you just need to talk to this girl." He nods in agreement with himself.

He's leaving. My jaw drops. "But she's crazy!" I squawk with weak righteousness, realizing this guy can't hear us through his homophobia.

His hand is on the door handle. "I'll give you some time to figure this out. Let us know if anything changes."

May

I can't sleep. Three dates last night, and I'm just lying in bed, thinking about him. Aching for him. My hands can't stay away from my pussy, clutching at it. I make myself cum, drift off for a bit, and then I'm awake again. His face, that sweet, kind face, looking at me. So helpless. It's insane what that boy does to me. I want him so bad. It's five a.m. I have to see him. Lunch. I can see him for lunch.

I get some coffee going and then wander to the mirror. Sleepy is a good look on me. My eyes are darker; the puffiness in my face makes it all cute and round. My roots are a little dark. But I have a box of blond and lots of time before lunch.

I'm standing in the bit of sunshine that's crept over the students' union building, warming my hands on an extra-large coffee, waiting for my sweetheart to walk by. No more lurking in the trees under a baseball cap now he knows I'm here.

My makeup is perfection—deep-blue eyeshadow and the pinkest, poutiest lip gloss. My little black dress fits like a second skin, with the *V* down the front squishing my tits together playfully. I'm wearing a black studded choker to add to the playfulness and red spike-heeled shorty boots. It's a shame it's so cold I have to cover up all this hotness with an overcoat, but at least I can keep it unbuttoned to frame the legs and the cleavage. We'll see how quick Ted dumps David after he sees this look.

I look good. Too good. Every red-blooded male is checking me out. It's like they know I'm not wearing panties.

The lunch crowd is starting to build even though it's only twenty to. I know it's too early, but I look over my shoulder to see if he's coming yet.

Ted

I stop in my tracks, recognizing the overblond hair, the lack of height, the look-at-me pose. The guys look back at me.

"You okay?" Tippy asks.

I look at them as if they are the surprise people in this scene and nod, yes, as a shiver runs through my body. I open my mouth, forcing out a lie instead of a scream. "Yeah, I forgot my wallet." Almost in unison, the group shrugs and walks away from me. Except Don. I guess he saw what I was staring at.

"I thought I saw her a few days back," he says.

"You what?" I'm whispering now, afraid she'll hear me.

He points to the trees lining the mall. "There, she was sitting against a tree. She's bad news, isn't she?"

I take a step back and then turn towards the lab, Don beside me. "Why didn't you tell me?" I mutter, loud enough for him to hear.

"I couldn't really place her. I just knew I'd seen her before. It's just now I made the connection."

As we walk back into Life Sciences, he touches my elbow, guiding me to his office. "Come on, let's call campus security."

I snort a raw laugh. "They won't do anything. I called the police yesterday, the guy pretty much laughed in my face."

"Yesterday?" he asks.

I tell him what happened. In his office, he points to a chair for me to sit while I continue my story. He takes his seat of authority on the other side and listens, his hand poised on the phone, waiting to make the call.

May

Weird. Ted's friends just walked by without him. Fucking dorks didn't even notice me. Where the fuck is he? My stomach just turned into an empty pit, and my heart fell in it. I turn around to see if he's coming down the path. I think I see him and the old guy walking away. Maybe he forgot something. I watch them as they become part of the crowd and disappear. I hear a clatter and feel a splash on my legs. My coffee cup. I guess I dropped it. I realize I'm shivering. I wrap my big coat around me, tying the belt with a tight single knot, watching as the coffee seeps across the ground soaking into my red booties. He's wrecked them. He wrecks everything.

Looking up towards Ted's building, I take a deep breath. Maybe this is better. I'll go to him. I light a smoke and start walking, my heels echoing above the sound of everything else.

There's a voice behind me. "Excuse me, miss?"

I assume I'm not the "miss" they are excusing. The toes of my right foot are damp from where the coffee seeped through, like these heels aren't hard enough to walk in.

Then a guy in a campus security uniform is walking beside me. His peaked cap falls past his ears, and the end of his belt flaps free, with the buckle cinching his pants at the last notch. He's a full head and shoulders taller than me, but he has the face of a fourteen-year-old, including the zits.

"Can we see some ID, please?"

I laugh at the royal *we* and continue walking. Suddenly,

someone is grabbing my arm on from the behind, and I stumble a bit on the shoes.

"Yeah, ma'am. You should stop." Not a royal *we*. The someone is Man-Child's security partner. She's got enough beef on her for both of them. She stands solid in her uniform perfectly pressed, a bit of a gut, and some whiskers sprouting on her chin, a tight bun tucked under her cap. The hand that grabbed me is now open and waiting. "ID?"

"Why?" I sputter, feeling rage begin its slow burn. "Who the fuck are you, and why do you need my ID?"

"Campus security, ma'am," Beefy one responds, touching her cap like a salute as she looks me up and down. "Please watch your language." Her hand is still out.

I don't have ID. "I left my driver's licence in the car."

"Okay," says Beef, all too eagerly reaching for my arm again. "We can escort you to your car or off campus. Whatever you like."

"You think I'm stupid?" I ask. "This is a public place. You can't just kick me out. I have as much right to be here as anyone."

"BC Criminal Code states, 'No one shall participate in sexual solicitation or receipt thereof for such acts where there is financial gain.'" Beefy looks me up and down again. "If you aren't for sale, I'll be a monkey's uncle." She smiles at her own wit.

I shake her hand off my arm. "Fuck you!" and walk away.

Beefy and Man-boy follow me off campus, keeping a distance. They stop and watch me get into my car, arms folded across their chests, looking all proud like they chased me away.

I sit up, proud myself, dig a Player's out of the pack on the seat. Puffing the tobacco to life, I take a deep drag and exhale in their direction, obliterating their smug faces with smoke.

I've worked hard the past couple of nights, so tonight's my treat night. I'm parked outside his building with a cheeseburger and a chocolate shake, watching their shadows break the light as they move around their apartment.

I wait. Wondering if one day he'll just walk out of that building into my car.

Actually, it's Thursday. They usually go to Superstore on Thursdays. Ted's gone solo the last few weeks. I'm guessing because of David's gimped leg. Sure enough, at around seven, Ted comes through the doors. He gets in the car, which is facing the opposite direction to mine. Cool. Maybe we can talk again. Find out what his plan is. As he passes me, I duck down. I take a final suck at my melted milkshake, the hollow slurp of the straw ripping into my quiet car space, and pull out of my parking space to follow him. I have to go to the end of the block to turn around, but I'm in no hurry. I know where we're going. As I drive by Ted's building, a taxi stops at the lobby doors. I make my U-turn, and when I pass the building again, there's David. Getting into the taxi.

What's he up to behind my Teddy's back? Or maybe they had a fight? My stomach flutters. What if this is it? Ted's kicked him out? Oh my God. I slow down, letting the yellow taxi pull ahead of me. And I follow them. My sweet one can wait. This is for both of us.

We drive along East Pender and then turn onto Nanaimo Street. It's dark, and the roads are wet, reflecting the streetlights with a distracting glare. But as we go deeper into warehouses and shipping yards, the streetlights start to disappear and the darkness becomes full, the shadows of buildings passing like impending doom. We are the only ones on the road.

The taxi drives into the gravel parking lot of a brick warehouse. I see a couple of streetlights up ahead and a flashing neon sign, spelling out the word *Tavern* in orange pulses. Above the word, the blue silhouette of a woman flashes through three positions as she humps a pole. No secrets about what's inside. Weird. Does David swing both ways?

David gets out as I drive past. I pull around the corner and park on the street.

Inside is dark. A spotlight and disco ball over the stage are the only lights; the rest is shadows. A few old men sit alone at tables, completely focused on the black-haired skeleton writhing around on stage. A light flickers across the room as someone lights a cigarette. As my eyes focus, I realize there are tables all along the wall, and they are full of people. I keep to the shadows, moving along the outskirts of the room, looking for David.

He isn't here. Maybe he's in the can. I contemplate ordering a drink. I wonder if a girl could get away with turning a trick or two here? I look at the bouncer standing beside the stage, meaty arms barely able to fold across his chest, and I decide not to take my chances.

The music ends, and the disco ball slows. Little miss skeleton scampers around the floor, collecting the bills tossed her way. One guy points and curls his finger at her in a come-to-me gesture, a pink bill—is that a fifty?—pinched in the fingers of his other hand. She glances over her shoulder at the bouncer and then steps towards the guy. The bouncer is beside them in two strides. The guy puts the bill in his mouth and lifts his face to the peeler, pointing at her lips. The bouncer rips the bill out of his mouth, handing it to the naked skeleton. She struts away. Perv man gets up and leaves the premises.

A slice of yellow light beams from the back of the room as a door opens. Two men stand in the light. They do a quick handshake and bump shoulders. It's David and some burly dude with long receding hair in a black T-shirt and leather vest. There's a wad of cloth sticking out the front of David's coat. Burly Dude points to it, and David stuffs it out of sight, buttoning his coat over the bulge. He heads to the door, not even acknowledging the braless waitress offering to take his order.

It's gotta be drugs or a gun. Guys like Burley Dude don't sell Girl Scout cookies. But what the fuck would David be doing with either? Those boys are way too pure to be getting high. And why would David need a gun? I guess it can be risky working at the pharmacy downtown. People are always hitting up drugstores because—drugs.

I'm deep in thought when an older guy, with a fisherman's beanie and a red-plaid lumberjack jacket, puts his hand on my shoulder. "Can I buy you a drink, sweetheart?" He smells of fish and whisky.

I look up at him. "It'll cost ya," I say, licking my lips and smiling.

"I know," he says.

I shrug. Might as well make a buck if he's offering.

Ted

It's Thursday night: grocery night. I look up and down the street before I get in the car. I still don't know what I'm looking for. I wish David were with me, but his leg is giving him hell today. He needs to just sit. Besides, it's been two days. Maybe campus security did frighten her off. Maybe she doesn't actually know where we live. Maybe she came to her senses and figured out I have no interest in her. Yeah, right.

I put my signal on and shoulder check before turning

onto the street. I see her just before she ducks down. I've seen the car before, an old and faded green Chrysler New Yorker with a dent in the back fender and rusting chrome. It's parked around the same spot, on the blackberry side of the street, facing our building about fifty yards down, in front of an old postwar cottage with rambling tea roses and overgrown crabgrass. But I wasn't looking for May before. It never even occurred to me to look for her. I keep my hands at ten and two, staring straight ahead and accelerating through the stop sign at the end of the block.

I drive around for what seems like hours, afraid to get out of the car, afraid to go home. I drive to the university; I drive to the Tsawwassen ferry terminal and then to the Horseshoe Bay ferry terminal, checking my rear-view constantly. There's no sign of her. I'm on the Upper Levels Highway when it dawns on me and I slam on the brakes—she was waiting for me to leave. I drive like I've never driven before, cutting in and out of traffic, way over the speed limit, running yellow lights. I'm kind of hoping to attract some police attention—they can follow me home, maybe catch her. Whatever she's doing. Poor David.

She isn't here. Her car isn't here. I look up and see the light on in our unit, and I feel the weakness of nausea in my jaw. I get out of the car, closing the door with a press instead of a slam. Part of me wants to run up the stairs; part of me wants to run down the street. I bite my cheek for strength and take the stairs two at a time. My key slides into the deadbolt as I turn the doorknob, but the door isn't locked. My hands are rattling. I open the door a crack and peek inside.

David looks over his shoulder at me from the couch. Then he's standing up. "What the fuck took you so long? I've been worried sick!"

I take a wide-eyed scan of the room before I come in and close the door, sliding the deadbolt in place and hooking the chain across the door. David looks at the floor and then locks my eyes, annoyance furrowing his brow, his hands rising, palms up. "Groceries?"

"I saw her," I say. I feel my skin pale as I say the words. David takes an awkward step towards me, his crutch still on the couch. "Her car. She was parked"—I point to the south end of the street outside—"right over there."

David freezes. The colour drains from his skin too. He reaches for his crutch and limps to the balcony.

"She isn't there now," I say, coming up beside him. We stand at the threshold of the French doors, peering down the street. "At least she wasn't a minute ago."

He puts his arm around my shoulder, and I rest my head against him. My crutch. My solid.

May

I try to be at Ted's place around suppertime, and I stay until I get a page for a client. Some nights, I don't get any calls, and I fall asleep in my car. Other nights, I work all night and I'm too fucked to bother with Ted. Friday nights are special though. I always come back after work on Friday nights, just to get a peek at my baby on Saturday morning, walking around the apartment with his shirt off. He looks for me too. He'll come to the window with his coffee in his hand and stare right at me. He doesn't smile though. He's too smart for that. David would know something is up.

Ted's being very careful that way. David looks at me from the apartment too, but he doesn't exude the love Ted brings me of course. David has rage on his face almost permanently. I don't think he's ever smiled at me. He knows too. It's only a matter of time before he loses Ted. When they drive by me, leaving the apartment, David glares at me, mouthing, "Fuck you," and sometimes displaying his middle finger. Ted stares straight ahead, all stiff in the shoulders and straight in the back. It must be so hard for him, knowing I'm here, listening to David talk to me like that.

I'm beginning to wonder what the plan is. It's been over a month, and Ted hasn't made a move. I think we need to talk again. Maybe he needs my help.

Ted

It's like we're onstage. We check the street every time we walk by the window until she arrives. Then close the curtains. We whisper more than we talk. Making love just doesn't even happen. At night, we sit close together in the dark, holding hands, watching TV.

Sometimes, she's still there in the mornings when we leave for work. Like she slept in her car. I refuse to look at her. David rants and threatens her as we drive by. She's always parked outside on Saturdays.

We've started looking for a new place, but it's difficult because how do we look at places if she's just going to follow us? And then we still show up for work every day. We aren't hard to find.

I know I have to tell Mom and Joe. May followed us to Mom's last week. Whether she knows it's Mom's place, I'm not sure. But we go there often enough that May is bound to figure it out. Joe doesn't know about May; at least, I don't think he does. I wonder how he will take it?

May

I get a set of boudoir pictures done for Ted's Valentine's gift. It's what women are doing for this year. The photographer gives you sexy outfits, and you pose in them. Then, if he likes you, he fucks you. He fucked me. Only because I let him though. I fucked him again when I picked up the prints. He gave me the prints for free. I told him to lose my number.

The pictures are so fucking hot. I wonder if I should start modelling?

Ted

I don't tell Mom. They're going to Palm Springs for a couple of months to wait out winter. I don't want her worrying about me. Hopefully, by the time they get back, this will all be over. On Valentine's Day, when we get back from a very romantic dinner at Giorgio's down the street, there's an envelope stuck in the door. I recognize May's handwriting and throw it straight in the trash.

May

The week before Valentine's is surprisingly busy. There are nights when I have to go home and take a bath, I'm feeling so chaffed. Some of these guys are just lonely, not horny. They want to talk and cuddle. I got no fucking time for that. Why the fuck would I want to hear about their ex-wife or how much they miss their kids—or worse yet, how their wife doesn't enjoy sex? "Not like you do," they always say. Like I'm loving trying to find their wilty little dick under their sweaty fat gut. I should give acting lessons to married women. That's what I should do.

I have to say, the whole escort thing is losing its charm. Maybe I'll take a couple of weeks off. Ted and I will be together soon.

Ted

David got his cast off on Monday, and it's amazing! He's driving and laughing and so full of good spirit. That smile of his is everywhere. Even this morning, when we drove by May on the way to work, his rant was full of fun. "You silly, silly bitch! He's mine!" He cackled, nodding his head side to side like a mad man and topping it all off by blowing a raspberry sprayed through his outstretched tongue.

We've ordered pizza from Benito's. Bacon, mushroom, green peppers, and shrimp—our absolute favourite; it's like heaven. We get our beer and put the pizza on the coffee table in front of us. I check out the street before I turn out the lights.

"She's there," David says, handing me a slice. It isn't a question.

I grin. "Yup."

He checks his watch. "Okay, that works."

We watch *NYPD Blue* and *L.A. Law*. Not really watching, just waiting. I keep looking over at David, his face reflecting the blue screen, and I get butterflies. "Are we really going to do this?"

He squeezes my thigh. "Fuckin' right we are!"

Still whispering. And listening. Finally, we hear the rattle of a muffler and see the reflection of lights on the window as a car drives by.

"That's her," David says, popping up to check the street. "Yup, she's gone."

We move fast. Sometimes, she's only gone a few minutes; sometimes, she's gone until after we go to bed. Our bags are packed. Any food we need we can pick up once we're out of town. I go down to the car and, throwing my backpack into the back seat, drive to the parking lot at the back of the building. We don't have our own spot, which is why we park on the street, but it works just fine. David is waiting for me when I pull up, holding the pizza box and his backpack. He tosses the backpack into the back seat and climbs in, balancing the pizza on his lap. We exchange mischievous smiles. I edge out of the parking lot and into the alley to take us down a few blocks before we take to the main roads. Harrison Hot Springs, here we come!

"You told them we'd be checking in late?" I ask.

"You don't have to whisper." He chuckles. "And yes, they're expecting us around eleven."

"Holy shit." I sigh, shaking my head as the tension I've carried for months eases off my shoulders. "Why didn't we think of this before?"

May

I've had a long night. It's four a.m., and I'm just pulling up to their apartment. My skin crawls with the odours of men and aftershave.

The car isn't here. What the fuck? Looking up, there are no lights in his window. That's normal. He should be sleeping. I turn into the driveway to go to the back of the building. No car. I feel a quiver of panic in my throat. I drive to the front of the building and park in my usual spot. My mind runs over the reasons why they aren't here.

He went to a party and got drunk. He moved. They had a fight, and one of them left in the car. There was an emergency, and he's at the hospital. The car broke down and is getting repairs. They went away on vacation.

I turn the engine off and sit, elbows resting on the steering wheel, my chin resting on my palms. My hands stink of condom and cock sweat. I look at them and wipe them on the seat.

There's a slam. It's Ted closing the door of a police car. I see him in my rear-view. His shoulders are broad, and he's got a confident strut as he approaches my car. I'm not afraid. I look back at the police car, but it's turned into a Camaro with the ghost car lights tucked up under the windshield. I watch as the pimply security guard from the university walks from the passenger side to the driver side. He folds himself to get into the vehicle. Another slam. Someone else is in the car. It's David. He sits in the back, hunched forward, and as they drive by, I see that his arms are pulled behind him, like he is in handcuffs. I wait for Ted to come to my window. But he doesn't come. He isn't on the street anymore. I look behind me, and I see his figure turn the corner at the end of the block. I fumble for my keys in the ignition, but I can't reach them. I can't reach them. He's getting away. Another slam.

I wake up. Blinking into the dull winter light. There's a couple unloading groceries from a Toyota across the road. The parking spot behind me is empty. I look into the side mirror. No Ted. No Camaro. No turquoise Honda. Just me. Sticky and cold. I start the car and light a smoke, leaning back, watching their window, waiting for the heat to kick in. My stomach growls and threatens to puke as the nicotine whorls me into consciousness.

It's ten a.m. Their curtains aren't open. Nothing is happening. Maybe they've gone for the day and I missed them. I'll go home and have a shower and get some food. Tears are rolling down my cheeks as I shift the car into Drive. My hands are shaking. Fuck, I should quit smoking. I stab my cigarette into the already full ashtray, knocking butts and ashes to the floor in a dirty cloud.

I'm back. It's six o'clock. I ended up getting an afternoon date, so I went home to shower again and got all prettied up for tonight. Now I have a tin plate full of special chow mein from the place Ted always goes to and a can of Kokanee. I figure I have a few hours to watch before work starts up. But it looks like nothing has moved. The car still isn't here. The apartment is dark. Sure, he has a life, but I know that life. I know he turns on the lamp in the living room when he goes out at night. He doesn't like coming home to a dark room. My Teddy's always been a little nervous in the dark.

I remember he went to the can one day when we were playing at my house, and while he was gone, I turned out the lights in my bedroom and hid under the bed. When he came back to the room, he thought I had left, so he started to walk away, but I called him back. "Ted! I'm here. Come find me!" And when he walked in and got close enough to the bed, I grabbed his ankle. He screamed. I laughed. When I turned on the light, there was a little wet spot on the front of his pants. I guess he still had some pee left.

I eat chow mein until the noodles start to congeal in the cold. Then I start the car, heater blasting, light a smoke— maybe I'll quit tomorrow—and savour my beer.

The old couple from the far corner unit on the ground floor come creeping out of the building, deep in conversation, walking as slow as a glacier. It's painful to watch. I want to poke them with a cattle prod to get them to speed up. She's wearing her usual: a yellowing blond pageboy wig, topped with a royal-blue fascinator, its lacy flowers dangling precariously over her right ear. Her face is powdered pink, and the rouge on her cheeks flames almost as red as her lips themselves. I guess blending is hard when you're all cramped up with arthritis. She clings to her husband, who is curled over a worn wooden cane. He wears a grey fur hat that gives him enough height to come up to her bent shoulders. He's clean shaven and as thick as she is thin. I can see the liver spots on his face from here. Their pace irritates the fuck out of me. They go out every Saturday night. I think they go for a drink at the pub down the road. Tonight, I can't keep my eyes off them. They remind me of Ted and me, how close we'll be when we've been married that long.

I wait until eight thirty. Still nothing. I get out of my car and cross the road. I can see the old couple down the street, already on their way home. I slip into the building, taking the steps two at a time to the third floor. The hallway smells like bubble bath, popcorn, and Mr. Clean. The linoleum-tiled floor is dotted with doormats. Some tenants still have Christmas wreaths on their doors. *Hockey Night in Canada* echoes into the hall.

I stop at Ted's door, number 320, running my hand over the smooth blue paint. There's a deadbolt. Of course. I go to the far end of the hall and step inside the stairwell, pulling two bobby pins from my hair.

Jake taught me before I got the job at Central Saloon. We would go into the middle-class neighbourhoods and take stuff. We popped CD players, some jewellery, cash if we could find it, and it's surprisingly easy to find. Everyone does the same thing, stashing it in the freezer or a sock drawer. It helped pay the bills. It also got me in the habit of pinning my hair and buying good-quality bobby pins.

I bend one in half—the wrench—and straighten the other—the pick—pulling off the goo at the end with my teeth. Stepping back into the hall, I listen and then go back to their door. Sliding the bent one in the bottom and pulling it to the left, I slip the pick down through the bolt and brush it up and out, feeling the lock pins slip up. The keyhole turns a little. The fourth pin is the jam. I stop for a second and listen, then apply a slow pressure to the seized pin, turning with the wrench pin. It slowly gives, and the wrench turns freely, opening the deadbolt. What a shitty lock!

I walk into darkness and grope for a light around the doorframe. There's a double switch under my hand, and I flip on the one closest to me. A light goes on overhead, sending a glow through the rest of the apartment. I smile.

The galley kitchen has a window opening into the living

room–dining room, like a snack bar. The little kitchenette that they moved from the window after I ran with Ted in the park that day is now wedged under the snack bar opening, and there are two barstools parked against the window.

Beyond that is a simple beige couch, a rectangular coffee table, and a portable TV on another, crappier coffee table. There's a poster of Elton John on one wall and a collage of concert tickets beside it. Plants hang from macramé hangers, and two big ones with giant leaves sit on the floor on the nonsliding side of the balcony doors. An entire wall is covered with a bookshelf made of cinderblocks and plywood. I shiver, remembering the snake in his bedroom so long ago.

I cross to the bedroom, turning a lamp on near the couch on my way. It's small. A double bed and two dressers crammed into the tiny space, no room for swinging cats at all. I open the curtains to the window that looks out to where my car is parked. They have always been closed. Even before they knew I was out there. The room smells of men. I don't feel any desire to lie on the bed that he shares with David. The thought puts a lump in my throat.

I open the drawer to the dresser nearest the window. Socks. I am about to open the next drawer when I see a photo of Ted's mom on the other dresser. There's another picture of Ted and David, arm in arm in clapboard and gowns, each holding a scrolled paper. They don't look much younger than they are now. It must be a university graduation. I knock the photos to the floor and start to dig through the T-shirts in the top drawer. What am I looking for? I guess I'll know when I find it. The second drawer is socks and underwear. He's a boxer guy. That's not surprising. Nothing fancy, just plaids, blues, and greys. I stick my hand in and root, stirring undies with socks, until I touch something cold and metal.

An old tin box, like they used to have for chocolates. The black and red paint has mostly worn off it, but there's relief of a bow and some cubes—I assume they were chocolate shapes —on the lid. I sit on the bed and pop it open. Inside is full of photos and odd things. A pink seashell, a beetle in a small, clear plastic box, pinned to a piece of blue spongy stuff. I take out a handful of photos and postcards, which uncovers a fucking snakeskin. I toss the box beside me on the bed. Things spill out. Fucking snakes. I walk out of the bedroom with the photos and close the door, taking a seat on the couch and turning on the second lamp on the end table.

The pictures are from back home. Black and whites. Some even have the pinked edges. A man with a pipe holding a baby bundled in blankets. The man is in suspenders and a white T-shirt, leaning against a car older than mine, from the '50s, I think. His legs are crossed. He's looking down at the baby like there isn't even a camera on him. "Daddy and his babies, '64" is written in pencil on the back. I look at the photo again and see the likeness to Ted in the man's posture and shape, long and lean. Big hands with long fingers, just like Teddy's.

I slip the photo inside my bra. Where is he? I miss him. My stomach growls, and I go to the kitchen to check out the fridge. There's a Labatt Blue in the door and a Heineken tucked away in the back, a jar of pickles, some Cheez Whiz, milk, and a carton of eggs. I take the Heineken, find some bread to make a Cheez Whiz and pickle sandwich, and chow down as I explore the rest of the apartment. Most of the books on the shelf are textbooks: chemistry, biochemistry, physics, and zoology. But there's other, not-so-boring stuff too. Not that I read, but I recognize titles, like *The Shining*, *The Lord of the Rings*, and *Shōgun*.

Washing the sandwich down with the rest of the beer, I go back to the fridge for the Blue. It's only then that it occurs to me—there's no real food in the fridge. But I know Ted went shopping with David on Tuesday. I watched him. I do remember thinking he didn't get much. He always gets four bags and a four-litre of milk. He only got the two litres this time. I should know enough to recognize a break in his routine.

And now I'm remembering the night I followed David. I lean back against a wall and scan the apartment. I go to the couch and lift the pillows, shoving my hand into its crevices. Then I check out the bedroom, under the mattress. I pull out David's dresser drawers one at a time, sifting through jeans, socks, and T-shirts, and checking underneath each drawer before tossing it on the bed. Then I tackle Teddy's dresser. Clothes are everywhere. I sit down on the edge of the bed, feeling certain now. Where the fuck would he hide a gun? The closet? The bathroom? I'm about to get up when I see a lump of duct tape wadded to the underside of the top of David's dresser where the top drawer had been. I reach in and give it a good tug —the tape and weight of the gun fall into my hand.

It's a Jennings .22 LR, exactly like the one I found when we were doing B and Es, and by the weight of it, it's fully loaded. Son of a bitch. Why would David need a gun? Is he planning on killing Ted? Does Ted have any idea? I check the safety and shove the pistol down inside my boot. Then my pager goes off. Playtime is over. I scan the apartment before leaving. Not much point in tidying up. I leave the bobby pins on the coffee table.

Ted

We're grinning when we turn onto our street. We had such a fabulous time! Hot springs, cozy dinner in the lodge, peace and nature and that beautiful, beautiful lake. All to ourselves. There was hardly anyone else there. We've been grinning all the way home. And the street is empty. She's not even here to ruin our high!

"God, I can't wait until I'm finished school and we can do that every weekend!" I say as we tumble up the stairs with everything in one load. I drop my bags at the door and fish for my key.

David comes up behind me and breathes into my neck, reaching around with his key in his hand. "I got this."

I turn the knob as he puts the key in the deadbolt. The door gives way without even a turn of the latch, and we stumble through. My throat tightens. The first thing I notice is the bag of bread open on the kitchen counter. Then the empty green bottle of Heineken on the coffee table. Then the photos scattered around it. "Oh God," I whisper, crossing the room and gathering up my memories, picking up each photo and pressing it to my chest. I'm shaking. I keep saying it. "Oh God. Oh God."

David watches me and then storms into the bedroom. "Fuck!" he shouts.

I go to him, still clinging to my photos. The bedroom is torn apart. Our clothes and dresser drawers are everywhere. David is digging through piles, muttering, "Shit. Fuck. Jesus fucking Christ."

I put my hand on his back. He jumps. "Hey," I say, realizing he's more upset than I am.

He finally stops, sits on the bed, and leans forward, holding his head in his hands, fingers clawing into his hair. He says something, but I can't make it out.

"Hmm?" I ask, stepping towards him.

"The gun!" he says. "It's gone."

"Gun?"

He looks up at me. "She took the fucking gun!" he snaps at me, as though I knew there was a gun, as though I knew she took it.

The pictures I'm holding fall to the floor as a wave of weakness washes over me. "What. Fucking. Gun?"

"The gun. I bought a gun," he says. He's shaking.

"Why?" I say, stepping away from him. "Why?" I'm shaking too.

"Oh, come on." He rolls his eyes to the ceiling. "To protect us from that crazy bitch."

"Now she has it." I state the obvious.

He nods.

"We have to phone the police."

He nods again, but then he shakes his head. "No!"

"I'm calling the police, David." I turn away from him, heading to the phone.

He catches up to me as I lift the receiver. "It's not legal. I think it might be stolen."

I lower the receiver. "What the fuck were you thinking?"

"I got scared. For you." He sits on the couch, stiff and straight, his hands clenching his thighs. "How do I protect you from her?"

I sit beside him and stare at the floor. "What if we don't mention the gun? She still broke into the house."

So we won't mention the gun.

It's ten o'clock before they arrive. Two of them. They smell like coffee and cheeseburgers.

"I'm Constable Ryan," the older cop says, "and this is my partner, Constable Rickland."

Constable Ryan is thick around the middle—is that a thing with cops? Her crisp black uniform puckers at the buttons, and her belt disappears into the folds of her waist. Her black hair is tied tight and straight at the nape of her neck, not a single stray hair. Her eyes are kind and searching. She seems like she wants to listen.

"Come in, please," I say as I step back into the kitchen. I offer them water, and David offers them a seat, pointing to the living room.

Constable Rickland, red headed and freckly, says he'll have water, and I start talking as I run the tap. "She was in here. There's the Cheez Whiz and the knife," I say, pointing to the mess she left on the counter. The bread bag is open, with slices spilling out. "We didn't touch anything in here."

David pipes in, "She drank some beer, too."

"She?" asks Ryan. "What makes you think it's a she?"

We move into the living room as we talk. "She stalks me. I've known her since we were kids."

Ryan and Rickland look at the photos piled on the coffee table. Rickland looks at me with a raised eyebrow. "This too?"

"Yeah," I say, "kind of, I—I piled them on the table. They were everywhere."

Rickland walks over to the bedroom, looks in, and then up at Ryan, signalling with his head she should join him.

She does, and when she sees the mess, she shakes her head. "Anything missing?"

I reach for David's hand, remember we can't do that, and shake my head in turn. "No," and then, "maybe a picture?"

Her face slackens with what must be disappointment. "I need more than that, guys. Anything? I can't just charge an acquaintance with breaking into a friend's house and drinking some beer."

"But she's outside every night! She even follows me to the grocery store." My heart is sinking into my stomach. It beats waves of nausea. "I— We can't live like this anymore." I sink down to the couch.

Ryan sits beside me. "Unless she assaults you, we can't lay charges." She speaks softly, like a mom. My mom.

I bite my cheek and close my eyes to block tears.

"But maybe we can have a chat with her." She takes her notebook and a golf-chit-sized pencil out. "She's never assaulted you, has she?"

I look to David, and he elicits the tiniest nod of permission, and I return it with the tiniest shake of my head. "No."

Ryan's eyebrows lower, and her lips tighten together. She looks to the ceiling and then back to me. She opens her mouth to speak, but Rickland interrupts. "You guys American?"

He's looking at the US flag over the bookshelf.

"Yeah," David responds. "We immigrated in 1983, right?" He looks at me for confirmation.

"Legally?" Ryan asks.

And the rest of us catch up to Rickland. "Oh my god, she's illegal," I say, turning to Ryan. "She's illegal!"

She's nodding. Almost smiling. "Okay, now we have something to work with," she says, licking the tip of her pencil. "When did she get here?"

"I don't know." I think back over the past few months and turn to David. "It was after you broke your leg, so after your birthday, right?"

David nods. "Right." He taps his forehead, like he does when he's trying to remember stuff. "Actually, a couple of weeks after. You went for a run—"

"No!" I interrupt. "Earlier than that. Don, Don Knudsen, my supervisor, told me he thought he saw her on campus before the run." I look at Ryan and give her the background, from when we first saw May in Seattle to when she showed up on campus and Don called security.

Ryan's smile fades. She's shaking her head. "Six months. Americans can stay six months without a visa or anything." She shrugs. "She has three months to go if she only got here in October."

My stomach sinks again. I look away from everyone, out the balcony window. David comes up behind me and puts his hands on my shoulders. I lean forward to avoid the touch. I feel cold.

"There's got to be something," David says softly.

Still staring out the window, I watch Ryan's reflection as she closes her notebook and stands, straightening her uniform with a brush of her hands.

"We can touch base with the RCMP?" Rickland asks his partner.

She nods. "We'll see if there's any warrants for her arrest down there. Maybe we can have her extradited." She shrugs again.

"What are the chances?" David asks.

Ryan raises her eyebrows. "How bad is she?"

I feel the slightest of hopes lifting inside me.

May

Ted and David's silhouettes are in the window, watching me. He knows I was in there, not like I tried to hide it. He shouldn't take off like that. Should I get out of the car? Maybe if I stand on the street, he'll come out to me. It's time. I can feel it.

There's a sense of thrill in my bones. I imagine Ted pushing David through the doors, over the balcony. Breaking him. And us driving away to live the rest of our lives hiding together.

Then I remember the gun. I can do this for us.

My hand goes to the cool chrome of the car door handle. It pops open, and I put a foot out onto the pavement. It feels like slow motion. Every sound is amplified. My breath. The rustling of my pant leg as I reach for the warm metal tucked in my boot. Tires on pavement driving past me. Wet and sparkly. I push the door open, gun in my hand, and stand up. And see the car that passed me was the police. Parking in front of the building. The silhouettes are gone from the window.

They called the cops? Really? Is this how we're doing it? Jesus fucking Christ. I flop back down in the car, throw the gun on the passenger seat beside a Big Mac box, and drive away.

Ted

It's hard to be in the apartment now that I know she can get in. I don't sleep. David paces as much as I do.

I know Rickland and Ryan tried to speak with her, but she just drives away as soon as she sees them coming. They have nothing to hold her on right now, except maybe her noisy muffler. I know they make an effort to drive by every night, but often as not, they've just missed her. Ryan stopped by last night to give us an update, but she seemed a little less enthusiastic. Like she'd been had—and not by May.

So we're doing the one thing we can do, and that's moving into a secure building. Who knows? Maybe we can even lose her for a bit.

We have Saturday's *Vancouver Sun* spread out on the coffee table.

"How about this? Two bedrooms, ground floor, secure building . . . Never mind. Ground floor would suck."

"Here's one, seven hundred and fifty a month, third floor, two bedrooms, fully renovated, gas stove? Wow! Includes cable and heat." I draw a big circle around the ad as I read.

David has his hand on the phone receiver, fingers poised, ready to dial. "What's the phone number?"

He dials as I read out the number and smiles at me as he waits for the connection. "Hello? Hi. I'm calling about the apartment . . ."

I hear the distant voice on the other end of the receiver. "It's been rented," and then a resolute click as they disconnect the call.

There have been a couple like that. Other good ones just have a busy signal at the other end.

We lower our standards and keep looking, finally finding a unit in Coquitlam—way farther out than we hoped—that's within our price range. David is nodding and smiling as he makes arrangements for a viewing. "Two o'clock works perfect. Yes, we can meet you at the front doors. Thank you."

He stands as he hangs up, going to the window and peeping out the curtains. "We're out of here, bitch!" he sings. I'm pretty sure she's not there, but we've taken to talking to her as though she's always outside on the street, watching us.

And I start pacing. "We'll need boxes. God, we've lived here a long time. And a truck. Who do we know?"

"I can start looking for a pharmacy in Coquitlam, get out of downtown." He stops midthought. "Do you think she'll follow us if we're so far out?"

I stop too, but I'm not letting her get to me right now. I laugh. "Of course she will. She followed me from Seattle, didn't she?"

May

They finally turned on their lights and pulled me over. They look like fucking Laurel and Hardy, only the fat one is a chick. She's the bossy one too. I kind of figured as much since she's the one who's always driving.

"Driver's licence and registration, please," she says, her hands on her hips at my window. The skinny one is standing at the back of the car on the passenger side. He's almost in my blind spot. Hardy looks like she might come to tears any minute, despite the scowl on her face. I reach into the glove compartment for the registration and then get my driver's licence from my purse. Jake always kept the car papers up to date. That way, if you get stopped, they don't have any reason to give you trouble.

Which is why Hardy looks disappointed when she reads them, but they're still American, so she asks, "How long are you staying?"

"Until you let me fuckin' go, dumbass," is what I want to say. But I restrain myself. "Gosh, I'd like to stay forever! It's so beautiful here. But I'm just here another couple of months."

She points the driver's license and registration at me, "I'm just going to check these out," and begins to walk back to her car, one hand resting on her holster.

I lean out the window, giving her my best chatty girl. "I've been thinking about applying for citizenship though. Do you think they would take a girl like me?"

Hardy shrugs. She doesn't look back. Judgy bitch. Laurel's at the front of the car now, inspecting the grill. When he lifts his head, I give him a little wave and a smile. He nods. No smile though. Fuck you too.

Hardy takes her time checking me out. Seriously, it takes about a half hour. At one point, I go to get out of the car, but Laurel steps in front of the door and puts his hand up, shaking his head. "Stay in the car, please, ma'am." I light a cigarette and blow the smoke in his direction. Then I wind up the window.

They've got nothing on me. I'm clean. The car itself is a little messy, but they can't bust you for that. Jake would never report it stolen. The car's in my name because he wanted to lie low in Washington. He figured if the cops didn't know he was there, with his record and all, they wouldn't bother him. He drove like a little old lady because of it.

When she comes back to the car, I wind down my window, but she doesn't hand me back my stuff. "Listen," she says. Her sad eyes look dark now, mean. "We know what's been going on with you and Ted Russell. It needs to stop." She nods at me, as though that will make me agree with her.

Stupid cunt. She has no idea what's going on with Ted and me. But I don't tell her that. Instead, with my smoking hand below her line of sight, I press my thumb against the cherry of my cigarette. The pain brings tears to my eyes in an instant. Hopefully, she can't smell the burning skin. I reach to the ashtray to stub it out. And then, eyes wet, lift my face to her. "But I love him!" I whine.

Like I figured, Hardy turns to mush when she sees my tears. "Oh, sweetie."

Laurel's head jerks up at the word *sweetie*, and he steps up to us, clearing his throat.

"Sometimes these things just aren't meant to be," Hardy continues. She looks over at Laurel, who is standing with his hands on his bony hips, frowning at her. She takes a deep breath and shakes her head. "You've got to let this one go, okay? For your own sake." She takes a step back, remembers she still has my licence and stuff, and passes it to me.

"Okay," I snivel, wiping my tears with the back of my hand to smear my mascara. Then I put on my brave-little-girl face for them and nod. "I will," I say, pulling myself tall. Why am I not an actress? "I can do this."

Hardy sets her mouth straight and nods with me. "You can do this." They both walk back to the squad car. I can see Laurel watching me as I drive away. I feel a little lump in my throat. I press my burned thumb onto my tongue to make it wet and then blow on it. The lump doesn't leave my throat for a while.

Ted

We move on February 1st, a Wednesday, which means we have to take the day off. Actually, most of the lab takes the day off to help us. Don has a truck and Tippy borrows his latest girlfriend's dad's truck, so it only takes two trips. The little Honda looks like an Amazon rainforest, full of houseplants, as I drive across town following the two trucks with the final load. We made sure May was gone before we started the packing frenzy.

We feed everyone pizza and beer, and it turns into a bit of a housewarming party while we unpack. David and I make the bed, shove drawers back into the dressers, call out directions, and grin at each other every chance we get. The new building is a step up from the walk-up. It's only about five years old, has a gym, and is right across from a shopping centre but just a couple of blocks from Burnaby Lake. It's gorgeous and stinks of fresh paint.

Tippy and Stephen are unloading books and knickknacks onto shelves in the living room; Don has taken charge of the kitchen, at his insistence. I keep looking out the balcony window, waiting for her to pull up. That's the other bonus of this unit. It looks out the back, and it's underground parking. She can't see if we're home.

We finally sit, there's a new, used sofa and chair donated by Don. They just bought a new set, or he used that as an excuse anyway. I know his partner was thrilled. So am I! This is a full sofa that folds out into a bed, and its pillows still have fluff, and the springs still have spring. It was a bitch to get up the elevator though.

I flop back onto the couch between David and Tippy,

with a freshly cracked beer. "Now we can have sleepovers!" I say, patting the cushion between us.

Tippy raises his beer. "Now we can do some serious drinking!" he says and takes a good guzzle. "And not have to find our way home."

Stephen is rubbing his chin onto his palm. I'd say he's rubbing his whiskers, but he only has about twelve. "How's this going to affect your other"—he clears his throat for effect—"relationship?"

Tippy snickers. Don glares, first at Tippy, then at Stephen. I blink, not sure what he's talking about.

"They know?" David asks.

"What?" I ask. My skin tingles in panic as my brain races over scenes of our life, trying to trace David's infidelity.

"That girl who is giving you trouble," Don clarifies, nodding. "I told them. For your own safety."

I don't know what to say. I look to Don, shaking my head, and then at David, who has assumed a full defensive posture, hands on his thighs, spine straight, scanning the room: from Tippy, to Stephen, to Don. I feel them all staring at me and drop my head.

"I didn't really want anyone to know," I say quietly.

"Hey," Tippy pipes up. "Joking aside, that girl is a little crazy. We met her, remember?"

"Yeah, sorry. I forgot you didn't know we knew," Stephen mutters.

"You need us to know," Tippy continues, "like Don says, for your own protection. We can give you a heads-up if she comes around."

"Well, you haven't so far," I grumble. "She's on campus all the time." I look up, finally, and spit words at Stephen. "She likes to follow me home from work. Then she sits outside our building half the night."

"She broke in when we went to the hot springs last month. That's why we're moving," David adds.

We reach for each other's hand at the same time. The solid grip of David's hand in mine is safety, as always. I sit back and relax a little, so does he.

Stephen adjusts his glasses, backstepping and trying to redeem himself. "I thought she might be the cause. You know, safety in numbers. Now it's out in the open, we can be a bit more helpful. Walk you to the car at night or hang out at the lab if you need to work late."

"Oh my god, this is embarrassing. No!" I say, standing up. "I am a grown man. I can handle her myself. It's just . . . annoying, that's all."

"*Annoying* made you move?" Stephen quips.

No one says anything. The silence is awkward, and I start to feel bad about rejecting their support. I know they mean well.

David cuts into the awkwardness. "I think it's a good idea."

I give him a sharp look. He shrugs. "I worry about you. And she is crazy."

"*Fatal Attraction* crazy," says Tippy. He leans forward. "Let's put a plan in place."

"She'll be gone by April, you know," I push back. "She can't stay in the country longer than six months, unless she applies for citizenship or a work permit or something."

"So? A lot can happen between now and then," says Don. "And you spend a lot of time alone in the lab."

Everyone is looking my way. "Fine," I say, and a feeling of relief melts tension that I didn't even know was there.

May

He fucking moved! What a freakin' hassle. Everything was going just fine, and then he moves. It's way the fuck and gone out of Vancouver. And the traffic is stupid. They actually have to drive almost an hour each way to get to the university and back. It was a week before I managed to follow them home without losing them in traffic. Plus, there's nowhere to park at their new place. And that's another thing; they're in this high-rise—I can't even tell what floor he's on. I watch him drive into the parkade at night and leave in the morning. But in between, I don't get to see him. Most nights, I just drive around the building looking for signs of him.

My car is dying. It was bound to happen, I guess. It can't handle the commute and all the idling in traffic. Yesterday it overheated on the "freeway"—where traffic barely hits ten miles an hour until you get past the fucking mess at Boundary Road—and I had to get someone to help me push it off the road. He also came back with a jug of water to top up the radiator and insisted on following me into Coquitlam. "To make sure you get home safe." When he asked for my phone number, I told him to go fuck himself.

It's been three weeks. I've stopped going to see him at night and started taking calls earlier. I don't even go to campus in the mornings. Then I do Friday nights and all day Saturday and Sunday with him. Another week, and I can get a car. I'm seeing one of my regulars tonight, Martin, who said he can get me a deal. How many blowjobs is a deal on a car worth? Whatever. I might look for a real job or something. I guess legally I'm only allowed to hang out in Canada for six months without some sort of job and a work permit and shit. Or I could go to school.

It's all too much paperwork. Maybe car-deal guy can help me.

His house is at the end of a street that leads into a ravine. It's a pretty lonely spot. there's some empty lots between him and the next house and he doesn't worry about me being discreet or anything. He'll often come out to my car to meet me. I think he's in his fifties. He wants the "girlfriend experience" most of the time, but every now and then, he just wants a hard fuck and for me to go away. Tonight, he wants two hours. That means girlfriend night. I'm wearing a classic A-line black dress with pearls and red lipstick. I look like a millionaire's wife: a fundraisers, cocktails-in-the-afternoon, tennis-on-Tuesdays kind of girl.

He walks down the driveway with a glass of champagne in his hand, shaking his head as he looks from one end of my car to the other. "You're not exactly discreet with that broken muffler, my love," he says, handing me the champagne. "You look lovely tonight." He gives me a peck on the cheek and takes my hand, which is nice because his driveway is gravel, and my heels are six inches.

We get inside, and he's kissing my neck, sliding his hand down my waist to my ass, sucking on my earlobe. His breathing gets heavier. Tonight's going to be an easy trick. I hold my glass steady, patiently waiting for the next sip. I always want to scream when it starts. Their touch is irritating; their foreplay, ridiculous. They never touch me like I want or need. Only Ted can do that. I remind myself about the money, close my eyes, and take deep breaths. They always think I'm extremely turned on, totally unaware that I would love nothing more than to wrap my fingers around their necks and squeeze them purple.

Martin leads me to the black leather sofa, his favourite spot for screwing, and takes my drink, putting it on the end table, beside his empty glass. Knowing the next stcp, I sit, spreading my legs a bit. He gets to his knees in front of me, reaches under my dress, and grabs my panties by the crotch, trying to remove them. This never goes smoothly. I try wiggling around to help him and finally end up taking them off myself. Every time. This might be part of the turn-on for him. Guys are fucking weird. Especially the old ones.

He does a pretty good job of getting me ready, and then he's on me. I let him go at it for a bit, wondering if I'm going to cum or not. Usually, if I think about it, I don't, so that fucks that up. I mean, it's always a bonus if I get a cum out of it. I pant and moan for him as I watch the clock on the wall over his shoulder. After five minutes, I start bucking my hips and grab at his butt cheeks with my nails. I moan and squeal and then arch my back hard, stiffening against him. Of course, it's too much for Martin. He cums like it's his first orgasm, falling back on his ass on the floor when he's done. I close my eyes and take some more deep breaths. There now, that part's over.

Then he's up, zipping up his fly, and off to the kitchen. "Do you want something to eat? A little more champagne?"

He comes out with a block of cheese in one hand, a box of crackers tucked under his arm, and the champagne bottle and a towel in the other hand. He hands me the towel, and I wipe myself off while he tops up our glasses. Sitting down, he puts his arm around me, kissing the top of my head. The after-sex snuggle is the absolute worst.

I look at the clock. So that killed fifteen minutes. An hour and forty-five to go. Fuuuuuck.

Martin sighs. "This is nice, isn't it?" The crackers are between his legs and the block of cheese on his thigh. He breaks off a piece of cheese and offers it to me. I'm hungry. I take it and shove my hand in the box to get a fistful of crackers.

I snuggle in while I chew. It's time to talk. "Yeah, my muffler is pretty bad. Pisses off the Johns, that's for sure." I feel his muscles tighten when I say "Johns." I forget that the girlfriend experience means they're the only one. Oops. I turn and caress his chest with my finger, tracing up along his throat to his lips. "I just don't want your neighbours to think I'm some kind of trash." I wiggle up and give him a kiss on the lips then slide back down.

"Aww, sweetie, have you seen yourself?" Yes, I have. "You are anything but trash. You're the classiest thing that's ever walked this street." He's right. But I still need a new car.

"Aww, you're so sweet," I purr, "but I do need a new car. That one keeps breaking down." I break off some more cheese for myself and munch down a cracker. He says nothing, just kisses my head and strokes my hair. The bastard's going to make me beg.

I uncurl myself away from him and sit upright. Fuck, I want a smoke. He won't let me smoke in the house though, and I'm pretty sure if I went out for one, it wouldn't help my cause. I down my champagne instead and hold out my glass. He looks a little surprised, but he empties the bottle into my glass, pretending to wring it out as the last drops fall. It's only half a glass. I knock it back. Fuck him.

He frowns. "Well, that's the end of that then." He's getting fidgety under my stare. "Maybe I should order a pizza?" He reaches for me and squeezes my thigh. "How about a gin and tonic, sweetheart?" He gets up to go to the kitchen.

"You said you would help me," I whisper. I can't decide whether to go into a rage or start crying. He's looking pretty easy to intimidate right now, but he's also very into being the big man taking care of his little girlfriend.

I hold my eyes wide until I can't anymore, then blink in the tears. By the time he gets back, I'm wet eyed with mascara dripping down my cheeks.

"Oh, sweetheart! What's wrong?" He sits down and wraps an arm around me again, pressing my face into his chest. *Don't fucking suffocate me, you idiot. Jesus.* I push away and sob, hiding my face.

"I-I just really need a car," I stutter. "I don't even know if I'll make it home tonight. I get so scared."

"No, no, no, don't you worry. It's going to be okay." He's reaching for me again. "Let's figure something out."

I brighten a little for him. "I have a little put by. Like maybe five hundred." Actually, it's two grand, but why not start low?

Martin chuckles. "That won't get you much of a car now, will it?"

I well up the tears again. God, I'm so good at this. "Won't it?"

He gets up and walks to the window, looking at my beater parked on the street. "You know," he says, taking a sip of his drink, "I could probably fix that thing up. Give it a paint job. It's a classic."

For fuck's sake, I don't want it fixed up. I want rid of it. It stinks. It dies everywhere. "But I need something now."

"How about we just trade? My car's in the garage. It's an '84 Chevy Cavalier. Good as new."

Seriously. How to purchase your very own hooker. "And what's that going to cost me?"

He turns back to me with a grin on his face like I just told him I love him. Shut that down right now, motherfucker. I return his grin with a stone-cold stare.

I am about to tell him exactly where he can shove his Chevy Cavalier when he responds, "A weekend."

I blink. A weekend what? With his cock in my mouth? I swallow the gag reflex that catches in my throat.

"We could go to Seattle," he says, shoving his hands deep in his pockets to hide his fresh erection.

I shake my head. "I won't go back to the States." Especially not to Seattle. Especially not with a John.

He nods, as though he's made some leeway. "Victoria then. It's gorgeous in the springtime." He lifts up onto his toes and raises his eyebrows. "We could stay downtown at the harbour. The Empress even."

He's begging now. That's better. I give him the tiniest of smiles and stand up. "Let's see this Chevy Cavalier."

He takes my hand and leads me to the garage.

Ted

She's gone. The move worked. The rotting old beater has disappeared from our lives, along with the crazy bitch behind the wheel. We haven't seen her in two weeks. She showed up at the new place a few times and then nothing.

I keep looking for her of course. I thought I saw her car a couple of times when we first moved here, but when we went down and walked around the building, it wasn't her. And I've been in touch with Constable Ryan. She hasn't seen the May Machine around at all. I guess, with her six months up, she went back to the States. I've started to breathe again. It's a good feeling.

May

It's been kinda fun the last couple of weeks: new car, new plates (with the help of a very naive Martin), a weekend in Victoria. I even changed my hair colour. The Johns are just loving the red! Not a fiery red this time, more Maureen O'Hara than Lucille Ball. I still give them fire though.

But Ted's lost me. He doesn't know my car, and he's looking for a blond. He usually stares straight ahead or turns away at least once he notices me, but these days, he just walks on by, yacking to David or hands in his pockets, deep in thought. I can't tell if he doesn't like the red or he truly doesn't recognize me. I suppose it's for the best though. I get to watch him, and he doesn't even know I'm here.

It's Friday, so tonight I followed him home. We stop to pick up beer and pizza at the little mall on Austin across from their apartment. They disappear into the liquor store for a minute and then come back out with a case of Old Vienna. Are they dancing? Jesus. They are. Ted is laughing so hard by the time they get to the car he's doubled over. David puts the beer in the trunk and puts his hand on Ted's shoulder. He says something, and they both go into fits of laughter again. It's like Ted doesn't even care that I'm gone.

They walk over to the pizza place, shoulder to shoulder. Practically holding hands. What about our plans? How does he not even feel me here, so close to him? I get out of the car and lean against the back end, arms folded. Waiting. Should I go in? Should I wait by their car?

Twenty minutes go by before he comes out of the pizza shop. They seem to have sobered up. I start walking towards them. Ted gives out a loud guffaw. Just like when we were kids. I'm getting tired of this. I take big strides across the parking lane, headed to cut them off. I call his name, "Ted!" but my voice breaks, and it comes out as a dry whisper. I call out again, but this time, I'm drowned out by a siren, loud and sudden.

There's red and blue lights everywhere. What the fuck? Two cop cars come into the parking lot from different ends. Adrenaline rushes through me, and I practically dive back to my car. I look over to Ted's car. David's got Ted by the elbow, opening the door for him. Did they see me? Did they call the cops?

Two more patrol cars drive into the parking lot, lights on but no sirens. There are uniforms sending people back to their cars and uniforms approaching the liquor store, guns drawn. I realize I'm gripping the steering wheel with white knuckles, slunk deep down in the seat to hide my head. I look like an ape. I sit up a little straighter so I can see over to the Honda. Ted's sitting in their passenger seat, tall and exposed, looking around like he's watching a parade. David is doing nothing to protect him.

The cops use a loudspeaker to talk to whoever's robbing the liquor store. Other officers direct cars towards the exits. I crawl out of my car, crouch down, and run to him. His head turns to look behind the car. He sees me. I trip in a pothole and stumble. He's looking straight at me. And then the car starts to move.

There's a voice behind me. "Miss? Are you with a vehicle? Can I get you to return to your car, please?" I run after the Honda as it accelerates away from me. Ted's turned away. A hand grabs my arm. "Miss? You're coming with me."

I yank away from the grip, but it holds firm, fingers digging into my bicep. "Let me go, you motherfucker!" I screech, turning to face the—fuck. Another fucking cop. I drop my fight and sigh, looking to the sky for an explanation. "Can I help you, officer?"

The cop is just another dildo in uniform. He keeps hold of my arm and leads me towards a black and white, its red and blue lights strobing over both of us. People are watching. Some guy comes up to us in a corduroy sports jacket and faded jeans. I wait for him to be reprimanded by the dildo too, but no. "She was running, sir."

Sir? Right. He must be a detective or something.

I give Sir some wide-eyed innocence. "Oh! I never even thought!" I bring my hand to my open mouth to cover my sweet surprise, then slide my fingers down to my lower lip before letting my hand drop.

He looks me up and down, popping his lower jaw from side to side, his mouth slightly open. He's sprouting a dark after-five shadow and has bags under his eyes that make him look two days too tired. As his eyes come back up to my face, his jaw pops forward. He gives his head a little shake. "Why were you running?"

"I'm so sorry! I saw Ted! From high school?" I say it like he should know who Ted is. I'm defaulting to ditsy blond here, despite the red hair. I think it's working.

"Can you tell me where this Ted is now?" asks the dildo, still thinking he's captured a prize.

"He drove away!" I whine, my lower lip sagging into a pout.

Detective Sir waves his arm like he's batting away a mosquito. "She's nothing. Let her go." And he's gone, leaving me with the dildo, who's still holding my arm.

I widen my eyes and give him a full-beam toothy smile. "I guess we're done." I give his hand a squeeze as I remove it from my body. "Ciao!" I walk away, swinging my arms and my hips so he has something to watch.

My car is the only one left in the parking lot that isn't a squad car. Apparently, this has turned into a hostage-taking. Fun. Uniforms direct me out, looking very impatient. Hey. Not my fault.

Ted

My research has taken a real turn for the positive. In November, I ran a range of twelve basic pH levels to figure out the lowest pH *Desulfovibrio desulfuricans* can tolerate before they just die. And they died in all of them. So then, I tried a higher range. And they still died. Then I changed the medium I was growing them in, varying pH at different concentrations of sewage. I finally found an ideal basic environment where they won't die: 18 per cent poo at pH 6.4. Now I get to start feeding them dimethylmercury, a fresh supply of which finally arrived on Wednesday. Tomorrow—I don't care if it's Saturday—I'm going to spend the day with my bugs.

I might just be giddy, but I can't stop laughing. David is in full form. Or should I say, Mrs. Simpson is. Today was his last day downtown. He's got a transfer to the Port Coquitlam location. He starts Monday. But today, Mrs. Simpson wasn't about to let him go so easy.

"'You young people are all over the place these days,'" he says in his Mrs. Simpson falsetto. "'How am I supposed to get my prescriptions filled?'" We're at the strip mall across the street from our building, picking up pizza and beer. David finds a parking spot and, continuing in Mrs. Simpson character, reaches out and squeezes my hand with both his. "'I have another granddaughter, you know. She's young yet, only twelve, but in a few years, she could make you a good little wife. I think she wants to be a doctor,' and the whole time she's doing this," David's caressing my hand in both of his, fingers reaching farther and farther up my arm. I pull my hand away because it tickles.

"I don't suppose you told her . . ."

"No, no, no, no!" David says as we both get out of the car. "She could never handle the fact that I'm already taken. Let alone that I have no interest in prepubescent girls."

"Or girls."

"Or prepubescent anything!"

"So then she asks me if I could come back once a month to fill her prescriptions. And slips a quarter into my hand. And she's winking at me, saying, 'I could make it worth your while, honey.'"

He's so funny. I'm laughing. It's Friday. Life is good. We

go to the pizza joint at the plaza and order the meat lovers and then head next door to pick up our beer. On the way out of the liquor store, he stops, reaches into his pocket, and hands me a quarter. He winks. "I can make this worth your while, honey."

I double over with laughter.

We put the beer in the trunk and go back to get our pizza. I love the wind-down of a Friday night. Another week is done. We'll watch a movie, eat crap, and talk about the future. Some nights, when it's nice, we go for a walk or a swim. Tonight, it's *Beetlejuice*—worth a second watch because it's hilarious. And we also have a vacation to plan. We're actually thinking about doing the West Coast Trail. It would be a week-long hike along the west coast of Vancouver Island. Don made plans to do it with his partner this year and invited us along.

Carrying the pizza out, warm cardboard on my arms, the wind is scented with ocean salt. "We should go to the beach—"

The parking lot explodes into sirens and lights. People are rushing to their cars. David takes me by the elbow and guides me to ours, the pizza sliding around in its box. He opens the door and puts me in the passenger side like I'm being arrested, hand on my head and pushing me down. Then he's beside me in the driver's seat.

"What the fuck?" I say, pizza still cradled in my arms, giggling with nerves as I look around the parking lot. Police cars are everywhere. Police are everywhere.

"Sorry, I guess it was instinct?"

"We have no reason to run from the police!"

David chuckles. "True." He's watching the rear-view mirror. "But we do have reason to run from whatever is causing five police cars to show up."

I turn around so I can look out the back window. Three officers have positioned themselves at the entry to the liquor store. Others are starting to direct traffic. "Wow, we just missed whatever's going on in there." Our hands reach for each other and squeeze. By now, everyone is in their cars, and we're being directed to the exit leading to Marmont Street. I see some motion to the side and it's someone running across the parking lot. An officer is chasing them.

"Go!" I say, looking straight ahead, reaching up to lock my door. "One of them's escaped!" We merge into the line of evacuees. When I look back, the officer has the person, a tiny woman, by the arm and is leading them away. I feel a little tingle of fear across my pecs.

David looks in the rear-view. "Huh," he says.

"Huh," I grunt in return.

"Not her?" he asks.

"No. Definitely not her," I lie.

May

I'm eating a donair and drinking Jack Daniel's tonight. Back here in the alley, you'd never know all that action is going on across the street. Craning my neck over the dashboard, I look up at what I've decided is Ted's place, then flop back and take another slug. The warm Jack tastes like piss. I should have got some ice.

My pager's buzzing, but I'm not leaving him tonight. That means I'm a no-show for nasally Norman. He's new last weekend. Rebooked after I fucked his brains out. No big loss. He didn't tip and whined about his divorce the entire time. If I were his wife, I would have dumped him in a week, not twenty years later. How can anybody stand that voice?

No. Tonight, I'm going to watch over my boy. Clearly, David isn't doing a good job.

Ted

David's got the weekend shift, so he's dropping me off. We eat breakfast together at the little table on the balcony. Our unit faces east, so we get the morning sun, and it feels almost hot in the little glassed-in deck. I stand up and lean against the rail, looking down at the alley. Cars are parked bumper to bumper across from the building. There's only one parking spot underground per unit, and most of the units have at least two people in them, and if they don't, they do on weekends. And everyone has a car. I think David and I are the only couple in the world who still commute together. He comes up behind me and wraps his arms around my waist.

"Contemplating suicide?" he breaths into my neck. "Cuz I know last night will be hard to top, but I don't think that's a reason to end it all."

I lean into him, willing my shoulders to relax.

"I don't know what got into you, but I'm willing to pick up a police scanner if that's the kind of thing that gets you there." He kisses me.

I turn to him, but I can't look into his eyes. Last night was crazy. I attacked him with everything I had. Before the pizza. Before we even got through the door. I needed to feel him in me. Solid, strong. Constant. Safe.

"Hey." He brushes the hair from my forehead, kissing the bare skin. "I'm kidding."

I hug him tightly, loving how my body fits into his. Then I push him away. "I'm just excited for today!" I say, prancing towards the door. "Dimethylmercury and I have a big date."

"Wow. I'm jealous."

"C'mon. Let's get out of here." And I am at the door, slipping on my shoes, my backpack shouldered.

May

I fucking passed out. My brain is wrapped in razor blades and rubber bands, and all the windows are steamed up like a bad dream. It's daylight. I'm shivering. Wiping off the windshield with the sleeve of my shirt, I see the little turquoise Civic motoring away down the alley. I start the car, slam it into Drive, and accelerate to catch up. But then, I slow the fuck down. They don't know this car. I should keep it that way. What's left of the twenty-six of Jack rolls out from under the seat. My stomach rolls with it. Jesus Christ, it's only nine o'clock!

Creeping the car out of the alley just enough to see them turn left toward the freeway, I reach for the bottle and chug down the last quarter. At least it's cold. They're headed into the city. I catch up at Brunette and slip in their lane a couple of cars back. The shivers fade as the alcohol and car heater kick in, and my shoulders start to relax. I grope for my sunglasses on the dashboard. The mountains scream white, black, and mist against the spring blue sky. I hope we're not going for a run.

Ted

I told David Tippy would be here, so I wouldn't be alone. But Tippy doesn't actually come in on Saturdays until around one o'clock, so I have two hours alone.

I love the lab when it's empty. The silence. The sticky sound of sneakers on tile floors. The succinct click of a cupboard door. The dry and true clink of glass flasks when you take them out of the autoclave tray. But nothing beats the Fine Young Cannibals when you've got a tedious job to do. I pop in a cassette and blast the tunes.

I get the fume hood set up, lay out the vials, and get the 18 per cent culture from the incubator and snap on a double layer of latex gloves. Then I head down the hall, with the key, to the locked fridge where the dimethylmercury is stored. "She Drives Me Crazy" follows me down the corridor, and I get a little boogie in my walk, chiming in with the chorus.

May

Campus is empty. I've actually had to park on the other side of the lot to be discreet. I'm using my binoculars to watch. And oh my God! You'd think they were never going to see each other again. I can see their faces pressed against each other. They've been in the car for five minutes. What the fuck? David is so clingy. He must know he's a second choice. Finally, Ted gets out of the car, and David drives away. Don't worry, asshole. I got it from here.

It looks like I finally get him to myself. My sweet boy. I rest my head against the car window as I watch him go into the Life Sciences building. It makes my heart ache to see him walk away from me all the time. He never looks back anymore. I wait. The little buzz I got from the Jack is fading back into a hangover. My stomach churns. Digging through the pile of crap on the passenger seat, I find a bag of Twizzlers and stuff a whole licorice in my mouth. It's cold and hard, and I think I'm going to choke. But the gag feels good. It brings tears to my eyes. And I know what I have to do.

Today's the day we make it happen.

I reach under the dashboard and wrap my hand around the cold metal piece tucked in the ledge. I've started to carry it with me. There's just too many creepy Johns. I realized the gun wasn't keeping anyone safe stuffed under my mattress. I wonder if he's going to fight me.

Chewing the licorice soft, I rub the barrel against my

cheek. Its smooth chill soothes the pain in my head. Sex would be good right now. Maybe we can do it in the lab. I smile, shoving the gun down the front of my pants.

Ted

I work, going through the motions. Pipette a sample into a vial, pop the lid down, spin the vial, pop the lid up, pipette a sample out, and squirt it into the next dilution. The little brown bottle of dimethylmercury is tucked safely at the back of the fume hood.

My breath is moist against the face mask. The fume hood roars its own storm, so I've turned the music up, but I can't resist bopping to the incessant funk of "I'm Not the Man I Used to Be" as it rocks to its conclusion. The music fades to a close, and there's a click. My instant thought is the tape has ended, but then the tin beat of "I'm Not Satisfied" begins.

She's here.

May

I press back into a doorway when the music starts. I can hear him singing, and when I peek out, he's walking down the hall. He might even have a dance in his step. And the song choice? Huh. I slip into the lab and step into the little office just inside the door. I angle myself so I am hidden by the door but I can still see through the window that looks out over the room.

When he comes back, he's got a Styrofoam box that he takes to the big chamber near the window. He turns on a switch, and a fan starts up, real loud. He turns down the volume on the ghetto blaster that sits on the shelf behind the chamber and puts on some safety glasses. Not a good look.

Then he opens the Styrofoam box and takes out a little brown bottle. Holding it up to the light, he shakes it and then puts it at the side of the chamber. His body blocks whatever else he's doing. But after a while, it looks like a dance. He reaches, moves sideways, moves the other way, and then reaches again. It's a little mesmerizing.

I haven't been this close to him since our run. I remember how he felt, even when he was struggling against me. His smell, the sure grip of his hands, his breath on my skin. I want it again.

I gently take the gun from my waistband, enjoying its weight in my hand, and I walk slowly into the lab. My heart is racing; I'm surprised he can't hear it, but he doesn't turn around. He never turns around anymore. It's like I don't exist to him. I raise the gun and pull back the hammer. Its click echoes into the room. The music has stopped, and he stops moving, but still, he doesn't turn to me. Another song begins. The tin beat matches my pulse. Does he even know I'm here? I am about to scream his name when suddenly he's coming at me. This is it! He loves me—he's going to kiss me—we're going to fuck right here on the floor. I lower the gun and open my arms. Something hits my shoulder, and I feel a cold splash on my cheek. I aim the gun again.

He's pushing me down. The gun flies from my hand and slides across the floor. I open my mouth for the kiss. He's pressing my face with latex-covered hands; they slip across my cheek and down my neck. I arch my back, wanting more, but then he's up and running away from me.

Ted

I panic and grab the bottle from the back of the fume hood, popping the lid open as I turn to her. I fling the entire thing at her face. It bounces off her shoulder onto the floor. And rolls away. She aims the gun again, and I rush at her, pushing her onto the spilled vial, mopping the floor with her body. *Fuck you, May*. Tears of rage roll down my cheeks. *Fuck you. Fuck you.* She's moaning, and I realize there's some wetness on her cheek. I smear it into her skin with my glove, wipe my hands on her shirt, and push her back into the ground as I rush to the safety shower, ripping off my gloves, my glasses, my lab coat, and my shirt as I turn it on, letting the cold water drench over me. Oh God. What have I done?

"Ted!" My name is coming from two directions. Tippy is stepping through the doorway from the hall. May is stumbling towards me, a wild smile on her face. She's pulling off her T-shirt.

"No! Tippy! Stay away. Call the police. The fire department. Don't come in! I've spilled it—I've spilled it everywhere!"

"Jesus!" Tippy says, hands up in defence, backing away.

"Get help!" I cry. I scan the floor for the gun. Where the fuck did it go?

And then she's in the water beside me, hanging onto me. I slip on the linoleum, and she's on top of me. Oh. There's the gun, in her hand. Water pours over us, running from the back of her head, across her cheeks, and dripping off her chin. I scramble out from under her, crawling across the floor. And there's fire in my leg. It's dimethylmercury, burning through my skin. No. My leg refuses to support me. I've been shot. She's shot me, and I'm bleeding like crazy. I smell sulphur and iron. I fight the puke rising in my throat.

Inhaling as much air as I can take, I hold it in for a lung-bursting beat, then exhale slowly. My eyes lock on her. I will not let her win. Not this time.

May

I reach across the floor for the gun. But then, a shower? My God, look at him! His naked wet skin. He just wants to play! "Ted!" I call his name, and it echoes across the room. But it isn't an echo. It's that black guy who fucked Kisha. I run to Ted, pulling my tank top over my head, unclipping my bra. Everything feels slow motion.

Ted calls across the room to him. "Call the police! The fire department!"

What? Fuck you, Teddy. Get the fuck over yourself. I stoop down to get the gun from the floor. Diving at him under the shower, I wrap my arms around him, pressing my bare tits against his skin.

"C'mon, Teddy. Stop this!" I'm crying as we fall to the ground, me on top of him. Just the way I like it. Water and tears are pouring down my face, hot and cold. "Please, baby." But he slithers out from under me. I point the gun and pull the trigger until it releases. The kickback slams through my arm and lands with a sharp jolt to my shoulder.

I hit his leg. He doesn't scream. Or anything. He just looks surprised. He holds the wounded leg straight as he reaches for a countertop and tries to pull himself up. My jeans are still on, cold and wet. My hair drips and clings in chunks to my face. My breasts are taut with goosebumps, nipples hard. Hangover? Gone. Nothing like a cold shower to clear the head. He isn't going anywhere. I smile and lift the gun as I walk towards him, loving the rush of power. I could do this for a living.

He mutters as he struggles to stand. I kick his good leg out from under him, and he falls onto his back. It's pretty cute, him lying there in a puddle of blood. So red and thick. It's in the shape of a heart, and the streak from where his foot slid looks like an arrow. Oh, cupid.

I stand over top of him, pointing the gun at his chest. "I could kill you right now," I say, calmly, my finger sliding along the smooth curve of the trigger.

Ted

My leg won't bend. I try to pull myself up against a lab bench, using all my upper body strength and my one good leg. She comes to me, gun aimed. And she's smiling.

"Get away from me, May." I'm almost up. I got her. She will die. She has dimethylmercury all over her face. She probably drank the stuff. She kicks my good leg, and I fall onto my back, cracking my head against the concrete floor. Blackness hovers at my temples as the pain of impact crawls up my skull. My mind flashes back to her kitchen, something hitting the back of my head. No. I close my eyes and shake my head clear. When I open them again, I start kicking with my good leg before I realize she's standing over me, gun pointed to my chest. She stumbles as my leg makes contact with her knee. I grab at her wrist and yank her to the floor just as the gun fires. The prospecting sound of metal hitting concrete rings beside my head.

She's on top of me again. Her teeth bared, her eyes bloodshot. She waves the gun in front of my face and snarls, "You. Love. Me."

She's pressing the full weight of her body onto the burning hole in my leg. The gun is still in her hand, but she seems focused on applying pressure. Is she trying to save me?

"No!" I whisper, hoarse and weak.

"From the day I saw you with that cat," she spits.

I shake my head, refusing to remember that lonely boy she befriended. I never loved her.

"You needed me," she says, jutting her chin forwards. "You've always needed me."

"I've never needed you, May," I say, my teeth gritted in anger. "Never."

"Yes, you have!" She looks across the room, pressing her knee harder into my leg. "And I've given you my whole life. You owe me."

May

I watch his pupils disappear under his eyelids, so just the whites are showing. Like a zombie. My finger is still on the trigger. Maybe he passes out and I— What? Drag him? To my car? I'm just winging it here. I thought this would be so much easier. I thought the gun would at least slow him down and make him see reason. But he has no interest in working this out. I can see that now. I guess the question is, do I?

He's kicking at me, his one leg going up and sideways. Is he having convulsions? His leg makes contact with the back of my knee. I'm falling. He has my hand and pulls me onto him. My elbow bangs on the floor. The gun fires. My skin tingles as the bullet pierces the tile beside his head like a hammer on a rock, then bounces away. Concrete dust whitens a patch of his hair. The fear rushing through me is like slow motion. I realize I can't' kill him. I watch his face, his beautiful blue eyes staring back at me, cold and angry. His perfect lips pressed so tightly together they are white. He can't hate me.

I feel the warmth of his blood on my knee and I press against his wound. The anger washes from his face as he winces. There you go, baby. I got you. "You. Love. Me." I spit the words into his face.

"No!" He can barely say the word because he knows it's a lie.

"From the day I saw you with that cat." I remember him, with that stupid paint roller wiping shit on the cat. My funny, lonely boy. How bad he wanted a friend. "You needed me.'" I remember how he followed me around when we were kids, desperate for me to look at him. "You've always needed me."

And he denies it. "I never needed you, May," he whines. "Never."

"Yes, you have!" How can he say that? My whole life, I've protected him. Protected him from bullies, from his own stupid ideas, from his homosexuality, from David. I've tried so hard to protect him from David. Even last night at the parking lot, I almost got arrested because David was putting him at risk. I grind my knee into his bullet hole. I want to hurt him more. I want to shoot him again. I look away, trying to gain control over the fire inside me. Stopping myself from slamming his head into the concrete floor. "And I've given you my whole life!" Damn him. I'm fucking crying again. I collapse on his bare chest, the gun wedged under his chin. I feel him tense up. His heart beats in my ear. My skin on his. I close my eyes and take a breath.

Somewhere under the screams inside my head, voices are shouting. We have to go. God, I'm tired. I take a deep breath and lift myself up again, grabbing a handful of his golden hair. "Let's go, Teddy," I say.

I get on my knees and reach for the counter, still keeping a grip on his hair. He turns his head in a weird angle as he uses his elbows to prop himself so he can twist around. He feels like a puppet under my hand. I smile.

Pain. Sharp and sudden on my wrist, and the gun is gone from my hand. The weight of Ted's body disappears from under the fistful of hair. It's all torn from his skull. No. Someone is squeezing my wrist so tight my fingers let go of him. People in plastic clothes and masks, breathing like Darth Vader, surround us.

Ted

She has the gun wedged under my chin, and her head is rested on my chest. Her skin on mine is oddly intimate. Her cold wet hair. Her warm breath across my bare nipple. The cold metal barrel pressing against my jaw. Every muscle in my body is tight. I try not to breathe in case it sets off the trigger. Is she falling asleep? My heart bangs loud over the din of my fear. And then she's up, pulling me by the hair. I feel the sharpness of single strands popping from their roots as I scramble to stand.

Suddenly, May is screaming, and I am in someone's arms, and there is lightness as my hair is freed and I float through the air. I hear the crinkle of paper and realize whoever is carrying me is wearing a hazmat suit. They take me back to the safety shower. The water is running warm now. Someone holds me up, and someone else pumps biosoap onto my hands. I scrub at my hands, my hair, my chest.

May watches me from across the room. She looks like she's about to pounce, but two people in hazmat suits hold her by the elbows. Her hands are behind her back, handcuffed, I assume. The door to the hallway is shut, and I can see the silhouette of a police officer's cap through its window. I turn away, lifting my face to the water.

One of the hazmat guys points at my legs. The other one comes at me with a pair of scissors and starts cutting the leg of my pants, the one with the hole in it, dyed red from the thigh down. When he passes the bullet wound, I feel like I'm going to throw up. He snips around it as though he does this kind of thing every day. He cuts through the waistband, and the pants fall around my ankles. A hand under each armpit supports me so I can hop free, completely naked. The water continues to flow, washing away blood as it drips, leaving just the red, meaty hole. I can't stop looking at it. Somehow, the pain feels like it isn't part of me anymore. I wonder if May is still watching. She would love this.

Finally, they turn off the water and lead me to dry ground, where someone hands me a towel and someone else starts drying my back. I look behind me. She's gone.

May

They carry Ted over to the shower. He sudses himself, his hair, his throat, his face. He looks my way, but it's like he doesn't see me. I press towards him, fighting the grip of the freaks holding me. I'm handcuffed. The freaks try to take me away, but I fight them, kicking at their ankles. I lose my balance, and they drag me backwards to the door.

When we get out into the hall, they slow down, let me get my feet under me, and turn me around. It's still daylight. Of course, it's still morning, but it feels like it should be midnight after so much blood and passion. I feel like I've just had an orgasm, my heart still crashing around in my chest, my body aching to hold my lover in after-sex bliss. My skin feels hot, despite the coldness of my wet jeans. A sunbeam from the main doors is the only light, hitting the tiles like a spotlight on a stage. We walk towards it.

They take me into a lab, just like Ted's, and lead me to a shower in the corner of the room.

"Take your clothes off," a woman's voice demands from under the weird suit. I didn't expect a girl under that getup. She unlocks my cuffs. She has a hell of a grip.

I smile, raising my eyebrows. "Really?" I ask, undoing my bra—this could be hot.

"You're contaminated," the other woman answers as a blast of freezing-cold water dumps over my head.

"What?" I shout. Contaminated? What does that mean? Because I'm a hooker? I peel off my jeans, but it's a fight because they're soaking wet, and the hazmat girls are still holding my arms. They take over, pulling down the thick denim and stepping on the legs so I can pull my feet through, stumbling. No worry about falling over though; they have hold of my arms tight.

The bitch on my right pumps soap all over me, and the other one rubs it into a lather. The slippery vinyl of her wet gloves slides over my hair and my face. She sticks her fingers into my ears and nose. The suds get into my eyes and burn. I try to shake her off, but her partner takes my hair and pulls my head back. Scrub-bitch works her way down my body, slipping between my legs when she gets there and sliding her fingers around my cunt.

That's it. I'm done with this. I bash my head into the bitch who's holding my hair. As she stumbles back, I slam my knee into scrub-bitch's face. The women fall to the floor, bringing me with them. The soap is everywhere, and they've let go of me. I'm on my knees. I get one leg up from under me and start to stand, but a hand grabs my other ankle, and I'm down again.

The water is off, and two more people are on me. My face smashes into the tile floor, and I taste blood as my teeth cut into my lips. "Ow!" I whine, "Take it easy! I slipped. I'm not going anywhere, I swear!"

The weight of my attackers lightens. Hands grip my arms and lift me to my feet. My shoulders feel like they're tearing out of the sockets. I whimper another, "Ow," keeping my head lowered. I get dried off. Then they're forcing my arms into a lab coat. My cuffs are back on. Someone throws a blanket over my shoulders. How nice.

"Okay, she's good to go," scrub-bitch says. I look up to see she's removed her hood and is peeling off her paper suit. Underneath, she's wearing a uniform. She's a cop. Huh. This is quite the to-do.

Two more uniforms come and lead me away. Both are nice, young, calendar-worthy rookies. They talk to each other as the lead me toward the door, laughing about some fun they had over the weekend, like I'm not even worth their attention.

Outside the building, the cold of morning still clings to the shadows. I'm covered in goosebumps. I wonder what their plan is.

"I have to pee," I say when we get outside. The oldest ploy in the world.

Ted

They put me on a stretcher to take me to the ambulance, which seems ludicrous considering I just fought for my life and then had a shower. The pain in my leg seems to brighten everything: the muffled sound of footsteps on tile as they carry me down the hall, the familiar squeak of the doors on the east entry as they open. I look around and see May being led across campus towards a patrol car. Panic rushes through my pulse despite the fact there's a cop on each of her arms. They stop, turn around, and start walking back to the Life Sciences building.

One cop is smiling. The other throws his head back in laughter.

"No!" I scream, sitting upright on the stretcher, but my scream is like a bad dream; it has no voice. They disappear back into the building.

May

They hand me off to scrub-bitch, and she puts me in a stall and pushes me down onto the toilet. I can hear the rookies out in they hall, still chatting and giggling like little girls.

She takes the blanket off my shoulders. "Go," she says,

standing in front of me with her hands on her hips like she's all that, watching in between my legs.

I pee. What the hell? I might as well do this on an empty bladder. I look at her all wide eyed and helpless. "Wipe me, please?"

She pulls off a wad of toilet paper from the roll and squats down in front of me. She reaches between my legs, and I launch myself overtop of her. A crack echoes off the walls. Again, I'm winging it here, ready to wrap my legs around her neck. Something. But there's no fight. She just slumps to the floor, and I ride her down, tucking my head so I land on my shoulder before I hit the floor. Seriously? This is too easy.

The cramped stall gives me leverage to turn myself around. Keys. Wow. Every movie I ever watched comes to mind. Do all handcuff keys fit all handcuffs? I'm on my knees on the hard, concrete floor, my face pressed against the stall wall. I lean sideways towards her, trying not to tip over, groping with my hands tied behind me, until I get my fingers wrapped around her belt. I follow it along her waist, trying to remember if her key ring was on her left or her right side, the side I'm on. But this is her gun side. And that's useless with my hands cuffed behind my back.

Key ring. Really? Maybe there is no key ring. Maybe that's just on TV.

This is ridiculous. I'm running out of time. I shuffle over to her other side and bend to reach for her belt again. Gravity wins this time though, and I am lying on her, the back of my head on her shoulder. But my hands are actually touching a cold metal ring. She moves a bit. Fuck.

My fingers find four keys. All big ones, for doors or something. And a whistle, I think. The handcuff key would be tiny and flat, like the ones for toy handcuffs. Oh, come on. It has to be here. I give the ring a shake and fumble through them again with my other hand. The whistle has a pointy end.

I wonder. Maybe I can pick the lock. I find the keyhole on one of the cuffs and stick the pointy end of the whistle in. The cuff pops open. Wow, I'm good!

I feel her body tense and her arms move. She starts to moan. I slam my elbow into her temple, and the tension disappears. I quickly flip around and get the other cuff unlocked. Huh. The whistle is actually a key. Oh well, I could've picked it if I needed to.

I'm out of the stall. Window. I need a window. Gun. Oh shit, her gun. I should get that.

A man's voice calls in through the entrance, "You okay in there, Margaret?"

Okay, forget the gun. I climb onto the sink counter and reach up to the window, which is one of those wind-open ones. I crank it as fast as I can and use the handle to pull myself up and peer through the hole.

"Margaret?" the voice calls again.

Using all my strength, I jump to the windowsill, launching myself into the open space. My heart sinks. I've landed on the crank arm. The metal spans the middle of the opening and juts into my stomach. Fuck. I try to squeeze myself through one side.

"Hey! Stop!" There's a uniform running towards me. He's got his gun out and aims.

I freeze. I'm looking straight into his eyes. He won't shoot. I'm not armed. His eyes are golden brown. A nice little cutie pie. Flirting is definitely my best option here. I smile at him and shake my head. "Yeah, you got me." I give a shrug, shoulders to my ears, head tilted, and a bashful, wide-eyed blink. There's a splitting sound behind me, and suddenly I'm falling. My first instinct is to grab at the windowsill, but I stop myself and let the fall happen. I land on my back, hard enough to slam the wind out of me.

Sucking giant hollow breaths, I crawl along the gravel towards some bushes. Above me, the window swings open. Cutie pie has his head propped against it to hold it open. His gun arm is hanging down the wall. "Stop! Freeze!" He's clearly new to this. He should've taken his shot while he had the chance. I step into a sprint. Fuck the bushes. I'm out of here!

Ted

David's here. His eyes are red rimmed and sunken. He would never cry in front of me. Not right now. His hand is beside mine on the cool sheets. I have an IV stuck in my arm, and the nurse is shaving my leg around the bullet hole. She's brisk and only speaks in efficient bites. I get the sense she might not approve of homosexuality.

There's been no news about May. When I saw those two officers walking her back to the building, they just looked too . . . nonchalant, like they didn't think May was anything to be concerned about. I tried to warn them.

"Could you"—she tries to hide her frustration—"maybe hold still?"

"Sorry," I say. I can't stop shaking. It's like I'm shivering from cold. But I don't feel cold. I tense up my leg and press it against the bed, hoping the tension will stop the shaking. "Will I be on crutches?" I ask.

"I should think for a bit, yes," she says.

I nod, listening to the final scrapes as she finishes up the dry shave.

"There. You're done." There's a sting overtop of the burning of the bullet wound as she wipes off the shaved skin with an alcohol pad. "They'll be in in a minute to take you to surgery." Then she turns to David. "I'm not sure how long it will be. You can wait in the lounge, or if you want to go home

—"

"No," David snips. I want to laugh at how controlled his voice is. He has zero patience for homophobes.

"Hmph," she grunts as she whips open the privacy curtain and leaves the room.

There are three other beds in the room. Two are empty, and one bed is a pile of messed-up sheets and blankets. I assume its occupant is wandering the halls somewhere.

I look to David and put my hand over his. His face is blank. I give his hand a squeeze, wanting to tell him I got her. Wanting to tell him she will die a slow, painful death. But I can't. To the rest of the world, this was all an accident. Nobody can know.

He blinks, and a tear wets his lashes. He looks away. "I shouldn't have left you."

I laugh. "Really? How could you possibly know what would happen?" I press my hands into the bed, trying to lift myself to a more erect position.

He jumps up and pushes a button on the bedrail. It lifts my legs. He pushes another button, and it lifts the top end of the bed. "Shit!" he mutters.

I'm laughing and wincing as he folds me in half. "Ow! Please stop!" I whisper.

"The down buttons are on the outside," a gravelly voice mutters. It's the empty bed occupant, making his way in a slipper-padded shuffle to his corner of the room. His IV stand rolls beside him like a dance partner.

David looks at me and shakes his head. A grin pours across his face, and it lifts a bit of the shadow that's been haunting the corners of my brain. We're safe, for now.

Or not. I look up to see Constable Ryan coming through the door. She isn't in uniform. A tall, skinny blond guy trails behind her, not Constable Rickland. "Hi, Ted," she says softly and then nods to David, "Hi."

I smile. "Constable Ryan? What—"

She interrupts me. "May got away."

"She what?" David snaps to a stand.

The mattress seems to lose its support as my body deflates. I nod. "Okay."

"I heard the situation over the radio. I knew it was you." She stands at the end of the bed, hand on her holster. "We'll have someone posted outside your door of course." She shakes her head, and her hands drop to her sides. "This shouldn't have happened."

"Damn right, it shouldn't have happened! What the fuck is wrong with you people?" David takes a step towards Ryan. The blond takes a step towards David.

"David, no," I say calmly. I shrug, as though it's nothing. "I saw them taking her back into the building. I tried to call out, but . . ." I shrug again, remembering the weakness of my shout. "I knew she'd try to pull something. I should have told you." I haven't told him the rest—that I bathed her face in dimethylmercury. I'm not sure if I'm ashamed or proud.

May

I stick out like a sore thumb. Whoever came up with that anyway? Sore thumb. I'm in a lab coat, naked underneath, walking around a university campus. Huh. I guess things could be worse. I could be in a shopping mall. But I feel awfully white, glow-in-the-dark white against all the green of these trees and bushes. Do I lose the coat? My car is out of the question. It's in the Life Sciences parking lot, surrounded by uniforms and squad cars. I slip deeper back into the little park only to pop out onto another road. A patrol car crosses at the end of the block, and I run across the road into a parkade.

A couple in scrubs walks by me. The girl gives me a little smile and nod. The guy, a stethoscope around his neck, is too involved in what he's saying to even notice I'm there. I keep walking. Three kids pile out of an old Mazda. The slamming of the car doors echoes on the concrete wall. One kid is wearing a lab coat; they all have backpacks. If I had pants on, I'd fit right in.

Maybe I should take one of these cars? I stand in the middle of the lane, deciding which one to go for. I'm startled by the slam of another door. It's a tiny little Asian girl. Her head is down as she walks away from her car. I approach her.

"Hey?" She looks up, surprised. Her glasses are Coke-bottle thick. "Do you know what time it is?" I say, pointing to my wrist. She nods, sliding her sleeve up to show me her watch. I realize she probably doesn't even speak English. Stupid cow. I reach for her wrist, ready to slam her to the floor, when a voice calls out. And then, there are two big dorky Chinese guys on either side of her. They speak rapid-fire Chinese. She smiles and giggles, and they all walk away.

Fine. I slip in between cars, trying door handles. *Click.* Nothing. *Click.* Nothing. Six cars later and I know I'm going to have to break a window. I look around for something heavy, which is stupid. Like there's boulders scattered around parkades. I shake my head at myself and head to the back side of the building. A vehicle is coming up behind me. I turn to see if they're worth taking on just as its siren blips. And I'm running. Tires squeal on the concrete behind me. I leap over a wall and land hard on some bark and shrubs.

A voice calls over the police car's PA system, "Wait! Stop!"

Well, that was well rehearsed. Of course I'll stop, now that you asked nice. I run across the road in front of me to a path between buildings. I get to a main road and slow down. There's a few cars, and I take my time crossing. I see the Earth

Sciences building—I'm not that far from the beach.

I smile. Wreck Beach even. Clothing optional. The perfect place to lose a lab coat.

Ted

Everything is light and shadows. Like opening your eyes under water. Pain. It radiates from my leg down into my toes and up, stopping cleanly at my hip. The clarity of what hurts and what doesn't—my healthy leg—makes acid rise from my stomach. I retch, and a hand comes behind my head, gently lifting me to cold metal on my lips. It's David.

"Uck. That's a fine way to come to." He laughs, gingerly walking the tray to the sink across the room. He dumps it, rinses it, and returns to me with a smile. I don't smile back. I'm just holding back whatever is left in my stomach.

"They said you might do that. It's from the anaesthetic." He pats my shoulder. "I'll go let Nurse Ratched know you're up."

There's a chuckle from across the room. "Jack Nicholson is a god," my roommate mumbles, catching the reference to *One Flew Over the Cuckoo's Nest*. David goes to shut the curtain, but then the roommate calls out, "How're you doing there, young fella?" I put my hand out to stop David and mouth, "No."

The distraction seems to make my nausea fade. I grunt, swallow down bile, and then squawk, "I'm okay." David gives me an are-you-sure-you're-okay look, and I nod. Then I puke again, no tray to catch it this time.

"Fuck," David says as he looks around for something to wipe me up with, raises his arms in despair, and leaves the room. "I'll go get help."

"You don't sound okay." My roommate chuckles again. "First bullet, huh?"

I retch again, but nothing comes up. I feel the puke cooling on my hospital gown.

"Well, aren't you a fine mess." A nurse walks in, followed by David. She's not Nurse Ratched. "Okay." She puts a hand on my forehead, checking my pulse at my wrist at the same time. Nodding briskly, but with a kind smile, she says, "Let's get you cleaned up."

May

As soon as I step onto the beach, I unbutton the lab coat and let it drop. Bodies are scattered along the sand and leaning against the bleached logs that sit above the shoreline. Some are dressed —a bikini bottom here and there or a very loose tank top— but most are completely bare, lying on towels in the sand or walking along the water's edge. There's only a few people in the water. It's still morning. The true heat of summer doesn't come down until the afternoon, and that's when people really hit the water.

It's odd to be so naked and have no one staring at you. To not have to worry about what will happen. I'll have to come by here sometime when I'm not being chased by the cops. I look behind me and walk to the water. The ocean breeze makes my nipples hard and my skin break out in goosebumps, just like in the lab. And the water is fucking freezing. I force myself to walk out to waist height and then squat down so only my shoulders are visible. Then I turn around so I can scan the beach.

People are arriving in swarms. Coming down the pathway, with bags and blankets. They stake out a spot on the sand and start stripping down to just their sunglasses. Most are old. And there are more men than women of course. My skin feels like it's stiffening from the cold. Finally, a woman stands up from her blanket, drops her sunglasses, and heads for the water. We have a swimmer. I watch her as I head to shore. She's probably going into the water to pee. Whatever. I hope she was wearing a dress. I exit the water as she gets her toes wet. She's a bit chunky, and her tits have a tired-looking sag that says they're going to deflate any day now. Not a beautiful woman.

I walk to her blanket and turn to see where she is before I bend down and start rooting through the pile of clothes beside her beach bag. Cut-offs and a black T-shirt. Fuck. The cut-offs will never fit me. But the T-shirt is big. Big enough. I grab it and continue walking. When I get to the path, I slip it over my head. It comes down a few inches past my ass, and voila, I have a dress. It's actually longer than some of the dresses I use for work. It's probably even sexy. I look down at my chest and realize it's got the Pink Floyd prism on it, from *The Dark Side of the Moon*. Cool. It isn't until I get to the parking lot that my feet start feeling raw. The water softened them, and its salt stings into all the little scratches and splinters I got from running. I love how adrenaline can make pain go away. I lift my face to the sun and let the heat soak into the black of my T-shirt. Now what? I can probably catch a cab home.

Then arms wrap around me from behind, and my body goes stiff as I recognize his smell.

"Not hard to miss that hot little body. What a nice surprise," Jake growls into the top of my head. "I guess little Kisha was more than just a good fuck."

"Jake," I whisper, as though saying his name quietly will make him less real.

He squeezes below my ribs until my feet lift off the ground. I can't catch my breath. "How've you been, sweetheart?"

We move towards the back of a faded-blue Town Car with Washington plates. It's backed into the parking spot so that the trunk is kind of hidden.

One arm lets go as he digs in his pocket for keys. I slam both my elbows into him and kick a heel up between his legs, but he just squeezes harder with the arm that grips. His free hand grabs a handful of hair and slams my head onto the trunk. Pains stings my eye as the bones in my cheek flatten against the hot dry metal. He lifts me off and pops the trunk. I start to scream, but his hand covers my mouth. Why is the fucking parking lot so empty? And then he just picks me up and stuffs me in, slamming the trunk on my arms and legs repeatedly until I pull them in. The trunk closes, and everything goes black.

"Jesus fuck, you put up a good fight, little girl," I hear him mutter. He taps on the metal above me a couple of times, and then the car door squeaks open and slams closed. The engine starts, and some DJ over the radio announces how hot it's going to get today. We're moving. There's cracks of light where the rust has broken through, and exhaust fumes seep in from somewhere. I feel like I'm going to puke.

Ted

I guess I'm here for a couple of nights.

David's gone to find us some real food. The mashed potatoes and Salisbury hockey puck they brought me at supper didn't seem fit for the kind of day we'd had, and I was craving a donair. Gunshot and all, my wish, apparently, is his command.

Don comes in with a miniature orange tree. The foliage hides his face until he sets it down on the windowsill. We smile at each other, tight lipped and tense. He cocks his head. "You good?" he asks. And I know this is how he will look at me for a long time. Waiting for something to show. Not wanting to say it out loud.

I just nod.

"You look like shit," he says.

I bite my lip and shrug. "Surgery. Bullet. All that." I scratch the back of my head, look back up at him and say, "I puked my guts out."

His face darkens with concern. But I shake my head and say softly, "You know that's not a symptom."

"That was fucking suicide, Ted," he says flatly. "The whole vial is gone," he continues in a whisper.

I raise my hands and smile. "I'm fine! Besides, they're starting chelation therapy tomorrow. DMPS. Two weeks. And who knows? I might get to puke my guts out some more." DMPS is the standard for getting mercury out of the system. It binds to the metal, and you pee it out. It binds to other things too, like copper, zinc, and magnesium, which a body needs to survive, so I'll be getting a fistful of supplements to go along with the DMPS. And it can cause nausea and vomiting. Can't wait.

"Don," David says, walking into the room with a bag of food. He puts the bag down and shakes Don's hand. "How are you doing?"

"I'm good," Don says, pulling the handshake into a hug. "What about you? This guy's just trouble, isn't he?" He looks at me over David's shoulder, questioning. Don steps out of the hug and squeezes David's shoulders, then turns his attention to the bag of donairs. "Donair King? Good call."

"Sorry about the lab," I say, peeling back the foil and paper wrapper on my meat sandwich.

Don shrugs. "Facilities was right on it. They're actually shutting down the entire floor for a few days to do decon." He shakes his head. "As far as the lab goes, they might replace the flooring."

I grimace, my mouth full of food. Guilt gnaws at my brain. I know Tippy was in the middle of some experiments, and Stephen had big plans of running some over the summer while he didn't have to TA.

"I think they're moving us into Monashie's lab. Tippy and Stephen will be thrilled, of course. A week off and then Patsy and Andrea." Patsy and Andrea are first-year grad students. They look like a pair of Barbie dolls.

"Ah, right. But how will Patsy and Andrea feel about it?"

Don just shakes his head and smiles. "And we're taking over the little seminar room in the back corner for office space."

We sit and chit-chat a while, but I can tell Don is thinking about the symptoms of dimethylmercury poisoning, not the conversation at hand. He keeps looking me up and down, searching my hands and my eyes for signs.

I'm holding steady. I really don't think any got on me, and I got under the shower right away. I'm good. I'm sure of it. Whenever he makes eye contact, I open my eyes wide, imploring him to stop.

May

It's so hot in here. We're on a gravel road, and the dust is choking me. Every now and then, he hits a bump so hard my body lifts and bangs down against the metal beneath me. We've been driving forever. My head feels like it's going to explode it aches so bad.

He slams on the brakes, makes a tight turn, and slowly moves forward. The car stops, and he gets out. I brace myself, ready to spring as soon as the trunk opens.

A click. Fresh air and sunlight blind me, piercing into my

aching head. I try to push myself up, but only one arm moves. The other arm and my legs are useless and numb from lack of circulation. A garage door closes, blocking the sun, and then Jake is reaching down for me. I try to grab at him with my good arm.

He laughs. "C'mon, baby girl. I have a space all ready for you." He tucks his arms under my body, grabbing my good arm from underneath, and lifts me from the trunk. Carrying me into the house as though we're newlyweds, he kisses the top of my head.

"You motherfucker," I mutter, and he lets go. I land hard on my back on tile-covered concrete. Sharp pain cuts away the numbness in my legs. I'm in a kitchen. Bright-yellow curtains frame blue sky in the window above the sink. The counter spills over with dirty dishes. I can smell old food and stale alcohol. The floor is sticky.

He puts his foot on my stomach, his boot pressing heavy enough that it knocks the wind out of me. Looking down at me, he sticks his bottom lip out into a pout and says, "You're hurting me, babe." He lifts his foot off my belly and kicks me in the side of my stomach. Hard. I curl away from him to protect myself as pee runs out of me in a hot stream.

"Fuck! What a mess!" He kicks me again, the toe of his boot landing between my butt cheeks. I swallow my puke, anger burning through me. I'll kill him. I'm not his baby.

"Get up," he says, hauling me up by the back of my shirt collar. He leads me to a door, opens it, and shoves me into a black space. I stumble, fighting to keep my balance as the door closes behind me. My hands find a wall. A deadbolt clicks. Light seeps through the crack at the bottom of the door. Watching the shadow of Jake's feet walk away, I exhale. But then he's back, and the crack of light disappears as he stuffs something against the door. I stand perfectly still. Pieces of pain remind me of the day I've had so far. The skin on my legs itches from pee. The floor under my feet feels clean and cold. I stink.

Peeling off the wet T-shirt, I throw it into the darkness and slide my back down the wall to sit, listening to my heart. I'm not afraid; I'm mad. Something with lots of legs crawls across my bare foot, and I jump back up, stomping at the floor until I feel the cold-legged body crush and pop against my heel. I'm shivering—but I'm not afraid. Jake loves me. I know this.

Ted

I'm guessing first-bullet guy is probably a lot tougher looking when he isn't in a hospital gown. God knows why he's talking to me. He looks like someone who'd beat up a gay man before he talked to one. And we haven't been that subtle.

He comes over after we finish our donairs and descends in an exhale onto one of the chairs next to my bed. David is nonplussed, looking at me, at the old guy, and back at me. Lips tight. I glance at David with wide eyes and then smile at our visitor.

He has a blurred tattoo on his forearm, hidden by the white hairs that seem to cover his entire body, except his face. Above the tattoo is a round scar. There's another scar, the same shape, near his collarbone. His head is shaved to a stubble, and the grizzle on the back of his neck makes me think of a hedgehog. Except meaner. He's all muscle and scars. He has a cigarette tucked behind his ear.

He points his head to the doorway. "I'm usually the reason the cops are parked outside the door."

I'm not sure what to say to that, but David is quick—maybe too quick—with a sarcastic bite. "You're a stalker?"

I think I gasp out loud. Tough guy just laughs and reaches out his hand. "Frank Rossi," he says.

David lifts off his seat to shake the offered hand. "I'm

David, and this is Ted."

I take my turn, receiving Frank's meaty grip with my spindly one. I give a firm squeeze. David and I make a point of a strong handshake. People don't expect it from the likes of us, and Frank acknowledges it with a tight nod.

Seconds drip by. Awkward seconds. I wonder why he came over here. Just to sit? Another wave of nausea comes over me, and I swallow hard. Frank grabs the little metal puke dish on my bedside table and hands it to me. "You going to puke again, kid?"

I swallow again and shake my head. "No?"

"What are you in for?" I ask. As soon as I say it, I cringe. What? Are we cell mates? I hear David exhale hard. I assume he's trying not to laugh.

Frank just nods. "Cancer." His gravelly voice makes the word sound like a cuss. "Started in my nuts."

"Jesus," David says.

I fight the urge to cover my genitals.

Frank takes the cigarette from behind his ear. He slides it between his thumb and index finger until it taps on his thigh, then flips it over and repeats the motion. "Some chick shot you?" he asks. There is no disdain in his voice. I might even pretend he sounds concerned.

"Mmm hmm," I say.

"Did she have good reason?" Now he's got the cigarette in his fist, like he's going to strangle it.

"No," I say.

"Other than she's crazy," David says.

Frank shakes his head. "Crazy's bad," he pauses for a beat, looking toward the window. "My wife went crazy."

David and I don't respond. I look for somewhere to look.

So much information coming from a very scary guy. Why is he sharing all this?

"She died." His voice cracks.

Oh God, please don't cry. He might kill us just so we don't tell anyone we saw his tears.

A deep, phlegmy cough rises up his throat. He covers it with the fist holding the cigarette, then wipes the fist on his pant leg. He leans into me, forcing me to make eye contact. "She couldn't handle my lifestyle, if you get my meaning."

That you are obviously a cold-blooded murderer and have your own crazy going on? Yes, I get your meaning. I nod, slowly.

He pulls away, hands on his thighs. "She didn't like our kind."

Our kind? Like him, me, and David have a common "kind"?

He mutters under his breath. "Faggots."

He's gay. Wow. Not what I expected. David seems to be turning red. I can't tell if he's holding back laughter, anger, or simply questions. He clears up my puzzling with a tart, "Bullshit."

Frank glares at him. The cigarette snaps in his hand. "Do you think I don't know that?" He glances around the room. "A guy like me? I've lived a lie." He looks down at the broken cigarette and straightens it so the break doesn't show. But when he lets go at one end, it flops in half again. He tosses it in the little paper bag taped to my bedside table, then rests his elbows on his knees and his forehead on his hands.

Is this some kind of deathbed confession? This is not something I need to know. Chances are he's killed more fags than he's made love to.

"Why us?" David is standing. Not just standing, he's in

fighting stance, legs ready to spring, fists balled at his side. "Why are you telling us this bullshit?"

Frank rises to meet him. His spine straight and strong. The veins in his arms appear as he clenches his fists. But then his shoulders relax, and his hands release. "Sit," he orders. And David sits. And I exhale.

The old man sits too. "Let me help," he says.

I feel a little rush of excitement—or is it fear?—tickle at my nerves. I find my voice. "Help how?"

"You tell me," he says, all business, his queer solidly tucked away. "Why'd she shoot you? Was she hired? What do you mean by *stalker*?"

I look over at David. He shrugs and nods. So I spill. No, I don't. I'd never tell a guy like this about the rape.

Frank seems to have grown in stature by the time I finish telling my story. His eyelids lower as he exhales his words in less than a whisper, "Crazy cunt."

I nod quickly in agreement.

"I can make that disappear, you know." He has his hands on his thighs, arms straight, looking very ready to talk business. "Just tell me where to find her."

My eyes open wide of their own accord, and I bite my lips, shaking my head. "No!" At the same time, I hear David's "Okay" beside me. I glare at him and turn to Frank. "No killing. That's bad."

Frank rolls his eyes, tilts his head towards the door, and whispers, "Shut the fuck up." He looks behind him and then smiles back at me. "No one ever said anything about killing anyone." He stares at me, eyes soft and questioning. I turn away. He sighs again, getting up from his chair. As he walks away, he looks like any old man, grey and wide, the ties of his hospital-issue housecoat hanging at his sides. "Black Ball

Billiards on Granville. If you change your mind."

May

I wake up to the glare and hum of fluorescent lights. The lights blink as they warm up. Or is it me? Light comes through the bottom of the door along with the smell of cinnamon and coffee. When the door swings open, Jake is standing there, hands on his hips, a giant smile on his face.

"Good morning, sweetheart! Ready for some breakfast?" He steps into the room and bends down, slipping his arms under my armpits and lifting me up into a hug. He buries his face into my hair and whispers, "Hey, did you have a good sleep?"

I don't answer. I want to kick him in the nuts and bite him, but instead I hug him back, weakly. "It was a little rough with the concrete floor and all."

"Yeah, sorry about that." Taking my hand, he leads me out of the room into the kitchen. "You know how angry I can get sometimes." He pulls out a stool at the island. I climb onto it. There's a dry piece of toasted raisin bread on a plate and a cup of black coffee in front of me, the barely recognizable fresh food wedged in amongst the dirty dishes. "See? I remembered your favourite!" he says, pointing at the toast. "Ever since you were a kid. Remember me sneaking it to you?"

I smile and fake a giggle. This is going to be just like working a John. It always has been with Jake. I guess that's why being an escort was such an easy job for me. I look into his eyes, biting my lip. "That's so sweet," I say, stroking a finger along his hand. "Got any butter?"

"Of course!" he says. I watch him as he turns away from me, feeling my face distort as though I've just smelled something worse than this kitchen. Making me beg for butter. *You fucker. I'll kill you. Just give me time.*

After breakfast, he takes me to his room and fucks me. He's like a virgin, his hands shaking with every touch, his breath short and nervous. It's quick. It isn't horrible. Something about his familiarity feels almost nice—like someone scratching a hard-to-reach spot on my back. I pump and grind and moan as he cums.

We're lying on our backs. I look at the ceiling and listen to his breath, waiting for him to start snoring. A yellow water stain blooms on the stucco near the window, and some of the stucco is scraped away. There's a spider web stretched across it, and the spider, big and black, is tucked behind it in the corner where the wall meets the ceiling. I hear a tap dripping.

Jake's breath gets deep and steady. He snorts and then makes a deep snore. I lift onto my elbows to watch his face. He's definitely down for the count. It reminds me of the last morning in Seattle. Going to see Ted. And that reminds me of yesterday. Wow. Was it just yesterday? I slump back on the bed, remembering everything in flashes. How Ted attacked me and then the shower. His naked skin under water. How he ran from me and how his blood puddled into the shape of a heart. I've got to get out of here. I need to get to him.

As though he sensed my pulse quickening, Jake's hand grips around my wrist. I lay back on the pillow and turn to look at him. His eyes have changed from lovemaking Jake to edgy Jake. "I thought you could get to work on that kitchen for me today." You don't realize how often a person blinks until they don't.

Ted

I can't help wondering where she is. If she'll show up again, or if she's already watching us, or if she's already too sick to do anything. Her car was towed from campus, so I think she has no transportation. The police know about the spill. It was an accident of course. They will be watching for her to be admitted to hospital, providing the hospital recognizes her symptoms and reports her.

Three weeks now, and I'm fine. My leg has mostly healed. There's still some pain and a limp, but it's getting better. Chelation is done, and I've stopped puking. And, so far, there's no tremors or spasms. It's a waiting game now. Waiting for something. Hoping for nothing.

Saturday. I'm sitting on the couch, flexing my toes and then my fingers, scrunching up my face and rolling my head in circles. Testing myself for signs of toxin. It's become a habit whenever I'm alone.

"How will you know?" His voice startles me. I look up to see David standing in the bedroom doorway in front of me. His face is still soft from sleep, and his hair is pressed down on one side. Both hands are tucked deep in the pockets of his flannel pants.

A wave of panic buzzes through my heart, and then it deflates into the fear I've been hiding. I shrug a tiny shrug, tears tingling my eyes. We haven't discussed this—the chance I was exposed.

"When?" his voice rises. "When can we exhale?"

"I'm not sure," I say, shaking my head. "A few months? A few weeks? A year?"

"And what happens if May dies? What then? Prison?"

It's like a slap in the face. Wow. He thinks I planned it. Attacking May. "No," I breathe. "Never." Did I?

We stare at each other across the room, David's jaw flexing as he clenches his teeth. Finally, he shakes his head and walks past me to the kitchen.

I listen to him clatter. A mug lands on the counter. Coffee pours. The toaster clicks down. I wait for him to come out, but he doesn't. His anger hums through the silence, interrupted by the simple sounds of him eating breakfast.

I get up and limp to the bedroom, calling out, "I think I'll go to the lab this afternoon." This means me taking the car, him driving me, or me catching the train into town. I'm okay taking the train if it means we don't have to do the silent drive together.

David returns the call. "We need to get groceries and a gift for Sheena and Kevin."

Sheena and Kevin are friends of ours, they're having a housewarming party tonight. I sigh as I dig through my dresser for socks. "Can't you do that? I really need to get back to the lab and do some catch-up." I'm still talking loud to send my voice to the kitchen, but when I look up, David's in the room with me.

His voice is soft. "You can't be in the lab alone." It's a new safety protocol when working with toxic chemicals. Or when you have a stalker.

"Stephen is there. And Paula's usually in on weekends."

"I was hoping we could do Granville Island. Maybe have lunch." He's looking down into his coffee mug as though it holds something more fascinating than dark liquid. It's an apology of sorts. This is going to drive us crazy.

I really need to get back to the lab. That's what I want to say. Not to hurt him or anything, just because I do. I'm way behind, and I've already taken three-weeks grace to let my leg recover. All my time has been deskwork, just writing and reading papers. And what am I supposed to write when I have no data? I feel like I'm just pretending to be a researcher at this point.

But, then again, why not enjoy life right now—just in

case? "You know what? That sounds perfect. A picnic with the seagulls?" I start looking for shorts instead of socks.

"Sounds good," David responds, still staring at his coffee. But then he looks up, and he's smiling—a tight smile, but a smile nonetheless—and nodding.

May

We're drinking coffee on the back deck. Crows are fighting in the fields surrounding us. Their constant noise is irritating as fuck. So's Jake's stare. This is our morning routine. Sex. Coffee. Sex. Breakfast. Then he goes out for the day, or we hang out and watch TV and smoke weed. People come visit. I watch them drive up in Harleys or big old Town Cars all polished enough that they reflect a bent-up version of the house. That's the only way I know what it looks like from the outside. I've been locked in here for weeks.

All the doors lock from the inside and the outside. I had a go at picking them the first time he left me alone. No luck. There's an alarm system in case a door does happen to open without him on the handle. Jake wears the keys around his neck on a string of braided leather, along with a feather that he uses to tickle me—he thinks it turns me on. Nothing he does turns me on.

I could probably smash a window to escape. But by the looks of outside, we're in the middle of nowhere. I stare out the window at the next house over while I do dishes. It's at least a mile away. Between us, it's just fields of . . . I don't know, maybe corn? I think of movies where people hide in cornfields. I wonder how far I could get before he caught me. No. I can do better than that.

Jake brought some of my clothes from Seattle. They're old and don't fit very well. Seems I've lost weight being an escort. My taste has improved too, apparently.

I'm wearing my worst-fitting jeans and a white T-shirt. It has a picture of something on it, but it's so worn you can't tell what it is. When I put it on, I made sure to give the neck an extra stretch and tear the hole in the armpit a little more. Now, while he stares at me, I lift up my arm so the hole shows. "Huh, looks like this shirt is ready for the rag bucket."

He nods a little and reaches for his smoke burning in the ashtray.

I pull at the waistband of my jeans. You could put a whole other me inside them. "None of my clothes fit," I say, sliding my hand inside my pants.

He blows out smoke to make room for words. "Don't wear any then," he says.

Fuck you. I tilt my head to the side. "You want me strutting around naked when your friends come over?"

He breaks his stare and looks out over the fields. Jake doesn't like the thought of sharing me. I breathe through his silent response. Waiting to tell him we need to go shopping. He looks back at me, and I swallow. His eyes have turned dull and dark. Shit. I brace myself for a blow, standing up and grabbing the coffee mugs, then putting them down, realizing my body is exposed to his attack. I go to sit back down but stop myself. I'm in control of this asshole. I exhale and step towards him. Straddling his lap and grabbing onto his shoulders, I press my tits against his chest.

"Maybe you should be put away when the guys come over," he says, but his voice is thick, and his cock is getting hard against me. His hands are on my waist.

I run my tongue along his neck and whisper in his ear, "Maybe we should just fuck?"

Three days later, we're in the car. At least I'm not in the trunk. We pull into the parking lot of a shopping mall. It's your basic tube of stores: tall brown stucco walls with plastic signs on the outside, and dimly lit with fake cobblestone floors on the inside. He leads me by the elbow past the food court and straight into Le Château.

A sales clerk leaps on us, offering to help. I want to say, "Yeah, can you help me? This guy's holding me hostage," but I'll wait for my moment. Jake points to some outfits on a couple of mannequins and talks about one in the window, draping his arm over my shoulders. "Those are the ones you wanted to try on, right, sweetie?"

I nod, trying to smile.

"Hmm . . . let's see." She looks me up and down. I can feel the judgment in her gaze, and I want to slap her. "You're about a size two, sweetie?" I nod again, imagining my fist hitting her throat. She saunters away, calling over her shoulder, "I'll set you up a change room."

Jake squeezes my shoulders and says, "Why don't you pick something out?" He's loving this sugar daddy game. I pick out a blouse and a sweater, as plain as I can find.

He stands at the door of the changing room, arms folded, looking mean. "Show me everything, 'kay?"

I know better than to try to run. Not the first day out. It's not as though I can really ask for help or call the police. Pretty sure my name is out there. I have to figure out where I am first. And where I'm going.

We settle on three dresses, a pair of pants, and the blouse and sweater I picked out. Jake is pretty pissed when he sees the bill. He keeps his hand on the back of my neck as we head to the parking lot.

He puts me in the car and hands me one of the dresses he picked out. "Might as well put this on," he says, locking and closing the passenger door. It's little and blue with spaghetti straps. Not super sexy, but I can pull it off. He actually waits outside while I contort myself into the dress in the passenger seat. Thank fuck I'm little.

When I stop moving, he gets in. He looks me up and down and nods, satisfied with himself. I look up to the sky and flop back against the seat.

He turns the key in the ignition and starts to roll out of the parking spot. "I think I'm going to take you for lunch. How does that sound?" He looks at me with the twinkle smile that he uses on the ladies. He thinks it's cute. It makes me nauseous, but that's just me.

"I don't have anything for my feet," I say, holding up the rotting sneakers he brought from Seattle.

"Wrong," he says, and he reaches behind his seat to retrieve a black stiletto, also from Seattle. He hands it to me.

I examine it. It's a favourite of his. He brought it home after a B and E he did with a buddy. He was super pleased with himself for finding shoes my size. I'm a size five. Little girl feet, he always says. Not easy to find slut shoes for little girls. He's wrong. He'd know that if he'd let me back to my old apartment to get my stuff. But that conversation stopped as soon as it started.

I state the obvious, "I'll need two."

"Yeah," he says. But he doesn't do anything about it.

Prick. I reach behind his seat and grope through rags and cheeseburger wrappers until I find the other shoe. There's something sticky across the toe strap, and I pick off the bits of cedar stuck to it. "Where're we going?"

He doesn't answer. Prick.

Ted

There's not much better than a sunny day at Granville Island. Except a cloudy Saturday. The crowds are smaller: more locals than tourists, people who actually go to the market because they get their groceries there.

We decide to put a basket of stuff together for Sheena and Joe. We buy wine, cheese, chocolates and candles, and a lovely little bluebird brass door knocker. We hemmed and hawed about the door knocker but decided it was too cute to pass up. Sheena's told me their new place looks like a little English cottage with old cherry and apple trees, tons of roses, and a front porch. I think a little brass knocker is perfect for it.

David was right; this is just what we need: to be out here enjoying our freedom. I inhale the sea air, tinged with exhaust fumes and gasoline from the boats nearby, and tilt my head back to enjoy the sun, weak though it is, on my face. Which makes me stumble, but David is there to grab my arm and steady me. He gives me an extra squeeze before he lets go. Vancouver is very open to its gay and lesbian population, but we're still not comfortable showing our affection in public for fear of being beaten up.

We head across the pier. No need to discuss where we're having lunch. Zabra's fish and chips takeout and then to the courtyard to watch the boats hum up and down False Creek, the seagulls hounding us for fries. A small aluminum boat passes with a very optimistic fishing net tucked under its bench seats. Followed by the *Hail Marie!* —an elderly looking wooden fishing boat that's been converted into a home. We can see its daisy curtains, drawn closed, with spices and an African violet in full bloom sit on the windowsill.

"Would you live in a boat?" I ask him, just to make conversation.

David rolls his eyes to the sky. "Too small," he says, shaking his head. "I'd go crazy! You've seen me prowling around the apartment. I can't wait until we can afford a real house."

His emphasis on *real* feels like a jab that I'm doing grad school instead of working. Or maybe I'm just feeling sensitive. "I'm sorry! But for fuck's sake, we're only twenty-one. Even if I was working, we'd still have to qualify for a mortgage. You think a bank would really look at us?"

He puts his hand on mine, which is reaching for a French fry. "Woah, there! Don't get all defensive," he says, looking over his shoulder as he continues to hold my hand. "I'm just saying, one day we can have a yard and some serious space to move around in. Can you imagine having a living room and an office? Instead of a living room that is an office?"

Okay. So I am being sensitive. I shrug. "You're getting sick of being crammed in our one-bedroom with me?" I regret it as soon as I say it.

"Stop it." He lets go of my hand. "I'm not looking for a fight."

I stand up, brushing the crumbs off my legs. Seagulls scatter. "Well, it sure feels like it," I say, turning to leave. I strut toward the market, listening for him to follow. Why am I doing this?

Behind me, there's more protesting from the seagulls, and I think I hear David cussing. Despite the aching in my leg, I quicken my pace and am up the stairs and searching for an entrance to get back into the market. I can see David out of the corner of my eye coming up the steps in big strides. Why am I being such a little bitch? The sharpness of my anger dulls as I merge into the thickening crowd and feel the loneliness of him not beside me. I let him catch up, stopping when he's beside me. People move around us like water. He's looking at me with his steady grey eyes, and I sink into them, like I have so many times, regaining my balance. The throbbing in my leg subsides.

"You're okay," he says. "We're okay."

I swallow and nod. "It's just—"

"It's a lot, babe." We both begin walking. I feel the back of his hand against mine.

May

We drive a while. His car stinks of the scented cardboard strawberry dangling from the rear-view mirror. It must be a fresh one. It reminds me of our drive from Timberland to Seattle. We were both so excited and full of fun back then. Gas 'n' dashes, fucking in parking lots, drag racing anyone who challenged us. We'd started the trip in a 1977 Trans Am, like the one Burt Reynolds drove in *Smokey and the Bandit*. I'd bought it a few years earlier, after I realized school wasn't getting me anywhere and got a job as a waitress at Hooters. We sold it when we got to Seattle to cover the first month's rent.

This Town Car is a little less used. I play with the electronic seat adjustment a bit and then try the window, despite the air conditioning blasting on my face. It opens a bit, then stops.

Jake looks over at me. "Yeah, I think that window's fucked." He returns his focus to the road for a few seconds, then back to me. He smiles, his old-time, best-friends smile. "You look really nice," he says, nodding with approval. I return it with a tight smile of my own. I don't think we were ever friends, but I still remember when we were in love.

He pops in the cassette that's been resting in the mouth of the player, and Lynyrd Skynyrd's "Free Bird" whines into the space between us. My skin tingles a little bit. It was always our song, which is stupid, because it's about goodbyes. My throat feels a little tight. We were something once, me and Jake. But he was never Ted. Jake wouldn't understand that though.

I put my feet on the dashboard and reach down the side of the seat to press the recline button.

Eventually, we pull into a parking space on Granville Street near the market. Jake gets out and walks around the car to feed the meter, then opens the door for me, reaching in to take my hand and help me out. I submit.

He holds my hand while we walk down the street towards the harbour. The streets are busy, but in a lazy Saturday kind of way: not big city lunchtime crowds, just people meeting for lunch and getting their errands done. Street people hang out in doorways and lean against piss-stinking walls, never in a hurry to go anywhere. It's just like downtown Seattle. Just like when me and Jake were new, when he first got out of prison.

And then we're in the market. It's crazy, like a surprise party when you walk through the doors—here's where everyone is hiding. It smells like food. Chinese food, apples, fish and chips, coffee, tea. I squeeze Jake's hand. Fuck. What did I do that for? I look up at him. He's grinning ear to ear. I try to look angry. "I'm starving," I say, loud enough for him to hear. "Are we going to eat or what?"

He laughs and shakes his head. "We can eat." Apparently, he thinks I'm funny.

We go to a place where there's these giant cinnamon buns under a glass case. A chunky grey woman with a permanent frown looks up at us. Jake holds up two fingers. She nods briskly and then shoves two cinnamon buns in a box, slaps a glob of icing on each one, and sprinkles them with cinnamon. I swallow my drool. She hands the open box to Jake and holds up five fingers.

Jake hands her a ten-dollar bill, and she turns to the till, but he waves her off. "No change. That's for you." Oh my god, really? My psychopath uncle has a thing for old women? She actually cracks a smile. Her teeth are black and grey. I'll have to try not to think about them when I'm eating. Then she picks up two napkins and hands them to Jake, looks at me, frown returning, and gives him a handful more. Like I'm competition or something.

We walk out without holding hands. Jake trusts I won't abandon the cinnamon bun, and he's right. We find a splinter bench overlooking the water and he hands me my bun. We eat in silence. The wind blows my hair into the icing. I have to eat fast so I'm not completely covered in sticky goo. Jake hands me a few napkins. I wipe off my hands and my face, but really, I need water to get the icing off. I don't want to say anything though. It's like if we don't speak, nothing changed. We're in Seattle. I didn't run. He isn't holding me hostage.

But then it's him.

I stand up, napkins flying off me into the wind. "Ted!" Jake has my arm, and he's pulling me back down. "Ted!" I cry out, one more time.

Jake yanks me down, digging his fingers into my arm. "Just try it, little girl," he growls in my ear.

I'm shaking. I call out one more time, over the seagulls, the wind, the crowd. Jake's grip tightens to the point that I wince. Ted slows down. I freeze, waiting for him to see me.

Then David walks up to him. My heart sinks. I see them touch. They look like they're going to embrace, but instead they start walking.

"It's him. That little fucker." This time, it's Jake's turn to stand up. He takes a step forwards, forgetting I exist.

I run to Ted and throw my arms around him from behind, almost falling to my knees. Fucking stilettos.

Ted stops. His hands are on my arms right away. I knew it. He's been looking for me.

"I thought this would never happen. I thought I'd never

see you again!" I whimper.

He pulls my arms from around his waist and turns to face me. He looks pale. What has David done to him? "May? Get the fuck away from me!" His voice rises as he backs away. His hands seem to be shaking. "The police—somebody call the police!"

David grabs my arm, and at the same time, I feel Jake's arm drape over my shoulder.

"Are these boys friends of yours, sweetheart?" Jake's fist is by my face as though he could put me in a headlock any second. He's staring at David. David lets go. Does Jake know this is Ted, the boy who broke my heart? Is he defending my honour in some weird, Jake-assed way?

David melts from his fighting stance and looks at his feet. But he straightens himself back up just as quick. It doesn't do much good. David is lean and muscular, but he's still a boy compared to Jake. I feel the sweat from Jake's armpit on my shoulder.

"Hey, don't I know you from somewhere?" Jake's talking to David.

I roll my eyes. He's got it all wrong. "No! It's not him." I point to Ted, who is searching the crowd of people who have slowed down around us. "It's—"

"No," David says, taking a step back. He shakes his head, "No," he says again, and he takes Ted's arm and starts to walk away.

Jake steps in behind them, dragging me with him and muttering, "You little fucker." But then he stops, and I look ahead to see a security guard coming towards us. "You're dead," he says. David's shoulders flinch, like he's expecting a blow, but Jake steers us away, back towards the harbour.

Ted

Her skinny little arms are wrapped around my waist, and she's crying. I feel the heat of her breath on my back. It's like I conjured her just by thinking. I pull away, turning to look at her. "May? Get the fuck away from me!"

David grabs her arm.

"Police—somebody call the police!" I try to make myself grab her other arm. We got her. We just need to hold her until the police arrive. But my skin feels like a wet mushroom, and my limbs won't move. Then this huge guy is beside her, wrapping his arm around her neck like she's a lamppost. David lets go of her.

People are slowing down around us. We can get help. I try to make eye contact with someone in the crowd.

May's buddy growls, "Hey, don't I know you from somewhere?"

I look back at the guy wrapped around May. He's looking at David, and David is looking at the ground. David takes my arm and starts leading me away. His hand is shaking. Uncle Jake? Is that Uncle Jake?

I hear the words, "You're dead," from behind us. David flinches.

May

I keep looking over my shoulder, trying to find his blond curls in the crowd, but they're gone. He just pushed me away. Again. My chest aches, and I realize my face is wet from tears. The wind blows my hair onto my cheeks, and it sticks there, with the help of the cinnamon bun icing. I can't see, but I don't need to. Jake's grip is still tight on my shoulder. I stumble beside him. My feet are numb. Stupid fucking shoes.

We walk around the market to the ferries and then start to make our way back to the car. I reach up to brush the hair off my face.

"No," Jake grunts, using his free hand to push mine down.

Ted

"Don't say anything," David says as he steers me around the security guard, who is trying to find the person who called for help. Me.

"What the hell, David?" I whisper the words. Is David involved in some kind of crime? Is he suddenly afraid of May? "We had her! Okay, you had her! You could've taken Uncle Jake easy."

He says nothing, looks over his shoulder, and quickens his pace. I'm practically jogging to keep up with him. "Do you know Uncle Jake?"

David sneers, shaking his head. "Uncle Jake? Is that what you call him?"

I'm guessing that's a yes, but he doesn't say anything until we're in the car and the doors are locked. He stares at the rear-view mirror and clears his throat. "He's the guy." I watch him swallow. He blinks, turns to me, and starts the car.

I raise my eyebrows, encouraging him to continue, but it's like the words are stuck in his throat. He wipes his palms on his shorts and then holds onto the steering wheel. He keeps staring at me with those big grey eyes, but his shoulders are slumped, and his knees are pressed together. He looks like a little boy who's told a lie.

"Hey," I reach out and stroke his hair. "What's going on?"

"He raped Stacey."

"What? No." I say no before my brain puts together what I already know. David's sister was raped. She was thirteen. "Oh God," is all I can say. I remember Jake at the playground with that little girl in the tunnel. Her panties. The blood. And that was a different girl, younger than Stacey. The weakness of nausea flushes through my skin. I reach for David's hand; he holds on tight.

"She was— Fuck, she was just a kid!" he says with surprise. "That fucking pig raped my sister." I watch as the frightened little boy melts away and an angry man pushes through. He lets go of my hand.

"So why did you let him go?" I whisper, not wanting to sound trite.

He shakes his head slowly. "The way he looked at me. It —it's how he looked at me the day I gave my testimony. Like he was going to kill me."

I wait for him to say more. Jake did look scary. I'm shaking my head, trying to understand, but it doesn't make sense. "Why not let the police take care of him then?"

"Geez, Ted, I never even thought of that!" David bites. He points back to the market. "Do you have any idea what it felt like to confront that memory? Here? In Canada?"

I don't. But I do know what it felt like the day May showed up here. Hopeless. I reach across for him. "I'm sorry. I-I just want May gone."

David nods his head in agreement. "And I want that creepy fucker gone too."

He takes a deep breath and pulls out into the street. My mind is racing. Why is Jake here? Why can't the police find May, but she can find us so easily? Why hasn't she shown up at the house? Or is it a matter of when? And, "What the fuck is he even doing here? Shouldn't he be on parole or something?"

May

Jake opens the trunk, his hand on the back of my neck. My stomach turns, and I feel the cinnamon bun dough inside me turn into a lump. I straighten myself up, ready for a fight. "No. Jake, please. No?" I try to sound strong and threatening, but instead it comes out like a whine. I clear my throat. "People will see."

He looks around. A couple is walking down the street, completely absorbed in each other. Across the road, three men stand around, talking and smoking. They have a shopping cart beside them, loaded with weird things: a small TV, blankets, a stuffed rabbit. Jake slams the trunk closed. "Get in the car."

I topple around to the passenger side and get in. The mood has certainly changed since our almost romantic arrival. I tug the stupid shoes off as he starts to drive and slide my feet into the familiar shape of my sneakers.

Staring straight ahead, I pull my knees to my chest. Ted. How do I get to you? God, if I could only have Jake's set-up. A house for just the two of us.

Beside me, Jake seems to have calmed down. He's listening to the music pumping out of the cassette and tapping his finger on the steering wheel. He sees me looking at him and reaches across to put his arm around me. I almost fall over as he pulls me towards him. He kisses the top of my head. "Sorry, I lost it back there. That little fucker put me in jail."

"David?" What does David have to do with him going to jail. Did Jake rape him too?

"Yup. Said he saw me with her." He shrugs. "She couldn't stay away from me. What can I say, right? Just a little cock tease." He squeezes me closer to him so I can feel his bicep press on my neck. "Just like you."

I don't know much about how things went down at Jake's trial. Just what Mom's told me. Jake talks about the girl sometimes. It usually leads to us having sex. "How did you know it was him? That was a long time ago. He was just a kid."

"Actually, I thought it was her dad at first. I'll never forget that guy. He stared at me the whole trial. He would stand up and watch when they escorted me in or out. I'd just stare right back at that fucker."

Jake takes his arm off my shoulder as he starts to merge onto the highway. When we get up to speed, he says, "So that's Teddy? That weird little kid you used to hang out with?"

I nod—even though he's not watching—and mutter, "He's not weird. He's beautiful."

Jake touches the brakes a little and looks over at me. "What? Are you fucking kidding me?"

"We're in love!" I snap back at him.

Jake throws his head back and laughs. "That didn't look like love to me, sweet thing!"

We drive in silence for a long time. I watch out the window as the mountains of blackberry bushes roll by on the side of the road, and fields and forests replace the suburbs that ooze from the edges of metro Vancouver.

We pull off the highway onto a feeder road that leads into familiar farmland, but he doesn't slow down. We're ripping over washboards and potholes at seventy-five miles an hour. His knuckles are white on the steering wheel. "What the fuck, Jake?"

He doesn't say anything. I grip onto the armrest and my seat, waiting for the car to blow apart on one of the bumps. My head bangs on the passenger window as we turn onto a gravel road, sliding sideways and fishtailing almost into the ditch.

Finally, he slams on the brakes, and I realize we're at the

house. He puts it in Park and just sits. I start to open the door, but he grabs my arm.

"What about us?"

Ted

I'm on the phone to Constable Ryan as soon as we get home. I get her answering service. "Tell her I need to talk to her immediately. It's an emergency."

The female voice on the other end responds with a tolerant tone, "Sir, this is an answering service. If you have an emergency, please call 9-1-1."

It would be funny if it weren't for the fact I'm hardly breathing for fear for our lives. "Umm. Okay. Not that kind of emergency. But do you think she can call us back today?"

"I will relay your message. Thank you."

The line goes dead. I hold the phone to my ear for a second longer than I need to. Now what? David is sitting on the couch with his head in his hands. His fingers dig into his skull. I sit beside him and wait. Forever.

I answer the phone, pacing, with the receiver in my hand.

"Ted," Ryan says, "how are you?" Her genuine concern makes me spill.

"I saw her. We almost had her, but then David . . ." David stands and steps into my path. We stand facing each other. "David and Jake—Jake's May's uncle—they know each other from the rape. We had to go. She's still here. Why haven't you found her yet? She's still here."

"Ted, slow down. You're not making any sense."

"Why haven't you found her yet?"

"There's not exactly a manhunt for her," Ryan says. When I don't respond, she continues. "It's busy. I'm following three different murders myself at the moment."

Ryan's not looking for May. No one is looking. No one cares. I tighten my grip on the receiver, but I can't find any words. She tried to kill me. I sidestep David and resume pacing.

She sighs. "I'm sorry. If it's any consolation, the local hospitals are still on the alert for her."

Oh my God. I actually forgot: she should be dying. I think back to how she looked. Did she look sick? I try to remember her movements, her face, anything that would show the dimethylmercury was taking hold. But all I remember is my fear.

"Ted, look, tell me what happened," she says. "Slowly."

I take a deep breath and exhale. *Stop being a panicky bitch, Ted. She's already dead. She should be, at least. Remember the deadly poison?*

I tell Ryan the entire story, including Stacey's rape and Jake's threat to David. "She knows where we live. What do we do now?"

"How did she look?"

"She looked"—I hesitate and shake my head, looking over at David, who is watching my side of the conversation —"fine. She was just fine."

"And this Jake guy, how is he in Canada?"

"I don't know!" My voice is loud and childish, but I don't care. "We didn't get a chance to catch up, did we? All I know is he is a child molester and a sick fuck and he threatened my boyfriend!"

"All right," Ryan responds in her calm, parenting voice. "Technically, you are out of my jurisdiction, but I'm going to get in touch with the RCMP. They'll be interested in this. They'll want to speak to both of you."

I take my tone down a few notches. "But what about May? She was in Vancouver. That's your city."

"I'll send out a reminder to keep an eye out for her, but really, Ted, from what I've read about that stuff, she's only going to last a few more months at the most."

"But she was fine!" I almost say, "I failed" but remember I wasn't supposed to be trying to kill May. It was all in self-defence.

"Well, like I said, we'll keep an eye out for her. And I'll get the RCMP out your way," she says, closing out our conversation. "How about I check in with you next week? See how everything's going?"

When she hangs up, I go to the bookshelf and remove a sheet of paper tucked at the end of a line of textbooks. It's the safety sheet that comes with dimethylmercury. I should have it memorized, but every time I read it, I get overwhelmed by the possibility that May might die. That she could be gone forever. That I might have committed murder. And I don't know how to feel.

"The symptoms are primarily characterized by loss of sensation in the hands and feet and in areas around the mouth, diminution of vision resulting in tunnel vision, ataxia, dysarthria, and hearing loss," the sheet reads.

Did she look like she was struggling to see? No, she found me in the crowd. Her vision is fine. Her hands were on my waist. I try to remember: did she squeeze my waist with her fingers? Did she stumble? "Severe poisoning produces blindness, coma, and death. There is a latent period of weeks to months before development of the poisoning symptoms." Weeks to months. It's only been three weeks.

"We need to move," David says, his voice crashing into

my racing thoughts. "Again."

I nod. "I know."

May

My toes are fucked from those stupid shoes. The big toe on my left foot and the three smaller ones on the right. Like they fell asleep and never woke up. I've tried rubbing them and soaking them in hot water, but they don't wake up. It's pretty annoying. I stumble a bit when I walk. I hope it goes away soon.

Jake's been high since we saw Ted and David. Some days, he lets me join him; other days, he tells me to go to my room: the laundry room. Some days, he fucks me; some days, he hits me. I have the laundry room set up a bit better now. Jake put an old mattress in there on one of his more amicable days. I've stashed some chips and pop in there and put pillows, a blanket, and a lamp in a corner. I have a bucket in case I need to piss, or worse, but mostly he doesn't lock me in unless he goes out.

Today is a day we're getting high. We're on the deck with our morning coffee, and it's a little chilly, so I have my hoodie on and a blanket wrapped around me. We haven't talked about David or Ted. He passes the joint to me, choking just a little as he holds it down. I take a nice deep toke and hold down as long as I can, wondering what today's high will bring. Fuck it. Why wonder? I exhale with a little cough and say, "I know where they live."

He lifts his head and nods, his face blank.

"Do you really want to kill him?" I ask.

Jake stands up, and I brace myself for a slap, but he just puts his hands on his hips and looks down at me with that empty stare and nods again. He turns away and walks to the rail.

Oh, fuck. Which *him* does he want to kill? "David, right?

You want to kill David?" Because killing David would be a major bonus for me on all fronts: David would be gone, and Jake would be in jail—I'd make sure of that. But killing Ted? I can't even think of losing him right now.

I watch the back of his head for a nod. Nothing. Okay, so this conversation is going nowhere quick.

I step up beside him, pressing my shoulder against him and reaching for the roach still burning in his hand. He looks at me and flicks it out into the backyard. Wow. I watch the little plume of smoke on the stubbly straw that was once a lawn, waiting for it to turn into flames. "I can help you."

"Yeah," he says. We both watch until the smoke disappears. Then he walks away.

It's been two days since I brought up David. Jake locked me in the laundry room and went out the first day. He came back late that night with a big bag of coke and a wad of cash bulging in his jeans pocket like an erection. Apparently, he was out making money.

We've been doing lines ever since. Neither of us have slept. Or talked, really. We watch soaps in the morning, reruns of *The Fugitive*, *MASH*, and *Alice* in the afternoons, and his endless collection of VHS movies at night.

We just did the last of it this morning as the sun came up, all bleeding red into the grey sky. I'm starting to come down, and I'm so tired. And sad. Now the clouds have come in all around, and it's started to rain. Why don't I just run away? What the fuck is wrong with me? I could steal the car easy. Jump off the deck. It's only about, what? Fifteen feet?

Jake's in front of me. "Okay. Let's do this."

"But I'm so tired," I want to say, but his eyes are dark and angry. They have been for days. So I reach for his fly, caressing up the seam with my finger. He grabs my wrist. Oh, fuck. Apparently, doing "this" wasn't fucking.

"What are you doing?" he growls.

For fuck's sake, I'm so sick of this misery he's wallowing in. "I don't know, fuckhead! Trying to read your fucked-up mind?" My ear explodes inside and out as he slams my head and I fall to the floor. Jake still holds my wrist with his free hand—it's twisted, and my arm burns up to my shoulder. I'm wide awake now and shaking with the pain. "No. Please, Jake? Stop."

He kicks me with a socked foot, just above my crotch. It's almost gentle without a boot on. "Go to your room," he says. Do I hear regret in his voice? "I need to figure this out."

I get up without looking back and head to the laundry room, grabbing the half-full twenty-six of vodka that sits on the counter on my way through the kitchen. Figure what out? How to kill David? Ted? Maybe it's me who has to figure something out. Like how to get out of here.

Ted

Another building, another move we can't really afford. This time in New Westminster. At least we're a little closer in. This place isn't as nice as the last one, but it's cheaper, and it's got a good security system, covered parking, and we're high enough up, even if all we see is the building next to us.

We've been staying at Don's since that Saturday. He's even traded vehicles with us so we aren't so easy to recognize. Tippy and Stephen did all the packing for us, and then we hired movers. The whole thing is costing us a fortune.

I'm hanging up a calendar from a box that contains kitchen stuff, books, and a handful of socks. Tippy and

Stephen's organizational skills leave a lot to be desired. I flip the pages to September and then realize we're actually in October now. I flip back to August—the twelfth is circled in red—and I count the weeks. Five weeks.

I wish I could see her. To see her realize the feeling in her fingertips isn't coming back. To watch her wonder why her eyes don't work or why she keeps stumbling.

David paces all the time. When he's not pacing, he's just sitting, staring. He helped move everything in, but he was more like a robot than a participant. No banter, no take-charge David, with his usual precise direction. I'm worried about him. We don't even know if Jake's threat is real. Why would a guy who managed to cross into Canada with a criminal record like his do anything to put his freedom at risk? But that family has some serious crazy going through their blood, so I shouldn't ask the logical questions. Just look at May.

I sit beside David on the couch and put a gentle hand on his shoulder. "Hey, babe," I say, "how are you doing?"

He doesn't respond right away, as though he has to pull himself back into the room to join me. He sighs and puts his hand on my thigh, giving it a squeeze. "I don't know."

"You're scaring me," I say, placing my hand on his.

"It's like I'm paralyzed." He turns to me. "How do you do it?"

"Do what?"

"May. You're constantly looking over your shoulder. She's been this dark shadow over our lives forever," he says.

"You said it right there. Our lives. I've always had you." I give him a nudge with my elbow, trying to lighten the situation. "Besides, you're the tough one here, not me, remember?"

He smiles. "I know! So what the fuck is wrong with me?"

He shakes his head. "It's like I've turned into an eight-year-old kid again."

"They shouldn't have made you testify."

He turns to me, his eyes calm and certain, like grown-up David. "It was the only way. I saw him with her. I saw him touching her. No one else did. He would have got away with it."

I flop back on the couch. "This is fucking exhausting! I'm so tired of running and hiding and living this stupid life where May's in control."

He stands up and starts pacing, running his fingers through his dark hair. "We have to leave the city—completely."

I'm stunned. The sun has moved so it's reflecting off the windows in the building across the alley, turning David into a moving silhouette.

"What about my research?" I ask.

He stops. "Find another sponsor."

No. "But I only have a year left." How can he ask that of me? "No one would take me on."

"Don will figure it out if you ask him to." He continues pacing, as though the movement of his body makes his brain work.

"But May's going to be dead in a year." It comes out without emotion.

He stops again, hands on his hips. "Unless that shit's contagious, that doesn't exactly take care of Jake, does it?" he snaps.

My palms are damp, and I wipe them on my thighs. More words come out of me: "Then I guess we kill him too," I shout. Where the fuck did that come from? Have I become some kind of cold-blooded murderer?

He steps in front of me, looking down, and my head

drops in shame. He walks away.

But really, what else is there to do? If Jake doesn't go to jail or get deported, we'll always live under his shadow. Even if either of those things happen, he won't get a life sentence for stalking, and he's already proven he can cross the border illegally. But if he's dead, he's dead. No more problem. Maybe I'm not a cold-blooded killer. Maybe I'm just solving a problem.

I get up and find David in the bedroom, sitting on the bed, his head cradled in his hands. I sit beside him. "It's actually not a bad idea, is it?" I'm whispering.

He says nothing.

"There's another vial left," I continue. "We don't even have to confront him. Just a drop on a door handle or something."

His head sinks through his fingers, and he pulls at his hair, hard. Then he straightens up but still won't look at me. "You don't think that would be the slightest bit suspicious?" he whispers too.

Of course I do. But it's also super effective. "So help me think of a better idea."

I expect a resounding no, but he's quiet. I look at his face, trying to figure out what he's thinking. Not always my best skill.

May

I don't even need a bag to run. I own nothing. Maybe some money. I'll need some money for sure. I get a flashback to when I left Jake in Seattle. That horrible little apartment. It was so easy to slip away. Back then, I might have loved him. But now? Fuck him.

Nothing hurts this morning. My bruises are starting to fade. Jake's been pretty much ignoring me since our last little event. No sex. No conversation. I sleep in my room, cook us meals, and do my chores: laundry, dishes, cleaning. He passes me a joint if I happen to be sitting beside him when he's smoking. He's gone out a couple of times and locks me in my room when he leaves.

He's asleep on the couch. I sit on my mattress in the laundry room, hugging my pillow, thinking. This shouldn't be so hard. But I don't even know where the fuck I am. Okay. Settle down. I do know where the fuck I am. When we came home that day, we left the highway at an Abbotsford exit. And we're close to the border. I saw a turn-off sign that said USA. But how do I actually get into civilization? It's just miles of fields and empty dirt roads out here. I don't even think I could get a taxi out this far. He's got to take me back into the city.

I bury my face into the pillow and scream. Not as hard or as loud as I want to. It's almost like I want him to hit me again just so I can trade all this frustration for the simpleness of pure pain. But we have to stop that shit. I have some sweet talking to do. I force myself to get up and get my pretty on. I grab a dress Jake picked out on that shopping day a million years ago and go to the shower. Jake opens his eyes as I walk by on the way to the bathroom. I nod. He nods.

It's been a while since I've taken a shower. I wash my hair twice and fill the empty conditioner bottle with water to get the last remaining bits, dumping it on my head and combing my fingers through my hair. The water is hot and delicious. I close my eyes too so I don't see the crusty black soap scum that lines the tub.

I put on a little eyeliner from a pencil I found down the side of the couch. Some chick must've left it here. It's olive green, not my usual black, but it looks okay. Kinda makes me look sweet instead of tough. That works for today. My hair is long and straight and does nothing. I have about three inches of dark-blond roots and then the last colour I had, Hepburn auburn, takes over, all faded and ratty. I debate whether I should cut it all off, but there isn't a decent pair of scissors in the house.

Jake's still on the couch. I bring him a cup of coffee. He looks me up and down as I walk towards him—how can he not notice? I'm looking pretty fine. I hand him the coffee and sit close beside him, tucking my feet under me. Our skin touches. I reach over him and take a cigarette out of the pack on the end table, giving him plenty of tits and skin to look at. He stretches his arm across the back of the couch as I sit back down. Bingo.

I light my smoke. He takes the lighter from my hand.

"We should do something today," I say, handing him the lighter.

He buries his face in my hair and reaches for my thigh. Okay, maybe we have to fuck first. I look up to him and slide my fingers through his hair, bringing my face to his and finding his mouth with my tongue.

We don't leave the couch. It's lazy, gentle sex. He almost feels vulnerable the way he holds me, kissing and caressing every part of me. I almost feel safe. I relax enough to cum, and he's right there behind me. After, we hold onto each other like we're friends.

I bite the inside of my cheek, blinking until the tears are real, and then let out a soft sob. Nothing. I do it again, making my body shake a little this time.

He gives me a little squeeze. "You okay?" Thank fuck. He still has feelings.

I wait a beat and then, with a little sniff, say, "Mm-mmm," and sniff again.

He leans up on his elbow, back against the couch, and caresses my belly. "I know. It's been kind of harsh this last little bit." But he doesn't say he's sorry.

Everything inside me wants to demand he take me to Ted right now. But that's going to just fuck things up again. Teddy seems to be a sore spot. All I need is for him to take me to civilization. I can find Ted myself. "I just want us to be back to normal, babe," I say, letting more tears drip from the corners of my eyes.

"I know," he says, again, stroking my hair, looking into my eyes and searching my face.

I look right back at him, trying to read him. Is he coming around? But then I realize he's trying to do the same thing. Read me. I force my lips into a smile and close my eyes, waiting for him to attack. But he doesn't. He just keeps caressing my hair. I'm that good. He has no idea. I let the smile fade, and I shrug, opening my eyes wide. "What if I get a job? What if I start pulling my weight around here?" I scooch up on my elbows, almost bumping heads with him.

He sits up, pulling his hands away from me and folding them in his lap. When he looks at me again, his eyes are cold. He shakes his head. "I don't think so, babe."

You motherfucking, cocksucking son of a bitch. I'm vibrating from the inside, fighting the need to kick him and claw at those horrible dark eyes. I look back at him, doing everything I can to breathe instead of scream. I could kill him right here and now. The thought surprises me. And it calms me. I nod, pressing my lips into a soft smile. "That's okay. I understand."

I reach my hand out to him, and he takes it. "I love you," I say. His grip tightens around my fingers. *Oh shit, he's going to hit me. Please no. I can't.* I close my eyes and take a deep, slow breath, bracing myself. But instead, he takes my hand to his lips and gives it a kiss. Stupid fuck. He believes me.

"I love you too, little one." He presses my hand to his cheek. "You just let me take care of things, okay?"

Yeah, I don't think so, asshole. It's time I take care of things. I lift myself up and curl into his arms.

Ted

Parts of me think this is a way bad idea. I keep looking at David to see if he's sure about what we're doing. He looks back at me like he isn't. But here we are, strolling along Granville Street, looking for Black Ball Billiards. I want so badly to hold his hand.

"There." I point down the street about half a block at a sign over the sidewalk. It's an oversized eight ball with two disproportionately small pool cues crossed behind it. I imagine it's some kind of flashing neon at night.

We continue walking, bumping against each other like we do when we're nervous.

We walk right past it without saying a word and continue north to the cleaner end of Granville. David tucks into the first bistro we see. We order hot chocolates and sit at the window, watching the shoppers.

"So," says David, shaking his head. "That went well."

We both smile, and I feel the tension start to fade from my skin. "Is that it then?" I ask. "We're leaving it?"

"Let's be real, babe," David says, brushing my hand with his. "We were actually going to ask a gangster to 'take care of things.' We could be in his debt for the rest of our lives. What's that going to look like?"

I don't know what gangster debt looks like. Could it be any worse than what we're dealing with now? We hatched the plan two days ago, but I've been thinking about it ever since the hospital.

David shrugs. "You've got what? One, maybe two more years? Maybe we do let it go. And then get the hell out of

Dodge."

"What about Jake? What about him killing you?" I whisper it because you don't talk about killing in public. "And May? She's already tried to kill me once. You don't think that will happen again?" The word *kill* lingers on my tongue like mouldy bread.

Meaty fingers clasp my shoulder and give it a squeeze. I jump out of my skin. I know the hand even before I know the voice. It's Frank.

"Does the word *discreet* mean anything at all to you, kid?" he asks. He pulls a chair from another table and sits with a groan, smiling, and says, "You looking for me?"

"No," I say, with the special squeaky voice I reserve for when I attempt to lie. "What makes you think that?"

"I heard your conversation." Frank winks at me. He's practically jovial. "That, and you're about a block away from my place of business."

David nods, his hands flat on the table. He's so much cooler than me.

"We just— We saw her again," I say.

"Only this time, she was with someone." David's words chase mine as we explain our most recent encounter with May.

When we're finished, Frank shakes his head. "Wow, you two. Nothing but drama."

David laughs. I don't. He's right. This isn't the average favour we're asking.

Frank rubs the stubble on his chin. "Don't worry. I've given this some thought." We wait for him to share that thought.

May

I'm doing dishes, thinking about weapons. The kitchen knives are useless. The sharpest one barely cuts through a sandwich. I have to find something else. I know he has a gun; he pulls it out to play with once in a while. Taking shots across the field. One day, he had some drinks and shot at the TV. He missed, and we slid the TV over a bit to hide the hole. The trick is getting my hands on it when he isn't looking.

I take the cast-iron frying pan and slide it into the sink, scrubbing at it with the Kurly Kate. It clunks loudly. It's not huge, but it's not small either. I lift it out of the water and wrap both my hands around the handle. I swing it like a baseball bat. But my numb toes make me stumble. The pan slips out of my hands and bounces off a cupboard before hitting the floor with a crash and sliding in a soapy puddle. There's water everywhere. I'm giggling when I bend down to pick it up. It reminds me of the day Teddy and I made love. Then Jake's feet are in front of my face.

He shouts, "What the fuck's going on in here?" But then he slips on the wet floor and lands on his back. Before I can think, I've got the pan in my hands, swinging it up over my head as I straddle him. His hands grab at my legs, pushing them outward, and I slide into the splits over his chest, bringing the pan down with a rubbery crunch onto his face. His hands let go instantly, and I lift the pan to take a second swing, but there's no need. A trickle of blood and clear stuff runs from his nose and frozen eyes.

Ted

David and I made love last night when we got home from our Frank encounter; the first time in ages. Since before Granville Island. And now we're sitting in our little hovel reading upscale magazines—*National Geographic* for him and *Nature* for me—pressed against each other like Siamese twins. Anticipating.

She's done for—either dimethylmercury or Frank's cronies. Frank didn't ever actually come out and say what "taking care of them" entailed, but I trust, based on his beefy, bad-man demeanour, it isn't going to be the nurturing kind of care. And I get the impression we don't owe him anything. Just knowing his secret is enough for him.

My fingers are starting to get numb from the glossy pages, and the magazine drops on my lap. I sigh with boredom. "What do you think? Should we get out and about today? Do Shannon Falls or Whyte Lake?"

David puts his magazine down on the coffee table and stretches into a yawn, draping his arm over my shoulder and pulling me close so he can kiss the top of my head. "That sounds like a fantastic idea. I vote Shannon Falls."

I reach up to stroke his face. He jumps as my fingers reach for him. "Ow!" he says, touching his cheek. "What was that for?" When I look up, he's holding his cheek. He pulls his hand away. Three red blotches are forming on his skin.

My fingers. The tips are still numb. I hold my hand in front of my face, slowly making a fist and then releasing it.

"Oh God," David says. He takes the hand and brings it to his mouth, as though kissing it will make it better.

That's it then. We didn't get it in time.

"We need to go to the hospital."

"No," I say, shaking my head as I touch the numb fingertips with the hand that still works. "Let's just go for that walk. Please?"

May

He didn't bleed much. I try to pull the chain with the keys from around his neck, but it won't break, so I have to lift his head and slip it off. His skull is like a boulder. Hair tangles in the chain, and when I finally get it off, tufts of it hang off the links. I smile to myself as I hold it up. Talk about dead ends! God, I'm funny.

I guess parts of me want to feel sad. He's family, after all, and I think we really loved each other at some point. It's taken me this long to kill him. That has to mean something, right?

No need to hurry now. I turn on the stereo, sit down on the couch, and take a couple of hits off the bong on the table. The high melts over me like a warm hug. I feel safe. I realize how long it's been since I've felt safe. Since he threw me into the trunk of his car. Fucker.

BTO's "Takin' Care of Business" comes on, and the beat forces me to dance. Hah! When was the last time I danced? My numb toes make my moves all funky because I keep losing balance, but that just makes me dance wilder. I throw off my housecoat and air guitar my way into the bathroom to take a shower.

Afterwards, I pack all the booze and weed I can find. Then I go into Jake's bedroom. Let's see what he left me. It smells like old sex and dirty sheets in here. There's a sock full of money in his sock drawer and a little Ziploc of coke —I think it's coke—under a lamp on the dresser. The drawer in his bedside table is a goldmine. There's a bag of pills—they look like bennies—and a Rolex. I dig deeper back and find a little velvet box. Inside is a gold ring with one huge diamond solitaire. Well, would you look at that? The stupid fuck was going to propose! Tears come into my eyes like I have a second brain that cares.

I look under the bed. It's just giant dust bunnies and lost clothes. Okay. Done here. I start to leave. But I hesitate. Didn't I catch him with his hand under the mattress once after he came home? I slide my hand between the box spring and the mattress on the side where he usually sleeps. His gun. How could I forget? A very nice gun—with a lot more oomph than that one I got from David. I check the magazine. Only one bullet missing. Huh. That works. I give the barrel a kiss and rub it against my cheek like it's a cock. The metal is cold and exciting.

Okay, boys, here I come. Ready or not.

Ted

Royal Columbian is a nightmare. Emergency is packed, and we've sat forever in this germ-infested waiting room. Clearly, I'm not dying fast enough to get any attention. Every time the emergency doors open, I hope it's May. I refuse to do this alone after all she's put me through.

It's three hours before we finally see a doctor. He pinches the ends of my fingers, makes a couple of phone calls, and then tells me to go home and connect with the specialist I worked with when I got chelation therapy. So now I have a business card, and I'm waiting for Monday.

David keeps touching me to see if I can feel. He doesn't say that out loud, but I can tell. He touches my thigh, rubs my feet; his hand is constantly on my shoulder or holding mine, even if we're in the kitchen making tea. As though he can stop my senses from leaving me if he hangs on tight enough.

I'm no better. I'm not being cool about this at all. My fingertips are still numb on both hands. I keep checking other body parts and moving my hand in front of my face, checking for tunnel vision. I'm in constant fidget. And eating. Apparently, my sense of taste can go too. So I keep tasting things. Last night we had Kentucky Fried Chicken with fries and gravy. Tonight, I want curry. I want to taste tacos before I can't and—oh, roast beef. What about Chinese food? Why did I waste that meal on Kentucky Fried? What's wrong with me?

Nothing, really. So far. Just my fingertips are numb. And I keep flexing them.

May

I'm tearing down a gravel road, hopefully in the direction of the big city. It's time to get my sweet Teddy.

Oh my God! It just dawned on me—I can follow Jake's lead and bring Ted back to the house in Abbotsford.

I can use the gun to convince Ted. Eventually, he'll remember how much he wants me. We can start fresh in the house. It's all set up so he can stay, and I don't need to worry about him leaving. The more I think about it, the more I thank Jake for showing me the way. And for setting everything up just so. I guess I should've done something with Jake before I left. He's probably going to start stinking in a day or so.

I look at all the stuff I loaded up in the back seat. Huh. I guess I'll have to unpack again. That's cool. I should buy some rope. Or duct tape—that's what they use nowadays right? What about David? Hah! That's pretty much a no-brainer. I just need to find him alone. I make a trigger and barrel with my hand and fire into the air. Yeah, David. This game is almost over. It's a nice way to honour Jake too.

A little lump starts to grow in my throat, and the road gets blurry from my tears. I push my foot down hard on the gas pedal, but my stupid numb toes lose their way, and my foot hits the floorboards. The car slumps to a crawl as I try to get my foot back on the pedal. Seems I've lost a couple more toes on that foot. How fucking annoying. Hopefully, it'll get better now I've got my freedom back. Probably just nerves.

Ted

The neurologist made room in his schedule for me this afternoon. The receptionist sounded almost excited at the prospect of me finally getting in touch. Sorry for the wait, folks.

The examination room is cold and white with a big poster of the nervous system on the wall beside the counter where there's a box of plastic gloves and a rubber ball. The examination table has stirrups. I can't even imagine why a neurologist would need their patient to put their feet in stirrups. There are no windows. Aren't specialists supposed to have windows?

My hands are rested palms up on my thighs. The feeling in the right pinky is completely gone now. On my left side, the palm has lost sensation. My arms shake as I force my fingers to flex. The right pinky doesn't move. David paces.

The door swings open, and Dr. Henry strides in, file in hand. "Ted," he acknowledges me like we're long-time associates who don't really know each other.

David reaches out his hand and introduces himself. "I'm David LeClair, Ted's . . . uh . . ." David hesitates and looks at me.

"Partner," Dr. Henry establishes, shaking David's hand and reminding us he's not a homophobe. "I remember you from the hospital." He sits on his wheely stool across from me, and David leans against the examination table. "Okay, so you're seeing some side effects?"

David snorts.

I hold out my hands. "I can't feel my fingertips," I say, flexing them again. "And my pinky, there"—I nod toward my right hand—"it won't move anymore." I swallow against the lump rising in my throat.

"Right." Dr. Henry writes a note on the lined yellow paper clipped to the front of the folder, then directs me up onto the examining table. David moves to the corner by the door, refusing to sit.

The doctor takes his little rubber hammer and taps at my knees, elbows, and ankles. Then he goes over my body with a dull needle, poking at different spots, my fingertips included. I'm supposed to let him know every time I feel a prick. Finally, he gets me to read the eye chart pinned to the back of the door. I make it to the second-to-last row.

Then he shakes his head. "Damn, Ted. I was sure we got it all."

I shrug.

"Um, okay," he says, distilling confidence with his *um* like nothing else could. "We've got to get you back on the DMPS." He scribbles some more. "And I'm going to add some DMSA this time. That might be what we're missing."

When he stands to leave the room, he touches my arm. "This is going to be rough, Ted. I'm sorry."

May

My heart is aching to see him. And my puss.

Three days. I've been parked here three days in a row. The car stinks of relish and French fries. And beer. And probably me. I haven't showered since I left Jake's house.

This morning, I sat in the parking lot outside the Life Sciences building, again, and watched everyone go in. That Tippy guy. The professor. The fat one. But no Ted. I walk through the building every day. They've moved their lab, but I found it. They're on the second floor now. The professor showed me on the first day when I followed him in. Not like I introduced myself or anything. I just followed him.

No one recognizes me. I have no makeup on, and I'm dressed like a student: jeans and a T-shirt. Plus, the limp from my stupid feet. True sexy, I'm sure. It's hard to be so low-key after being hidden away so long. People don't usually ignore me when I walk by, but I guess that's a good thing right now.

I start the car. I need to get some food and maybe hit up a rec centre for a shower. The sock full of money is in the glove compartment. It hardly has a dent in it. I think I've spent thirty bucks since I left Abbotsford. Maybe I should splurge and get a hotel room? But I have to find him. I have to.

As I'm backing out, I see a couple hugging in my rear-view mirror. They're the same height, and I think that's why it catches my eye. As they untangle themselves, I see they're both guys, one has a beard, and the other—well, he's just got way too much nose and chin to be a chick. They remind me of Ted and David. My fingers grip the steering wheel, and I want to back right into them. Fuckin' David. He fucked everything up.

Holy shit! David! That's right! I know where he works. If I find David, I find Teddy. I smack my forehead with my palm. *Really? Three days it took you to figure this out?* I rip down Westbrook Mall towards West Sixteenth. Here we go, girl. It's almost over.

David works in a little pharmacy behind Safeway on North Road. I expected something way fancier than that for him, being that he's a genius and all, but it turns out he isn't all that fancy. He still makes good money, I bet.

I back into an angle spot across from the strip mall and pop across the road to the bakery for a scone and a coffee. The lady at the till gives me a dirty look and wrinkles her nose when I hand her a fifty-dollar bill. Bitch. I know I stink, but that's not her business. She's probably wondering why a homeless person has a fifty. I stick my tongue out at her when she hands me the change. She doesn't know me.

Now, I wait.

Ted

David's back at work today. The apartment is freezing, and I'm pacing, partly from frustration and partly to keep warm.

I've got some stomach cramps, and I feel like I'm going to barf every now and then. And the chelation is like chemotherapy—it makes my immune system weak. So David wants me to stay home this week. Not that I can do much in the lab anyway.

I'm trying to analyze data that's useless. I need to run a couple more experiments before I have anything worth working with. My fingers aren't letting that happen. Hell, I can't even hold a pen. This entire master's degree has been an absolute joke. One disaster after another, thanks to May. I'm surprised Don even lets me continue. Let alone the cost. I keep pacing, pulling at my hair.

Pulling my hair. It's a habit I've started since the numbness came on. I feel the strands stretch across the patches of skin on my fingers that still work. It feels good. Grounding. Another wave of nausea hits me, and I double over with cramps, grabbing onto the end of the couch. Then I sink to the floor on my knees.

It doesn't hurt that much. But the nausea is exhausting. And the fear. That's exhausting too.

Fuck. Is this it? Is this how it's going to end? I close my eyes, leaning my head against the couch, willing tears to come, but for some reason, they don't. I just sit there with my eyes closed. There's no sting to my eyes. There's no sob rising up my throat. Me, who cries at the drop of a hat, can't cry over my own death? Has the organic mercury clung to my emotions?

I blink rapidly a few times, testing the dryness of my eyes, and finally open them. The sun has managed to make its way through the sliver of space between the buildings in our back alley, into our window, delivering a ray of sunshine right beside me in a very ethereal way. How very cheesy. All of it.

I pull myself up and walk to the kitchen. I can be such a drama queen! I'm not going to do that with what might be the last days of my life. I will make myself some peppermint tea. I will be strong and positive. For David and for me. Maybe this isn't it, but if it is the end, I'm going to make the most of it.

David has left the kettle full, so all I have to do is plug it in. A bottle of Pepto-Bismol sits on the counter. I take a chug of the pink minty paste while I wait for the kettle to boil. Once it does, I use two hands to pick it up and pour the water into the mug. My hands shake with the effort, so much so that the hot water spills all over the counter. I slam the kettle down and slam it down again. It cracks at the handle. My face burns with rage, and every muscle in my neck gets ready for a long, loud scream. Instead, I close my eyes and inhale deeply. The steamy mint of the tea, enhanced by the Pepto-Bismol and the settling of my tummy, reminds me of my resolve. I will not freak out.

May

It's getting dark by the time David emerges from the drug store. I didn't recognize him at first. His usual walk—like he's going somewhere important, and no one had better get in his way—seems a little different. He's wearing a navy pea jacket, and his hands are in the pockets. His shoulders are hunched.

He folds himself into a little orange Chevy S-10. What is with these guys and ugly vehicles that are too small for them? My Town Car is bigger than his truck. I follow him down the little street and onto the main drag. He heads for

Lougheed Highway. It seems super dark outside. Like there's a fog on either side of me so I can't see my side mirrors. I stay pretty close; I don't want to lose him in the traffic. No way he's going to recognize me in this beast, especially in the dark. I'm wearing a black beanie of Jake's I found in the back seat, and it smells like him. Alive him, not dead him. I feel a little ache in my chest, but it disappears pretty fast.

David turns off in New Westminster. Huh. So they did move. That's one thing—once Teddy and I are together, we're going to settle down. I'm sick of moving. I want to live in the same place forever, like people on TV do. And it'll be a nice place too. Ted's so smart, he'll get a good job easy. I can do something too. Better than waitressing. I could be a realtor maybe. One of my clients was a realtor. They make loads of money. Or I'll work in a bank somewhere. We'll be rich together.

Now he's stopping at a liquor store. I park across the lot and turn the car off. He's in there forever. Finally, he comes out with a case of beer and a brown paper bag. He gets in the truck, and I see his silhouette bring one of those mini liquor bottles to his lips. Then he slams the steering wheel with his hands and rests his head on it. I smile. Trouble at home, Mr. Perfect? Nice.

Once he stops his temper tantrum, I follow him as he drives down a few more streets and into a back alley. It's a neighbourhood packed with apartment buildings. A couple of old cars are parked along the side that we have to squeeze past, and it looks like a homeless guy has set up camp next to one of the dumpsters that lean against the buildings. Wow. Why would they move here after that fancy-ass place in Coquitlam?

David disappears into a parkade. I zip in behind him before the door shuts and then lag back. He doesn't seem to notice. I park my car in the first empty spot I find. Apparently, it belongs to apartment 12B. "Eat shit" is spray-painted in green on the concrete wall in front of the spot, only someone has tried to paint it over with grey, to hide it. It's a light coating of grey though, and it just looks like a frame. I get out of the car and listen for sounds of David in the parkade.

A vehicle door slams. Hopefully, that's him. I scoot, bent down, towards the sound, hiding—or should I say bouncing?—between vehicles and concrete pillars. My feet make a slap on the concrete like flip-flops because of my toes. I mostly walk on my heels now. It's like walking on stumps, only half of my right foot has feeling. My left is a little better. I still feel a couple of toes. But I stumble all over the place; I must look like a drunk. Then I hear the ding of an elevator. I run towards the Exit sign where the sound seems to come from. I get there just as the number light above the elevator door reads eight. And it stays there. I smile and close my eyes. Wow. I exhale and nearly fall to my knees with relief. That was way too easy. It feels like I've been holding my breath all this time, since that day in the lab, with the gun and the shower. We were so close that day.

Ted

I've set the table with a tablecloth and fancy napkins, and I've taken the steaks out of the fridge and spiced them ready to barbeque. I take a bottle of red from the booze cupboard in the kitchen and the corkscrew from the drawer. One look at the corkscrew, and I realize I won't be able to use it. I'll just put them on the table. David can deal with it.

On the way to the table, I stumble. There's something on the floor; I've tripped on it twice already. I look down, dragging my foot over the rug, looking for a bump or a wrinkle. It feels weird, like the floor isn't there in spots. My heart begins to race, and I grab onto the back of the couch. Oh, fuck. Oh, fuck. My toes are gone.

I stand perfectly still and wiggle—or try to wiggle—the digits on each foot. My big toe and second toe on the right foot are good, but I can't bend the last three. Only the pinky toe on my left foot isn't working. So far.

As though I'm suddenly crippled, I use the couch for support, take careful steps from the back to the front, and lower myself onto the cushions, corkscrew and bottle still in my hands. I feel winded. Sucker punched right in the solar plexus. My eyes water. Yay. The tear factory still works.

Strong. I said I'd be strong. David can't see this. My watch says it's 5:12. He should be here any minute now. Do I get up and risk tripping? Or do I just sit here? There's asparagus in the fridge. I could get that ready. No, I can't. That would require stupid fingers using a knife. But I can get a frying pan ready with some butter. I can do that. Come on, Ted. Keep going. I tap the wine bottle with the corkscrew, willing it to open, and then put them on the coffee table in front of me.

Getting up is no problem. Walking to the kitchen is no problem. I'm fine now that I understand my toes aren't able to help me walk. This is easy. I turn the radio on in the kitchen, and the CBC *Drive Home* show is on. They're interviewing a veteran of World War II.

May

I'm going to celebrate. Steak and lobster at the Keg. And a hotel for a nice, long bubble bath. Might as well get ready for the rest of my life. I clamber back to the car. The driver's door is open. I didn't close it when I was sneaking up on David. I slide in, humming the Kinks's "You Really Got Me."

I can't breathe. The smell of denim and gasoline hit me before I realize there is an arm wrapped around my neck and something hard in my ribs. I wriggle and beat back with my elbows as the arm pulls me against the headrest. Jake. He didn't die. Oh God. The pressure on my throat gets harder, and I fight to catch air, bucking and flailing my arms. I can't scream. I can't get enough air. "Jake. No!" I squawk. I'm not sure if sound is coming out. Blackness is coming to the corners of my brain, like I'm drifting off to sleep. "Please—"

"Don't kill her." It isn't Jake's voice. "I don't think he wants us to kill her."

The tension eases on my throat, but there's a jab in my ribs. A gun.

"You gonna drive?" the voice attached to my attacker grumbles.

"Nah. Let her drive," the first voice says. "She's all set."

I turn my head slightly to look in the rear-view. There are two men in the back seat. Neither one of them is Jake.

"You heard him," the second voice growls. He sounds like someone's got an arm wrapped around his throat too. "Drive." The gun pokes deeper into me.

I cough as I try to speak. "Where?"

The two men look at each other. They haven't a clue what they're doing.

"Jake's?" I ask.

"Black Ball," the dickwad with the gun says.

The other guy says, "Who's Jake?"

Dickwad and Meathead direct me along the East-West Connector, then onto 99 to Oak Street. We hit green lights all the way, fucking incredible. All I need is one red light. Finally, at Granville, they tell me to turn left, and we miss the light. Cars are moving all over the place. We're in the middle lane of the road, and the advanced green stops flashing. I inch closer to the vehicle in front of us. I grip the steering wheel super tight so they don't see my hand shake. I slide the other hand to the armrest, clenching it into a fist.

Ted

When I hear the key in the door, I'm still in the kitchen, contemplating a bottle of vodka in the liquor cupboard. I hate vodka, but it's a screw-top, and that's inviting. I lean against the counter, bracing myself with my palms and digging my heels down, so there's no need for toes to balance.

"Good evening, noble warrior," I chirp, tilting my head as he walks through the door.

"Hey there." David sighs. He has a brown paper bag, a six-pack, and a very tired face behind his smile.

"I see you've brought alcohol, sir. I can't begin to express my delight!" I press hard into the counter, erecting my posture, and continue to be ridiculously jovial. "I'm preferring the offering in the brown bag, I believe; although—be forewarned —there is a lovely shiraz on the table."

David has the brown bag by whatever's in its' neck, and there is a clatter of glass as he puts it on the kitchen counter.

"Oh, my! Do I sense more than one bottle in that parcel?" I giggle with nerves and embarrassment. My jovial idiocy isn't working, obviously. I'd hoped some silliness would help ease the misery we've both been coping with, but he isn't buying it, and the whole thing just seems awkward.

He steps towards me and puts his hand on my waist. I'm still shaking with giggles. He rests his forehead on mine; his other hand slides down my arm, gently grasping my wrist.

"How you doing today?" he asks.

"Good," I croak, then I repeat it in a whisper, as I nod our heads up and down, "good."

He exhales a warm breeze over my face.

"How about you?"

He pulls me closer and buries his head into my neck. I feel his head shake, no. I lift my hand to stroke his hair, stupid on so many levels. I have no fingers to stroke with, for one thing, and for another thing, my hand was holding me up. I slide between David's legs as I lose balance and wrap my arm around his neck to catch myself. No need, of course. He's got me in his solid arms.

"Whoa!" he says, catching me around the waist as my heels try to gain traction on the floor. If only I were wearing socks, this would seem so much more normal.

David doesn't say a word. With my arm over his shoulder, he grabs the paper bag from the counter and wraps his other arm around my waist, leading me to the couch. He sits me down and slides a mickey of McLaren's out of the sack, followed by two mini bottles of Southern Comfort.

He cracks the tops off the Southern Comforts, handing one to me. Enveloping it with my fist, I chug it like an elixir, feeling the warm blanket of alcohol seep through my insides. He smiles and nods before knocking back his own tiny bottle.

"Did I see steaks on the counter?" he asks.

I nod. "All seasoned and ready to go."

Apparently, we're not going to discuss my body's latest antics. I'm okay with that.

"Cool," he says and marches out to our tiny deck to light the barbeque.

I look at my feet and then my hands, willing myself to get back up and help with dinner.

May

I hardly feel my fingers as they slide to the door handle—they feel like stumps, and I have to look down to make sure they're wrapped around the little chrome latch.

"Hey!" Dickwad shouts, poking me with the gun again. I snap my head up, looking in the rear-view and then realizing the advance green arrow is flashing ahead of me and the car in front has disappeared. Fuck. Then my hand spasms and pulls at the latch. The door pops open quietly. I catch my breath, take a quick glance again in the rear-view and, leveraging myself against the steering wheel, while pushing against the door and the accelerator, launch myself onto the pavement as the car rolls into traffic.

Not as planned. Not as fucking planned. There's a crunch of metal. I'm assuming the car hit something. The pavement is cold and wet, and there are way too many tires close to my face. Horns honk. I'm supposed to be screaming, but somehow, I'm winded, and the air won't come to my voice.

Behind me, I hear Dickwad and Meathead's muffled shouts from inside the car. Then a strip of fabric is tickling my face, and hands gently hold my head. I can smell the musk of a man's crotch. I open my eyes. It's a tie. The fabric is a silk tie. It smells like cigars.

"Is she okay?" a woman's high-pitched whisper asks.

The man cradling my head answers, "Call an ambulance."

I hear heels clicking away from me as the woman shouts, "Someone call an ambulance!"

"You're going to be okay, sweetheart," the man says, stroking tears from my cheeks with his thumbs.

Of course I'm going to be okay. I got away from Meathead and Dickwad, didn't I? My body is cramping with the cold from the rain-soaked asphalt. I try to curl up in a ball, but the hands grip tighter on my head. "You need to stay still, sweetheart."

"I'm cold," I mutter, fighting against him. Fucking control-freak men. All of them. I would claw his eyes out if it weren't for my escape plan. I clench my fists. My fingers on my left hand are asleep. No wonder I couldn't get them around the door handle.

"Stop it. She's fine!" It's Heels.

A perfumed blanket of silk and wool falls on me. Chanel No. 5.

"This oughta help." She's given me her coat. I can't help but smile. I like that woman.

Tires begin to move again on the wet pavement, and I hear sirens in the distance. Car doors slam, and I wonder where my captors have run off to. I make a mental note to avoid anywhere called Black Ball.

Ted

It's dark when I wake up. I hear David in the kitchen: the coffee machine gurgles, dishes clatter. I look for the sleeve of light that slides under the door of the bedroom from the rest of the apartment. Why hasn't he turned on the lights? I roll onto my side and look towards the door. There. A glimpse of light registers in my brain, and my sense of disorder settles. But then the light disappears again. I hold my head very still and move my eyes, finding the light and freezing on it.

"David!" I call out. Maybe it's a scream. Something to cut the darkness. The door opens, and a circle of light appears. I don't move my head. "David," I repeat his name softly. Then he's sitting beside me, hand on my shoulder.

"My eyes."

"Fuck."

We sit there, very still. I try not to blink in case whatever light there is disappears. Forever.

It's happening too fast. Last night my feet. Now this. It's like someone keeps punching me.

Then David is up. "What are you wearing? Can you dress yourself? I need to call the pharmacy."

I turn my head and find he's riffling through my underwear drawer. "What are you doing?" I ask, still not blinking—I think.

"And Dr. Henry. Where's his card? We'll just go straight to Vancouver General. No point in fucking around anymore."

"David. Wait," I say in a voice way calmer than the situation allows. "It's only been a couple of days. The chelation might not be working yet."

He stops and turns to me, looking like a man possessed at the end of my tunnel vision, with a hard smile and his eyes wide. "No," he shakes his head. "No, Ted. They have to do more."

Finally, my eyes squeeze closed. I hope he's right, that there's more that can be done.

May

I've been here all night. A tube in my arm and wires stuck to my body. The beeping of the machine is driving me batshit crazy. Apparently, I'm waiting for a CAT scan or an MRI or something. They are worried I've done something to my brain or my spine. That's why my legs stopped working after the accident. And the numbness in my hands has taken over my whole arm. It's stupid. I told them my feet were already fucked from the shoes. And my hand is probably a sprain. Dickwad was pretty rough with me, and I did put up a good fight. But this is a safe place to be for now.

A perky little nurse comes into the room with my breakfast. "And how are you this afternoon, Diana?" I smile at the fact she thinks I'm Diana. I have no ID, so I just picked a name to work with the whole hospital thing. Diana, the inappropriate princess.

"Because we aren't sure if you need an anaesthetic yet, you still only get clear liquids for lunch." She rolls the eating table overtop of me and begins to crank up the bed so I'm upright.

"I'm not hungry," I say when I see the apple juice, some kind of broth, and a bowl of green Jell-O cubes on the food tray. I catch my breath like I've been running.

She blinks thick mascaraed lashes at me. She's cute in a bucktooth kind of way. I feel a warmth in my crotch. Funny how boredom always makes me horny. I wonder what that's about?

I put my good hand on the back of her thigh, close to her ass, as she adjusts my pillow. She stands up straight and blinks again. I smile. "I could kill for a cigarette though," I say, sliding my hand a little closer to her butt cheek. She jumps away, and I laugh out loud.

"There's no smoking in here," she squeaks, and I watch her scurry out of the room. I turn back to my Jell-O. Fuck. So gross.

Then a shadow crosses the door, and there's a man at the foot of my bed. Not a doctor. He's big like a barrel. And old. He's got thug gear on: a leather bomber jacket and a tie. He puts his hands in his pants pockets and puffs his chest, which would be laughable except for the gun handle that pokes out of his jacket when he does this. Another fuckin' Jake-man? Jesus fucking Christ. We stare at each other for an entire year before he takes a seat in the corner.

"I could scream, you know," I say, poking my plastic spoon into the Jell-O cubes. Weird. I'm catching my breath again, and for sure this old fart isn't turning me on.

He nods. "And I can tell them who you are."

Jake reported me? That's fucking ballsy. "He kidnapped

me," I whisper. "He held me hostage for weeks. He—"

"That poor kid didn't do a goddam thing." The thug man stands up. He's still speaking softly, but his hand is on the butt of the gun, and he seems twice as tall as he did when he sat down. "He's just trying to live his life, but you? You can't leave him the fuck alone!"

"What are you talking about?" I have to stop to take a breath. "Jake has been on me since I was a little girl!" I choke on my words like I'm going to cry.

"Jake?" He pulls his head back and squints like he just inhaled something awful. "Your uncle? No. I'm talking about Ted. You obsessive, crazy bitch."

I catch my breath on his name. Ted. I smile and sob at the same time. "You know my baby? My Teddy?" I inhale a shaky breath. "Oh." I reach a hand out to this giant stranger. "Thank God. Oh, thank God." And here I thought he was my enemy. "I'm so sorry. I didn't realize you were here to help me." I'm literally panting I'm so excited.

The thug backs away, shaking his head. I scramble to get out of the bed, forgetting my legs don't work.

I almost fall out, but Thug Man jumps forward and catches me. I cling onto his arms as he lifts me back to the middle of the bed. My cheeks get hot, and I'm grinning like a goof. But then he lets go, shaking off my grip, and walks towards the door, his pointer finger raised and his head tilted.

"We've got a room set up for you right here, Mr. Russell," a voice in the hallway calls out. And there he is. My Teddy. In a wheelchair. Rolling past my door.

I squeal.

Thug Man turns back to me. This time, his gun is out, held at his belly button and pointed at me. He shakes his head. "Shut the fuck up."

Ted

On the plus side, I swear the feeling in my right toes is coming back. I try to wiggle them as we roll down the long green hallway that is Vancouver General. It's extra green because I'm wearing sunglasses. I'd wear a blindfold if I could; the tunnel vision is so weird, but David doesn't think that's safe.

It didn't take them that long to process me at admissions. Dr. Henry gave them a heads-up, and there's an IV waiting for me in neurology. But they insisted on the wheelchair. My vision problems are apparently a safety issue.

We follow the male nurse into a semiprivate room, and he offers me a hospital gown and pants. David steps between us and says, "We'll let you know when he's ready," as he pulls the privacy curtain across the young nurse's stunned face.

I take off my sweats, leaning on David for support, and let him help me put on the pyjama bottoms, but when he unfolds the gown and holds it up for me, I snap it away from him and finish dressing myself. I waffle between needing him and hating his nurture. It doesn't seem to faze him; he's so focused on my happiness. Sometimes, I wish he'd just get mad at me instead of being so kind and understanding.

I climb under the icy tight sheets, sunglasses still on, and wait while David summons the nurse again.

"Well, don't you look cool?" Frank's grizzled voice startles me, and I turn my head to focus him into my narrow line of sight.

David's silhouette is behind him. "Look who I found," he says.

I smile, feeling a weird sense of safety knowing Frank is in the room. Not that May can get at me here. I'm pretty sure she doesn't do hospitals. "What are you doing here?" As soon as I ask, I shake my head as though to erase the question. My hand goes to my mouth. "Are you . . . ?" Sick again? Following up on a botched murder? Visiting a dying relative? How any of it is my business even, I don't know, but I feel like he's a friend, so I finish my sentence. "Are you okay?"

He points his head to the wall behind him. "Right next door. She's here."

My blind eyes pop wide, opening my circle of vision only slightly. Holy shit. Holy shit. Holy shit. Is this another attack? Did she somehow weasel Frank into her fold? How does she know I'm here?

He shrugs. "The boys told me they had her, but she jumped out of the car." He shrugs again. "I just chased the ambulance. She's pretty fucked up. Can't walk." He grins a bit when he says this, but then he points his chin at me. "What's this?" he asks, as though my condition is a thing separate from the person he is talking to.

David pipes up, "It's the dimethylmercury."

Frank's brow furrows. "That shit you told me about?"

I nod. "I lost feeling in my fingers about a week back and some of my toes last night," I explain. "Now my vision is going."

Frank rubs his hand over the bristles of what looks to be a day-old beard, then slides his fingers through the thin rails of hair on his scalp.

"You think that's what's wrong with her?" he asks.

I turn my head to see David. We nod at each other. But there are no smiles.

May

Thug Man walked out of the room. He must be getting Ted.

Or maybe a wheelchair for me. I hope Teddy's okay. He must have fallen and sprained an ankle or something. Oh well. At least I'm here to help him. Talk about signs! No wonder I was getting horny earlier. He was probably already in the building by then. The energy we create when we're near each other. It's spectacular. I practically expect my body to heal just being this close to him. I rub my wrist between my thighs, willing the feeling to come back to my hand. And I wait. I still can't catch my breath. This is crazy.

Where's Thug Man? What's taking him so long? There are wheelchairs all over the place. And Ted isn't too far. I heard him going into a room right close. The machine beside me whines and sighs louder and louder. I try to press the nurse call button that's pinned to my sheet, but my hand is fucked.

"Nurse!" I holler, slamming my useless fist against the buzzer. "Nurse! Someone!"

A boy in blue scrubs glides into the room. "How can I help you, Diana?" he asks in a sarcastically efficient voice. I sweep the food off my table, but my arms feel like they're in casts. The broth in its stupid cup crashes to the floor, but the Jell-O bowl just flops onto my lap, and green cubes roll into the folds of my sheets. The apple juice didn't even fall off the table.

The boy stares at me and then leaves the room.

"I need to go next door! I need to be with him!" I slam my sausage arms against the table and then rub them against my body, trying to remove the wires that hold me down. The feeling of nothing enrages me. It's like I'm being pulled away from my own existence. I slam my head back against the pillows again and again.

Taking a deep breath, I scream, "Teddy! Teddy! I'm here, baby!"

Ted

The scream from down the hall has a distance to it, like it's stretching to meet my ears, disconnected from its source. My ears recognize it before my brain registers what I'm hearing. My name. May's voice. Then nothing. I ache to hear it again. Why?

David goes to leave the room but stops at the doorway and comes back to my side, taking my hand. "You okay?"

"Is she dying?" my voice asks. It too sounds disconnected. Is my brain starting to break down? The room feels cold and still.

Frank steps up to my bedside, his shadow obliterating David's. "I'm pretty sure that's what's happening, buddy." His hand hovers over me as if to touch me in comfort, but then he drops it to his side. He whispers, "You want me to speed up the process?"

I look at them both, then turn my gaze to the doorway where the hallway lights beam into the room like the fabled other side. I shake my head, no, straining to hear her voice again.

Is this how it ends? With her screaming my name on the other side of a wall?

Dr. Henry strides into the room, interrupting my emotions with his white lab coat and clipboard in hand. "Hi," he says, examining the clipboard.

David and Frank back away from the bed, letting the doctor approach. He takes my hand, gives it a squeeze, and then puts the clipboard on top of me. "How are you doing?" he asks, digging in his breast pocket for his penlight. He looks at me, then the clipboard, and moves the clipboard to the side table. The light from his penlight explodes into my eyes. My entire inner eyeball glows like an eclipse around the light beam. It's smoother than I expected—sensations like this should be ragged, shouldn't they? It hurts enough I push his hand away.

"Okay," he says, nodding. "That's not a bad thing."

I let out a sigh. "It feels like a bad thing."

"They're going to hook you up to an IV, and we'll continue with the chelation." He checks his watch, looks behind him at the doorway. "I've got a new patient next door. I'll come back and check on you in a bit."

He turns to leave, but when I say, "It's her," he stops in his tracks.

"The other victim?" he asks.

I want to correct him, especially seeing the surprise in David's and Frank's eyes. Victim. Hah. But I don't. "The person who was exposed the same time as me, yes."

"We've been waiting for her," Dr. Henry says as he hustles out of the room.

May

I stopped hollering. No one is listening to me. Thug Man hasn't come back. I don't think he's going to. I have to figure out a way to get to him myself. I'll have to work on a better relationship with that nurse boy.

I close my eyes, but then a shadow hovers over them, and I open them again to see a doctory-looking guy with a lab coat, a stethoscope, and gorgeous hazel eyes standing over me.

"Hi," I say sharply.

"Hello, May," he says. "I'm Dr. Henry."

"Diana," I correct.

"Right," he answers. "Seems you've had exposure to dimethylmercury, am I right?"

This guy's fucked. He doesn't even know who I am. "Wrong. Next doctor, please." I glare at his surprised look. "You have the wrong patient."

He checks his clipboard, looks at the end of the bed—I guess there's a tag there—and then back at me. "No, May, I don't. I've been working on Ted's exposure for some time now. You were with him when it happened. I'm assuming you've been exposed too." He holds his hands up. "Mind if I touch you?"

This guy is so full of shit. "What's that di-whatever-it-is?" I ask. "What do you mean *exposed*?"

"Let's just call it mercury poisoning, shall we?" the doctor responds, groping me as though I did give him permission to touch me.

He looks at my chart again. "You certainly have the symptoms." He seems excited.

"What symptoms? What are you talking about? When did me and Ted get mercury on us? At that market, with Jake?"

"When did you lose feeling in your feet?" he asks.

Oh my God, it was the market. Where was that? Granville? My feet started fucking up that day. Did David poison us? Or Jake? They're both jealous of me and my Teddy. Oh, my poor baby. "Is Ted okay?" This is my fault. Oh fuck. It was Jake. He probably got some on David too. That's why he wasn't in a hurry to kill him.

"Will it kill him?" Then it hits me like a slap, and my voice drops. "Will it kill me?"

The doctor looks at my face, not at my eyes, and tilts his head a little bit. But he doesn't answer. Instead, he turns and walks away. "I'll get you started on some chelation drugs," he says as he leaves the room.

Ted

Dr. Henry isn't gone ten minutes before he's back, nodding his head. "It's definitely her," he says. "She's in a bad way, Ted." He touches my arm as though he's delivering devastating news.

A lump forms in my throat as I turn to see David and Frank nodding in unison. David makes eye contact and suppresses a smile. I shake my head and look away. I look towards the door. "What now?" I ask.

"You need to call the police," David pipes up. Frank straightens his stance at the word *police*.

Dr. Henry squints, then takes his hand off me like I'm fire. "Right, yes. Sorry, I forgot."

I forgot too. I really just want to see her. It seems like it's been ages since we've been together. No. I just want to see her die. Right?

May

Nurse Boy hangs a plastic bag of liquid on the hook above me, changing it out from the empty one.

"Why can't I go next door? If we're both sick with the same thing?"

"I'm not sure," Nurse Boy puzzles. "I'll ask, okay? Probably just keeping the boys from the girls—but if you two know each other—I'll see what I can do."

I want to hug his pimply little face! "Aww, thank you, sweetheart. It's really all I want."

Especially if I'm dying. "Do you think we're dying?"

The boy looks up. "We?" Then he seems to figure it out.

"Umm." He goes back to sticking a needle into the tubing that flows my way. I feel nothing at first, and then the cool of the liquid reaches my feeling parts. Nice. I feel like it's fixing me.

As he cleans up the leftover bits and pieces, I nudge him. "Go do Ted now, okay?"

He smiles proudly. "Already done. He's kind of a regular around here."

A regular? Ted knew he was poisoned? Then it was David who did it. And then he felt guilty and got Ted to the hospital for this treatment stuff. How could Ted forgive him for something like that? Jesus. And he's in the same room with David right now. How can this be happening? I should be there. I start hollering again.

Ted

It's only about a half hour before Constable Ryan shows up. She's alone, and she's smiling.

"Why do I keep finding you in hospital, Mr. Russell?" she says, sauntering up to my room.

I smile back. She's exactly who I want to see. She can help us. David steps up and shakes her hand. Frank mutters something about food and leaves the room.

"Thanks for coming," David says. "We're just going to grab some food. Back in a bit."

"I've set an officer up outside her door. But I don't think she can walk, so you're good. Do you want me to see if we can get you on another floor?"

I shake my head. I think that's the opposite of what I want. Then I hear May's voice screaming my name again. "Teddy! I'm right here! Don't let him get you!" Her crazy almost feels normal under the circumstances. It feels like life.

Ryan smiles. "That girl's mad about you," she says.

"I know." I nod.

She pulls up a seat beside me. "How long are you here for?"

I shrug and feel the weight of my reality sitting on my shoulders. "I might be done," I confess. "It doesn't make sense. I feel fine, except, you know, my vision." I wave my hand over my eyes. "But this stuff, this dimethylmercury. Once it's in, it's in."

I don't cry. I keep not crying, and it's weird. All the little shitty things that have happened, where the tears come without concern for my composure, and now they're gone.

Constable Ryan looks at me with all that empathy she always has, and she squeezes my hand. "Anything I can do, Ted. Anything."

May

Doctor Hazel Eyes is standing outside my door with two other doctors. I can hear their voices but can't make out what they're saying.

Three fucking days. I can't breathe. What the fuck is wrong with me? Is it the stuff they're pumping into me? My lungs are like balloons stuffed in a pillow. I can't get any air in them. The only time I stop thinking about trying to breathe is when I'm puking. Which is definitely from the stuff they're pumping into me. The doctor said it would make me puke.

And still no Teddy. I need him so bad. I hope he's still here. I hope he's still sick. Then we can be sick together. Maybe even die together. How very Romeo and Juliet. I'd be okay with that.

"May?" Dr. Hazel Eyes is back. I watch him put his hand on my arm. "I think it's best we put you on a ventilator at this point, okay?"

I don't know what that means. I blink in response.

"It'll help you breathe, sweetie. Make you more comfortable." He brushes the hair away from my eyes, finally touching a place I can feel.

It reminds me of my mom that day I had the black eye, and I flinch, and he pulls his hand away. I shake my head. Don't stop. I want him to touch me.

He thinks I'm shaking my head about the ventilator. "It's our best bet right now. Really."

I nod to show him my agreement and then say what I always say, "Ted?"

He looks at me like I'm the saddest thing in the world. I probably am. "He's doing okay. Don't you worry."

Ted

The tunnel vision is going away, I swear. I feel okay. Just nauseous. Really nauseous. And tired of sitting in the hospital. I've had lots of visitors. Constable Ryan comes by every day. Stephen and Tippy showed up yesterday. Stephen got all choked up and had to leave. Don was here this morning with yet another plant. And of course, David comes here straight from work and sleeps in a chair.

Dr. Henry says he wants me to stay at least a week. Just to keep an eye on everything. Then we'll continue treatments for a few months. May is still next door. She stopped calling for me a while back. The doctor doesn't seem to want to give me updates, but Constable Ryan, as promised, goes in May's room every day. Today, she told me May's on a ventilator.

That's it then. It's almost over.

May

That cop. She's here again. Thumbs on her belt, tits sticking out as far as her gut, all tough and sneery. She thinks she's all that. I tell her to fuck off every time I see her. This time's no different. Except this giant tube down my throat. Fuck off, you big, fat cunt. Can't you see I'm fucking dying here?

Ted

I find myself listening for the ventilator the rest of the afternoon. Every now and then, I think I hear it, but then some other noise floods over it before I can hone in.

David brought goulash tonight for supper. It's awful—he didn't get it from Kozak's—but he's committed to the bucket list. Something different each night. Even though I'm okay. I swear. I don't need a bucket list anymore. I'm weak because every mineral in my body is getting sucked out of me. And I really hate food right now. But I'm fine.

He balances his bowl on his lap, and I sit up in bed with my stupid little table taking sips from a plastic spoon. His slurps drive me to distraction. My slurps drive me to distraction. I just want to hear the ventilator.

"I think the new cashier quit today," David says between slurps.

I want to scream at him to shut up, but instead I look over at him and feign interest.

"I thought I smelled alcohol on her a couple of times, but I didn't say anything. And then one of the customers today right out and asked her what she had to drink for breakfast this morning!"

Funny. I laugh politely.

"So, after the customer goes, I say, 'You know you can't drink on the job, right?' and she says, 'Yes,' but then she slams the till closed so hard it slid off the counter." David wipes his mouth with a napkin, which is a good thing because he was dribbling, and it was starting to bug me. "So, I'm sitting there with my jaw on my lap, figuring out a polite way to say, 'You're fired,' and she just storms out the door!"

Hah. I laugh again and shake my head. I don't want to be mean. I just want to hear May.

David senses my mood and stops talking. I still only hear the odd swish. Is that what a ventilator sounds like?

May

I guess I'm dying? I don't have to breathe anymore. This ventilator thing is doing that for me. I don't even pee anymore —there's a tube down there for that. I feel nothing but my brains.

Jake has the frying pan. There's blood around his neck, like a necklace, dripping down his chest. He's just wearing underpants, and they're white and stained and his dick is peeking out through the pee-flap. He's standing over me. But it's not me. It's David. I'm just watching. Jake lifts the pan to take a swing, and I look back at David, and I'm laughing, but it isn't David anymore. It's Teddy, and I scream and dive over him to take the blow.

Then I wake up.

Tears roll down my cheeks, all hot and wet, and make the collar of this dreadful hospital gown wet. They seem constant.

I've never thought about being dead before. It feels so wrong. He's supposed to be with me. Holding me, in this end of our forever.

Or maybe it's the beginning of our forever? Maybe there's

a heaven and an eternity and Teddy is dying too and this is how it's all meant to be. Of course.

Teddy has the snake from the bedroom. And he wants me to touch it. But I'm so scared. Ted keeps saying, "Don't be scared. I'll protect you." But I don't believe him because Jake is with him, and David is holding my arms behind me, whispering, "He would never hurt you."

David is standing in the doorway. Hands folded in front of him. Watching me. His face is cold and still. I'm awake. I must be, because I feel the wetness of my collar. He turns and walks away. And I remember he was here before. Maybe more than once. That means Teddy's still here. I love how my heart aches for him. It feels good. It feels like life.

Ted

"I thought she was in a coma, but then her eyes opened," David says. "Freaked me out!" He's sitting on the edge of my bed. He rubs my leg. "You should go take a look. You might find it inspiring." He chuckles a bit, sees I'm not laughing with him, and stops awkwardly.

At night, I hear the machine over David's snores. It's like an off beat to the rhythm of his breaths. It keeps me awake like a dripping tap. I want to see her. I can. Nothing's stopping me.

I've walked around the floor plenty of times. But I always turn around before I reach the room before mine, her room, and walk the other way.

Tomorrow, I go home. The tunnel vision has subsided, thank God. My sunglasses are off. My fingers and toes are still numb though. Dr. Henry says the feeling might not come back. But he's happy with everything else and keeps apologizing for not being more aggressive with my treatment right from the start. I don't care.

May

He's here. Oh my God, he's here. His skin. I can smell his skin. There's a rush through my body. Hot, sudden feeling. My heart feels like it's going to explode. I shake my head hard. I need to get this stupid breathing tube out of me.

He's standing beside me. The sheets move. He's touching me. Oh my God. I close my eyes, trying to feel, but open them just as fast. He's still here. Our eyes make contact, and I try to nod my head. Yes, baby, yes. You came to me.

Ted

I slide out of the bed, the cold tiles reminding my feet about the useless toes. Light from the nurses' station illuminates the window in the door to my room. I walk to the light and pull the heaviness of the door carefully towards me, opening it only enough so I can slide through. I don't want to light up the room and wake David.

Out in the hall, it seems darker. The only sound is her breathing machine. I walk towards it. Towards this weird feeling of joy and fear that's messing with my head.

Her door is closed. The cardboard name tag identifies her as May Carlisle. It's printed in black felt pen, like the name tags on the coat rack in second grade. I remember her smile when the school day was done and we'd go grab our coats. She was always smiling at me. I remember how it used to make me feel safe. I push open the door, feeling the weakening of the chelation on my bones.

May

I beg with my eyes for him to touch somewhere I can feel. I tilt my head for him to touch my face. But he doesn't understand.

"I'm sorry," he says.

Why are you sorry, baby? It's okay now. We're together. I watch his face. He's thin and tired looking. Then it dawns on me; he's walking. He's not sick like me. I thought he was sick. I thought we were dying together. What the fuck, Ted?

Ted

She's just a body under sheets. Not May. But the fear inside me doesn't stop vibrating. And the ache I've had since I knew she was here gets stronger as I move towards the bed.

She's got tears running down her cheeks, her sobs making a horrible choking sound through the tube, and her hospital gown is soaking wet like she's been drooling. She shakes her head violently when I first walk up to her, but then she calms down and just stares at me. I stare back.

It's just May. She has no makeup on. Her eyes are soft and tired. She looks like a child. I squeeze her arm over the sheets and slide my hand under, so I can take hers. It's limp and cold. She closes her eyes. If she hadn't made such a fuss when I came in, I would think she was dead. Already. The thought hits me hard. She nods her head at me.

She knows. She knows this is my fault.

"I'm sorry," I say, squeezing her hand. Her eyes turn cold.

May

You killed me? Why the fuck would you kill me? I'm yours. I've always been yours. I feel the hurt in my chest. Like I can't catch my breath. But this stupid machine keeps breathing, in and out, in and out. My cheeks burn with rage, and the salt from my tears makes the skin feel tight.

But now he's crying and shaking his head. "I am so sorry," he whispers. "But you just wouldn't stop, and I needed you to stop. I couldn't live like that anymore."

One of his tears drops onto my face, and he brushes it away with his thumb. As though he touches me every day. And I realize what he's trying to tell me.

Ted

Her anger is such a familiar feeling. Just the look in her eyes makes me want to run. But I can't. I won't let her die angry. And there it is. She *is* dying, and I killed her and I'm so happy it's over and I'm so terrified to live without her.

"May, I'm so sorry. But you just wouldn't stop, and I needed you to stop. I couldn't live like that anymore. I lost it. You. In the lab with the gun. It was—" I'm crying. Those tears that wouldn't come are here now, in full force. She's crying too, and I grab a tissue from the nightstand and wipe her cheeks dry. The ice in her stare melts away, and I swear she's smiling at me.

I smile back and bend down to kiss her forehead and give her a hug amongst the tubes that invade her.

I pull up a chair and take her hand again. She's fallen asleep. I'll just sit here for a while.

May

He didn't mean to kill me. It was David he was trying to get with this poisoning thing. He must have got it at the market and was just getting ready. I probably interrupted him when I grabbed him at the market. Teddy would never hurt me. I have to learn to control my temper. I try to smile at him, to let him know I understand.

He smiles back. Of course, he knows me. He knows I'm smiling. He knows I forgive him. It's us. It's always been us. He bends down to kiss me, like he always does, and I close my eyes. Then he presses his cheek close to mine and whispers, "I love you, May."

I feel warm.

PLEASE REVIEW
THIS BOOK

Not to beg or anything, but please, if you enjoyed this book, give it a review. Reviews are extremely helpful, especially to new authors.

You can review May and Ted on any Amazon marketplace.

Also, if you would like to keep up to date with my latest antics and upcoming publications, please visit my website at jdrobertsonbooks.com.

AUTHOR'S NOTE

I can only imagine what it was like to be a gay man in the last quarter of the twentieth century. I do know that I went to school with boys who came out later in life, and my heart aches for them and what puberty must have been like for them.

Some people may think I don't have a right to write about what these men dealt with. Which is why May and Ted isn't about that. David and Ted's love story is based on all the love stories I've known, because I know love is love, no matter who you are.

If the language in this story seems offensive, please know it had to be, because that's what it was like back then. I am a firm believer that history can't be candy coated, lest we forget how far we've come and how much further we need to go.

ACKNOWLEDGEMENTS

Like any author, my list of thank-yous is endless.

Thank you to all the members of the Inkhorn Writers' Group who encouraged me in those early chapters. You gave me the confidence to keep writing.

Thank you to my sons, Adam Stockdale, Brad Beecher and Tory Borsboom. Adam, my first reader for every chapter, thank you for your honesty, your support, your knowledge and your patience. Brad, fellow struggling artist, thank you for listening when I doubted myself and encouraging me on the days when all I could see was a blank page. And Tory? Just thank you, you warm my heart.

Thank you to my beta readers: Alison Cude, Deepa Menon, Dejan Ozegovic, and Jason Young. Your feedback and enthusiasm meant everything!

Thank you to my editor, Maggie Morrison. Holy cow, you caught so much! Thank you for making me look good (or reasonable, at the very least)!

Thank you to Katherine Foster and my sister, Chris Worsley, for holding my hand when things get rough. And thank you to Elyse Gratton, Leslie Lerat, and Natalie Stubb, because how could I leave you out?

Finally, of course, thank you to my husband, Bill, for being my rock, for believing in me, and for loving me, every single day.

ABOUT THE AUTHOR

J. D. Robertson

J. D. Robertson is a retired corporate writer. She lives in Edmonton, Alberta, with her puggle, Charlee, and her husband, Bill. May and Ted is her first novel.

Made in United States
North Haven, CT
14 April 2023

35437405R10202